P9-BZT-257

The door to the waiting room slid open . . .

. . . and a scent immediately caught her attention. It was incredibly familiar, one that she knew almost as well as her own. She rose from her chair, determined to stand even though she felt so weak-kneed from astonishment that she thought she would fall.

The owner of the scent scuttled in with that bizarre, familiar, semi-pirouette walk that his tripodal form required.

"Arex!" she fairly shrieked, and leaped the distance of the room toward him. He enfolded her in his three arms and she felt, rather than heard, amused laughter in his chest.

"Greetings, M'Ress," Arex said. . . .

STAR TREK NEW FRONTIER®

GATEWAYS

BOOK SIX OF SEVEN

COLD WARS

Peter David

Based upon STAR TREK®
created by Gene Roddenberry

POCKET BOOKS

New York   London   Toronto   Sydney   Singapore

For information regarding special discounts for bulk purchases, please contact Simon & Schuster Special Sales at 1-800-456-6798 or business@simonandschuster.com

The sale of this book without its cover is unauthorized. If you purchased this book without a cover, you should be aware that it was reported to the publisher as "unsold and destroyed." Neither the author nor the publisher has received payment for the sale of this "stripped book."

This book is a work of fiction. Names, characters, places and incidents are products of the author's imagination or are used fictitiously. Any resemblance to actual events or locales or persons, living or dead, is entirely coincidental.

An *Original* Publication of POCKET BOOKS

 POCKET BOOKS, a division of Simon & Schuster, Inc.
1230 Avenue of the Americas, New York, NY 10020

Copyright © 2001 by Paramount Pictures. All Rights Reserved.

 STAR TREK is a Registered Trademark of
Paramount Pictures.

This book is published by Pocket Books, a division of Simon & Schuster, Inc., under exclusive license from Paramount Pictures.

All rights reserved, including the right to reproduce this book or portions thereof in any form whatsoever. For information address Pocket Books, 1230 Avenue of the Americas, New York, NY 10020

ISBN: 0-671-04242-4

First Pocket Books printing October 2001

10 9 8 7 6 5 4 3 2 1

POCKET and colophon are registered trademarks of Simon & Schuster, Inc.

Printed in the U.S.A.

COLD WARS

1

AERON

THE ZARN FINALLY DECIDED that if he did not get the matter settled, he was never going to be able to get any sleep.

It was not a decision that came lightly to him. The Zarn was a proud individual, and disliked intensely having to admit to any shortcomings or weaknesses. Certainly not being able to slumber was one such. Furthermore, he was going to have to seek aid from the Zarna, who had the temerity to lie peacefully next to him, snoring away contentedly. She had denied any number of times that she snored, and he had insisted with equal vigor that he, and not she, would be in a superior position to make such a determination. Such was the female's intransigence, however, that she refused to accept his word—*his word*—of this particular shortcoming of hers. Yet there she stubbornly lay, snoring blithely away. He wished, not for the first time, that there was a way to put an end to her snoring, and he further wished that he was not so besotted with her, even after all this time, that he could not bring himself to deal in any harsh manner with her.

The Zarn rolled over, studying the shape of her pale back, the jutting spine ridge exposed and alluring as ever. He ran his elegant fingers along it, not with a steady, brushing touch, but instead a series of light taps along the edges that he knew would rouse her, even in her sleep. Her hips twisted slightly with subconscious pleasure, and she made a little humming sound. "What are you doing?" she yawned thickly, but with the slightest sound of amusement in her voice.

"Nothing," replied the Zarn, sounding utterly innocent. He made no pretense of his own wakefulness, but instead simply lay there with his head propped on one hand. "I am doing nothing except regarding the magnificence that is your body."

"Mm-hmm," she said, in a tone that both managed to convey that she Was Not Amused, and yet simultaneously made him aware that she did, indeed, find it just ever so slightly funny. She wasn't looking at him, instead keeping the spine presented. It was a provocative decision, and she knew it to be so, but acted as if it wasn't. She managed to push the last vestiges of sleep from her voice. Her dark green eyes, solid and pupil-less, glowed in the darkness with that eerie luminescence so characteristic of the Aeron race. "All right, my husband . . . you have awakened me. Satisfied?"

"I? I intended no such thing," he assured her, sounding suitably stricken. He wasn't fooling her for a moment, of course, but after so many years together, they had developed little verbal rhythms that were as much a part of their union as sex or trust or anything else. "What sort of husband would I be if I thought I could disturb your much-needed rest whenever it suited my fancy?"

"You would be a ruling husband," she pointed out, "a Zarn, to be specific. And I would be your endlessly patient Zarna, wondering why she had been awakened while miraculously keeping a level tone."

He touched the fluttering membrane at the base of her throat in a vaguely suggestive manner, but she gently pushed his hand away. "Enough of that," she said firmly. "You did not rouse me from a perfectly sound slumber simply to feign interest in play."

"It's hardly feigned."

"Perhaps," she allowed, "but neither is it your concern. I know you too well." She now sat up, curling her knees to just under her chin. "Speak to me of what is *truly* on your mind."

"If you know me as well as you claim, then you should know without my having to tell you."

"Very well," said the Zarna evenly. "You're worried about our eldest son."

The Zarn looked at her with open admiration. "I am well and truly impressed," he admitted.

"It was not that impressive a feat, much as I would like to pretend otherwise." All of the banter, the teasing amusement in her voice had given way to seriousness. She was nude in bed next to her husband, and yet one would have thought from her deportment that she was fully robed and gowned, and seated in her Place of Discernment in the main courtroom. "The relationship between you and the Zarnon has become more strained with each passing day. The Zarnon is no fool. He knows that you are disappointed in him."

"My disappointment arises from his own conduct and my judgment thereof." The Zarn swung his legs out of the gentle liquid bubble that served as their bed and stepped onto the floor. Even in the warmth of the Palace, the coldness of the night could be felt in the air. He slid his feet into slippers that sat near the edge of the bed, and pulled on his dressing gown, which hung nearby. His wife, the Zarna, clearly preferred the warmth of the liquid bed, and made no move to exit it. "He knows his duties, and appears unable to live up to them. In theory, he is to become Zarn after me. . . ."

"In theory," the Zarna pointed out. "But to the Zarnon, it is not quite as easy as all that."

"Why not?" demanded the Zarn with irritation. "He is given the best of everything. The best teachers, the best training. All his young life, he has been provided every opportunity to live up to that which is his birthright. He should be proud. Instead he . . . seems to resent me. I do not understand."

"Tell me, my husband," the Zarna said slowly, apparently aware that she was treading on delicate ground. "How did you feel . . . about your own father?"

The Zarn shrugged indifferently. "I felt nothing for him one way or the other. He was my father and taught me my duty. I lived up to it. I ask nothing more of my own son." His pale face flushed with slight annoyance. "Are you now claiming that I have been an inadequate father? For if you are, I cannot help but take offense. I have labored mightily to be a far better father to the Zarnon than ever my father was to me."

"And you have succeeded," she assured him soothingly. "There is a very close bond between you and your son . . . deeper, perhaps, than even you know or understand. And in that bond may lie the problem."

He stared at her blankly. "I do not follow."

"All of the duties for which he is trained," she explained, "are predicated upon one thing: his assuming your duties after you are no longer capable of doing so, either because of incapacitation or death. Apparently our gentle son does not desire to dwell on such things."

The Zarn was not a stupid person, and even though it took him a few moments to process what the Zarna was saying to him, in time he finally understood. "He does not wish to dwell on my passing."

She nodded. "That is exactly right."

He stood in the middle of the dimly lit room. It was ornately furnished with many ceremonial trappings from the long line of Zarns who had preceded him in office: robes and headdresses and similar adornments, all carefully mounted and labeled with gleaming plaques beneath them. It had never occurred to the Zarn that being part of that line was not the greatest honor that any creature could hope for. He had often said that death held no terror for him, for in many ways he was already immortal. No matter what happened, he would join the line of illustrious Zarns who had overseen the fortunes of the planet Aeron, a marvelous little globe of blue and green hanging in the depths of what had once been called Thallonian space. It now appeared, though, that his successor, the Zarnon, felt differently.

The reality of it was a good deal for the Zarn to take in all at once. He eased himself down onto the edge of the bed, shaking his head. "I find that . . . difficult to believe. . . ."

"Why so difficult? You have worked hard to be a caring and supportive father. The Zarnon wants only to please you, to gain your approval. And yet his greatest opportunity to do so can only occur after you are in no position to grant that approval. He is conflicted and frustrated. To his mind, he is being groomed for a position, for a duty, that will commence with failure. You will not be able to tell him that he is a good Zarn, nor will he be able to show you what he is capable of."

"He has overanalyzed the situation," the Zarn said, but he sounded a bit uncertain, and that was most unusual for him. He loathed any hint of uncertainty; he would rather make a wrong decision quickly than a considered decision slowly. "He has created in his mind a no-win scenario. That is hardly worthy of a ruler."

"He is *not* the ruler. Titles such as 'Zarnon' aside, he is simply a frustrated young man who wants to make his father proud, and has no true idea how to go about doing so."

"Well, what would you suggest . . . ?"

"I am but the humble Zarna. You are our esteemed ruler. It is for you to decide."

He had no ready answer. He simply lay back on the bed,

still in his dressing gown, his hands behind his head. He considered the matter for a considerable length of time, during which his wife's steady breathing did little to convince him that she had gone to sleep. When he finally spoke again, it was half an hour later. "I know what you are suggesting."

"Do you?" she said with amusement in her voice, making no pretense of having been slumbering.

"You do not fool me in the least."

"I don't?" Her tone had not changed.

"You are suggesting that I retire as Zarn. That I step aside and hand the office over to the Zarnon." His eyes narrowed as he spoke, and he did not sound any too pleased at the notion.

"I have suggested no such thing," replied his wife.

"Zarns retire when they are incapacitated. When they are unfit and unable to serve in the office."

"That is true," she allowed, but then added after a moment's thought, "However, that is not any sort of a rule. Merely a custom . . . and an unfortunate one at that."

"Unfortunate?" He was thunderstruck. The Zarna had always been second-to-none when it came to respect for traditions on Aeron. "Why unfortunate?"

"It is not my place to—"

"Bellanaria," he said abruptly.

It brought her up short. The Zarna could not remember the last time he had addressed her by her true name. It made her realize just how much they had lost sight of that which they once were, and instead become simple extensions of their offices. Perhaps, she mused, that was part of the problem. As parents they knew what was right and true, almost instinctively. As Zarn and Zarna, every decision they made had to factor in what was best for the world of Aeron.

He had spoken sharply, and when he repeated the shortened version of her name, a more gentle "Bell," it was with as much compassion as he was capable of mustering. "Bell . . . why do you say it's unfortunate?"

Normally the Zarn did not like to hear anything against the traditions of their world, but it was quite clear to the Zarna that he was making an exception this time. She knew she had to speak as carefully as possible; who knew how long his mood would last? "Well," she said after several moments' consideration, "you really need look no further than the history of our world, do you? The beginning of a young Zarn's reign is always fraught with difficulties. Skirmishes, wars always seem to break out, until such time as the new Zarn gets a more secure grip on his people."

"Isn't that unavoidable, though? No matter how carefully a successor may be trained, there still has to be a time for him to learn, correct?"

"Yes, but look who he learns from: those who were advisors to the Zarn before him. Advisors who always seemed to act in the best interests of the Zarn and Aeron while the Zarn was alive . . . but once the Zarn they initially served passes, they always strive to grab whatever personal power they can. It happens time after time, and each Zarn, later in his career, appoints people who he thinks won't fall prey to such self-serving motivations. Yet it recurs. Such is Aeron nature, I suppose."

"And what would you suggest," he asked, "to break this cycle?" But he said it with the air of someone who knew the answer before he asked the question.

She took a deep breath, feeling as if she were launching herself off a precipice. "Step aside for your son. Instead of ruling as Zarn, be content to serve in an advisory capacity." She saw the expression on his face then, which spoke volumes in its silence. It seemed to say, *You think I'm not doing the job. You've lost faith in me.* It almost broke her heart to see that in him, and she made certain to keep a tone of love, affection, and respect uppermost in her voice. "You would not be driven by desire for power, because you would already have walked away from power, set it aside willingly.

Other advisors and chancellors will not attempt to foist their own agendas upon the Zarnon . . . I'm sorry, the new Zarn. You will be able to guide the young Zarn in the ways of his office. Help give him the sort of on-the-job training that is the only way a new Zarn can truly come to understand his duties. As opposed to previous Zarns, who have always had to weigh the self-interest of their advisors into decisions, the new Zarn will be able to trust you—his father—implicitly. And in turn, it will give him the opportunity to show you what he can do. To earn your respect, your approval, while you are still here to give it."

"And when he has no need of me?" asked the Zarn. "Sooner or later, my presence will cease to be a comfort, and instead be a shadow that he cannot escape. That is certainly not desirable."

"When that time comes," she replied readily, "why . . . then you will just have to focus your attention on the rest of your family. We do have other sons, as well as two daughters. And a wife . . . a wife who enjoyed hearing you speak her true name just now." She stroked his arm, gently, adoringly. "A wife who would very much appreciate the opportunity to have you all to herself. Sometimes when I climb into bed with you, I feel as if I'm here with the entire population of Aeron, for your attention is split in so many directions at once. If, on the other hand, it were just us, oh, the pleasure that would bring me. And for that matter, the pleasure I could bring you . . ." She let her voice trail off, but there was a teasing look on her face.

"You present a very . . . compelling argument," he said after a time. He had been propping himself up on one elbow, watching her as she had spoken, and she'd felt as if that gaze were boring deep into her soul, dissecting her molecule by molecule. Then, to her utter astonishment, he said, "I will do it."

"What?" she managed to get out. "You . . . you don't wish to discuss something of such importance with . . ."

"With others? Those who might feel disenfranchised, or believe that I am making decisions based on lack of trust in their abilities? No, I see no need to discuss it with them." He was nodding, although it seemed more to himself than to anyone else. "I am the Zarn. I am the leader of the Aeron. I am the one who makes the decisions, and once a decision is made, I see no reason at all to consult others. The things you've said to me make infinite sense; why should I waste time discussing the matter with those who will make less sense? Or who will strive to explain to me why you are wrong? I do not think you are wrong, and furthermore, if you are . . . I do not wish to know about it."

"You will really do it?" she asked wonderingly. "Our son means that much to you?"

"Do you really have to ask that? Or are you simply looking to me to affirm that which you already know?"

She laughed at that. "The latter, I imagine. I suppose I'm just that transparent. If I were any more so, you'd be able to see right through me."

"That would be most unfortunate, considering that I am quite pleased with what I am seeing now."

"Oh, are you?" said the Zarna teasingly, even as she arched her back and pressed her nude body against his, bringing the sensitive spine ridges within easy reach of his hand. She brought her lips down on his exposed belly, which she knew he liked.

He smiled and moaned softly even as he said, "Tomorrow is going to begin a new and extraordinary day in the history of Aeron."

"I have a suggestion," she said, lifting her lips momentarily. "How would it be if we made a little history of our own tonight?"

"Such as . . . endurance records?"

"I was thinking that very thing."

He moved against her, wanting her, needing her, hiding well his nervousness over the prospect of turning over the ultimate authority on Aeron but—at the same time—not regretting it for so much as an instant.

So involved with one another were they that, at first, they didn't notice the crackling in the air. But then it caught their attention, and the Zarn sat up, drawing his dressing gown tightly around him even as he tried to locate the source of the sound. "I have never heard anything like that before. . . ." he said, looking to the Zarna for confirmation. She shook her head, similarly befuddled.

Then the noise, which had seemed to be coming from everywhere, abruptly coalesced into one section of the room, approximately ten feet away. The air rippled and the Zarn and Zarna gaped as, incredibly, a hole appeared to open up right there in front of them. It seemed about seven feet across, rippling, and although it was still possible to see the opposite side of the chamber through the hole, the distortion of the air itself gave it an opaque look.

All of it happened within seconds, and even as the Zarn shouted for his guards, even as he heard the comforting pounding of feet toward the doors of the bedchamber, the center of the hole darkened, and armed and armored men charged through. There were ten, no, fifteen of them, maybe more, and the sigil painted on the armor could not have been more familiar to the Zarn. Serpent-like creatures intertwined with one another, heads back and ready to spear each other with jagged fangs.

"Markanians!" he shouted, clearly still not believing what he was seeing. The Zarna looked back and forth frantically between the intruders and her husband, even as she gathered the sheet around herself.

The soldiers, adjusting to the dimness of the room, turned and trained their sights on the Zarn. Their helmets were all-encompassing, obscuring their features and making them seem that much more formidable. The Zarn, for his part, was startled but unafraid. "How did you get here?" he demanded. "What is this . . . this bizarre gateway that brought you here? You will depart immediately; I will not tolerate this—"

He got no further. The foremost Markanians extended their armored fists, and there was just enough time to see the glinting barrels mounted on them. Then they roared to life even as they spit out death. The pulse blasts hammered into the Zarn, sending him flying off his feet, the screeching weapons-fire drowning out the screeching of the Zarna. The Zarn slammed against the far wall and was grotesquely supported there a moment, several feet off the ground, by nothing except the sustained impact of the shots that were pounding his helpless body. It had taken mere seconds for his white dressing gown to become thick with blackness. They continued to fire, following his body down as it slid to the ground, turning it into a mass of flesh and bone and sinew that was barely recognizable as anything sentient, much less something that had until moments before been the supreme ruler of the world.

The main chamber door was locked and was bending inward under the pummeling of the guards outside. The Zarna leaped off the bed, blanket still around her, lunging for the door to open it. It was happening so quickly, so quickly, that the Zarna thought for a moment that it was all a dream. That she had unknowingly slid back into slumber, and a nightmare was playing itself out for her. This belief sustained itself for exactly as long as it took the Markanians to train their weaponry upon her and rip her to pieces. The sheet slipped away, but it didn't matter as the blasts shredded her lovely body, which seemed to explode upon the blasts' impact. She wanted to scream *Not my children, leave my children alone!* And perhaps somewhere in her head she did so with such force and gusto that she actually thought she'd said it. But she hadn't. Instead, all that emerged from her throat was a muted, vague mewling sound. She tried to crawl over to her husband, everything else forgotten—her own life, her children, all of it. The only thing she was thinking at that point was how much she wanted to touch his hand one final time. Then she heard one final shriek of blaster fire that seemed concentrated on her head, and oblivion claimed her.

At that precise moment, the doors to the imperial bedchamber were smashed open, splintering upon the impact of the guards' bodies. There were three of them, and they had pump-action pulsers under their arms. But they were clad in light armor, largely ceremonial in nature, and they stood no chance against Markanian shock troops outfitted in heavy-duty battlewear. Plus they were frozen in shock for crucial seconds as they beheld the horrific scene awaiting them: the shattered bodies of the Zarn and Zarna upon the ground, blood everywhere, and the assassins who somehow had managed to slip past the mansion's security systems as if they simply weren't there.

They brought their pulsers to bear, even managed to get off a couple of shots, although all they did was glance harmlessly off the Markanian armor. The Markanians, for their part, only required seconds more to dispatch the Aeron guards than they had needed to murder the Zarn and his wife.

The lead Markanian wasted no time. "There will be more, and they won't be as easy as these were," he said. "Don't get cocky. Let's finish this and leave."

The Zarnon was up and out of bed, hearing the shots, looking around in confusion. He was a young man, slim, with coiled muscles, and normally a look of quiet intelligence, which had—in this case—been replaced by a look of barely controlled panic.

Then the door to his chambers was blasted open and he

lost control of the panic, along with several bodily functions. He did not, however, have to live long in that disgrace, as the Markanians cut him down where he stood.

Kreb and Toran, the twin boys just in their teens, huddled on a bed, clutching each other. There was a scrabbling under their bed, and Kreb hissed at the source of the noise. "Stay under there!"

"Come here, too!" came back the female voice from beneath. "There's . . . there's shooting and killing all over—! Can't you hear—?"

"We don't run, Tsana," said Toran firmly. "You stay there. No matter what happens, don't make a—"

The door burst open. The boys looked startled, then relaxed for an instant . . . and then two precisely placed blasts hammered through their faces. They pitched backward off the bed and lay silent.

Moments later, quick footsteps moved away from the room . . . and from under the bed scrambled a young and terrified girl. She knew she should have stayed under the bed . . . but thick liquid was dripping down and coalescing under it, and she knew what that liquid was, and she'd rather die than huddle in a pool of her brothers' blood.

Her mind already shutting down at all she had seen, Tsana staggered away.

The Markanians burst apart several more doors, killed several retainers and a clothier who had the misfortune to be a guest for the night, and then blasted open yet another room to see a teenaged girl clambering out the window. She was halfway out, and froze, the wind whipping her long hair, and there was quiet pleading in her eyes, but it was clear from the set of her mouth that not a word of begging for her life was going to emerge from between her lips. She wore a thigh-cut nightgown that revealed muscular legs. The lead

Markanian took a step forward, tilting his head slightly, assessing her.

"You look like your mother," he said at last.

"Did you kill her, too?" The question was asked flatly, without emotion.

He saw no reason to sugarcoat it at this point. "Yes. And now we're going to kill you."

Her face hardened and the pleading vanished from her eyes, to be replaced by utter contempt. "No, you won't," she informed them. She turned quickly, thrust outward with those muscular legs, and vanished from the window. The Markanians dashed across the room, their heavy boots cracking the delicate tiling, and they looked out and down. The young woman was lying in the courtyard eighty feet below, dark liquid pooling beneath her, her body twisted in such a way that it was clear, even from up there, that she had not survived the fall. Nor, obviously, had she expected to.

"She wished to die on her own terms," muttered the lead Markanian. "Something to be said for that."

"And for that as well!" said the trooper right behind him, pointing. Then they all saw it: a squad of Aerons, charging across the courtyard, and, unlike the palace guards, these were clearly from some sort of standing army. They were heavily armed and outnumbered the Markanians by at least three to one.

"Time to leave," said the leader.

But the trooper behind him was hesitant. "I think there was one more," he said. "We might not have gotten the entire family."

"I said it was time to leave, Pmarr," the leader repeated, more forcefully this time.

"But we might not have gotten all of them! I think there are others—"

"Our intelligence on the matter is uncertain at best. We were fortunate that the plans of the mansion were as accurate as they were, or we wouldn't have gotten this far." His voice rising in anger, he said, "We need to keep our priorities in order. Now come along!"

He did not stand there and debate it further with Pmarr, for the soldiers below had entered the building and even now their footsteps could be heard echoing up the steps. The Markanians bolted back down the corridor, not even glancing at the destruction they had left in their wake. The floor was littered with shards of doors smashed open, and pieces of the wall carved out by blasts littered the floor. They all crunched underfoot as the Markanians passed.

But as they approached the former chambers of the Zarn and Zarna, Pmarr slowed. "What do you think you're doing!" shouted the leader.

"I thought I saw someone behind us. . . ."

"Yes! The damned soldiers! Now get to the Gateway! I told you, we need to keep our priorities in order!"

"I think it was something else," Pmarr insisted. "Smaller . . . a child . . ."

"Leave him!"

"I think it was a girl. . . ."

"Leave her, then! Our job here is done—!"

"Not while even one of the imperials lives!" Pmarr shot back hotly. He yanked off his helmet and faced the leader. His skin was mottled blue, as was typical for his race, and his crescent-shaped eyes blinked furiously sideways. His hair was thin, gold strands that almost looked like a skeletal hand spread across the top of his head. "That was the plan! Perhaps you have lost sight of that fact, but I have not! It will not take long to—"

"It will take just long enough to get someone killed. One of the goals of this endeavor was to subject our people to minimum risk . . . even fools such as you, Pmarr! And I have spent more than enough time here talking about it! Now come!"

He did not hesitate, but instead crowded in with the others

to the bedchamber. "Pmarr!" he shouted over his shoulder. "We are not going to wait for you! We are not going to hold the Gateway open! You come now, or you do not come at all!"

Pmarr started to turn toward the bedchamber, toward the glowing escape-way through which the other Markanians were dashing. Each time one would pass through, the Gateway would glow slightly and emit a little hum of energy, as if it was cheerfully consuming those passing through instead of simply transporting them back to their point of origin. And then he saw it again—the small form at the end of the corridor. A girl, yes, definitely a girl, and he took a few steps toward her. She was staring at him in wonder, as if she couldn't quite believe that she was seeing what she was seeing. The fact that he was about to kill her didn't even seem to register. The child appeared to be in shock. Well, that was hardly surprising, what with her entire family dying around her. The fortunate thing was that she wasn't going to have to be in shock for very long.

He started to raise his gauntlet blaster, and suddenly, from down the corridor, there was the high-pitched whine of an Aeron weapon. A split-second later, a glowing ball of light came from behind the girl, miraculously bypassing her and homing straight in on Pmarr like a lethal sprite. He tried to run, his bravado suddenly disappearing as his jeopardy became far more real to him, but it was too late. The energy ball grazed the corridor slightly, ricocheting off it to gain speed and power, and then smashed into his upper thigh. He felt the impact even through his battle armor. He staggered, dragging the numbed leg, and then a second blast whipped around the corridor and slammed into him in nearly the exact same place as the first one. The thigh armor cracked, and so did Pmarr's upper thigh bone, and he went down with an outraged screech.

It was his last, desperate determination to try and annihilate the child at the far end of the corridor, but then soldiers pounding down the hall toward him blocked her from view. He started to bring his weaponry up, but the lead soldier shouted, "Don't move!" and Pmarr, much to his own annoyance, complied with the harsh order. He lay there, immobile, already planning what he was going to say when grilled for information. There was no doubt in his mind that he was going to tell them absolutely nothing. The secrets of the Markanians were going to remain secrets with him. Let them do to him what they will; he would not bow nor crumble in the face of adversity.

The lead soldiers charged into the bedchamber of the Zarn and Zarna, vaulting over the fallen bodies of the palace guards, and Pmarr grinned ruthlessly as he heard the wails and lamentations that issued from within. *The Aerons make mewling sounds like so many women,* he thought grimly. *How they ever stood up to us for any length of time, I haven't the faintest idea.*

"How did they get in here? How was it possible?!" The soldiers were shouting at one another in utter frustration, and Pmarr understood instantly. The Gateway had closed, leaving no trace of their entrance or exit. He had been left behind. He felt a flash of anger toward his leader, but quickly had to admit that he had brought it upon himself. The simple truth was that he was just going to have to make the best of it.

The soldiers reemerged, and one of them, who bore markings on his armor that appeared to indicate some sort of higher rank, shouted briskly, "Search the building! See where they've gone!"

"You won't find them," Pmarr informed him. He felt proud saying that. He was giving nothing away on that score. He wasn't going to tell them how he knew that they had disappeared. He wanted to taunt them with the knowledge. Make them aware that no matter how they begged him, or threatened him, or tortured him—yes, even tortured him—no matter what they did, he was going to give them no details into the masterful plan that had allowed the Markanians to lay low their ancient enemy.

The ranking soldier looked down at him. His helmet encompassed his face completely, as did the Markanian helmet, though the frontpiece was clear. Yet, despite the transparency, most of the commander's face was cloaked in shadow. Only his eyes were clearly visible, burning with an ominous inner light . . . which would, of course, have frightened Pmarr if he'd been of a mind to *be* frightened. Which he wasn't.

"No, you won't find them," Pmarr went on, "no matter where you look, no matter how hard you search. And I will not tell you a thing of how—"

The commander took two quick steps forward and kicked Pmarr twice in the face, savagely. The first blow smashed in his nose and cheeks; the second broke his entire lower jaw and knocked out five teeth.

At that moment, Pmarr suddenly wanted nothing more than to tell the Aerons anything they wanted to know. Unfortunately, the Aerons displayed no interest in anything that Pmarr had to say, nor would he have been capable of communicating, beyond incomprehensible grunts.

Desperately, Pmarr started to raise his arms, to try and aim the weapons that were atop the gauntlets. He never even saw the slash of the bladed weapon, which had been pulled from its scabbard by the second-in-command (not that Pmarr recognized him as such from his markings). The bladed weapon was customarily utilized only for ceremony, but the second-in-command kept the blade so sharp that any hair that chanced to float across the blade would be neatly bisected.

It was that sharpness that made the difference as the blade sliced through the air and through Pmarr's gloved wrists. There was the acrid smell of something burning—circuitry in the gloves—and then Pmarr's hands fell off. The cut had been so smooth that it was slow to register on him. Once the reality sank in, a good few seconds later, that was when his screaming began.

The Aerons were not a reticent race, and did not hesitate to express whatever was on their minds. As a result, they went to work on Pmarr with uninhibited gusto. It would have been impossible to say how long he'd actually been dead before they stopped pounding on him, at what point in the battering his soul had actually fled the body. They might have gone on for quite some time longer if a horrified scream hadn't soared above their shouts of fury and interrupted them at their gory pastime.

The scream came from within the bedchamber, and several of the soldiers dashed in, realizing even before they got there that they had completely forgotten about the young girl. Instead, they had allowed themselves to be completely caught up in their bloodthirst. The girl, for her part, was standing in the middle of the room, her arms rigidly at her sides, her fists curled into balls, her face ashen. The scream didn't sound like anything an Aeron female would produce. Instead, it sounded much more like the wounded and horrified howling of a stricken beast.

She was not looking at the tattered remains of her parents. Instead she was staring straight ahead, her eyes not focused on anything. It was as if she were looking deep into herself and saw within images that she knew she would never be able to erase from her mind.

The soldiers looked at each other uncomfortably. They knew who and what she was, but had no idea how to proceed. They were men of war and destruction, not prepared— by temperament or training—for dealing gently with a traumatized child. The commander took a tentative step toward her, stretched out a hand. "Tsana," he said.

She kept screaming even as she twisted and spun from him, moving so quickly she might as well have been composed of light. She dashed past them and sprinted down the corridor, still screaming. The soldiers simply stood there until the irritated commander said impatiently, "Go after her!" and then, dissatisfied with the way they were standing there, took off after her himself. Several of his men trailed him.

The girl he'd called Tsana ran into another room, a room that the commander recognized instantly as the bedchamber of the Zarnon. The screaming didn't halt, but instead escalated, and she dashed right back out before the commander could draw near her. He barely gave a glance into the room, knowing that he was going to see the blood-spattered corpse of the Zarnon. It had, after all, been there moments before and wasn't likely to have gone anywhere. "Tsana!" he called again, even as she ran into another bedchamber.

The screaming stopped.

Immediately concerned, the commander and his men ran into the room. There was nobody there. The window was wide open, a steady breeze wafting through and causing the drapes to flap. Three quick, long strides carried the commander across the room and, with trepidation, he looked out and down. He saw the crumbled body of the Zarn's eldest girl, and was relieved to see that Tsana's was not next to it. The commander withdrew into the room and glanced around, trying to determine where the girl might have gone. His attention was immediately drawn to the bed. It was large and ornate, with carefully made yellow sheets, as if the bed was expecting its owner to lie down in it sometime soon.

Two of the soldiers went to either side of the bed, nodded to each other in coordinating the effort, and lifted the bed clear of the floor. And there, on the floor, was the girl. She was curled up, trembling slightly, staring off to that same place that could have been either inside or outside of her head.

It was in the commander's nature to be brusque, but the child's clearly damaged state cut through that demeanor. He gestured for the soldiers to move the bed away completely, which they did, and then crouched near her. "Tsana," he said softly. "It's safe. It's perfectly safe now."

Except he knew it was a lie. Somehow Markanian soldiers had gained entrance into the mansion. It had been cursedly stupid for them to beat the one captured Markanian into a bloody, useless mass; they had given in to the blood-fever of the moment, and now they were going to pay for it, because they were going to remain in ignorance of how the Markanians had achieved the massacre. More than that, though . . . this little girl, like any other, drew security from her family. But her family lay in bloodstained shreds, and she—not quite a woman, hovering just on the cusp of it—would never know anything resembling security again.

Tsana whimpered to herself slightly, giving voice in a light, singsong tone that might have been echoes of a lullaby her mother had sung her, and then lapsed into silence. And nothing that any of the soldiers did could stir her from it. The commander picked her up; her body was stiff, as if death had already claimed it and the muscles had seized up.

"It will be all right," he lied once more, and wondered how anything would be all right for the child, ever again.

2

DEPARTMENT OF TEMPORAL INVESTIGATIONS

THE OFFICE WAS relatively spare in its adornments. A few chairs that were reasonably comfortable, carpeting that could stand to be replaced, and a desk at which the receptionist— a junior lieutenant—was seated. His face was somewhat pinched-looking, as if he were sitting on a tack. He seemed to be rather determined to focus on the files on his computer screen, but he kept glancing in the direction of the individual who was occupying one of the chairs. He was trying to be subtle about it, and failing rather miserably.

She knew he was interested in her, intrigued by her. She could always tell. She could smell it. The increased hormone levels, the pheromones—whatever it was that someone was giving off, the scent was as strong as burning meat to her.

"Excuse me," she said after what had seemed an interminable amount of time. Probably welcoming the opportunity to have an excuse to do so, the lieutenant j.g. looked her full in the face. Her voice was low, almost purring. "I'm still feeling a bit . . . disoriented. I was under the impression that I was to have a meeting with Admiral Gulliver at seventeen hundred hours. I . . . could be wrong about that, I admit. I'm still a little fuzzy on the way things are being done hereabouts, Lieutenant . . ."

"Vickers. Robert Vickers. Bob. You can call me Bob," he said quickly.

"Bob. If you could just check and—"

"I've already checked," he assured her. "You did have an appointment, yes, and the admiral is running a little late . . . plus, he's waiting for someone. . . ."

"Waiting?" Her brow furrowed. "Who is he waiting for?"

"He didn't say. I'm afraid he doesn't tell me all that much," Vickers said apologetically.

Mentally, she shrugged, deciding that Vickers wasn't going to be of much help. She further decided that if something about the circumstance didn't change within the next few seconds, she was going to get up and leave and . . .

And go where?

For about half a second there she had felt a degree of hope. It would have been wonderful if she were actually able to accomplish something, go somewhere, do something. But that hope had quickly faded as the crushing reality of her difficulties closed in on her once more.

Dead. Dead, they're all dead, and you should be, too. What are you doing here? Why can't you be dead, too? What possible purpose can there be to continuing in this . . . ?

Then the door to the waiting room slid open, and a scent immediately caught her attention. It was incredibly familiar, one that she knew almost as well as her own. She rose from her chair, determined to stand, even though she felt so weak-kneed from astonishment that she thought she would fall.

The owner of the scent scuttled in with that bizarre, familiar, semi-pirouette walk that his tripodal form required. Indeed, among various quarters it had caused him to acquire nicknames ranging from "Top" to "Merry-Go-Round" (and even "Dreidel" on one occasion). His thin neck extended a bit further than its normal length as his craggy, crab-like head turned in her direction. Something vaguely resembling a smile played across his lips. "Fancy meeting you here," he said in that slightly vibrating voice of his which, once upon a time, she had found rather grating. Now it was the most wonderful sound in the world to her.

"Arex!" she fairly shrieked, and leaped the distance of the room toward him. He enfolded her in his three arms and she felt, rather than heard, amused laughter in his chest.

"Greetings, M'Ress," he said.

"It's you! It's really you!" She shook her head in disbelief, her great mane of orange hair swaying from one side to the other. Her furred muzzle was crinkled up in that way she had when she was grinning, and her fangs were bared—not in threat, but in surprise. Her pointed ears atop her head were flattened down, as if she were expecting to be petted, and her limpid green cats' eyes were wide with joy. "I never thought I'd be so happy to see anyone in my life, much less you!"

Arex digested the sentiment and finally said, "I believe I shall choose to take that as a compliment, as oddly phrased as it might be."

"But what are you doing here! Have you . . ." She gasped, not daring to believe it, gripping his bony shoulders with such force that she quickly eased up, lest she break them. "You've come to take me back. That's it, isn't it? I'm not trapped in this time. There's a way to return to our century."

Arex was about to reply, but then the door to the inner office slid open. An avuncular-looking gentleman with a salt-and-pepper beard and a gleaming forehead smiled at the two of them. "Greetings," he said. "I'm Admiral Gulliver. Welcome to the Starfleet Department for Temporally Displaced Officers. Come in, come in, both of you."

Understanding dawned upon the feline officer as she turned her gaze toward Arex. He nodded in silent confirmation of that which she was already figuring out. "You're . . . trapped here, too?" she asked, but there wasn't very much question in her voice.

He sighed. "Shuttle expedition that fell through a wormhole. You?"

"Landing party expedition that stumbled across a time gateway of some sort."

"Yes, yes, most unfortunate," Gulliver said in a neutral tone . . . so carefully neutral, in fact, that it caught M'Ress's attention. It made her feel as if there was something that he wasn't saying. But before she could pursue it, Gulliver said, "If you'll . . . ?" as he gestured once again for them to enter, not bothering to repeat the invitation out loud.

M'Ress preceded Arex into the office, but she was already feeling despondent over the situation. For one joyous moment she had thought she had a way out of her predicament, only to discover that Arex was in the same fix that she was. Humans liked to say that misery loves company, but having experienced it, she could now say with complete authority that all misery loved was a way to stop being miserable. Having someone to share your grief didn't accomplish a damned thing.

As opposed to Arex's scuttling walk, M'Ress moved with delicate, feline grace, one foot carefully placed directly in front of the other. Early in her career she'd worn boots, but had never been able to find a pair that was truly comfortable, and eventually she'd shed them in favor of going barefoot. Her own natural pads provided more than enough protection, and it added a nice element of stealth to her approach that she found preferable to clonking about in Starfleet-issue footwear. In this case, however, her movements reflected her despondency; she actually made noise padding across the carpet, which was most unusual for her. She didn't care.

Gulliver circled behind his desk, rolling out his chair so he could sit while continuing to speak in a very pleasant tone. "I've always imagined it Starfleet's bit of whimsy, assigning someone named Gulliver to oversee a department in charge of unusual travels. Don't you think so?"

"I suppose," said M'Ress, looking as blank as she felt.

"It seems most . . . amusing to me," Arex affirmed.

Gulliver looked from one to the other. "You've never read *Gulliver's Travels,* have you."

"Should we have?" inquired M'Ress. "Is it autobiographical?"

"Wha—? Oh . . . no," and he laughed. "I didn't write it. A man named Jonathan Swift did. It's a novel about a fellow who finds himself in some very strange places, and he's endeavoring to get home."

"In that respect, I can definitely empathize," said M'Ress. As was her habit, she stretched out the *m* just a hair, making it sound as if she truly enjoyed saying the word. She leaned forward, her long, leonine tail whipping around behind her, showing her momentary excitement. "And . . . is there a way? For us, I mean? To return to—"

But her feelings sank once more when Gulliver began shaking his head. "I'm sorry. It's quite against Starfleet Temporal policy."

"*Against policy!*" Her ears twitched. "But . . . there are ways to time travel in a controlled fashion. James Kirk did it, several times. . . ."

"Including one time when he obtained whales and saved the earth; yes, we're all quite aware of the legends of the good captain," Gulliver said patiently.

"He wasn't a legend to me. I knew him. I served under him. And if he could do it—"

"Then you should be able to do it?" He shook his head again even as she nodded hers. "Again, I'm afraid not."

"But what difference will it make if I return home?"

"We don't know. And that is the problem. You see, M'Ress, Starfleet Temporal policy is as follows," and he leaned forward, fingers interlaced on the desk. "When it comes to temporal displacement, all things happen for a purpose."

"That's predestination." She blew air impatiently between her teeth. "You're telling me that there's some greater being manipulating our lives and making a shambles of them in as creative a manner as possible?"

He chuckled and said, "We tend to leave that decision to the individual. The point is, you're here, now. According to our records, you vanished over eighty years ago. That's the reality of our universe. The same with Arex, some,"—he double-checked the files—"seventy-one years ago."

"And if we unvanish, what difference will it make?" demanded M'Ress.

"We don't know." It was Arex who had spoken. When she looked at him in obvious surprise that he seemed to be taking the admiral's side, he simply shrugged. "This is my second time having this discussion. I volunteered to be here when I heard you were coming through, for old time's sake."

" 'Old time' is all I have left to me," said M'Ress bleakly. "I still can't believe that my returning would pose any sort of risk. . . ."

"You said it yourself, Lieutenant," Gulliver reminded her. "You served with Captain Kirk. He learned firsthand the difference that even one person could make. Starfleet . . . indeed, the Federation . . . is bound by the Prime Directive to do everything within its power to maintain the status quo, if you will, of all worlds. The reality of the worlds of the here and now includes one Caitian, Lieutenant Shiboline M'Ress, and one Triexian, Lieutenant Arex Na Eth, having disappeared without a trace. That must remain the case. I'm sorry."

"Are you?" M'Ress said, making no endeavor to keep the

bitterness from her voice. She felt as if she wanted to scream, as if she wanted to explode in all directions at once. But all of her training, her very nature, prompted her to keep her own counsel. She did not want this . . . this stranger to see how upset she truly was, so instead she reined herself in and tried to keep her voice as neutral as possible. "When someone is truly sorry, they endeavor to make things better. Are you going to try and make things better for me, Admiral? Better for Arex?"

"We already have been doing so, Lieutenant," Gulliver said patiently. "You certainly have firsthand knowledge of that. The education—"

"Yes, yes, I know," sighed M'Ress. "I wasn't trying to be dismissive of the reeducation program you've been utilizing. Sleep-teaching, psi-teaching, all manner of specialized learning tools you've been using to make me aware of how much I've missed. But . . ."

"But what?"

"Well, it's . . . it's made me aware of how much I've missed."

Gulliver didn't comprehend, but Arex clearly did. "Admiral," he said softly, "much of the joy of what we do is derived from the discovering of it. It's as if . . ." He paused, trying to come up with a workable comparison, and then he smiled. "Let us say that you have a child. A son. So one day you're at home, holding the newborn infant in your arms. Then you put it down, walk out the door, thinking you'll be back in fifteen minutes. Well, one thing leads to another, and the next thing you know, you return and it's fifteen *years* later. So there's your son, all grown, smiling, welcoming you back to the bosom of your home. And he sits you down and tells you everything that he's been up to in the intervening decade and a half. So there you are, appreciating all that . . . and glad to see how tall and strong he's grown . . . but at the same time . . ."

"At the same time," Gulliver interrupted, smiling sadly,

"you're overwhelmed with regret for not having been there to see it all happen."

"Yes," M'Ress said. "Exactly." She shifted in her seat and looked at Arex. "Thank you. Thank you for expressing it so well."

"I am pleased I could be of service," said Arex.

"Well," said Gulliver, sounding quite regretful, "there's nothing we can do about the time lost. Still, if you'll allow me a bit of humor: I have every confidence that you'll land on your feet."

M'Ress winced visibly. "That would be a cat joke, would it not? How nice to know some things remain consistent."

"M'Ress has heard them all," Arex told Gulliver by way of explanation. "There are very few Caitians in Starfleet . . . or at least there *were* few when we were there. And when she would encounter new individuals, they would invariably make a reference to, or joke about, earth felines, always thinking they were the first to come up with it. It's always meant in gentle jest, with no nastiness attached to it . . . but it becomes repetitive and even tiresome."

"So let us be clear with one another, Admiral," M'Ress said, leaning forward, furred fingers interlaced. "I have one life, not nine. I have never been killed by curiosity, my parents do not live in a cat house, my mother did not rock me as an infant in a cat's cradle, the preferred Caitian method of self-defense is not cat-boxing, I do not deposit my earnings into a kitty, if I am trying to be delicate about a subject I do not pussyfoot around . . . shall I go on?"

"I would really prefer if you did not," Gulliver assured her. "My apologies. I didn't realize I was walking on such thoroughly trod ground. Let's . . . try things from another approach. Would you like me to arrange for you to visit your native Caitia? Granted, they're not members of the Federation . . ."

M'Ress tilted her head in surprise, her ears visibly rising as if something most unexpected had been said. "Caitia . . . *isn't?* But . . . but we were when I . . . at the time I left."

"That's true. However, Caitia has undergone a number of changes in leadership. Matters continue to remain fickle on your homeworld, I fear."

"Well, that would certainly be typical. So they simply left the UFP . . . ?"

"Not quite *that* simply, actually," said Gulliver. He called up a file on his computer, and M'Ress looked longingly at her homeworld, floating on the monitor screen. His finger ran down a series of dates. "Two years after your accident, they left the Federation . . . but eventually there was a shift in Caitian leadership and politics, and so they requested, and received, permission to rejoin . . . except, as soon as they were in, they . . ."

He started to laugh.

M'Ress looked at him in confusion. "What is it?"

"Well, obviously, when they were in, they wanted out . . . and when they were out, they wanted back in, and out again, and in once more, because that's what happens with . . ." His voice trailed off as he saw the utterly bemused stare M'Ress was giving him. He cleared his throat, composing himself. "What happens with a . . . volatile world . . . such as, uhm . . . yours."

"Oh," said M'Ress, aware that there was something she was missing, but not wanting to pursue it lest there be jokes about curiosity again.

"In any event, it's quite likely they'll be rejoining at some point in the near future. In the meantime, your status as a Starfleet officer remains 'grandfatherered,' as they used to say. And a visit to Caitia can be arranged. . . ."

But M'Ress shook her head, a sad smile playing across her lips. "I don't see the point, really. My family, my friends, are all quite, quite dead. My people are not the longest-lived, you see. Unlike, as I recall, the natives of Triex," and she inclined her head toward Arex.

"That is true," Arex said, trying to sound modest. "I have, in fact, been in touch with my parents, eleven brothers, and thirteen sisters."

"And—?"

"They were unaware I was gone."

M'Ress and Gulliver gaped at him. "I'm sorry, did you say . . . unaware?" asked a stunned Gulliver. "How could your parents be unaware that you were gone?"

"Because I have eleven brothers and thirteen sisters," said Arex reasonably, his head craning forward on his thin neck. "Who between them have, I might add, given my parents eighty-three grandchildren. I suspect they were grateful for one less name to remember. Besides, my people are not quite as conscious of time as yours are. Then again, our lifespan averages several hundred years, so that's going to happen. We're not as driven by—"

"We get the idea, Arex," M'Ress said irritably. Then she took a deep breath. "I'm sorry."

"No apologies necessary," he assured her.

She nodded once and then returned her attention to Gulliver. "I cannot speak for Arex, but as for me . . . to be honest, I'd rather be returned to active duty as soon as possible, *if* that's possible. For if I have to spend excess time dwelling on all that's happened, and the unfairness of my predicament . . ."

"You do, in fact, speak for me," said Arex. "I've been undergoing the same retraining program that you're presently involved with, M'Ress. And I'm assured by Admiral Gulliver here that the program can continue, under medical supervision, while aboard a starship. I would just as soon do that, if that is permissible."

"It is the job of this department, Lieutenants, to accommodate time-displaced personnel whenever it's possible. I think this is certainly one of those instances where we can make it very possible. And, by great good fortune, there's a starship captain already asking after you."

"Is there?" M'Ress glanced at Arex to see his reaction, but he looked just as surprised as she was.

"Yes. As a matter of fact, she should be in my outer office, presuming she's punctual . . . and from all that I hear, she is very much that. Vickers," he called, raising his voice slightly.

Vickers's voice promptly came back over the interoffice comm unit. "Sir?"

"Is our esteemed captain here?"

"Yes, sir."

"Send her in, please."

M'Ress and Arex reflexively rose, as courtesy and protocol required. The door to the office hissed open and a smiling woman with curly, strawberry blonde hair and a look of quiet authority entered the room. Promptly Admiral Gulliver rose and said, "Captain Elizabeth Shelby, may I introduce Lieutenants Shiboline M'Ress and Arex Na Eth."

The woman introduced as Shelby smiled at each of them. It struck M'Ress as not quite a sincere smile. It wasn't *in*sincere. It was just . . . all business, that was it. It was as if this Captain Shelby had allotted a precise number of seconds to the smile and, once those seconds had passed, the smile could be dispensed with. She wasn't, M'Ress decided, unkind. She was just very focused.

She nodded at each of them in turn and then said, "Please, sit." They did so. She remained standing, draping her hands casually behind her back.

"Captain Shelby has just been put in command of the *Trident*," Gulliver said.

Without blinking an eye, Arex said, "The *Trident*. Registry NCC-31347. Newly commissioned *Galaxy*-class vessel."

"That's correct," Shelby said, looking surprised, but not too surprised. "It would appear Starfleet speed-teaching techniques are all that I've heard. A pity they're not used at the Academy. We could all graduate within six months."

"There's something to be said for savoring the learning process," said Gulliver.

Shelby nodded absently as she returned her focus to the time-displaced officers. "I've looked over both your files. Impressive. Very impressive."

"I'm afraid they're a bit truncated," M'Ress said. Without thinking she curled her legs up underneath herself in a somewhat protective manner. "Suggestions of careers that might have been, rather than what were."

"Perhaps. But they showed a great deal of promise. And you come highly recommended."

"Really. By whom?"

"By Captain James T. Kirk."

Arex and M'Ress exchanged looks. "He's . . . *alive* . . . ?"

"Apparently not. But he had a good deal of foresight, Captain Kirk did. Remember, both of you disappeared under rather curious circumstances. Eventually Captain Kirk learned of your misfortunes, and the esteemed captain thought highly enough of you to prepare extensive and copious recommendations for you in the event that either or both of you should be found. I don't think he was anticipating the rather unlikely happenstance that you would both turn up here and now, within weeks of each other. Then again," she shrugged, "perhaps he did. My understanding of him was that he was a rather remarkable man."

"He was most definitely that," M'Ress sighed, with the air of one who held close to her heart an emotion so unrequited that she had never even given full attention to it. Then she blinked thoughtfully. "It . . . is a rather odd circumstance at that, isn't it? That we should both return around now."

"Perhaps. Or perhaps . . . not so coincidental," said Gulliver.

"Meaning?" asked Arex.

Gulliver leaned forward once more, looking even more serious than before, and with all the gravity he could muster he said, "I have no idea."

"Oh. Well . . . that's helpful," said M'Ress.

"The universe, Lieutenant, is like an intricate painting. Sometimes, if you step back far enough, it makes sense."

"And how far back would we have to step in order to make sense of our current situation?" she asked.

"Well, for starters," Shelby told them, "you can step aboard the *Trident*."

Arex leaned back and drummed his fingers on one of his legs. It was a nervous habit that M'Ress had always found irritating. Now she found it oddly comforting. It was amazing what a difference a few decades could make. "You'd want us on your ship, even though we were recommended by Captain Kirk?" asked Arex.

Shelby looked puzzled at that. "Why wouldn't I?"

"Let us not mince words, Captain," Arex said politely. "I have read essays, opinions by Starfleet officers of more recent vintage. A number of them have been highly critical of James Kirk. I've seen him referred to as a cowboy, a maverick, a madman, a fabricator of mythic proportions. Why would you be interested in people who served under a man such as that?"

"Because," she replied evenly, "*I* served under a man such as that. It was the best experience of my life, even if I didn't realize it at the time. His name's Mackenzie Calhoun; he's the captain of the *Excalibur*."

"Really?" M'Ress laughed. She found herself liking the woman's candor. She even liked her scent. Relaxing slightly, she said, "He sounds interesting. I'd like to meet him. Is he single?"

"Married."

"Ah. Well, men like that never stay married. I feel sorry for his wife."

"I'll tell him you said that," said Shelby, "the next time I'm having conjugal relations with him."

M'Ress opened her mouth, then closed it. Arex was clearly trying not to laugh. She wondered if he'd known that this Calhoun was Shelby's husband. Probably. And the bastard had let her walk right into it.

"Did I just talk myself out of a posting to your ship?" M'Ress finally managed to say.

"Not at all. Frankly," Shelby told her, "I have the oddest feeling you're going to fit right in."

3

AERON

WARMASTER BURKITT STOOD over the unmoving form of Tsana, slowly shaking his head. He had been doing nothing but that for quite some time, and Gragg was waiting for Burkitt to say something—anything—but nothing seemed forthcoming. Burkitt simply stayed right where he was, head going back and forth.

As far as Gragg was concerned, Burkitt was the kind of man who could only be a warmaster, who could only become some sort of leader. Every aspect of his personality radiated confidence and an unvoiced—but nevertheless palpable—demand that others follow him. Although he was no giant, he nevertheless seemed to tower above others in his deportment and confidence. Indeed, Gragg was physically taller and more imposing than Burkitt, with wide shoulders and a blocky head that seemed to fit seamlessly onto his shoulders without benefit of neck. Nevertheless, if one were looking at Gragg and Burkitt standing together, there would never be any doubt as to who was in charge.

Gragg, who had been the commander of the soldier forces that had interceded, belatedly, in the slaughter of the imperials, was still having trouble believing in the reality of his world. Only two nights ago, the floors of the mansion had been awash with blood. As if observing the proceedings from a far-off distance, he had mentally "watched himself" as he had picked up the trembling body of the young girl and hurried off with her to a proper medical facility. Such had been Commander Gragg's confidence in Aeron medicine that he had been certain—naively certain, to be sure—that she would recover in no time. She just needed rest, isolation, and support.

Well, she had received all three of those things. And the Aeron days, normally cold this time of year, had warmed up appreciably, as if to provide that much more comfort for the people of Aeron in general and Tsana in particular. Tsana, the sole survivor of her imperial family.

Burkitt and Gragg went quite a ways back. Gragg remembered Burkitt when he, Gragg, had been simply a raw recruit, and Burkitt was the most intimidating, ruthless, and also efficient commander the armed forces of Aeron had ever known. For reasons that eluded Gragg to this day, Burkitt had seen potential in Gragg and chosen to mentor him to a large degree. As a consequence, Gragg had risen through the ranks until he was now holding a rank equivalent to what Burkitt had possessed when they first met. As for Burkitt himself, he was still as intimidating as ever. They had fought together, gotten drunk together . . . Burkitt had even introduced Gragg to the first female he'd ever coupled with. But still, those black, fiery eyes set against the pale skin were enough to make Gragg feel once again like the rawest of recruits whenever they focused on him and there was cold fury burning within them. Fury such as he was displaying now, for instance.

"Still no change in her condition?" asked Burkitt.

"None." Gragg shook his head. "God only knows what horrors have invaded that child's mind."

"Running from horrors doesn't help. The only way to deal with them is to meet them head-on."

There was not the slightest trace of sympathy in his voice. Gragg looked at Burkitt and said, carefully, "Warmaster . . . she is but a child."

"And childhood is when the preponderance of learning is achieved," Burkitt replied, his voice a low rumble that seemed to originate from somewhere around his knees. "If one does not learn emotional toughness when one is of a young age, it is most unlikely one will develop it in old age. And it is a trait Tsana can and must develop. You seem to have forgotten, Commander: She is our only surviving imperial. By tradition and by law, she is to be the next Zarn." He snorted. "Look at her. Look at the face of leadership for Aeron."

A small trickle of spittle was hanging from the edge of her mouth. Her eyes were wide open, but still staring inward.

"Doesn't give you much hope for our future, does it?" asked Burkitt.

Gragg looked forlornly at the helpless child. "And what is the law for a situation such as this?"

"If an imperial is incapacitated . . . which is certainly the case here . . . then the nine Counselars are to choose a regent from among themselves to rule in the Zarn's place."

"And how is this choosing to be done?"

"That," sighed Burkitt, "is the regrettable aspect. There is no single proscribed procedure. The usual result is that the Counselars employ methods that begin with politicking and, more often than not, result in a full-blown, unholy war. Such is the way of things when a Zarn is alive, but incapacitated. Now, if the Zarn is killed . . ."

There was a significant pause, and Gragg looked at Burkitt curiously. "If the Zarn is killed . . . ?"

"In that case . . . the Warmaster is given charge."

Gragg could not quite believe it. "Why—?"

"Because," said Burkitt with grim amusement, "the law-makers reasoned that an assassinated Zarn meant that we were either at war, or caught up in events that would send us spiraling toward war. The selections by the Counselars are perfectly adequate if old age or illness fells a Zarn . . . but if a Zarn is cut down, it was supposed that war was inevitable. At such a time, the oldest and most experienced military hand on Aeron would naturally step in to guide our people through such . . . unfortunate times."

"Meaning you."

"Meaning me."

His gaze shifted uncomfortably from Burkitt to Tsana and back again. "But the Zarn . . . at least, the new Zarn . . . yet lives. So you are saying by the letter of our laws . . ."

Slowly the warmaster turned to look at his longtime fol-lower, his eyes glowing but unreadable. "I am merely one of the Counselars, with no more or less influence and power than any other. If, however, Tsana were to die . . . and it would be supposed that the poor distraught child simply gave up her hold on life rather than live with the shocking events she had witnessed . . ."

"Then you would be the unquestioned power on Aeron."

Burkitt nodded.

For what seemed an eternity, the two old soldiers stood there, staring at the girl who might well have been thought to be dead, were it not for the slight rising and falling of her chest. Then, without saying a word, Burkitt picked up a pil-low. He scrunched it lightly between his large fists, as if test-ing its heft, and then he started to lean forward to press it down over the girl's face.

The soft hum of a weapon stopped him. Silently, Burkitt turned to see Gragg standing there, his weapon leveled at him. There was the slightest flutter of what appeared to be fear visible in Gragg's eyes, but if he was indeed daunted, it did not translate to the mildest hesitation in his aim. The gun was unwavering.

"Put it down, Warmaster," he said.

And Burkitt smiled approvingly. "Good. Very good." He tossed the pillow aside.

Gragg looked at him askance. He didn't lower the weapon so much as a micron. "Very good?"

Burkitt approached him as if coming to a child to congratulate him on achieving a high mark, and rested his hands on Gragg's shoulders as he would a trusted confidant, rather than someone who had just been aiming a weapon at him. "There will be dark times ahead for Aeron," Burkitt informed him. "There will be those who will desire to throw the rule of law aside. In that way lies pure chaos, and we will eat ourselves alive and destroy ourselves long before we've had the slightest opportunity to see retribution upon our foes. I desired to see whether you had respect for that law."

"So . . . this was intended to be some sort of . . . of test . . ?"

"Yes. Just so. What . . . ?" Burkitt actually appeared to have a surprised look. "After all the years we have worked with one another . . . after all that we have achieved . . . do you know me so little, Gragg, that you think me capable of smothering a helpless child in her sickbed?"

"As you said yourself, Warmaster . . . there are dark times ahead." He bowed politely. "It is not for me to say whether they have not, in fact, already arrived."

Then they heard noises, chanting, in the distance. Gragg went to one of the windows and looked out. What he saw was not entirely unexpected, but, nevertheless, it was somewhat amazing. There were people, as far as the eye could see. They were marching in slow but orderly fashion, waving to one side and then the other, their arms stretched toward heaven in supplication.

"A Mourning March," he said, by way of informing Burkitt. "I have never seen one so massive, though."

"Nor will you again, let us hope," said Burkitt. "You attended the funeral?"

Gragg shook his head. "I felt it better if I remained on post here, along with the rest of the protective force. There is nothing to say that the Markanians would not return in an endeavor to complete their grisly work. Tsana needed to be protected."

"Indeed, she did. But you loved the imperials as much as any other good Aeron."

"I . . . did, Warmaster."

Burkitt looked at him askance, a sympathetic expression working its way across his face. "Including, particularly, the eldest daughter. What was her name—?"

"Jylla," Gragg said tonelessly.

"I thought it was my . . . imagination that you seemed to be spending a preponderance of time with—"

"The imagination was indeed the province of our relationship, Warmaster, I assure you. There was nothing further than that, there could never . . . be . . ." His voice trailed off.

He patted Gragg affectionately on the back. "Yet while she lived . . . there was hope, however forlorn it might be." He said nothing for a moment, allowing Gragg his quiet but noble pain. Finally he observed, "Funerals and mourning are not for the dead, you know. The dead cannot hear us, no matter what all the theologians might say. They are for the living. I suggest you join the march, Gragg. It will help alleviate some of the pain you are feeling just now. Eliminate, no . . . but alleviate. It will set you on the path toward healing."

Gragg was listening to this, nodding in acknowledgment . . . and then he stopped and looked at Burkitt with a suspicion that he couldn't quite disguise. "And . . . if I were to do that . . . you would . . . ?"

"Remain here. The funeral was most impressive, as I said. The ceremonial torches, the lamentations, the musical crescendos . . . an impressive send-off to a family that was much beloved. There is only so much mourning, though, that even the sturdiest of warriors can endure." He looked at him curiously, something in Gragg's tone clearly alerting him to concern on the commander's part. "Why, Gragg? Is there some difficulty if I—?" Then he stopped talking, and Gragg couldn't help but wonder if he was simply feigning surprise or was genuinely startled to perceive what was running through Gragg's mind. "Ah. You fear to leave Tsana with me. You believe I will kill her in your absence."

"I thought you were trying to kill her in my presence, Warmaster. Why should my absence be any more daunting to you?"

"But as I assured you, Gragg . . . that was merely a test of your own loyalty." He took a step forward, arms folded, and said, "I now trust your loyalty, Gragg. Your loyalty to the laws of our people, and your loyalty to me. If we are to continue serving as warmaster and commander to one another . . . you are going to have to make it clear that you trust me as well. Otherwise, how will either of us know whom to count on in the dark times? Would you have me swear an oath?"

Gragg's impulse was to look down and shake his head. Instead, he fought that compulsion toward subservience and, meeting Burkitt's look, he said, "Aye. I would."

"Very well," said Burkitt, apparently not the least bit perturbed. "I swear an oath, upon my honor and upon the lives and honor of all those I hold dear, that no harm shall come to Tsana if it is within my capability to prevent it. Satisfied, Gragg?"

In truth, he wasn't. But he could not think of any way to further challenge the matter without straying well into the realm of insult. So he gave a terse nod, turned, and headed out to join the Mourning March.

There were soldiers at the door and he could easily have told them to go in and keep an eye on Burkitt, but that would not have accomplished anything in terms of displaying trust. He did say to them, though, "Keep a listen for any Markanian intrusion. Remember that they penetrated the mansion's inner security once already. A second time is eminently possible." It was only after he had departed to join the march that he began to kick himself mentally. All unintentionally, he had just given Burkitt the excuse for a cover-up that he might have needed. If Burkitt disposed of Tsana while Gragg was gone, he might turn around and try to find a way to blame it on the Markanians.

He thought of poor, helpless Tsana lying there. And he thought of Jylla's broken and bloody body where he'd discovered it in the courtyard. At first he had thought that the Markanians had flung her to her death, but then he'd come to the decision that she had probably chosen to end her life on her own terms, rather than let the invading bastards do whatever they wished with her. After that he thought about the Markanians, and how much he hated them.

The night had turned, the air stinging in his lungs as he walked. He didn't acknowledge it; he simply ignored the cold. As he blended in with the marchers, his thoughts continued to tumble against one another. Despite what Burkitt had said, he did not feel the grieving for his departed Jylla diminishing, nor did he experience any less sorrow for the comatose Tsana, not to mention the other slaughtered members of the family. His hatred for the Markanians, on the other hand, swelled. He felt as if blood was rushing to every part of his body, exciting him, galvanizing him, making him see the reality of the world with greater clarity than ever before.

They must die. The words went through his head, straight and clear and with utter certainty. *They must die so that we can live in safety and peace. They must die because of their crimes against us. They must die . . . because the bodies of the Zarn and his family cry out for it. They must die . . . because they are Markanians, and our ancient enemy, and we thought we could coexist in the galaxy with them . . . but obviously we were wrong. And because we were wrong, the*

*Zarn and his family paid for it with their lives, and they must
be avenged.*

So angry and black were his thoughts that, by the time
he returned to the imperial mansion, he had almost forgotten that he had not expected to see Tsana still alive. Yet
when he walked into her chamber, there she was, safe and
sound. It took him a moment to realize that her continued
existence was a matter of some surprise to him. Burkitt, for
his part, was seated several feet away, studying what appeared to be some sort of report, his legs crossed in a casual fashion. He glanced up at Gragg with only the mildest
of interest. "Surprised to see her alive, Commander?" he
asked.

"No, Warmaster."

"Don't lie to me."

"Yes, Warmaster."

He sighed heavily. "And yet you trusted me sufficiently to
hope that I would heed my word. I suppose I shall have to
take my triumphs where I can. Have you been dwelling on
the Markanians, Commander?"

"I have, yes," said Gragg, with an air of someone who was
relieved not to have to prevaricate or overanalyze every
word he spoke before actually speaking it.

"And your conclusion?"

"They must die."

"Yessss," said the thoughtful warmaster. "I have come to
much the same conclusion. The question, though, is: How?
They are, after all, upon another world. Deposited there during the great exodus thrust upon us by the Thallonians, all
those many, many years back. We do not have a space fleet
at our disposal."

"Neither do they," Gragg pointed out.

"Which prompts one to wonder, not for the first time:
How did they get here?"

"I do not know," Gragg said. Then he considered and continued, in a slightly scholarly and singsong voice, "However . . . whatever method they chose to arrive here . . ."

"We can somehow utilize in order to go back after them," said Burkitt, and Gragg smiled eagerly at the prospect. "That is precisely right, Gragg. We will learn how the Markanians accomplished their assault upon us, and we will turn it back upon them. Then, and only then, will the memories of the Zarn and his family be avenged. Only then will we be able to stand proudly and call ourselves Aeron."

Tsana, for her part, continued to lay there in silence, with a little more spittle running down her face.

4

EXCALIBUR

MACKENZIE CALHOUN HAD been determined to wait until everything was "just so" before taking this final step. Now, however, as he looked around the ready room with satisfaction, he decided that the time had come.

He scratched absently at his chin, the bristles of his beard wiry beneath his fingers. Such was the nature of his crew that they felt no trepidation about weighing in with opinions on his facial hair, whether solicited or not (and, in this instance, most definitely not). And they were saying uniformly the same thing: lose it.

Granted, it was not the most elegant growth ever sported in the history of Starfleet. It was patchy in places, and there were also a few bits of gray coming in. The major problem was that there was dead skin in the area of the vicious scar that ran down the right side of his face, and no facial hair was growing in there. So no matter what, the full beard was going to have an uneven look to it. That was one of the things he liked about it. Not only that, but it was somewhat nonregulation just because of its unevenness. He liked that aspect of it even more.

"After all," he said out loud to no one, "if Eppy isn't going to be around to remind me that I'm out-of-bounds, then I'm just going to have to remind myself."

This, of course, was enough to depress him a bit. But he pushed his way past it, deciding that dwelling upon it was certainly going to accomplish nothing. Instead he decided to focus on that which pleased him: namely, the final touch.

He reached into a cabinet and withdrew a package that was carefully wrapped in oilskin. It was an old-fashioned means of protecting the contents, but then again, in many respects, Mackenzie Calhoun—former warlord of the planet Xenex, who, as a teen, had spearheaded a revolution that had overthrown his world's enslavers—was something of an old-fashioned man. He unwrapped the package until finally it lay, gleaming and perfect, on his desktop.

There was a chime at his door. "Come," he called.

Burgoyne 172, the Hermat chief engineer of the *Excalibur,* entered. S/he moved and spoke with hir customary relaxed style, one that always seemed to be laughing ever so slightly at those who were disconcerted over the presence of Hermats. S/he looked with interest at the subject of Calhoun's present attention. "Nice sword, Captain," s/he observed.

"Thank you. We go way back."

"Planning to use it to shave yourself?"

Calhoun laughed. *"Et tu,* Burgoyne?"

"It was just a question," Burgoyne protested, the picture of wide-eyed innocence. "I wouldn't want you to shave."

"Oh, really? Why not? Have you got a betting pool going as to how long before I get rid of it?"

"Well . . . yes," s/he admitted. Defensively, s/he added, "I have to find some way to make the money back I lost on the pool over when you'd come back from the dead."

"Really? Who won that?"

"Lieutenant Beth, down in engineering. The rest of us, we figured if you'd survived, you'd turn up quickly, discovered in a floating pod. She was the only one willing to bet on you long-term."

"How nice. I'll be sure to send her a fruit basket in appreciation for her loyalty."

Calhoun was pleased that it was something they were actually able to joke about. In point of fact, when the previous vessel called *Excalibur* had been blown to bits, Calhoun himself would have been the last person to put any money down on his own survival. That he had managed to get out of the ship at all was a miracle, the nature of which he had not been fully able to comprehend even after all this time. He had then spent months marooned on a far-off world before managing to obtain a vessel and return to Federation space . . . with a young orphan boy named Moke in tow, having promised the boy's dying mother that he would take care of him.

But really . . . how do you fit all those circumstances into a betting pool?

"Did you come here for the sole purpose of inquiring after my face, Burgy?"

"Ah. No," Burgoyne said, as if having momentarily forgotten the reason for hir presence. "I actually came to tell you that Holodeck B is set up for the holomeeting. It's scheduled to start in just under five minutes."

"Good, good. Burgoyne, you have the honor of being present at a singular and usually private ceremony."

"Private? Why private, Captain? Does it have a deep personal and spiritual meaning?"

"No, it's just that nobody except me is remotely interested." He took the sword by the hilt and sliced it through the air. From the corner of his eye he saw Burgoyne take a cautious step back. "Problem, Burgoyne?"

"I would just rather not be bisected, Captain, if it's all the same to you."

Calhoun turned and mounted the sword onto a bracket he'd already attached to the wall just behind his desk. "I've had this sword for a great many years, Burgy. Took it off the man who gave me this scar, as a matter of fact." He studied his image in the gleaming blade.

"So the reflection in the sword has doubtlessly aged a bit since you first looked in there."

"Actually," said Calhoun with a bit of satisfaction, "whenever I look in it . . . I see myself exactly as I was. It's practically the only place I can do that. So . . ." He turned to Burgoyne, gesturing to the chief engineer to sit. Burgoyne looked slightly puzzled, obviously believing that s/he had no further business there. That pleased Calhoun; he liked to keep people off balance. Burgoyne sat, and Calhoun did likewise. "I'm somewhat curious, since you seem to be knowledgeable in all things having to do with pools. What's the current betting on who my first officer will be?"

"Smart money's on Soleta," Burgoyne said promptly. "She's the science officer, she's sharp, she's logical, she keeps her head in difficult situations. Granted, she's a lieutenant, but you could bump her up in rank."

"Mmm. And the outside money?"

"Well, the outside money has Comman—uhm, Captain Shelby reconsidering her post as captain of the *Trident* and instead returning to be your number one. I mean, the two of you are married, after all."

"So some people on this crew actually think Shelby would accept a demotion and go back to being my first officer." He laughed softly at the notion. "They don't know her very well, I think."

"Captain, pardon my asking, but . . . don't you miss her?"

Calhoun felt slightly taken aback by the question. "Miss her? Of course I miss her. That's why it took me so long to put my sword up. Because I don't do that until I feel that everything is right, and without her here, it didn't. . . ." He sighed.

Leaning forward, as if wanting to take advantage of this unusual private moment between hirself and Calhoun, Burgoyne asked, "Tell me, Captain . . . did you marry her just so you could be certain you'd still have an attachment to her? Because you were afraid that, with her off on another ship, she'd forget about you?"

Calhoun looked up at Burgoyne, and his purple eyes were unreadable, as if he'd just pulled a cloth over them. "You know, Lieutenant Commander . . . I think we'd have to know each other a bit longer, and a bit better, than we do, for me to answer that question . . . or for you to ask it."

That was more than enough for Burgoyne to realize that s/he had overstepped hirself. S/he cleared hir throat a bit too loudly and said, "Sorry, Captain. So, umm . . . Holodeck B, any time you're ready. I'll just . . ." Without finishing the sentence, s/he rose to leave.

But Calhoun didn't match the action. Instead, still seated, he said, "Just out of curiosity: Where did the number-one favorite put *her* money?"

"You mean Soleta? About first officer? She didn't. She said betting is illogical. For what it's worth, though, Lieutenant Beth told me that Soleta agreed with her."

"On what?"

"Well . . ." Burgoyne's mouth drew back in a smirk, exposing the tips of hir fangs. "You're going to laugh."

"Try me. I could use a laugh."

"Well . . . Soleta said you'd offer it to me."

Calhoun promptly laughed, and Burgoyne, visibly relaxing at the amusement from hir captain, joined in. "That's very funny!" said Calhoun, once he'd recovered himself.

"I know, I know."

Eyes glittering in amused awareness of the impact his next words would have, Calhoun said, "She's right."

The laughter died in Burgoyne's throat, and s/he gaped at him. "Wh-what?"

"In a command situation, no one knows this ship and what it's capable of better than you. And considering this vessel is a *Galaxy*-class 'hot rod,' you're certainly the right one to press it when matters become dire."

"But . . . but . . ." Burgoyne was stammering.

Calhoun proceeded to tick off reasons on his fingers. "You're intelligent, you're capable, and you're not afraid to ask me crass questions which, on occasion, you *will* have to ask. Furthermore, you're intensely loyal. Don't say that you're not; I saw how you were with our Doctor Selar, and I've heard about how you fought to retain custody of your son, Xyon. You've forged a relationship with Selar, practically through sheer willpower alone. That's what I want to see in my first officer."

"But, Captain . . . I doubt very many people on this ship see me as command material."

"Perhaps, Burgy. But your rank should attend to the 'command' aspect. I will be issuing a field promotion to 'Commander.' As for the 'material' part, I leave that entirely in your capable, and occasionally clawed, hands. Now then, I have a holoconference to attend to." At that point, Calhoun rose from behind his desk. Burgoyne was still standing, looking stunned.

Calhoun stuck out his hand and Burgoyne, reflexively, shook it. But there was no muscle in Burgoyne's arm, as if the strength had been drained out of it. "When you appointed Commander Shelby as your second-in-command, did you just 'inform' her that that was the way it was going to be, whether she wanted it or not?"

"No, of course not. She had an option. So do you."

Burgoyne looked visibly relieved. "So . . . I have the option of turning it down?"

"No, *she* did. You have the option of taking on the post now or later."

"Oh. Well . . . in that case . . . I guess I'll take it now," Burgoyne said weakly.

He patted hir on the shoulder. "Good thinking."

Burgoyne was shaking hir head in disbelief as Calhoun headed out. "And here I had money down on Soleta."

"That was a shame," said Calhoun, pausing to turn and address Burgoyne. "The reason she wasn't betting was because I asked her for what she thought would be the most logical choice, and she said you. We'll make a formal announcement later. By the way—you have the conn." And with that, Calhoun swept out of his office.

Burgoyne stood there a moment longer, trying to take in what had just happened. Then, slowly, as if walking on razor blades, s/he stepped out onto the bridge and looked around. It was just the same as always. There was the crew: Mark McHenry at conn, Robin Lefler at ops, the massive Brikar, Zak Kebron, at tactical. Soleta was at her science station, and she was glancing over at Burgoyne with a raised eyebrow. She probably already knew. Damn her.

Taking a deep breath, Burgoyne walked over into the lower well of the bridge, stopped at the command chair, and rested hir hand on it. Then s/he swung one leg over and sank into it. Even though the chair was not remotely elevated, s/he felt as if s/he were looking down from on high.

S/he looked around. Everyone was staring at hir.

McHenry leaned back and whispered, "Does the captain know you're sitting in his chair?"

S/he closed her eyes and tried to figure out who she wanted to throttle more at that moment: McHenry or Calhoun.

The holodeck looked no different than it usually did. The glowing grids were visible, and there was a faint humming of controlled power. Calhoun stood in the middle of the room, looking at the relative emptiness and wondering whether there hadn't been some sort of screwup.

He tapped his combadge. "Calhoun to Burgoyne."

"Burgoyne here. Come to your senses already, Captain?"

Calhoun smiled and shook his head. This was going to be a most interesting partnership. "If you mean in regards to you, no. I'm just wondering: Did you say the holodeck is set?"

"Yes, sir."

"Is there anything I have to do to activate it? What program do I tell it to run . . . ?"

"None, sir. Not this time. The computer is rigged directly into the signal that's being transmitted from Starfleet headquarters on earth. As soon as the connection is made, the holodeck will automatically activate and you'll be in the middle of the holoconference."

"Which is originating from San Francisco."

"Yes, sir. The 'hosts' are Admiral Ross and Captain Picard."

"And we in turn are going to be interfacing with other captains from all points throughout Federation space."

"Yes, sir, that's correct. Several dozen."

"Then would you mind explaining to me," Calhoun asked slowly, "how in the hell—given the unavoidable lag-time involved in a transmission of any distance—this is going to be conducted in anything approaching 'real time'?"

There was a pause. "It's somewhat complicated, sir."

"Give it to me in ten words or less."

This time Burgoyne didn't hesitate. "Magic."

"Magic?"

"Yes, sir. Magic."

"And that's supposed to suffice, is it?"

"I'm certainly hoping it does, sir. You'd need five years at Starfleet Engineering school to understand the technical issues. Plus, you said ten words: This leaves nine left over."

Calhoun was suddenly glad that no one else was standing there who might be able to see the look of annoyance on his face. "I can think of two more I'd use if we weren't on an open frequency. Burgoyne . . ."

"Yes, sir?"

"Forget I asked."

"It's forgotten, sir."

Calhoun shook his head as the communication went out. This entire holoconference thing had come up most unexpectedly. Details had been sketchy at best. He'd heard rumors that the agenda of the meeting had to do with some sort of "gateways," but beyond that he knew very little. This alone was extremely bothersome to him. Then again, if Shelby were around, she'd probably be asking him if the thing that was bothering him most was that he, the great Mackenzie Calhoun, was going to have to find out what was going on at the same time as a bunch of "lesser" captains. Shelby had this annoying habit of making everything relate to Calhoun's ego and allegedly overinflated opinion of himself. She had an even more annoying habit of pretty much being right. But Calhoun had the equally annoying habit of never admitting when she was right, so it all evened out.

Suddenly there was a shimmering of the air around him, and the power hum sounded as if it was being channeled in some direction.

And then, just like that, he was not alone.

He was slightly startled by the suddenness of it, but he hid his discomfort with his customary sangfroid. He suddenly found himself surrounded by—just as advertised—several dozen fellow captains, as well as a few commanders and an admiral.

"Hello, Mac," said a soft voice next to him.

He turned and smiled. "Hello, Eppy. This is interesting."

He reached toward Shelby, and she instinctively took his hand. Their fingers interlaced . . .

. . . and passed through. There was no "ghosting" image, no transparency. But the hands moved through each other just as the same, like wind and air. It was as if she were there, but not there, all at the same time.

"Holos don't have substance outside their respective decks," she said with a soft sigh. "The technology's not quite that sophisticated . . . yet."

"Too bad," he replied. "If it were, we could—"

"I know where your mind is. We still haven't had a proper honeymoon—"

"Ohhh, now, Eppy . . . we had fun on Xenex."

"I almost died, Mac. So did you."

"But we didn't. That was the fun part."

She rolled her eyes even as she chuckled. "See, that's the nice thing about being married to you, Mac. The things about you that once infuriated me, I now find amusing."

"Particularly when they're at a distance?" he suggested.

She grinned at that. "Well, *I* certainly didn't say that, but I wouldn't entirely rule it out. . . ."

His gaze sought out and found Jean-Luc Picard across the room. Picard was talking to an admiral whom Calhoun didn't know, but took to be this "Ross" Burgoyne had mentioned. Ross was slightly older than Picard, with dark hair flecked with gray and eyes that seemed to have lost their vigor. His uniform was not entirely flattering to his waistline, but it didn't seem to concern him.

As for Picard himself, well, aside from a very slight whitening of his hair (what there was of it), the damned man never seemed to age. Picard inclined his head slightly in greeting, and Calhoun returned the silent gesture. It appeared to Calhoun that Picard had either been present at, or even directly responsible for, every major turning point in Calhoun's life. It had been Picard who had first talked a young M'k'n'zy of Calhoun into joining the Academy; Picard who had convinced the older, cynical Mackenzie Calhoun that he should return to Starfleet and take on the *Excalibur;* hell, it had been Picard who had performed the wedding ceremony when he'd married Shelby. It made Calhoun wonder if what they were going to conference on now was going to have the same sort of impact.

Shelby had turned and was now talking softly to a woman whom she'd addressed as "Garbeck," and he recognized the name instantly. Garbeck was the first officer who had stepped in as captain of *Exeter* when Shelby had taken command of the *Trident* (well, actually, of the *Excalibur,* but that was something else entirely).

Beyond Garbeck, Calhoun saw what appeared to be a female Bajoran. What struck him as odd was that she was not wearing a Starfleet uniform, but rather that of what he took to be the Bajoran military. That came as a bit of a surprise. An older man whom Calhoun did not recognize was next to her, and judging from the way they were interacting with one another—their body language and such—Calhoun suspected they had arrived "together." The older man was Starfleet, but held the rank of commander.

"Good afternoon," Ross began in a deep voice. Many returned the greeting, some nodded; one, a Vulcan, offered his people's customary salute. "It's nice to know our relay systems are fine-tuned enough to allow holoconferences like this to occur. It certainly beats trying to find parking orbits for all of you." He smiled, but the smile faded quickly when the mild joke failed to generate so much as the slightest reaction. Calhoun glanced at Shelby and mouthed, *Tough room.*

Apparently realizing that, Ross obviously dismissed any further notions of levity. "I'm placing you all on yellow alert until further notice." He let that sink in before continuing. When he did, his voice seemed to get even more serious. "As for why we're doing this, we have a new problem. A few days ago, the Federation Council was approached by a group of beings who identified themselves as the Iconians."

The name meant absolutely nothing to Calhoun. He glanced once more at Shelby. She wasn't looking at him, but instead at Ross, and he could tell instantly from her expression that she knew precisely who these "Iconians" were. At that moment she glanced at him, clearly to see how he was taking the news. Calhoun managed to muster a grave look in his eyes, one that he hoped conveyed sufficient appreciation for the gravity of the situation. Apparently it was enough to convince Shelby that he fully grasped the seriousness of this bit of news, as they exchanged "knowing" nods.

"Captain Picard," continued Ross, "would you please detail what we know of the Iconians?"

Thank you, Calhoun thought.

"Of course, Admiral." Picard's head had been slightly cocked, like an attentive canine, but now he straightened his uniform and looked out amongst the sea of holoimages. "The Iconians were known to exist in this quadrant of space some two hundred millennia ago. Their culture and technology were unparalleled in that time period, but records about them are scant. About a decade ago, Captain Donald Varley of the *U.S.S. Yamato* determined the location of their homeworld in the Romulan Neutral Zone, but was lost along with his ship when a destructive Iconian computer program inserted itself into the *Yamato's* mainframe. Even after all this time, the technology on the Iconian homeworld remained functional—including the Gateways.

"These Gateways provide instantaneous transport between two points that could be meters or light-years apart. Two functional Gateways have been found over the last few years: one on the homeworld, which I myself destroyed rather than allow Gateway technology to fall into Romulan hands; and one discovered by the Dominion in the Gamma Quadrant, which was destroyed by a joint Starfleet/ Jem'Hadar team from the *U.S.S. Defiant.*"

"Thank you, Captain," Ross interjected. Picard appeared slightly annoyed that Ross had interrupted, but said nothing. Ross went on. "The Iconians who have now come forward have offered us the Gateway technology for a price. The Council is considering the offer, but it's a bit more complicated than that. First, they are offering the technology to the highest bidder; similar offers have been made to governments throughout the quadrant. Clearly, this could have a devastating impact should any antagonistic or ambitious government obtain the technology exclusively.

"Second, and most immediate: The Iconians have chosen to demonstrate how useful the Gateways can be by activating the entire network. Gateways have opened up all over the quadrant and beyond. The Iconians have seen fit to withhold how to control them, and they have chosen not to provide us with any form of useful map."

As Ross paused, several of the officers began speaking up, tossing out questions, and offering comments of their own. Shelby, it appeared to Calhoun, was lost in thought.

Ross continued, and the group grew silent. "As the Gateways came on-line, we immediately began studying their output, trying to get a handle on how they work. We became rather alarmed at some of the readings, so turned the study over to the Starfleet Corps of Engineers. We now have a preliminary report."

Calhoun saw a newcomer "arrive" on the scene, stepping through unseen doors. He was an older man, with thick gray-white hair and a bristling mustache, and a walk that seemed as if it would have been at home on the swaying deck of a schooner.

"Captain Scott, thank you for joining us," said Ross.

The name immediately clicked for Calhoun. This had to be the legendary Montgomery Scott, whom Burgoyne had spoken of on occasion. Shelby, from her reaction, seemed to know of him as well. A pity the other people who had served under Kirk weren't there; it would have been old home week for them.

"It nae a problem," Scott said. Calhoun had to listen carefully; the man's accent was going to take some getting used to. "Those Gateways, to be blunt, are behavin' in ways we never imagined. It seems that when they exhaust their power, they tap into any other power supply that's available. Like pussywillows here on Earth, that seek water and break into pipes to find it. These Gateways are so beyond our ken tha' figuring out how they tick and stoppin' them will be almost impossible."

Ross looked even more concerned. "Do you mean, they could tap an entire planet's resources and drain them dry?"

Scott took a deep breath. "Aye. Worse, for those worlds using predominately geothermal or hydraulic power, their ecosystem could be compromised. We don' have all the figures in yet, but one o' my ships is measuring solar consumption. My fear is some stars might be destabilized by additional power demands. It's a very nasty bit o' business," he concluded.

"All the more reason for us to mobilize the fleet. Duty packets are going out now with specific sector assignments. We'll need to maintain the peace. Some of our scientific vessels will be working with the S.C.E. to determine just how severe the problems might become. Captain Solok . . ."

The Vulcan captain seemed to step forward.

"I will want you and your crew to begin monitoring all incident reports from Gateway activity. If the Iconians won't give us a map, I want to make one."

"Understood. I should point out that it will not be complete, and therefore not entirely accurate."

"Noted," Ross said. "I'll take whatever we can get, since it's better than the nothing we have right now." He turned to the Bajoran and the commander standing next to her. "Colonel, Commander, our scientists have done some preliminary mapping based on the Gateway power signatures, and we've discovered something very interesting out your way. We're estimating no Gateway activity within ten light-years in any direction of Bajor."

"The wormhole," the commander said, his eyes narrowing.

"We think so, yes."

"It could be the Prophets protecting this region," the female Bajoran spoke up.

"That's certainly a possibility," Ross admitted. "Vaughn, given your experience with the Gateways, I want you out there, finding out why there aren't any Gateways near Bajor. Is it something natural? Is it the doing of the aliens—that is to say, the Prophets?" he amended with a contrite glance at the Bajoran. "What properties are being displayed, and can they be harnessed beyond your sector?"

"You're hoping we can turn it into a practical countermeasure."

"Exactly."

"I was unaware, Admiral, of any encounters with Gateways beyond those by the *Enterprise* and the *Defiant*," said Picard.

With a look at her first officer, the Bajoran said, "Neither was I."

"It was a few years ago," Vaughn said neutrally.

Ross gave Picard a reassuring look, although Calhoun—in watching it—felt a little less than reassured. "The relevant portions of Commander Vaughn's mission will be declassified, in light of the present emergency."

Picard nodded. "Good."

Ross and the Bajoran colonel started discussing another assignment of DS9's relating to the evacuation of a world called Europa Nova, but Calhoun was watching Picard. Picard, in turn, was staring at Vaughn. He had the feeling Picard was suspicious of Vaughn for some reason, but, naturally, he had no idea why.

Then his attention snapped back to Ross when he heard his own name mentioned. "Captain," Ross was saying, "you and the *Excalibur* will go deep in Thallonian space. There's a concentration of Gateway signatures that bears investigation."

"We don't habitually go shallow in Thallonian space, Admiral. 'Deep' is our status quo. Can you give us a bit more of a hint than that?"

"We'll forward the coordinates to your science officer."

"Thank you. What do the Gateway signatures say, by the way? 'With all our love, the Iconians'?"

This drew a few scattered guffaws. "Captain," said Ross, "I'm obviously referring to energy signatures, not autographs, and this is no laughing matter."

Adopting a demeanor almost as serious as Ross's, Calhoun archly informed him, "You're only saying that, Admiral, because your joke didn't get a laugh."

"Admiral," Shelby cut in quickly, firing a glance at Calhoun, "if I may . . ."

"Please do, Captain," Ross said pointedly.

"I have a new crewman on my ship. She came to me through the Temporal Displacement Office, and she described the means through which she got here as a sort of 'gateway.' I don't think she used the term in the 'official' capacity you're using here, but it may well be the same technology."

Ross amazingly looked even more grim. "Transporting through time *and* space? These things may be even more powerful than we had previously imagined. Was she on the Iconian homeworld or in the Gamma Quadrant?"

"I don't believe it was either, sir. She'd filed a report with the TDO; obviously it wasn't passed along to you."

"Damned paperwork trail," commented Picard. "Thanks to modern technology, the left hand can be oblivious of the right hand's activities with greater efficiency than ever."

This drew more chuckles, and Calhoun commented, "Careful, Picard. He hates it when other people get more laughs than he does."

"Captain!" Ross snapped.

"Yes, sir?" said several people at once.

Ross sighed and spoke to Shelby even as he directed an impressively withering look at Calhoun. "In light of the current situation, Captain Shelby, speak with this crewman and see what further details you can learn. Send a report directly to me, if you'd be so kind."

Ross then turned and started giving assignments out to others, particularly near the Klingon and Romulan borders, as Shelby said in a low voice to Calhoun, "You just love making new friends, don't you?"

"Why do people take an instant dislike to me?" asked Calhoun, all innocence.

"It saves time," replied Shelby.

He laughed softly at that, and then, more seriously, whispered, "The crewman you're referring to . . . is it M'Ress? The Caitian?"

Shelby nodded. Calhoun had known about her; he was the one who had suggested M'Ress as a possible crew member for Shelby.

Then Calhoun's attention was caught by the silence in the room. Ross had stopped speaking, and instead was taking all of them in with a single glance. "These will be trying days ahead of us all. I want to keep in constant contact, and I'll be reachable any time you need me. Good luck."

Realizing the conference was almost over, Calhoun suddenly wanted to turn to Shelby, to say things to her. He realized he'd been standing there the entire time and not once told her he loved her. But when he looked her way, she was already gone. They all were. The connection had been severed just that quickly.

"*Grozit,*" he muttered in annoyance. Seeing Shelby had simply served to remind Calhoun of just how much he missed her. He wondered if she felt the same way, and then he forced himself to bring himself up short. He had promised himself that he was not going to miss her. He had his life, she had hers. The marriage was an acknowledgment that they were forever intertwined, but it was most certainly not an excuse for moping around.

"I love you." It was Shelby's voice. He looked for her, but she wasn't there, except in his imagination . . . or perhaps it was some sort of residual signal held over from the meeting.

Just to play it safe, he said, "I love you, too," and hoped that—if it was, in fact, a stray signal of some sort—he hadn't just said something untoward to Admiral Ross . . . or Picard . . . or especially that female Bajoran, who looked like a very tough customer indeed.

5

TRIDENT

M'RESS COULDN'T TAKE her eyes off him. It was only the abrupt snapping of fingers, practically in her ear, that drew her attention back to the matter at hand. The snapping fingers belonged to First Officer Katerina Mueller. Tall, imposing, vaguely Teutonic, and rather chilly, she had dark blonde hair tied back in as severe a style as M'Ress had ever seen. She also had a nasty scar on her left cheek that she seemed to bear with a good deal of pride. M'Ress had found herself taking an instant dislike to Mueller for reasons she couldn't even begin to comprehend. That was how M'Ress tended to work: on instinct. However, M'Ress still felt very much the displaced traveller through reality, and couldn't help but feel that it was not her place to judge Mueller, the first officer. Curiously, Mueller preferred to be addressed by the rank of XO, an abbreviation for executive officer. In Starfleet, it was the term customarily assigned to the night-side officer who was the functional equivalent of the first officer. No one was quite sure why Mueller preferred it that way—probably because she had spent so much time with the rank herself—but the night-side first officer, Lieutenant Commander Tang, didn't seem to care one way or the other, so XO it was.

In any event, it was M'Ress's job to try and get along with Mueller (and, for that matter, with everyone else), rather than decide arbitrarily who she was and was not going to find palatable. So she swallowed her distaste for the unlikable woman and determined that she was going to try and put behind her all her sad memories of those she had lost and focus on . . . on . . .

. . . on the bleak, hopeless existence of being a stranger in a strange land . . .

Well, *that* way certainly lay madness.

All of these thoughts and more had been moving through M'Ress's brain as they had been awaiting the arrival of the ship's science officer. Seated in the conference room (*Lounge! They called it conference lounge now. She had to keep reminding herself of that*) besides M'Ress and Mueller was Captain Shelby herself. They had been making idle small talk while waiting for the science officer, most of which centered around how M'Ress was adjusting to her new home.

Terribly. I feel eyes on me wherever I go, and people whisper to each other as I go past, "Is that her? That's her, isn't it? The Caitian relic from a century ago. What's it like for her? How's she managing?" I feel like an oddity, a freak, which is what I am, and this will never be my home because I have no home, I'm just this piece of spacefaring flotsam that happened to wash up on your shore.

All of that went through her head, even as she smiled and said, "Everything is going just fine, Captain. The crew's been receptive, patient, and helpful. Things couldn't be better." She was impressed with herself because she really hadn't ever been much of a liar before, but she was apparently getting quite adept at it. She was aware that her ears were flattened against the top of her head, a sure sign—for anyone who knew her—that she was uncomfortable or nervous. But these people didn't know her, didn't know a damned thing about her. Unconsciously she licked the backs of her hands and smoothed her hair down.

Even as Shelby nodded, apparently pleased and satisfied with the response, M'Ress felt as if Mueller's gaze was boring into her, capable of seeing right through her dissembling and calling her on it at any moment. But Mueller remained as silent and distant as the icebergs of which she reminded M'Ress.

M'Ress shifted slightly in her chair, trying to get accustomed to the fit of the new uniform. It felt far stretchier than any she'd known before, and she didn't like the feel of the fabric against her fur. Her own people had very little patience for clothing; their fur provided them all the protection they required. But she was in Starfleet, and as such she felt constrained to wear the appropriate accoutrements. There was nothing in regulations, though, that said she had to like it.

Then the door hissed open and a gentle, almost amused-sounding voice said, "Sorry I'm late."

"Why should now be different from any time in the past?" Mueller said tartly.

M'Ress looked up at the individual who had just entered, and it was as if her mind had suddenly gone blank.

Since M'Ress was Caitian, it would have been only natural that her standard of beauty would be formed by those of her own race. All of that went out the window, though, when she saw the man standing in the doorway. He was tall and muscular—she could tell even though he was in uniform, because the cloth almost seemed to adhere to him, tracing the lines of his abs. His face was nearly triangular, his chin strong, his eyes slightly slanted and drawn back, his nose aquiline. His skin tone looked like pale gold, and he sported a mane of red hair that swept back and down, although it was neatly cropped just above his collar. But the skin itself seemed almost to glow with . . . what? Health? Power? It was impossible for her to say. And the eyes, upon closer inspection, actually seemed to sparkle. It was as if he did not have retinas, corneas, or other normal ocular parts. Instead, it seemed—upon close inspection, crazy as it sounded—as if his eyes were comprised of tiny sequins, an inner circle of silver surrounded by an outer circle of blue.

It was at that point that M'Ress heard the impatient finger-snapping from Mueller in her ear that forced her attention back to the moment at hand.

"I'm sorry . . . what?" M'Ress said desperately, feeling mortified that she had so utterly zoned out of the moment.

"Lieutenant Commander Gleau was just apologizing for not having met with you earlier," Shelby said. She seemed more amused than anything by M'Ress's temporary "departure" from the meeting. "You have, after all, been assigned to the science department."

"I've been remiss," said Gleau. M'Ress might have been imagining it, but it seemed as if there were bells tinkling when he spoke. "As the captain said, my heartfelt apologies. Organizing a science division is a rather daunting task, wouldn't you say?"

He was asking M'Ress. She said the first thing that came to her mind: "If you want me to say that, then, yes." Then she heard the words that had come out of her mouth, and wanted to crawl under the table.

"That's nice to see: cooperation," said Shelby. "Lieutenant Commander, it's my suspicion that Lieutenant M'Ress here has never met a Selelvian."

M'Ress shook her head mutely. "I . . . read about them . . . you . . . them . . ." M'Ress managed to say. "Along with about fifty other new member races that joined the Federation in my . . . my absence . . ."

"I'm one of the first in Starfleet. There are some"—and he seemed to cast a glance in Mueller's direction—"who feel uncomfortable with us around, because we exude a high degree of . . . what's the word . . . ?"

"Bull?" Mueller suggested.

"Charm," said Gleau. "Some simply call us the Elves, after a mythical race of beings who had the power to charm the pants—and just about anything else, it seemed—off humans of old Earth. An amusing nickname, don't you think?"

"Hilarious," said M'Ress, still captivated by his eyes. Her ears were perked straight up, and her tail was extended. She became aware of the outward signs of excitement, and her cheeks flushed furiously. This time she was incredibly grateful that the significance of her outward reactions were lost on those looking at her.

Mueller *harrumphed* rather loudly, bringing matters quickly back on track.

"Circumstances have arisen, Lieutenant," Shelby said, "that might directly pertain to you. You described the device that catapulted—no pun intended . . ."

M'Ress winced inwardly but kept her face neutral. "Understood."

". . . catapulted you to our time as a sort of 'gateway.' If that is truly the case, yours may well be the first encounter on record with such a device. We need to find out as much as possible about it."

"If that's the case, why don't we simply go to the planet where it was located? I mean, my understanding is that we're one of two vessels here in Sector 221-G, the other being the *Excalibur.* Certainly our presence won't be missed here for a little while. . . ."

"Just tell us, if you would, what happened," said Gleau. Even though he was all business at this point, she still felt as if she could drown in his very presence.

"Well," she said slowly, shifting in her seat, "truthfully, there's not much to tell. It was shortly after I'd been reassigned off the *Enterprise.* I was serving on a science vessel called the *Einstein,* and we had found some unusual energy signatures off a world called Ceti Alpha VI. When we arrived, a landing party—I'm sorry, away team—"

"Use whatever terminology you're comfortable with," Shelby said.

"An away team," continued M'Ress, "consisting of myself, Lieutenant Wexler, and Ensign Levine, went down to the surface to investigate it. We found what can only be described as a sort of . . . of pulsation in the air." She paused in wonderment, recalling the sight as clearly as if it happened yesterday, which she realized, subjectively, it practically had. "It was just there, right there, in an open area near some rocks and outcroppings, and there were what appeared to be controls set within its proximity. The only thing I can think of is that it was running through a sort of self-test—"

"Self-test?" said Mueller.

"Some types of equipment, when not in use, go into a kind of standby mode," Gleau told her. "Every so often, however, they will activate themselves and run themselves through a series of self-diagnostics, just to make certain everything is in working order should the equipment need to come on-line. It sounds to me as if that was what the lieutenant and her team stumbled over."

Shelby nodded, taking this in, and then asked, "What happened next?"

"Well . . . I approached the device, using my tricorder. I was trying to get readings off it, see if I could determine the power source." She was holding her hands up as if the device were in them still. "And then the tricorder . . ." She paused.

"The tricorder what?" asked Gleau.

"It was as if . . . as if it interfaced with it somehow. Activated it, perhaps. Either kicked it into active mode or—worse—self-defense mode. The next thing I knew there was some sort of massive energy discharge, and a burst of colors like a rainbow exploding in my head. It . . ." She stopped for a moment, composing herself, all too aware that she was describing the last moments of what had been her "real" life. Feeling their eyes upon her, she steadied herself and continued. "Then the world roared around me, and I was hauled off my feet and through the . . . gateway, as I called it. Everything seemed to twist and expand and contract, all at the same time, and the next thing I knew—"

She paused again, this time with dramatic impact. "And then—?" prompted Gleau.

She laughed curtly. "And then I was in Dublin."

"Dublin?" said a perplexed Mueller. "Dublin . . . *Ireland?*"

"Yes."

"On Earth?"

"Unless they relocated Ireland to Vulcan recently, yes."

"So . . . you suddenly found yourself in Dublin, Ireland . . . on Earth . . . a century into what you would consider the future," said Gleau wondrously.

"You don't have to sound quite so thrilled about it," M'Ress told him. For a moment she felt slightly annoyed with him . . . and then instantly felt guilty because she'd dared to feel that way. What *was* it with this guy?

"You'll have to excuse Mr. Gleau," Shelby told her, leaning back in her chair. "He tends to be rather enthusiastic about scientific discoveries, anomalies, and the like. As you might suspect, we prefer to consider it merely part of his charm."

"As opposed to behavior bordering on the childlike," noted Mueller.

Gleau did not appear the least bit chastened by Mueller's faintly scolding tone as he said, "It's just that Ireland is an interesting site. I've made a hobby of ancient Earth myths and peoples, for obvious reasons. I wonder if beings used that gateway to come through to ancient Ireland . . . beings who might have been the basis of those referred to as 'leprechauns.' "

"Very amusing," said Mueller, who didn't sound amused. She turned to M'Ress. "What then?"

"Then . . . not much. I contacted Starfleet. Was brought to the Temporal Investigation Department. One thing led to another and . . . here I am."

"Yes. Here you are," said Shelby, scratching her chin thoughtfully.

M'Ress felt as if she was letting them down somehow. As if she should have more information that she could provide them. She leaned forward, her tail twitching, and she said, "As I was saying . . . if we could return to Ceti Alpha VI . . ."

"That might prove problematic," Gleau informed her.

"Why?"

"Because there is no Ceti Alpha VI."

She blinked, confused. "What? But—"

"Your 'interface,' as you call it, with the Gateway apparently set off some sort of alarm, which in turn set off a chain reaction," Gleau explained, looking rather apologetic to have to tell her. "At least that's what the records of the *Einstein* indicate. It's our suspicion that you stumbled onto more than just a Gateway world. There may have been other technology there, hidden, waiting to be restarted by the race that had planted it there. But when you came upon it . . ."

"It blew it up . . . rather than let it all be discovered, probed . . . the whole planet, gone," Mueller finished.

At that moment, M'Ress felt something inside her die,

just a little bit. "Oh," was all she managed to get out as her throat constricted.

Gleau leaned forward and rested a hand atop hers. In another circumstance, she would have been all too aware of the warmth his touch generated. As it was, though, she could not remove the black shroud from her mind. "You were hoping," he said softly, "that we could return there . . . that you could find that Gateway, reprogram it . . . and get back to your own time."

"That would, of course, be a violation of regulations," Mueller reminded her.

And something in her tone, something in the flat and unsympathetic way she said that, caused M'Ress—just for a moment—to lose control. Slamming the table with her open hand, she snapped at Mueller, *"To hell with regulations and to hell with you!"*

Mueller's face might have been carved from granite for all that she reacted to the outburst. Shelby said sharply, "Lieutenant—!"

At that moment M'Ress absolutely didn't care what Shelby did to her. "Am I done here, Captain?" Her lips were drawn back, her fangs bared. She hadn't intended to appear threatening, but that was how she looked, nonetheless.

If Shelby was at all intimidated, she didn't let it show. She looked as if she was about to say something else, but instead her face softened slightly, and Shelby told her, "Yes. You're done."

"Thank you. A pleasure meeting you, Lieutenant Commander Gleau. We must dash my faintest hopes of normality again sometime." And with that, she padded quickly and ever so quietly out of the conference lounge.

Idiot! Idiot idiot idiot! She excoriated herself mercilessly as she barreled down the corridor. Even though she was moving in a manner that felt akin to a freight train, she nevertheless made almost no noise. So stealthy was she, even in her ire, that people jumped in surprise as she seemed to materialize right behind them. They hastened to get out of her way, and she ignored them. *What the hell kind of impression was that to make?* It wasn't enough that she was someone out of her proper time and place; now she was going to poison the well of the era she'd been stuck in? What an absolutely flaming stupid way to conduct herself!

But was she to be blamed for it? Really blamed? The circumstances she had been thrust into were just insane! How was any reasonable being supposed to survive? To keep one's head screwed on, one's perspective in the right place, given what she had to deal with? There was no way, absolutely no way that someone who had simply been yanked out of their proper time and place and deposited elsewhere could just fit in. There was—

Laughter.

She heard laughter from up the corridor. Loud and boisterous, and normal, oh so normal. She had almost forgotten what normal crew interaction, people enjoying each other's company because they belonged together, could sound like. She headed toward the noise and saw that it was coming from within the armory. Somebody was leaning right in the doorway, and as a result the doors were staying open. He was laughing along with the others within, and M'Ress felt somewhat cheered by it. . . .

And then she heard a familiar voice saying, "So there we were, all the officers having been reduced to the ages of children, running around . . . it was insanity! You haven't lived until you've seen Starfleet veterans making comments like, 'Are we there yet?' and 'He made a face at me!' "

Still more laughter as Arex held court, easily entertaining the roomful of security officers. Arex, who was as time-displaced as she was, and didn't seem to be aware of it. She had forgotten about him, or perhaps simply blanked it out because it was so frustrating to her. Arex, unlike M'Ress, had shown a stunning knack for adapting to the new environment in which they'd found themselves. His psych profile had come back clean, and his compatibility with the world around him had been so complete that he'd been installed as security head of the *Trident*. It was a position that he had taken to with utter facility.

Arex spotted her standing outside, peering into the private lounge used by security . . . the lounge referred to informally as "the Pit." "M'Ress!" he called. "I was just telling them about the time—"

"Yes, I heard what you were telling them." She folded her arms and looked slightly disapproving. "The crew turned into children and we all almost died. Very funny. I'm sure there are dozens of near-death experiences you can turn into hilarious anecdotes."

Arex didn't miss a beat. "Oh, more than dozens, I'm sure. Want to help?"

She wanted to wring his scrawny neck, was what she wanted to do. Instead she said, "I have to get back to the science department," and she bolted from the Pit as quickly as she could.

She hated the words that had been coming out of her mouth. She hated the type of person she was becoming in order to have said them. She hated the way people were looking at her, and the way she was looking at herself.

And as new laughter reached her ears from behind . . . laughter that she was convinced was at her expense, even though it very likely wasn't . . . most of all, she hated her life.

"That could have gone better, XO," Shelby said scoldingly.

They had remained in the conference lounge while Lieutenant Commander Gleau went on about his duties. Shelby hadn't needed to tell Mueller that she wanted her to remain; Mueller simply knew. That was the way she was.

"I'm shocked you would say that, Captain," Mueller returned drily. "And here I thought Lieutenant M'Ress's outburst was the height of professionalism."

"She's been through a good deal, XO, and a little understanding could go a long way to—"

Mueller rose from her chair even as she thumped an open palm on the table. "I knew it. I knew it would come to this."

"Come to 'this'? What 'this' are you talking about?" inquired Shelby, genuinely puzzled.

"This business of having to watch ourselves with a crewman. Of having to take some sort of extra care not to upset her or disturb her because of her," and she made quotation marks with her fingers, "'special circumstances.' "

"You're overreacting, Kat," Shelby told her.

"No, I don't think I am, Elizabeth," Mueller replied. She was circling the room, as was her wont when she was annoyed about something. "The simple truth is that everyone on this ship—everyone in the galaxy—has their own individual problems, their own set of circumstances. We cannot afford to start treating one crewman differently, more tentatively, from another. We have to expect the same level of competency, the same level of professionalism from each of them. The moment we start bending on that, the moment we give one crewman some sort of preferential treatment over another, we risk undermining the entire chain of command."

"I think you're overdramatizing things a bit."

"Overreacting, overdramatizing. But perhaps I'm also overright."

Shelby, watching the determined annoyance of her first

officer, still couldn't quite suppress a smile. "Is that a word? Overright?"

Mueller paused a moment and then said, with utter certainty, "No. But it could be if I wanted it to be. And I'm not overreacting or overdramatizing."

"Yes, you are," Shelby said with calm insistence. "I hardly think that displaying some simple understanding and compassion for a woman who has lost everything she ever knew is going to send Starfleet tumbling into chaos."

"It's easy to make light of it," said Mueller. "Don't you think I'd rather display sympathy for her than be a hard-ass?"

That was a bit more than Shelby could take. "No," she replied, "I think you rather like being a hard-ass."

Mueller paused, and a smile touched the edges of her mouth. "All right, fair enough," she said. "But if I weren't, you wouldn't want me for your second-in-command."

She had to admit to herself that there was some validity to that. "True enough," she allowed, but then said firmly, "but there has to be a balance, Kat. A balance between hardlining on the regs and going soft. I wasn't able to achieve it with my previous second-in-command on the *Exeter*. One of the reasons I wanted you—"

"Is because I'm just that damned fabulous," Mueller said, deadpan.

"There's that, of course. I also believed that someone capable of being in synch with Mackenzie Calhoun would also be in synch with me. I'd like to think that was part of what influenced you to accept the position."

"There was that . . . and the fact that I thought Mac was dead when I took the post," Mueller told her.

Shelby looked at her askance. Something in the way she had said that . . .

"Kat?" she said slowly, cautiously. "Are you saying you'd rather have served as Mac's second-in-command? Stayed with *Excalibur?*"

"Actually, I would have preferred to stay on night side," Mueller replied. "I never had any particular ambition to graduate to the post of second, much less command. But I was beginning to feel pressure to advance—"

"From Starfleet?"

"Bugger Starfleet. From my mother."

"Ah," Shelby said, suppressing a smile. "Understood."

"However, once you and Calhoun were married, I felt it would not be wise for me to work directly with him. He is a good and faithful man, but sooner or later . . . well . . . it would have been inevitable."

Shelby leaned back and stared at her. She wasn't quite sure she was hearing what she was, in fact, hearing. "Are you saying that, had you taken a position as second-in-command on *Excalibur,* Mac would have wound up cheating on me with you?"

"Of course," Mueller said, with such confidence that Shelby could scarcely believe it. "You know perfectly well that he and I had a relationship before. Sex would have been a natural outlet for the pressure of duty, and we would have been logical partners for one another. I doubt very much Mac would become involved with any other in his crew; he would consider it inappropriate, from a command point of view, if nothing else. But he and I, well . . ." She shrugged. "And I admit, when it comes to him, I do not always act in the wisest manner. Far better for all concerned this way."

Shelby was amazed at the woman's forthright way of addressing the subject. "So you're saying that, even had he endeavored to be faithful, you would have approached him and he would have been unable to resist."

"That's correct."

"Well, well," Shelby said, after a moment to take that in, "it appears someone has a rather inflated opinion of themselves."

Without a word, Mueller reached back and undid her hair. She shook it out, long and blonde, tumbling around her face and shoulders. As a few stray strands danced around her face, she moistened her lips, giving them a pouting, provocative look. Her cobalt-blue eyes seemed to drill right through the back of Shelby's head. Mueller leaned forward on her elbow, and Shelby detected a faint aroma of jasmine coming off her that she hadn't noticed before.

Her voice was low and throaty and laden with the images of sweaty and twisted bedsheets as she said, "Men want me . . . and women want to be me. Any questions?"

Inwardly, Shelby couldn't decide whether Mueller really *was* as utterly irresistible as she was making herself out to be, or whether she was just the most egotistical individual she'd ever met. Or both. But was it really ego if one could genuinely deliver on the boasts? Opting not to consider it too closely, lest she come up with an answer that she wasn't going to like, Shelby said with admirable cool, "No . . . an order. Ease up on M'Ress."

Mueller was visibly surprised. She let out an exasperated snort as she leaned back and started to put her hair back in the bun. "I wasn't going hard on her, Captain. And have I ever said that you occasionally suffer from single-mindedness?"

"Yes, you were, and yes, you have."

Mueller sniffed with mild disdain, and then the intraship com system hailed them. "Shelby here."

"This is Takahashi," came the familiar drawl from Romeo Takahashi up at ops. "Got a message incoming from planet Thallon 18."

"Thallon 18." She looked to Mueller.

Immediately Mueller rattled off, "Thallon 18: one of a group of worlds in Thallonian space with no star or planetary designation other than the simple numbering system. Used primarily by the Thallonians—when they were in power—for colonizing and, in some cases, as punishment worlds. Residents of the varied worlds tend to rename the planets to suit their own tastes, but the 'official' designation is how we list them. In this particular case, Thallon 18 is a class-M world, populated for the most part by a race calling themselves . . ." She paused a moment, and Shelby could almost see her thumbing through a mental file of index cards. "The Markanians."

"Are we live with them, Hash?"

"No, Captain. Recorded transmission only."

"Pipe it down here, then," she said.

"Coming down."

The screen in the conference lounge immediately flared to life, and an individual who seemed rather aged appeared on the screen. At least that was what Shelby garnered from his general attitude and deportment, since it was hard to tell simply from looking at him how old he might be in Markanian years. His skin was mottled blue, his eyes sideways crescents that seemed to have bits of dried crust in the edges. He had no hair, but instead what appeared to be streaks of lighter color in the very skin of his head, which might once have been occupied by hair. "Attention, Starfleet vessel. I am Furvus," he said, "of the ruling council of Markania."

"A.k.a. Thallon 18," put in Mueller.

"I know, Kat."

"We have a situation on our world that we believe will be of interest to you," continued the one who had identified himself as Furvus. "It is our understanding that the Federation is here in what was once Thallonian space for the purpose of keeping the peace, and preventing outside forces from exploiting various worlds. Matters have occurred on our world that, I believe, fit that criteria."

"Let's hope so," murmured Mueller, and Shelby knew exactly what she was referring to. They had received summonses from three different planets in the past weeks, and in each case it had involved matters that were either sublimely trivial or outside their purview as a starship. The worst had been the high monarch of Bixilfiz, who—it turned out—had wanted Shelby to be the mother of his child. Putting aside that Bixilfiz biology wasn't remotely compatible with human (what with them being a race that looked somewhat like overgrown earthworms), it had quickly become apparent that the whole thing was a stunt designed to make his mate jealous. It had worked a bit too well; in anger, she had retaliated by falling upon him and devouring him.

"Our situation," Furvus continued, "is related to what can only be described as an advanced sort of transportational device, called a . . ." He paused, wanting to get the word right. "A Gateway, I believe," he said.

"Freeze," Shelby said instantly, and the image of Furvus obediently froze in position. She looked at Mueller significantly, for she had already brought Mueller up to speed on the nature of the holoconference from the previous day.

Shelby was pleased to see that she was so in synch with Mueller, that Mueller didn't even have to wait to be prompted. "Mueller to conn."

"Conn. Gold here," came the brisk reply.

"Mr. Gold, set course for Thallon 18."

As per his custom, Lieutenant Mick Gold didn't bother to wait for the inevitable subsequent order to actually send the ship hurtling off in the direction he'd set it for. Instead he simply said, "On our way."

"Let's listen to the rest of the message," Shelby said briskly, "and then I want to get on the horn with Mac. I'll want Si Cwan's input on this, too."

"Impressive," said Mueller thoughtfully. "No mention of this 'Gateway' business for centuries, and then all of a sudden, we have Gateway ramifications and scenarios coming out our ears."

"Maybe you could solve it," suggested Shelby, "by leaning on the table, letting down your hair, and speaking in a husky voice to the Iconians."

Mueller's expression didn't so much as twitch. "Perhaps I will at that."

"And, Kat . . ."

"Yes, Captain?"

"You couldn't have seduced Mac, no matter how hard you tried."

Mueller laughed softly. "You're probably right, Captain."

As for Shelby, she wasn't quite so sure, but was pleased she wasn't going to have to find out.

6

AERON

BURKITT WAS NOT AMUSED, even as he expertly guided his glider through the expanse of the Outer Swamp.

The Warmaster was partly annoyed with himself, having let himself be pulled into a situation that he could have—indeed, probably *should* have—dismissed out of hand. But the entire proposition had seemed just interesting enough to ensnare his attention, and he had to admit that the conditions of it . . . a meeting out in the desolate swamp, coming alone, all of that . . . was serving to pique his interest in this business.

Truthfully, he had other concerns that should have taken precedence over this meeting. There had still been no change in Tsana's condition. As he had further surmised, the Counselars were already beginning to jockey for influence and position, and it was anyone's guess how all of this was going to turn out. So when this "opportunity" had presented itself, Burkitt could just as easily have dismissed the entire proposal out of hand. That, in fact, had been his first impulse. "I don't have time to play games and agree to clandestine meetings in the middle of swamps!" he'd said impatiently.

Yet here he was. Which made him either the biggest fool or the canniest individual on the planet. Well, maybe it was a little bit of both, when you got right down to it.

Whoever this mysterious "Smyt" was that he was supposed to be meeting with, he certainly knew what he was doing. He had given specific coordinates for Burkitt to arrive at, and sure enough, as Burkitt approached them, there was a sizeable clearance up ahead. As opposed to the marshland, which dominated the area, here was a nice little vacant island that would easily accommodate Burkitt's personal vessel. He shut down the antigrav, switching to glide-and-land mode, and expertly guided the small ship into a landing. He'd always been rather proud of the vehicle; despite its size, it was quite fast and very agile, capable of outrunning and outpowering far larger vessels. The last thing Burkitt wanted to do was botch the landing and sink the ship in the swamp.

He also saw that there was someone waiting on the island for him. He didn't appear to have any sort of vessel with him, and Burkitt couldn't help but wonder how in the world he had gotten there. The individual was at the far end of the island, standing with his back to a grove of trees, giving Burkitt ample room for setting his vehicle down, which he did with practiced ease. Once settled, he didn't get out immediately, but took the time to study the person with whom he had this most unusual appointment. He was just standing there, looking rather placid. At first Burkitt thought that it was a trick of the light, but no . . . the fellow's skin was genuinely pale yellow. He had no chin to speak of. His hands were draped behind his back, his expression open, even pleasant. He seemed as if he felt utterly in control of the situation. That, of course, was enough to make Burkitt suspicious.

After deciding that he'd made the man wait long enough, Burkitt emerged from his vehicle and stepped out onto the island. His nose wrinkled as the smell of the swamp hit him. The air was thick with noxious fumes and the smell of dead and decaying matter. He swatted at the air, assorted insects immediately coming from nowhere, converging on him as if sensing a potential new source for nutrition. This Smyt, by contrast, didn't seem bothered by them at all. Either he had remarkable self-control, or else the insects didn't want to get near him. Burkitt wasn't pleased about either prospect. The sun was low on the horizon, and the Warmaster suddenly had no desire to remain there any longer than necessary.

"Smyt?" inquired Burkitt.

"I'm impressed that you came," admitted the other. "I was worried that you might think this to be some sort of trap."

"I still do consider that a possibility," Burkitt said evenly. That much was evinced by the fact that Burkitt was keeping his hand resting comfortably and securely on the butt of his weapon, which was tucked in his right holster. "And I can assure you that, if this is a trap, you will not live to see it sprung."

"I appreciate the sentiment, however misplaced your caution is."

"Caution is never misplaced; just occasionally unnecessary in retrospect."

"Well, you will certainly discover that this is one of those times." He bowed slightly. "I am, indeed, Smyt, and I do appreciate your coming."

"And was this godforsaken meeting ground truly necessary?" asked Burkitt testily.

"There might have been other possible meeting grounds,"

admitted Smyt. "But this was what came to mind. Security was of uppermost concern to me."

"My headquarters is secure."

"As was your imperial mansion, I daresay," he replied pointedly.

Burkitt scowled at that. "How do you know of that?"

"Well," said Smyt, with a coarse laugh that grated on Burkitt's ears, "how could I not? Your entire world is in mourning for the loss of its imperials."

"But you are not of this world. That much is apparent simply by looking at you."

"Yes, yes. Very observant. I am," and Smyt bowed slightly, "an Iconian."

"Really."

"You do not appear impressed."

"Appearances can be deceiving."

"Ah."

"In this case, however, they are not."

"Ah," Smyt said again with a smile. "A dazzling riposte. Most, most amusing."

"I do not consider any of this amusing," Burkitt made sure to let him know. "And if you do not come to the point of this nonsense within the next minute, I am going to take my leave of you. And whether I leave you in one piece when I do so is something that I have not yet come close to deciding."

"So testy," Smyt said scoldingly. He appeared to be entirely too jovial, as if all of this was just some great game to him. "Very well. I have something that I think you will consider to be of great interest."

"Really."

"Yes, really." He folded his arms, and when he spoke again, he did so with the air of someone who knew the answer he was going to get before he spoke. "How would you like to strike back at those who assassinated your imperials?"

Burkitt's eyes narrowed, although he did all he could to keep his face as neutral as possible. "You have my attention," he said noncommittally. "Keep talking."

For the first time, Smyt moved. He stepped to one side, and Burkitt now saw that there was something behind him. It had been hidden by the lengthening shadows of the trees behind Smyt, and Burkitt mentally chided himself for such an amateurish slip. If Smyt had been concealing a weapon there, Burkitt would have been dead where he stood.

It did not appear to be a weapon, however. It seemed to be a . . .

. . . well, truthfully, he didn't know what the hell it was. It seemed to be an array of metal tubes, inextricably intertwined, looking almost like a free-form sculpture. But there were no welding marks on it that Burkitt could discern, and since he'd done such sculpting in his youth as a hobby, he would have been in a position to know. It was almost as if the thing, which came to about waist-high, had . . . grown into its present shape.

He also noticed that there were some sort of controls upon it. At least that's what he thought they were. There were several pads, slightly raised on the surface, on one of the upper grips. Burkitt had no clue how they might have controlled the object, or even what the thing's nature was.

"Intrigued, aren't you?" Smyt said, clearly pleased with himself. He patted the oddly shaped thing, almost as if it were a child that he was eminently proud of.

"You're in danger of losing my attention," Burkitt warned him.

"Aren't you going to ask me what it is?"

"This is nonsense," said Burkitt angrily, his impatience overwhelming him. "Speak plainly or we've nothing more to—"

"It's a portable Gateway. The only one like it in existence."

Burkitt stared at him blankly. "A what?"

"A Gateway. It enables the user to go to whatever preset coordinates he desires. Basically, it takes one point in space-time," and he touched his thumb to forefinger, "and another point in space-time," he did the same with his other hand, "and pulls them toward one another until they're like this." He interlinked the thumb and forefinger from his two hands to form what amounted to a bridge between his hands. "And when that union is made, the user can cross over."

"So you're saying . . ."

"I'm saying," Smyt told him, "that you can use this device to launch an attack on those who annihilated your beloved imperials. You do not have space-flight capability; but this will solve that. In fact, you'll be in a superior position to many who *do* have space vessels. Here, the trip is instantaneous. You're here . . . then you're there. Then the controller just brings you back."

It was at that moment that everything snapped into focus for Burkitt. "Of course," he whispered. "It was you."

"Me?" Smyt affected a puzzled and innocent look.

"This was how the Markanians got into the mansion. They used this device. This 'one-of-a-kind' device of yours. Which means you sold it to them."

"I am stunned, sir!" Smyt said, apparently doing his level best to, indeed, look stunned. "I have come to you in the spirit of sharing—"

"Of sharing. You mean that you're going to provide this device to my people out of the goodness of your heart."

"Well, now . . . I didn't quite say that," he demurred. "This is a unique item, after all. There is such a thing as supply and demand. If there is a demand for this Gateway, should I not be the one who benefits by providing the supply? Especially when that supply is limited to one. But if you're willing to make it worth my while . . ."

"You," Burkitt informed him, "are under arrest."

"What?" His eyes widened. "Simply for endeavoring to transact a deal? That doesn't seem quite fair." He didn't sound the least bit perturbed at Burkitt's announcement, and that alone was enough to infuriate Burkitt all the more.

"You are under arrest for providing a lethal device to a known enemy of Aeron. . . ."

Smyt laughed disdainfully at that, leaning against the device and looking very relaxed with the situation. "You have no proof that I provided anything to anyone. And in any event, the device itself is not lethal. It simply transports. I have no control over what people do once they're transported."

More than anything at that moment, Burkitt wanted to see Smyt lose some of that insufferable smugness. "And you will be charged as an accessory to multiple murders. You are going to come with me—"

And suddenly, just like that, there was what appeared to be a weapon in the Iconian's hand. He had produced it so quickly that Burkitt had absolutely no idea where he'd even pulled it from. But it was trained upon him, the barrel unwavering, and if Burkitt even tried to draw his own weapon, he'd have no chance to get a shot off before Smyt blasted him.

"This is truly a shame, Burkitt," said Smyt, and he actually sounded genuinely apologetic. "I was expecting more from a warmaster such as yourself."

"Then far be it from me to disappoint you," replied Burkitt. "Look above you."

Smyt laughed. "Oh, please. Do you seriously think that I would—"

That was all he managed to say before Gragg and three other soldiers dropped overhead from the trees behind him.

Smyt yelped, and then he was slammed to the ground, his

face shoved into the marshy dirt. He tried to get out a shout of protest, but only succeeded in getting a mouthful of dirt. The soldiers then hauled him to his feet, and he staggered, confused for a moment, trying to sort out what had happened.

Burkitt strode toward him slowly, taking his time, savoring the moment. When he was quite close to Smyt, he said, "Was this more the kind of thing you were expecting from a warmaster . . . such as myself?"

"You . . . you had them planted here . . . before I came . . ." Smyt managed to say. He spit out some dirt that had wedged in between his lips.

"As soon as I received your communication, yes. They hid there for many hours. I would guess that they do not appreciate your having made that assignment necessary. Do you appreciate it, Commander Gragg?"

"No, sir," he growled, and he shook Smyt ever so slightly for good measure.

"See there, I thought not. Commander Gragg here will escort you to a lovely holding facility back in the city. I, in the meantime, will confiscate this . . . device . . . of yours. I'm sure our scientists will be most delighted to have an opportunity to examine it."

"Your scientists," Smyt said, rallying his bravado for a moment, "will kill themselves. You have no idea of how to operate it, and you have no comprehension of the danger."

"We learn very quickly."

Gathering his scattered reserves of nerve, Smyt told him, "What you will learn, Warmaster, is that you're not as clever as you think you are."

Burkitt ran his fingers along the curves of the device. It seemed warm to the touch. "We were clever enough to apprehend you," he pointed out.

"That was not so much your ingenuity as my overconfidence. I shall not make that mistake again. You, however, are making a huge one now."

"I suppose we'll just have to live with it."

Smyt looked at him in a way that abruptly made Burkitt's spine feel cold.

"No. You won't," he assured him.

7

EXCALIBUR

LIEUTENANT CRAIG MITCHELL, second-in-command of engineering, gaped in disbelief at Burgoyne. Mitchell was heavyset, bearded, and his brown hair was its customary unruly mop. "You're not serious about this, Burgy," he said.

"I am perfectly serious about this, Mitchell," replied Burgoyne. S/he looked around the table at Ensigns Torelli and Yates, and the recently promoted Lieutenant j.g. Beth. Outside the engineering room conference lounge, the rest of the crew was going about its business, briskly keeping the mighty engines of the *Excalibur* in working order and devoid of computer viruses and gigantic flaming birds. "As second-in-command, I'll be spending the majority of my time on the bridge. To all functional intents and purposes, Craig, you're going to be chief engineer."

"Permission to speak freely, sir?"

Burgoyne looked at him with bemusement. "I'm sorry . . . has there ever been a time when someone considered—even for a moment—not telling me precisely what was on his or her mind?"

"Permission to—"

"Yes, yes, go ahead," Burgoyne said.

"I don't know that I'm ready for this."

"Trust him, Lieutenant Commander," Beth urged. "He's really not ready for it."

Mitchell fired a glance at her. "Don't help me, okay, Beth? I'm reasonably sure I can plead my own inadequacy."

"You're being astoundingly modest, Mitchell," said Burgoyne. "It's rather unlike you."

"Well, I'm just contemplating what it will be like with you not around here all the time, keeping everything in order. I just . . ." Mitchell cleared his throat and did his best to look needy. "I don't think I'm up to maintaining this place at the demanding standards you've set."

Burgoyne sat back in hir chair, eyes narrowing, as if s/he was visually dissecting Mitchell. "Is that a fact?" s/he said slowly, obviously unconvinced.

"A harsh fact to admit," Mitchell said sadly, "but one I'm prepared to live with." There was a uniform nodding of heads from around the table.

"I see." Burgoyne tapped hir sharp fingernails on the tabletop for a long moment, and then said, "This would not, by any chance, be some sort of . . . oh, I don't know . . . resistance to my promotion, would it?"

Protests immediately came from around the table. "No!" "No, sir, not at all!" "Definitely not!" was chorused by all of them.

"It couldn't be," continued Burgoyne, "that you think I'm the wrong choice to be the second-in-command of this ship. That I lack sufficient . . . what would be the best word . . . ?"

"Maturity?" suggested Mitchell.

"Experience?" said Beth.

"Stability?" said Yates.

"Self-control?" said Torelli.

Burgoyne couldn't quite believe what s/he was hearing. "Is *that* what you think? After all this time working under me? Do you think so little of me as chief engineer that—?"

"Burgy, we didn't say that we actually *believed* any of those things," Mitchell quickly said. "We were just . . ." He looked to the others for help.

"Floating possibilities," suggested Beth.

Mitchell clapped his beefy hands together in triumph, as if Beth had just explained the mysteries of the universe in under five words. "Floating possibilities! That's it exactly."

Burgoyne leaned back in hir chair, and there was genuine sadness in hir eyes. "I am disheartened. Extremely disheartened. That you'd think so little of me—"

"We don't, Lieutenant Commander," Beth said earnestly. "It's—"

"*Commander,*" Burgy softly corrected. "It's 'Commander' now. I would prefer not to have to remind you."

There was considerable uncomfortable shifting of feet under the table. "Commander," Beth corrected herself, "the truth is, we'd really hate to lose you around here. You're the best engineer I've ever served under. Ever. And it's just, well . . ."

"Well . . . what?"

"You don't seem the command type," Mitchell blurted out.

"And what 'type' would that be?"

"Someone who's less . . . well . . ."

"You."

It had been a strange voice that had interrupted. They looked up to see a Bolian standing in the doorway. His eyes were deep-set on either side of the bifurcation that was unique to Bolians, and his blue face was a bit blubbery, although, curiously, the rest of his body was rather trim.

"Less me?" said a puzzled Burgoyne. Glancing at the ranking pips, s/he said, "Ensign, if someone is going to insult me, I insist that they at least serve with me for six months, minimum."

"No insult was intended, Commander," he said in a voice that was slightly wispy. "I was simply saying, 'You,' which was going to be followed in short order by, 'would be Commander Burgoyne?' But then I realized you were in the middle of a discussion, and was loathe to interrupt."

"No, it's quite all right. Your timing is actually rather appreciated." S/he gave a pointed look at hir subordinates, who abruptly seemed less than anxious to meet hir gaze. "What can I do for you?"

"I am reporting to you, as instructed," he said with a slight inclination of his head. "I'd been assigned to ship's general services, but since you're relocating to the bridge, I was placed here. I assure you I am quite conversant with all technical aspects of—"

"Yes, yes, I'm sure you are. Otherwise I doubt you'd have been assigned here," said Burgoyne, sounding a bit more snappish than s/he would have liked. There was no reason to be short-tempered with the newcomer, after all. "You'll be reporting to Lieutenant Beth for duty assignments," and s/he indicated Beth.

Beth rose from her chair, extended a hand, and said, "Welcome to engineering, Ensign . . . ?"

"Pheytus," said the Bolian.

There was a slight guffaw from Yates, quickly squelched. Beth, her eyes even rounder than usual, said, "Pardon?"

"Ensign Pheytus."

"Pronounced . . ." She clearly couldn't quite believe it. "Fetus? Ensign Fetus?"

"Yes, that's correct," said Pheytus. His hairless brows puckered in confusion. "Does that present a problem?"

"No, no . . . not at all," Beth said quickly, but it was obvious to Burgoyne that she was trying to stifle her amusement.

Mitchell said, "Welcome to engineering, Ensign Fetus."

"I'm sure we'll have plenty of womb for you here," said Beth.

That was it for Yates and Torelli; they burst out laughing. Mitchell masterfully kept a straight face, as he always did. As for Beth, her lips were tightly sealed, but her shoulders were shaking in silent mirth. Pheytus could not have looked more bewildered. "Am I . . . missing something here? Am I unwelcome for some reason?"

"Definitely not," deadpanned Torelli. "Having you here will be a labor of love, and if you need anything, we'll be at your cervix."

More laughter. Pheytus wasn't taking offense; he was too puzzled to do so. Burgoyne, however, more sternly than s/he had ever spoken before, said, "All right, that's more than enough."

"If I have given offense in some way—" began Pheytus.

This time it was Yates who piped in. "You'd be sick about it in the morning?"

"I said that's enough!" The thunder, the anger in Burgoyne's voice was so uncharacteristic that it was enough to startle the others into silence. "Ensign Pheytus, that will be all." Pheytus bowed again ever so slightly, turned and left, shaking his head a bit as he did so. Burgoyne glared at hir command staff. "And you say *I'm* immature?"

"I'm sorry. That could have been handled better," admitted Mitchell.

"Oh, do you think so? Really?" Sarcasm was dripping from every syllable. "You people cracking jokes, and you, Mitchell—they answer to you now. By sitting there and smirking, even though you didn't join in, you tacitly endorsed it." S/he shook hir head, making no secret of hir annoyance. "I have to say, people, I'm less than impressed by what I've seen today. I've worked too hard forging one of the best engineering staffs in the fleet. And today I've seen you become disconcerted by everything from my promotion to the unintentionally funny name of a new crewmember. That is unacceptable, people. *Unacceptable,* as in, I won't accept it." S/he glared around the table at them, one at a time, and one at a time each of them lowered their gaze rather than return it. Tapping the table with one of hir claws, s/he continued, "I demand, and expect to receive, the very best out of my crew. I strongly suggest you don't disappoint me a second time. Is that clear?"

There were scattered murmurs of "Yes, sir," from around the table.

And something in Burgoyne bristled ever so slightly. "I believe I asked, *'Is that clear?'* "

This time the "Yes, sir," was in unison and quite vocal. S/he nodded once, approvingly, but s/he was still annoyed with them and made no effort to hide hir feelings.

Then the com beeped. "Engineering, Burgoyne here," s/he said.

"Commander, we're almost ready for our communication with the *Trident.* As second-in-command, you should be there."

"On my way, Captain."

S/he rose, gave one final annoyed look at the rest of them, said "Unacceptable," one more time to underscore hir annoyance, and then headed for the conference room . . .

. . . and managed to hold hir laughter over the tragically named "Ensign Fetus" until s/he got into the privacy of the turbolift.

"Interesting choice," was Shelby's initial reaction.

She was smiling at him from the viewscreen of the conference lounge. It was all Calhoun could do to resist placing his hand against the screen. It would be unnecessarily over-sentimentalized, and it wasn't as if the curvature and coldness of a screen would do anything to simulate the softness of her skin.

"I'm pleased that my choice meets with your approval," Calhoun replied.

"I didn't say *that*," she demurred. "I mean, honestly, Mac . . . do you really think that Burgoyne is even remotely Starfleet command material, let alone an appropriate first officer of the *Excalibur?*"

"One never knows about these things unless one tries," he said reasonably. "I'm sure that, as scruffy and savage as I was, I hardly looked like Starfleet material twenty-some years ago. And as for the 'appropriateness'—"

"I know where you're going with this," Shelby interrupted with a small smile. "How appropriate was it for you to put your former fiancée in place as second-in-command? That's what you were going to say, wasn't it?"

"More or less. That's why I had to marry you, Eppy. It got to the point where there was no use in my even opening my mouth anymore; you knew everything that was going to come out of it before I even said it."

"Sure way to get out of a rut."

The door to the lounge hissed open and Si Cwan entered. Calhoun never got over how Si Cwan didn't seem to come into a room so much as fill it with his sheer presence. Tall, red-skinned, with his mustache and beard meticulously trimmed as always, the current Thallonian ambassador and former Thallonian royalty looked to the viewscreen, bowed slightly, and then said, "My apologies. I value punctuality, and did not intend to be late."

"You aren't," said Calhoun. "Captain Shelby and I started early so that we could take a few minutes to . . . compare notes."

"I see," Si Cwan said neutrally. If he was ascribing some other meaning to "compare notes," he didn't indicate it. "And Commander Burgoyne . . . ?"

"Right behind you."

The towering ambassador stepped aside, allowing Burgoyne to pass. Burgoyne nodded hir head slightly to Si Cwan, who returned the gesture. "Since I have not had the opportunity to say as much to you earlier, Commander: Congratulations on your promotion."

"No smart comments regarding it?" Burgoyne asked with mild curiosity.

Si Cwan raised a ridge where, on others, an eyebrow would have been. " 'Smart comments'?"

"Well, most others seem to have volumes of opinion on the subject regarding my suitability."

"Commander, you seem to forget that Captain Calhoun, in the time that I've known him, had the good sense to allow me to remain upon this vessel after my creative means of boarding her—"

"The word you're looking for is 'stowaway,' " Shelby commented from the screen, "and it wasn't this ship, it was her predecessor."

"Be that as it may," Si Cwan said mildly. "The point remains that he made the remarkably intelligent decision to keep me as part of the crew in an ambassadorial capacity. He has made one wise choice after another since then. Who am I to second-guess his abilities at this date? No, I can say with quiet, and yet firm conviction, that any decision made by our good captain is one that I will wholeheartedly and unreservedly support."

Burgoyne stared at Si Cwan for a long moment, obviously aware that s/he was missing something. Calhoun waited patiently, confident that Burgoyne would tumble to it, and in short order Calhoun's confidence paid off as Burgoyne thumped a hand against hir head. "*Of course!* You had money down on me in the pool."

"Better than that: a side bet with Kebron. A hundred credits, ten to one odds," Si Cwan said with satisfaction. "Ah, the expression on that rock-hided buffoon's face was truly priceless."

"Kebron never changes expression," Burgoyne pointed out.

"I know. But I could tell he was seething inside. His

money was on Soleta. Apparently they went to the Academy together, and he allowed sentimentality to sway his better judgment."

"This is all very enchanting," said Shelby sarcastically, "and fortunately enough, I have absolutely nothing else to do aboard the *Trident* except listen to you people chatter on about whatever enters your heads. However . . ."

"Point taken, Captain," said Calhoun with appropriate formality. "All right: Care to bring us up to speed on the distress call you received?"

She did so, with her customary efficiency. When she finished, Calhoun stroked his beard thoughtfully. Si Cwan was shaking his head, already looking somewhat discouraged. It was not an expression on his face that Calhoun cared to see. "Cwan," he said, "I can tell already that you have some knowledge on this subject. Care to share it with the rest of us?"

"Knowledge is power, Captain. And I can only assume you do not keep me aboard this vessel simply for my dazzling personality."

"Go with the assumption," said Calhoun. "So . . . Thallon 18 . . . ?"

"The problem is not Thallon 18 . . . or at least, that is not where the problem began," Si Cwan told them. He leaned back in his chair and, as was his habit at such times, casually rubbed the circular tattoo in the middle of his forehead as if he were stimulating the memories directly from his brain. "A hundred years ago, there were two races on a single world—a world called Sinqay—and the two races had been enemies for century upon century. They absolutely could not coexist, no matter what anyone did. Do not think we did not try. As much as many of you wish to characterize the Thallonian empire as dictatorial, such was not the case. There were any number of times that our involvement simply focused on not only trying to keep the peace, but encouraging other races to keep that peace with one another."

"You were saints," Shelby said with exaggerated conviction, "and no one in the Thallonian empire ever did anything in less than a perfect and philanthropic manner."

"That is true," said Si Cwan, utterly ignoring the irony. Shelby rolled her eyes. He ignored that as well. "In the case of Sinqay, however, well . . ." He shook his head. "It was almost as if the two races either had a death wish, or were just utterly infantile, for they proved unwilling to share their world. Peace talks would drag on, and then when final accords seemed on the brink, something would happen, the peace process would fall apart, and bam!" He slapped his hands together with such force, it was as if a small thunderclap was unleashed in the room. "Just like that, there would be war again. In time, the warfare became so violent that weapons of mass destruction were unleashed. Tens of thousands were killed, and the two races were on the verge of bombing each other into nonexistence. So," and he cracked his knuckles in leisurely fashion, as if he was only just warming up, "we Thallonians opted for a drastic solution. We took the warring races and relocated both of them."

"'Relocated'?" asked a slightly puzzled Calhoun.

Si Cwan shrugged as if it were the most commonplace matter in the galaxy. As if the "relocation" was as casual as changing one's boots. "It was not a tremendous chore for us, for our technology was so advanced over the two races."

"And aren't *we* masters of our galaxy," Shelby said drily.

Once more, Si Cwan did not rise to the bait. "You are forgetting, Captain," he said politely, "where *we* were . . . and where *they* were . . . in terms of development. Indeed, where we were in comparison to most of the denizens of Thallonian space. Our technology and abilities were far, far beyond anything that almost anyone else had throughout our sector. Only the Redeemers came close to matching us, and even they were loathe to take us on head-to-head."

"Yes, you're all wonderful, that's why you're still in

charge," said Calhoun, and he took some mild pleasure in seeing Cwan visibly wince from the verbal barb. There was never any harm in taking the Thallonian down a peg when the situation warranted it. He continued, "If you wouldn't mind continuing, please."

"Well . . . to make a long story short—"

"Too late," muttered Burgoyne. Calhoun was breathing a silent prayer of thanks that Kebron wasn't in attendance.

"To make a long story short," Si Cwan repeated even more slowly, casting an imperious glance around the table. "We moved both of them to separate worlds that we had terraformed. We placed one race, the Markanians, on the world designated Thallon 18. On Thallon 21 we placed the other race, the Aerons."

"And they couldn't get at each other?" asked Calhoun.

"Let me guess: no means of space travel," said Burgoyne.

Si Cwan nodded. "Exactly. You see, you may all take space vessels for granted, but these two worlds knew nothing of such things. They had managed to launch the occasional odd satellite or two, but interplanetary travel was simply beyond their technology and know-how. We, of course, were not about to provide them such secrets. Oh, we knew that eventually they would figure it out. Sooner or later, they would develop technology enabling them to move from one planet to another at faster-than-impulse speed. However, it was our hope that, in doing so, they might find a more constructive way to live their lives than bicker over ancient hostilities."

"And that hasn't happened," Calhoun correctly surmised.

With a heavy sigh, Si Cwan shook his head. "Unfortunately, we underestimated the depth of hostility they felt for one another. Every so often, we would send in observers to interact with them, feel them out in terms of how they regarded their former enemies. In this case, absence—human truism to the contrary—did not make the heart grow fonder."

"Well, there's another human truism," said Shelby,

"which says you should never go to sleep angry. That's apparently what happened here. You separated two races, angry over issues that went unresolved. As a consequence, they spent year after year stewing on them without being able to address them."

"Considering their means of addressing them had historically been to try and annihilate one another, it's something of a small loss," said Si Cwan with a shrug. "Be that as it may—the separation at least prevented them from killing each other."

"Yes, well, it would appear that has changed," said Shelby. "As far as we've been able to piece together, what's happened is as follows: The Gateway technology has enabled the ancient enmity between the two races to move to a new level. According to the residents of Thallon 18—the Markanians—a Gateway was used to launch an attack against the Aerons. Just about the entire ruling family of that world was wiped out, plunging the world into a serious power struggle. It's the Markanians' concern that, once the Aerons get matters of rule settled, the first thing they're going to endeavor to do is retaliate."

"That will be difficult," observed Si Cwan, "considering the Aerons still do not—to the best of my knowledge—have any means of spaceflight."

"But the technology of the Gateway is out there, Ambassador," Burgoyne said. "And it's a funny thing about technology: Once it's out, it's damned near impossible to tuck it back away."

That was one thing that Calhoun had to admit about Burgoyne: S/he had a unique mastery of understatment.

"Meaning that you think the Aerons will find some way to lay their hands on a Gateway and return the favor," said Shelby.

Burgoyne nodded. "I don't see how they wouldn't."

"For what it's worth, the Markanians agree with you,

Commander," Shelby told hir. "And they want to try and head that off before it happens."

"Given the Aeron track record," said Si Cwan, "it is extremely unlikely that they are simply going to nod their heads and shrug off the attack that was made upon them. If they find any means of retaliating, they are going to take it, and they are not tremendously likely to listen to anyone telling them otherwise."

That was not something that Calhoun was particularly enthused about hearing. He leveled his gaze on Si Cwan. "Are you saying," he asked, putting enough of a challenge into his tone that he hoped Si Cwan would rise to the occasion, "that you would be incapable of convincing them otherwise?"

He was pleased to see that the effort was not in vain, for Si Cwan bristled every so slightly and replied, "No, I'm not saying that at all. I'm saying it would be difficult. But 'impossibility' and I do not tend to get along."

"Your modesty continues to dazzle even me," said Shelby.

Cwan inclined his head slightly, as if accepting a compliment.

Calhoun, for his part, felt some miniscule degree of triumph, but there was still a long way to go in this matter. "All right," he said slowly, "here's what I suggest. Captain Shelby . . . since you were contacted by Thallon 18, I'd recommend that you head there, so that you can establish for yourself the severity of the situation. At the same time, the *Excalibur* will go to Thallon 21—"

"Captain, as I recall," Shelby reminded him, "that is not exactly the assignment that was given you by Starfleet in regards to this Gateway problem."

He'd had a feeling that Shelby was going to bring that up, and he certainly hadn't been disappointed. *Curse this inability I have to be wrong,* he thought glumly as, out loud, he agreed, "No, it's not. However, the *Excalibur* comes loaded with some fairly handy extras, including some long-range autoprobes. We'll fire them to the deep space coordinates we're supposed to investigate and gather preliminary information as to these Gateway 'energy signatures' they want us to look into."

"I doubt they're going to be satisfied with a mechanized exploration, Captain. My assumption is that they wanted your input."

He knew that Shelby wasn't going to let this go easily. On the other hand, there was some measure of "safety" for him in knowing that there wasn't a whole hell of a lot she was going to be able to do about it. "You're undoubtedly right, Captain," he agreed, "but it's my belief that, since we can't be in two places simultaneously—at least, not without bringing the starship *Relativity* down on our heads—our time would be better spent trying to head off a planetary conflict." He saw Shelby purse her lips, a sure sign that she knew he was right, and then pushed for resolution to the problem. "Besides, considering a Gateway seems to be involved in that conflict, this strikes me as a more solid lead than investigating energy signatures."

Shelby inclined her head slightly. "Whatever you say, Captain."

That was easier than I dared hope. "My, my—married life has mellowed you, Captain Shelby," said Calhoun with a smile.

"Not at all. It's simply liberating, not having your decisions be my problem anymore. He's all yours, Burgoyne."

"Thanks a lot," said Burgoyne.

"Stay in touch, Captain," Calhoun told her.

"You, too, Captain. *Trident* out." Her image blinked off the screen.

Calhoun drummed his fingers on the table for a moment, then glanced at Burgoyne. "I didn't hear you disagreeing with my decisions regarding Thallon 21."

Burgoyne was quiet for a long moment . . . so long that Calhoun began to wonder if he should have left well enough alone, rather than knocking the fact that Burgoyne had offered no protest. But then Burgoyne said, with a shrug, "That's probably because I agreed with your decision. Our priority has to be the preservation of life. The extension of a pointless feud is hardly of benefit to anyone."

"Oh. Well . . . good," Calhoun said with an approving nod. "A first officer who agrees with me. I could get used to it."

With eyes half-lidded, Burgoyne said, "Well, don't."

At that, Si Cwan emitted a low, rumbling noise that passed for laughter. "Captain, I believe you've just been warned," said Si Cwan.

"You know, Ambassador . . . I believe I have."

8

AERON

Smyt was awakened by the screaming, as he knew he would be. The screaming, the rumbling, and the overall sense that a final and complete doom had come not only for the residents of Aeron, but the very planet itself.

The cell in which he had been residing had not been especially dank, or even all that unpleasant. Nevertheless, despite the adequate furnishings, it remained a cell. It was in an underground bunker, with no windows and only recycled air to breathe. The furniture, while functional, was nothing more than that. A chair, a small table, another chair (which he had drawn across from the first one and propped his feet upon). Otherwise it was relatively barren, and there wasn't much for Smyt to do to occupy himself.

That was all right with Smyt, however. He had a very clear idea that time was on his side. So he would simply sit in the middle of the cell, cross-legged, eyes closed, allowing his intellect to drift in and out of awareness. He would take his mind far, far away, where no cells could reach it, where no imprisonment could hold it. It helped him to remember that these were simple planet-bound creatures, scrabbling about without the slightest idea how to achieve any of the goals to which they aspired. While he . . . he and his people . . . they were so much more.

But he was jarred from his self-satisfied reverie by the doomsday noises occurring outside his cell. Smyt brought himself down, down, until he was fully awake and back to full attention.

He listened thoughtfully, dispassionately. In his mind's eye, he could easily picture the chaos that the noises were suggesting. He vaguely wondered whether anyone was dead, and if so, how many. Whether any Aerons had died or not wasn't all that important to him; it would simply give him an indication of how humbled they would be when they finally came crawling to him. If he waited a few minutes more, then undoubtedly there would be some deaths, and that would get them nicely softened up.

So he waited a few minutes more.

Then, satisfied with the degree of discord that had been unleashed above, he began rolling up the sleeve of his left arm. It looked no different than his right arm, and any medical scan of it would have detected no difference. He ran his long, tapered fingers along the inner forearm, found the ridge he was seeking, and tapped it once. There was a soft whirring of servos and a small panel slid open on the arm, revealing an equally small array of controls. There were several lights blinking, indicating that everything was functioning as anticipated.

He shook his head. "Idiots," he murmured. He had done nothing to instigate the insanity; no, no, the Aerons had more than done that to themselves. On the other hand, he had certainly done nothing to prevent the catastrophe from being unleashed. There was no better way, he reasoned, to convince them of the necessity for dealing with him directly, rather than shunting him away into some sort of prison.

He reached into the exposed section of the arm and deftly manipulated the controls. It was not the easiest of chores, considering that the ground was rumbling beneath him, but ultimately it did not take long at all. Within moments the trembling had subsided, and Smyt smiled with quiet confidence. He could practically sense the relief flooding over everyone within the area of the test site . . . indeed, very possibly everyone on the planet, even those who did not comprehend what had just happened.

From that moment on, it was just a matter of time.

He closed the control panel, rolled the sleeve back down, and returned to his meditative state. He knew that, sooner or later, they would be coming to him, and he wanted to be in a calm, imperturbable frame of mind when they did so.

As it happened, it was sooner rather than later.

The brisk sound of footsteps approaching rousted him from his inner contemplation, and he had just managed to recall his consciousness to full wakefulness when the doors to his cell slid open and a familiar figure was standing there, accompanied by several guards.

"Good day to you, Burkitt," said an unnecessarily jovial Smyt. "And how are you doing with the Gateway? All the testing procedures go as smoothly as you could have hoped?" He inclined his head slightly, displaying a false air of concern. "You look somewhat haggard, dear fellow. Has there been a problem?"

Burkitt said nothing at first, merely glared at Smyt. It was all Smyt could do to keep a self-satisfied smirk off his face, but he knew he was dealing with delicacies. He did not wish to annoy his customer, particularly considering how obviously aggravated Burkitt was at that moment. So he said nothing, waiting for Burkitt to break the silence.

"Leave us," Burkitt said, and although his gaze was fixed

upon Smyt, the comment was clearly addressed to the guards. They promptly did as they were told, while Burkitt stepped into the cell and allowed the doors to close behind him. Smyt could see that the warmaster was trembling with barely suppressed rage, but gave no indication that he was the least bit concerned. "Do you know what happened?" Burkitt demanded. "And did you know it *would* happen?"

Smyt, who had been planning to lie, saw the look in Burkitt's eyes and immediately intuited that any attempt at prevarication would not bode well for him. Smyt was by no means an imposing figure, and yet he managed to draw himself up and look at least mildly impressive. "I know that *something* happened," he said with brisk efficiency. "I'd have to be deaf, dumb, and blind to be unaware of that. Precisely what it was, I've no idea, nor did I know exactly what results your mucking with the Gateway would trigger. You could have actually lucked onto the proper functioning of the device. I wouldn't have expected you to do so, you understand, but anything is possible. I think I can safely assume, however, that that isn't what occurred."

"No. It's not," Burkitt said tersely.

Smyt settled back, still fighting the impulse to smile at Burkitt's obvious discomfiture. "Tell me what *did* occur."

Burkitt took a deep breath, and Smyt could see that Burkitt was fighting back the anger that had threatened, however momentarily, to consume him. "We're not altogether certain. The controls appear to be encrypted, but our scientists were certain they had managed to crack it. It was . . ." He placed one hand on one of the chairs, leaning slightly on it, but not sitting. "It was supposed to be a modest test of the device's capabilities. It's not as if we were intending to use it to launch a full strike against the Markanians. We wanted to do nothing more than use it to transport a test device from one side of our world to the other."

"And instead . . .?" prompted Smyt, when Burkitt didn't immediately continue.

"Instead," said Burkitt, looking shaken just from the recollection, "when the Gateway was activated—as near as we can determine—it appeared to lock onto a sun."

"Onto a *sun?*" Smyt was doing an excellent job of sounding surprised. He was quite pleased with himself, chalking it up to his meditative skills. "Which one?"

"How would I know?" Burkitt said testily. "It was hot, it was bright, and it almost killed us all. Thank the gods no one was standing near the Gateway when it started up."

"The Gateway has a protective filter for just such a mishap," Smyt said, as if what Burkitt was telling him was news to him. "If it had not prevented the heat from getting through, you, everybody there, half the damned planet would have been incinerated."

"That much is true, apparently," admitted Burkitt. "But what the filter couldn't keep out, as it so happened, was the star's gravity. The gravimetric force that came through . . . it started pulling up everything around it. Huge pieces of the planet, the upper portions of a nearby mountain peak . . . it was as if a giant vacuum had been turned on and was sucking in everything in sight. The control center building was trembling, being pulled apart by the power of it. Pieces of it went flying, got sucked in despite the distance of the device. Our scientists were trying to shut it down, but weren't succeeding in doing so." He paused a moment, as if gathering himself. Apparently he was having trouble relating what had occurred, as if he couldn't believe it even though he had been an eyewitness to it. "Not only that, but the power of the star was beginning to affect the very tectonic plates between the planet's surface, triggering quakes, and . . ." He shook his head, and for a moment—just a moment—he trembled slightly. Smyt found himself admiring the warmaster's self-control; had he witnessed as catastrophic an accident as

Burkitt had, he doubted he would be able to address the recollections of it with such equanimity. Burkitt steadied himself then and said, with remarkable cool, "If they had not managed to shut it down . . . the entire planet would very likely have been sucked into the thing."

"Was anyone hurt?"

Burkitt licked his dry lips. "Several of my people. They were trying to get the scientists to safer ground . . . as if there *were* any safer ground. As the building came apart, several were killed by falling rubble . . . and a couple more were just . . . just hauled away. I felt . . ."

"Felt what?"

Burkitt let out a long breath. "I felt the gravity pulling at me. I would have gone next . . . been pulled through the air, into the Gateway, hurled right into the fiery core of a star . . . and then it just . . . shut down."

"With no warning?"

"I can only think that whatever steps our scientists took to disconnect it eventually kicked in. Either that," he added thoughtfully, "or there was some sort of built-in override or safety shut-off."

Suddenly his eyes narrowed and he stared at Smyt. It was a gaze that made Smyt feel extremely uncomfortable, and he began to wonder if, somehow, he had underestimated the Aeron warmaster. For a moment, he expected Burkitt to grab his arm, rip it open, and expose the controls hidden away therein. But then the moment passed, and Burkitt leaned back, letting out a soft sigh of relief. "Whatever the reason . . . it stopped. And we were spared what could easily have been the most cataclysmic mistake in the history of our people."

He said nothing more for a time. Finally Smyt could take the silence no longer. "So . . . now what?"

"Now?" He laughed bitterly. "Well, I had an interesting meeting with my fellow Counselars, I can certainly tell you that. Half of them wanted to have me put on trial for posing a deadly threat to our world. The other half insisted that, although the concept of striking back at the Markanians was a sound one, that we were foolish to proceed without the aid of the individual who best knew how to operate the Gateway. Even though," he added, "it is my conviction that that individual—namely you—is endeavoring to play one race against the other. I do not trust you now, Smyt, any more than I did before."

"And may I ask what the final resolution of your Counselars was?"

Burkitt rose and walked around the cell, hands draped behind his back. "When I said they were evenly split, that was not exaggeration. And obviously, I was not about to vote for my being put on trial."

"Meaning you have elected to trust me," Smyt concluded with clear satisfaction.

"I have elected to do no such thing," Burkitt said, giving Smyt that same uneasy feeling he had before. "Your price—presuming it's reasonable—will be met. And you will be working directly on the Gateway, showing our scientists the proper way to operate it. However, we will make certain that you are positioned directly in front of the Gateway when next it's opened. If, in an attempt to subject our world to destructive forces, you open the portal to a star, or a black hole, or some other 'inappropriate' destination, you will be the very first to meet whatever fate you intend for the rest of us."

Smyt laughed unpleasantly. "There's certainly nothing like a trusting atmosphere to provide a conducive environment for scientific exploration."

Smiling grimly, Burkitt assured him, "Then take heart, for I can promise you nothing like a trusting atmosphere. On the other hand, if you consider the terms unacceptable, we can simply destroy the Gateway now and leave you to rot."

At that, Smyt was seized with silent fury. "The Gateway is my property. You have no right—"

And suddenly Smyt was off his feet, Burkitt lifting him with one hand and slamming him up against the wall. His voice choking with fury, Burkitt snarled, "Several of the soldiers I lost were men I trained myself, from their youth. They were like sons to me. I take their loss very, very seriously, and as much as I hold myself responsible for what happened to them, I condemn you all the more." And with each subsequent pause, he thumped Smyt against the wall once more. "So I do not—suggest—you speak—to me—of your—rights." He unclenched his fingers then, and Smyt slid to the floor. "Do we understand each other?"

Smyt coughed several times, and then said, "Perfectly."

Then Burkitt hauled him to his feet, and Smyt flinched against an anticipated blow. Instead, Burkitt simply said, "Good. Then let's get to work."

9

MARKANIA

"THANK YOU FOR COMING," Furvus of the Ruling Council of Markania said for what seemed the hundredth time. His forehead was beaded with sweat, and he dabbed at it with a cloth, forcing a smile as he led Captain Shelby and Lieutenant Arex past the ornate columns leading to the inner chamber of the Council. Outside there was a cold rain falling, and a fairly stiff wind blowing. Shelby was wearing a Starfleet-issue windbreaker over her uniform tunic, against the weather. Furthermore, Shelby had to walk carefully, because the rain had caused the walkways to become quite slick. Yet, despite the weather, there seemed to be a fair number of citizens out and about. That was made more understandable when she learned that a steady rain and chill winds were more or less the standard state of the weather thereabouts. If the people of Thallon 18—or Markania, as they termed it—remained indoors waiting for a sunny day, they'd likely never go outside at all.

Interestingly, Arex didn't seem the least impeded by the

inclement weather. Perhaps his three-legged structure gave him additional traction. Whatever it was, he moved with utter confidence across the slick flagging that led up to the council building.

"The rest of the Council is waiting within," Furvus said, gesturing ahead of himself. "They all want to thank you for coming." Shelby couldn't help but observe that she had never seen, in all her career, a planetary head who appeared more concerend about being liked than Furvus. That, she mused, was never a good attribute for a leader to have. One simply couldn't be concerned about whether he or she was liked. *Well, that certainly puts you on solid footing, doesn't it?* Shelby's mind commented in a snide fashion. She airily told her mind to shut the hell up.

"Will the thanks be *en masse,* or individually?" inquired Arex.

Shelby fired him a look and he promptly silenced himself, although there was a hint of a smile on his wide lips.

Totally missing the sarcasm, Furvus bowed slightly to the security head and said, "Whichever you would prefer."

Shelby had trouble believing that Furvus could possibly be that dense, but such seemed to be the case. "Neither will be necessary," Shelby said promptly. "I think you've made your appreciation abundantly clear."

She was finding it even harder to believe that this "Furvus" was any sort of a genuine leader of the world. He seemed extremely tentative, bordering on being apologetic for his very existence. Yet the Markanians that they passed appeared to hold him in proper esteem, bowing their heads slightly as they went. Perhaps the Markanians were culturally trained to prize humility above all else. That being the case, Furvus could probably be king for life.

As they walked down the corridor toward what she assumed was the council chamber, she noticed a series of mosaics artfully crafted into the wall. As benign an attitude as

Furvus was putting forward, she was seeing a very different view of the Markanians from the wall-works. She saw a blue-skinned race that she took to be the Markanians, locked in combat with another race. They were very pale in hue, but there was nothing in their depiction that indicated any sort of physical weakness. What Shelby found of even further interest was that the mosaics seemed to cover a significant span of time. In some of them, the combatants were armed with little more than cutting weapons and clubs. From those very primitive beginnings, up through to relatively modern times, with the enemies having at one another with energy-blasting weapons, Shelby was witnessing generation upon generation of enmity. "What a waste," she muttered to herself.

Arex obviously heard her talking under her breath and looked at her with curiosity, but she didn't offer any sort of clarification, nor was it his place to request it. Instead he simply continued to move alongside her, noiselessly, as her security escort.

Yes. Yes, noiselessly. That was the most remarkable thing about him: how he didn't seem to walk so much as he glided. She had it on reliable authority from Starfleet that Arex had been absolutely devastating in both hand-to-hand and weapons simulations while he was being appraised for Starfleet duty. His scores had literally been off the charts, and his installation as head of security had been a natural fit.

Would that M'Ress had proven as natural. Unfortunately she continued to seem out of place, having difficulty fitting in. Every time Shelby happened to wander past the Caitian, she seemed preoccupied and distant. She supposed she couldn't entirely blame M'Ress. She was, after all, in a time and place that was not her own. That would have been enough to drag down even the most gregarious of souls . . . except for Arex, whose basic upbeat nature didn't seem the least bit perturbed by his new circumstances.

Well, she'd always heard that cats don't travel well. That

notion made Shelby smile, and she reminded herself that she should share the observation with M'Ress. Certainly M'Ress would find a cat reference amusing. She probably had a very good sense of humor about such things.

Furvus appeared to notice where Shelby's attention was focused. "Impressive array, is it not?" he said, slowing his pace.

She nodded. "Very much so."

"Would that it were not." He sighed heavily. "I am afraid, Captain, that you have wandered onto a world caught in a true schism."

"We haven't 'wandered' into anything, Furvus . . . I'm sorry, do you have a title of some sort? President? Honorable?"

"I am simply Furvus," he said, once again sounding almost apologetic. "Once . . . once our people were most enamored of titles. And of war," and he indicated the mosaics. "And I fear that time is coming once again. Which is why I, on behalf of the Ruling Council, asked that you come. Our thanks for your coming, by the way."

She'd lost count of the number of times he'd said that. "Thank you."

They walked through a large set of double doors, and Shelby could hear what sounded like urgent discussion on the other side, which promptly lapsed into silence when they entered. There were two more Markanians seated at a semicircular table, and they fixed what looked to be urgent gazes upon Shelby and Arex when they entered. One of them looked at the two Starfleet officers and asked, "Which one would be the leader?"

"I am Captain Shelby," she said. "This is Lieutenant Arex." Not for the first time, she regretted that Si Cwan had chosen to remain with the *Excalibur*. This was the precise sort of situation where the knowledgeable Thallonian would come in handy.

"I am Vinecia," said the Markanian on the right-hand side of the table, and, indicating her associate, "and this is

Clebe." It was only when the Markanian had spoken, with a voice lighter and far more delicate than that of Furvus, that Shelby came to the conclusion that Vinecia was in fact female. "We wish to thank you most profoundly for coming."

"Yes, I suspected you would," said Shelby. She looked around for a place to sit and found none. Instead, the Council members rose and came around from behind the table, standing in an orderly formation. Wonderful. Apparently the Markanians believed in conducting affairs of state on their feet. It seemed to make a certain degree of sense in a perversely logical way. It was easy for people to argue about matters when they could do so while positioned on their backsides. But if one had to stand the whole time, there was that much more incentive to try and address matters in a succinct and straightforward manner, if for no other reason than to get off one's feet.

"So . . . you spoke of a Gateway," Shelby said.

The three of them nodded, almost in unison. "However," the one called Vinecia said, "for you to understand the significance of the Gateway problem, you must know a little about our world's circumstances."

"I think I know a bit about—"

She didn't even get the entire sentence out; as if she hadn't spoken, Vinecia turned to her right and prompted, "Clebe?"

Clebe was apparently quite accustomed to public speaking, for he promptly launched into a narrative that sounded rehearsed. "For many hundreds of years, we shared a paradisical world called Sinqay with another race known as the Aerons. Due to Thallonian interventions, we were removed from our homeworld and placed on another planet, as were the Aerons."

"Yes, I know th—" she began to interrupt.

Clebe continued as if she hadn't opened her mouth. "The Great Separation occurred one hundred years ago. During that time, our race became sorely divided against itself. There were, and are, those of us who look back upon those warlike times with great chagrin. We see it as the wasted opportunity and resources of a people too immature, as a race, to fully appreciate the futility of war and the cost and pointlessness of extended mutual destruction."

"Good for you," said Shelby, and Arex nodded approvingly.

"However," continued Clebe, "there are others—youngers of us—who feel that our race has lost its way. It is believed that the destruction of the Aerons was a holy mission put upon us by the gods, and that, in failing to complete the mission, we will bring the wrath of the gods down upon ourselves. For we are the Selected Ones of the gods, and to stop at anything less than total annihilation of our enemies is to be less than sanctified in the eyes of the gods."

"I hardly see where your gods would only give approval if another race was wiped out."

"Your own gods never issue such dictates?" inquired Furvus.

Before Shelby could answer, Arex piped up, "Actually, in the earth scripture known as the 'Old Testament,' there are numerous instances where the God of that particular tome demands that entire peoples be obliterated, and even wipes out cities and the whole of humanity when He's so inclined."

"Arex, you're not helping," Shelby said a bit testily.

Arex simply bobbed his head slightly and said, "Apologies, Captain." But he sounded more faintly amused than anything. She supposed she shouldn't have been surprised. Arex had, after all, served under Kirk. So he was certainly not going to be daunted by disapproval from any modern Starfleet captain.

"The point," said Clebe, "is that the people of our world are sorely divided on the issue. There are those who very much are in agreement with the philosophies of Ebozay, and believe that—"

"Wait," Shelby raised a hand, halting the torrent of exposition. "Ebozay? Who would Ebozay be?"

"The leader of the opposition," Vinecia said patiently. "For several years now, he has stirred up feelings of unrest.

We tolerated it for two reasons: One, because the Council has already preached tolerance in any event. And two, for as long as Ebozay and his followers could not actually reach the Aerons, his complaints and warmongering could only go so far and no further. If there is no brew in the kettle, there's no harm in allowing someone to try and stir it as aggressively as they wish, since they cannot possibly spill it upon themselves and cause injury."

"But then this Gateway thing came along." Shelby moved her weight from one foot to the other, even as she interlaced her fingers directly in front of her. "Where did it come from? Who brought it?"

The members of the Ruling Council looked at each other nervously, shifting in obvious discomfort. "We do not know," Furvus admitted finally.

"You don't know?" She couldn't quite believe it. "A device turns up that enables your people to make an attack on another light-years away, and you have no idea where it came from?"

Furvus shook his head. "Whoever brought it to this world was very canny in his choice of allies."

"You say 'his.' Could it be a 'her'?" inquired Shelby.

"It could be an asexual creature spat up from the primordial ooze, Captain, and we'd still have no idea," said Vinecia. She sounded a bit testy. "All we know is that we, the Ruling Council, were not approached."

"Nor should that be surprising," admitted Furvus. "Ebozay has staked out the philosophical territory of a bellicose attitude toward the Aerons. He and his followers believe the Aerons to be guilty of war crimes."

"And are they?" Arex asked.

"Technically," replied Clebe. "Then again, that is the way of war, is it not? Each side accuses the other of crimes. This much, though, is indisputable: Whatever 'crimes' were committed occurred at least a century ago, by beings on both sides who are long dead. Advocating an assault on those living today on behalf of 'crimes' committed by those who died yesterday is certainly a pointless waste of time and resources. Nevertheless, this is part of what Ebozay's position hinges upon. He contends that the souls of those who fell to these 'crimes' a century ago will never rest until some sort of restitution is made. A life for a life, lives for lives."

"I believe I speak with reasonable authority, if not utter certainty," Shelby said sarcastically, "in saying that the dead absolutely will not give a damn. They have more important issues to concern them—"

"Such as being dead," Arex offered.

"—than obsessing about some sort of balancing of cosmic scales. That strikes me as more the province and interest of the living than the dead."

"I would tend to agree," Furvus said mildly, "but unfortunately, Ebozay and his associates would not agree. He claims the agonies of the departed keep him awake at night."

"Oh, God," moaned Shelby. "And your people fall for this line of malarkey? No offense intended, Honorable Council Members, but are those you govern *that* stupid?"

"People want to believe in something, Captain," said Furvus, sounding quite weary. "They are so desperate to believe in something that often it seems they'll believe in anything. In this case, that includes whatever it is that Ebozay is feeding them. We have open petitions to the Council twice a week, and at those petitions there are always followers of Ebozay, lobbying us to take a more aggressive stance toward the Aerons. Always we have resisted in the past."

"After all," Vinecia said, sounding quite reasonable, "what purpose is there to declaring war on a world we cannot reach, and getting everyone worked up about it as well? Except that decision is being taken out of our hands."

"So you're saying," said Shelby, leaning against the table (unsure of whether it was a breach of protocol and not especially caring at that moment), "that it was Ebozay and his followers who embarked upon the assault?"

The three Council Members bobbed their heads in unison. "We believe that is exactly what happened."

"How do you know it was a Gateway?"

"Oh, we have some among Ebozay's followers who are still loyal to us," Clebe said with a measure of visible pride. "They described the technology to us, told us what the inventor called it—"

"Inventor?" Her eyes narrowed. "You said you didn't know who brought it here."

"We don't know for certain," Furvus said primly. "We haven't actually met this 'inventor.' We did not wish to give you secondhand information."

Shelby moaned inwardly. "Tell me everything, rumors or not. This inventor . . . is he a native of your world?"

"No," said Clebe. "Thin, yellow-skinned—"

"An Iconian," she said immediately.

The Council Members looked at one another in puzzlement, and Arex said in a low voice to Shelby, "I am unfamiliar with this race, Captain. Do they pose a security threat?"

"Only to the entirety of the Federation."

"Ah," was all Arex could think of to say in response to that.

"He arrived here some time ago and immediately gained the confidence of Ebozay and his followers," Furvus said. "And why not? Ebozay likely saw him as something of a godsend. He has been seeking to acquire power all this time, and along came someone who might very well be able to provide him with it. One cannot build a political power base on impossibilities and flights of fancy. As long as the desire for vengeance against the Aerons was nothing more than a vague need, Ebozay's influence and abilities were limited. But now that he is actually capable of giving his followers that which they most desire, his powers grow exponentially."

"Where is this 'inventor' now?" demanded Shelby. "I think

I'd like to speak with him." To herself she added, *Oh, yes, definitely . . . I'll be wanting to talk with him. These arrogant blackmailers, who are threatening the security of the entire Federation . . . I'd like to have a long, personal talk with them and try to emphasize the folly that they're embarking upon. And if common sense fails, perhaps I can emphasize it with a brick.* She was more than aware at that point that she was starting to sound like Calhoun, but something within her simply didn't care, and even took pride in that. But she was sorely disappointed by the next words she heard.

"We do not know, I'm afraid," said Furvus.

She didn't let her disappointment show, however. Her face impassive, after a moment's consideration she said, "I'll want to meet with this Ebozay. Him and his followers. I think it's necessary to explain to them that these Gateways present a far greater threat than they realize."

"Yes, yes, that would be excellent," Vinecia said immediately, and there were bobbing heads from her associates, clearly in agreement with her. "If there is any way that you could get Ebozay to listen to reason—"

"However," Shelby added, "I cannot interfere in your internal politics. If there's a shift in the philosophical direction of your people, I'm not in a position to enforce the status quo. I can't *make* your people want to keep you in office. It seems to me that—"

At that moment, there were explosions directly outside, followed by screams and sounds of confusion.

"Captain, stay here!" Arex said immediately, moving swiftly in the direction of the disturbance. But Shelby was not about to accept orders barked at her by anyone, even if it was a crewmember who was charged with keeping her safe. As fast as Arex was, Shelby motored past him at a flat-out run. "Captain!" Arex called once more, but she was already approaching the corridor with the war mosaics, which in turn opened out to the main courtyard.

She skidded to a halt, almost slipping on the rain-soaked flagging, and what she saw stunned her.

Armored men, everywhere. The armor itself was gray and looked fairly sturdy, enough to resist all but the most concentrated blasts. But it was also obviously lightweight, for the soldiers were moving extremely quickly, whipping around energy-pulse weapons and opening fire on anyone and everyone they could find.

The Markanians were panicking, and she couldn't blame them. Women and children were screaming, with no endeavor being made on the part of the attackers to discriminate between them. The armored men shouted no war cries. Instead they moved with brisk, ruthless efficiency, and there were more—

—pouring out of thin air.

Shelby couldn't believe it, but there it was, right in front of her. The air was shimmering as if it had been sliced in two, and more soldiers were emerging from what could only be described as a rift in reality. There was a low hum of power accompanying it; she could feel the vibrations right through her boots.

The quick movement to her immediate right caught the corner of her eye. Later, Shelby would have no idea what sort of instinct caused her to drop to the floor, but that was precisely what she did. She hit the ground, flattening—and that was the only thing that saved her life as an energy bolt from a weapon passed right through where she'd just been standing. One of the gray-armored men was standing no more than five feet away, having come up around and to the side, and the fact that Shelby had evaded the blast was nothing short of miraculous.

It was not, however, going to be enough, as her assailant swung his weapon down and prepared to blow a hole in her the size of her fist.

And then, just like that, the armored man was in the air.

Arex's three arms were suspending him with no sign of strain at all, and the Triexian's multiple hands processed the attacker with the efficiency of a meat grinder. The assailant did not know where to look first as one hand held him immobile, a second yanked his weapon from his hands, and a third ripped his helmet from his head.

It took Shelby only an instant to recognize the species that the torn-away helmet revealed. After all, she had just been staring at them on the mosaics that decorated the inner wall. It was an Aeron, and he did not look any too happy.

He tried to twist around in Arex's grasp, but it did no good. Arex, his thick lips drawn back into a very unpleasant smile, whirled the Aeron around, pinwheeling him with facility and then smashing his head directly into the floor. The Aeron let out a groan and slipped into unconsciousness.

Even as the action occupied no more than a couple of seconds, Shelby was already tapping her combadge and saying with extreme urgency, "Shelby to *Trident!*"

"This is Mueller," came the immediate response, and from the sound of her tone, it was obvious that the ship's first officer had been about to send a communiqué to her captain, and that Shelby had only narrowly beaten her to it. "Captain, we're detecting energy pulses—"

"We're under attack, thanks to hundreds of years of resentment and a Gateway," said Shelby. Phaser fire practically screamed in her ear; attackers were starting to notice Shelby's presence and, not only that, but the building that housed the Ruling Council. They were focusing their attention on it now, and only Arex's pinpoint blasting from his phaser was keeping them back. Their armor was obviously capable of protecting them from Markanian armament, but they clearly weren't up for withstanding phaser blasts. With one well-placed shot after another, Arex—who was standing behind a column for added protection—was keeping them at bay. But he was not going to be able to do so forever, that much was clear. "Kat, I want a five-second burst from the ship's phaser banks, wide beam, heavy stun, in a one-hundred-meter radius, except for the building I'm standing in. Fire at will!"

"Five seconds, aye, Captain."

"Captain!" It was Arex's high-pitched voice shouting a warning. Shelby had been standing behind another of the columns, which provided some momentary shielding, but now another attacker was coming up right behind her, moving in from the side. He was not, however, wielding an energy weapon of any kind. Instead he was swinging a sword at her. Shelby threw herself backwards, bending at the waist as if she were ducking under a limbo bar. The air hissed above her as the blade cut across, slamming into the column and taking a sizable chunk out of it. The split-second dodge was just enough time for Arex to take aim and fire, and the intensity of the phaser blast knocked Shelby's attacker literally heels over head. He hit the ground and lay still, the blade clattering out of his hand.

Then from overhead came a shriek of energy that caused all battle in the main courtyard to freeze for a moment as everyone—attackers and targets alike—paused and tried to determine from where the sound was originating. Abruptly the sky, the very air itself, flashed with sustained amber brilliance. Shelby reflexively shielded her eyes from it, even though she was not at risk. Precisely as she had requested, the blinding light held for five seconds, and when it faded, no one was left standing. One or two of the armored men were on their knees, swaying, trying to command their stunned bodies to rise to the occasion, but they did not succeed. Instead they pitched forward and lay still, about as threatening as a field of dust bunnies. The only sound left in the air was the humming of powerful energies—the open Gateway, hanging in the air, source of all their problems.

Shelby felt a cold, burning rage within her. She would have scolded Mackenzie Calhoun severely if he had done what she was about to do. But Calhoun wasn't here and she was, and she was nursing enough anger in her bosom to justify—to her mind—her next words. "Arex," she ordered, and she pointed a quivering finger at the open Gateway. "Shoot that damned thing."

Arex did not hesitate. Instantly he took aim and fired upon the Gateway. The phaser blast went straight in, vanishing into the rift, and Shelby took grim amusement at the notion that— on the other side of the Gateway—someone might very well be getting a faceful of phaser stun at that moment. At the very least, she told herself, it would be a nice warning to prevent the people on the other end from sending through reinforcements.

The tactic could not have worked better, for within seconds after Arex shot at the Gateway, the hum of energy abruptly ceased, and the Gateway vanished. Now there was no sound save for faint and distant moaning from those fallen in the courtyard, and the steady beat of the rain coming down—even harder, it seemed.

Shelby immediately tapped her combadge. "Shelby to sickbay. We've got wounded people down here. Send out a field unit immediately."

"Permission to bring down a security force to round up the attackers," Arex asked briskly. She had to give Arex credit; he thought ahead. After all, with everyone within a several block radius having been put to sleep by the powerful phasers of the *Trident*, it wasn't as if there were a lot of spare troopers around to get the job done. And the fact was that the attackers needed to be secured before they awoke. Shelby gave a brief nod, and Arex promptly summoned a squad of a half-dozen men. That was more than enough for them to secure binders upon the attacking troops, who seemed to number about twenty or so.

By that time the medical team had also materialized. Shelby was not the least bit surprised to see Doc Villers herself leading the team. She was impossible to miss; age had not slowed Villers, nor bowed her in the slightest. Mueller had highly recommended Villers from a time when they had served together on another vessel, and it was easy to see why. Villers was an extremely commanding figure, white hair cropped short, massively built. If she hadn't been human, she would have made a convincing Brikar. Within seconds Villers had an efficient triage under way, seeing which of the fallen citizens were hurt the worst, who could benefit from what sort of medical care, and which of them were beyond help.

The Ruling Council had now emerged, and was looking over the fallen Markanians with obvious regret, and at the unconscious troopers with not a little fear. "Don't worry, they can't hurt you," Shelby assured them. "My people are attending to that."

"Oh, they can hurt us," Furvus assured her.

"How?"

"By their presence."

Shelby didn't understand at first, but then, from a distance, she heard shouts and war cries and howls of fury. She and Arex exchanged puzzled glances, but Clebe was able to explain immediately. "Ebozay's people," he said with a mixture of confidence and despair. "I recognize their rhetoric anywhere."

He was perfectly correct. From behind the buildings, from beyond outcroppings, the followers of Ebozay were emerging. They were, almost to the man, tall and muscular and moving with determination and confidence. They had meager weapons with them, yet they were wielding them with such verve that one would have thought they possessed the greatest weaponry in the cosmos.

She was able to pick Ebozay out immediately. His brow was ridged, his skin a deeper blue than any on the Council— perhaps the skin lightened with age. Moreover, there was something in his eyes . . . "the madness of leadership," she had once heard Calhoun call it. "Anyone who takes it upon himself to marshal people to a cause has to be a little insane.

To paint that large a target upon yourself, to willingly take on the responsibility of people counting on you . . . what sane individual would do that?"

"What about being a starship captain?" she had asked him.

He'd smiled and said, "Not all starship captains are good leaders. Only the slightly crazy ones are."

"Considering you're slightly crazy, that's a rather self-serving definition."

"I wouldn't say that."

"You wouldn't say it's self-serving?"

"No," he'd corrected her with a glimmer in his eye. "I wouldn't say 'slightly.' " And then he'd laughed, and she'd never known, from that day to this, what to make of that laugh, which was probably the way he preferred it.

"The madness of leadership . . ." Yes, definitely, there it was in the eyes of the one she suspected was Ebozay. Not only that, but he was not looking at any of the wounded, dead, or dying members of his own race. Instead his attention was entirely upon the fallen attackers. She could see from where she was standing that he was seething with anger.

"Aerons," he snarled in a voice choked with fury, and the hated word was taken up by, and repeated by, others who were standing near him. They had their weapons unslung and were waving the barrels around, as if daring one of the fallen attackers to attempt another assault.

Ebozay spun when one of the Starfleet security guards moved into his peripheral vision, and he started to bring his weapon to bear reflexively. But Shelby's voice cut across the moment like a saber: *Put it down!*

He swung his attention over to Shelby, and it seemed to first begin to register on him that there were offworlders aside from the hated Aerons there. It might have been that the relative paleness of the skin—the most visible association between the terran members of Starfleet and the Aerons—had thrown him off for a minute. He realized his mistake then, but did not seem especially inclined to be the least bit apologetic. Nor did he lower his weapon immediately, as she'd ordered. The entire situation seemed rife with problems, and Shelby wasn't about to let any of them happen. "I said, put it down," she repeated no less firmly, looking Ebozay straight in the eyes and showing not the slightest fear.

"Who are you?" Ebozay demanded. The weapon stayed where it was.

There were several ways Shelby could have played it at that moment. She knew that Calhoun would have been perfectly capable of simply pulling out a weapon and dropping Ebozay where he stood, just as a personal test to see if he could . . . or out of a sense of pride, taking offense at the tone of Ebozay's voice. Shelby, however, chose to play it slightly cooler. "Captain Elizabeth Shelby, of the Starship *Trident*. We're here at the invitation of your Ruling Council . . . and we're also the reason that there weren't any more casualties than there were."

"You?" He glanced around.

"Ship's weaponry, from orbit."

He looked up, as if in hope of catching a glimpse of the vessel. It was all she could do not to guffaw.

"And you are—?" prompted Shelby.

"Ebozay," he said, speaking his own name with such passion that it sounded as if he had coughed it out. By this point he had lowered his weapon, but the *Trident's* security people—who had not taken their attention from him from the moment he started waving weaponry in Shelby's direction—continued to watch him warily. Then Ebozay took a step forward and pointed angrily at the members of the Ruling Council who had now emerged. "And if you serve those cowards and fools," he snarled, indicating the Council, "then you are no friends of ours, nor of the people of Markania!"

"We serve no one except Starfleet," Shelby corrected him, "and through them, the United Federation of Planets."

He made a dismissive wave, then turned to his own troops. Shelby wondered where the hell the Council's own military arm was, and why they weren't involved in any of this. "Kill the Aerons," he said briskly, and swung his own weapon toward the head of one of the fallen raiders.

"No!" Furvus immediately called out.

Ebozay's lip curled disdainfully and, without looking away from the Council Member, shouted, "Pick targets and kill them. Wipe them out as you would insects."

"I believe the gentleman said 'no,' " Shelby interrupted, and she spoke with such force and confidence that Ebozay's men paused momentarily, obviously unsure of what they should do. She walked toward Ebozay, still showing not the slightest fear of him. He stood a head and a half taller than she, but one would have thought she was the one looming over him. "And since it was *my* weaponry, *my* people, and *my* ship who delivered these assailants into your hands, I believe I have some say in this as well."

"You have no say at all."

"Really?" She was standing directly in front of him.

"Yes. Really. You are an offworlder. You have no rights, and you have no power here."

"Don't I?" Without hesitation, Shelby tapped her combadge. "Shelby to bridge."

"Bridge. Mueller here."

"Kit, I need you to do something for me."

There was a slight pause, and then Mueller said, "Waiting on your order, Captain."

"There's a gentleman standing approximately two feet in front of me. Have the transporter lock on to him, would you?"

"Transporter locked on."

Shelby was pleased to see Ebozay's expression of superiority slip ever so slightly. Without batting an eye, she continued, "Good. Give me a ten count and then beam him off the planet."

"Where to?"

"I don't care. On second thought, set for maximum dispersal. Scatter his molecules all over the quadrant. Count down to begin on my mark . . ."

"You're bluffing," said Ebozay.

"Mark," she said. "Shelby out." Then she looked blandly at Ebozay and said, "Ten . . . nine . . . eight . . ."

"You wouldn't dare!"

"Seven . . . six . . ." She seemed unfazed by his wrath.

"If anything happens to me, my men will open fire on you!"

Shelby didn't look especially worried about the prospect. "Five . . . four . . ."

"This is an outra—!"

From all around them in the air, there was the distinctive humming sound of transporter beams flaring into existence. "Three—"

"Lower your weapons!" Ebozay abruptly shouted. "Back away from the Aerons!"

Without missing a beat, Shelby tapped her combadge. "Shelby to bridge. Belay that last order."

"Aye, Captain. Cancelling transport orders. Shall we power down the transporter?"

"Keep it on-line . . . just in case," Shelby said with an unmistakable air of warning. Ebozay glowered at her, but said nothing. "Shelby out." Shelby then draped her hands behind her back and circled Ebozay as if she were inspecting him. She felt as if the balance of power had just shifted to her. "You know who I serve, Ebozay. Who do you serve?"

"We serve the people of Markania!"

"Really?" said Shelby, folding her arms and looking at him scornfully. "The way I see it, you're far more interested in the Aerons than your own people. You've wasted all this time sparring with me over the privilege of killing your attackers, who are, at the moment, helpless. In the meantime, your own people are injured and you don't seem the least interested in attending to them. That's being left to my people, as you can see."

"We are not trained in the art of healing," Ebozay informed her.

"Now's as good a time as any to learn. Dr. Villers!" Shelby called.

Villers strode through the drizzle that was still coming down. Her size and build were such that Ebozay was visibly taken aback. "Doctor, the honorable Ebozay here has brought you some extra hands."

"Good," Villers rumbled in her customary brusque, no-nonsense manner. "Let's get this done."

Seizing one last moment of bravado, Ebozay stabbed a finger at the Council Members and called to them, "See? See where your policies of nonaggression have gotten us? The Aerons attacked us because they knew we were weak!"

"The Aerons attacked because you attacked them!" Furvus snapped back. It was the most iron in his voice that Shelby had yet heard. She was a bit relieved; at last he was starting to sound like a genuine leader. "You and your revenge-crazed followers, who seek restitution for something that happened generations ago!"

"My followers represent the will of the people of Markania!" replied Ebozay. "The sooner you realize that, and cede leadership to me, the better off we shall all be!"

Furvus said nothing in response, which disappointed the hell out of Shelby. This was the moment for the Ruling Council to establish firmly just who was in charge. By allowing Ebozay to have the final word, by allowing his rant to remain unanswered, Shelby felt as if Furvus had practically turned over the keys of the kingdom to his opponents, and it was now just a matter of time. But she said none of that, because it wasn't her place, and besides, it was too late.

Ebozay then allowed himself to be guided away by Doc Villers. Shelby quickly crossed back to the Council, gathered just inside the entrance to the Council building and looking a bit shaken, but also determined. "You handled that quite deftly, Captain," said Vinecia.

"I shouldn't have had to," Shelby said. "Where the hell are your own soldiers? Your own enforcers of the law?"

Vinecia suddenly seemed very interested in looking anywhere except directly into Shelby's eyes, and Furvus stepped in. "The vast majority of them," he said, reluctantly acknowledging it, "stand with Ebozay. Something of a warrior class, you might say, with their own rules and philosophies, many of which are not exactly in tune with that which we represent. They have served the Council out of a respect for tradition . . . but over the last several years, their interest and allegiance has been far more stimulated by the modern words of Ebozay than the old words of the Council."

"We are considered . . . antique. Out of date, out of step," Vinecia said bitterly. "There are those who feel we have very little to offer modern Markanians."

"We do not have a regular standing army," said Furvus. "We can largely thank the Thallonians for that. We are, after all, the only race upon this world, nor do we have anything of sufficient value to attract the interest of offworld attackers. We hold a very, very narrow mandate among our people, Captain. Barely half of our race is content to remain out of war, out of trouble. But there are nearly as many who are— and there is no other way to put it—bored. They seek diversion from that boredom, and Ebozay and others have more or less convinced them that the diversion lies in evening the scales with the Aerons. Unfortunately, there can be no evening of scales in a true war. All that happens is that either side of the scale becomes more heavily laden—"

"Until eventually the scale breaks," said Shelby tightly. "I think your heart is in the right place, Furvus. However, I'm not so sure about the rest of your people. I think it best if we deal with one problem at a time, however. These fallen members of the Markanians . . . where do you want them?"

"We have a holding facility. I can show you where it is."

"Good. We'll get them stored away. Then, Furvus, if it's permissible by your Council . . . I'm going to start scanning your planet."

"For what?"

"For two things: Energy traces or signatures traceable to a Gateway . . . and any life-forms that are not Markanian. I don't know what an Iconian's life-form readings look like, but I'd guess that they're significantly different from your people."

"How long will that take?"

"How long?" She sighed. "Quite some time. There's no shortcut to doing it; we have to scan each populated section, one life-form at a time. But I don't see where we have a good deal of choice. Do you?"

He shook his head sadly. "Truthfully, I see no other options. I apologize for putting you to all this trouble. And Captain—"

"Furvus, no insult intended," she said tiredly, "but if you were about to thank us for coming . . . please . . . don't say it."

Furvus didn't say it.

Lieutenant Commander Gleau, science officer of the *Trident,* blinked those luminous eyes of his several times, and still couldn't quite remove the surprise from his face. "A bioscan, Captain? Of the *planet?"*

On the bridge, Shelby settled into her command chair with a sigh. "You heard me, Mr. Gleau. We're looking for anything non-Markanian."

"Very well, Captain, but I think I should inform you that such a scan will take approximately—"

She put up a hand, silencing him. "I don't care how long it will take approximately, or even precisely. I want it done."

"Aye, Captain." He tapped his combadge even as he started toward the turbolift. "Gleau to Lieutenant M'Ress."

"M'Ress here," came back the immediate reply.

"Meet me in the sensor scan department. I have a bit of a specialized job I need done, and I'm drafting you to help."

"On my way."

It might have been Shelby's imagination, but it sounded to her as if M'Ress was *extremely* enthused with the idea of working directly with Gleau on a project. She supposed that she couldn't blame her. Truth to tell, if Shelby weren't captain and weren't married . . .

You wouldn't want to go there, she warned herself. *Gleau's reputation precedes him. The last thing you'd need is to be a notch on someone's belt.* And then she smiled. *Still . . . what a belt that would be. . . .*

"Captain?" It was Mueller, looking at her oddly.

Shelby promptly shook off the reverie and said, "Nothing. Just thinking. It wasn't all that long ago that I went to a planet's surface and, within five minutes of my getting there, we were under assault by killer insects in an attack masterminded by another race. So I go down this time, and the next thing I know, a Gateway opens up and we're under assault from another race. I'm going to start getting a reputation as a jinx. I'll be *persona non grata* on every world in the quadrant. By the way, XO, good job with the transporting bluff."

"Bluff?" Mueller's face was blank.

"Yes. I'm pleased that you picked up on it so quickly."

"Picked up?"

Shelby's mouth thinned. "When I called you 'Kit.' Instead of Kat. I addressed you by a fake name, and that prompted you to realize that I was signaling you that the orders I was about to give you were fake."

"Ah."

"Ah?"

"Well, to be honest, Captain, I just assumed you got my name wrong by accident."

Shelby paled slightly. "You mean . . . you were ready to

beam someone up and disperse them all over creation, on my orders?"

She stared at Shelby as if the captain had lost her mind. "That's why they're called 'orders,' Captain, not 'requests' or 'suggestions.' "

Letting her breath out in a very unsteady sigh, Shelby ran her fingers through her hair and muttered, "I almost had someone killed, just to prove a point."

To which Mueller shrugged and said, "If you're not going to kill someone out of self-defense, that's certainly the third best reason to do it."

Shelby was about to ask what the second best was, and then wisely thought better of it.

10

EXCALIBUR

BURGOYNE STOOD IN SICKBAY, looking in bemusement at Ensigns Yates and Pheytus. Yates and Pheytus were each sitting on the edge of a diagnostic table, and neither seemed to know quite where to look. They certainly didn't want to look at each other, but neither did they want to meet Burgoyne's gaze. So they contented themselves with looking randomly around sickbay. Yates's left eye was swollen, and there was a greenish bruise on Pheytus's right cheek. Lieutenant Beth was nearby, shifting uncomfortably from one foot to the other. Nearby, Dr. Selar stood with arms folded and her patented disapproving stare. Annoyingly, Burgoyne found that s/he was unable to meet her level gaze. The reason it was annoying was because s/he felt as if s/he had no reason to feel chagrined. Yet s/he was.

Every syllable dripping with incredulity, Burgoyne finally broke the silence by demanding, "Yates . . . Pheytus . . . you got into . . . a fight?"

"That's not exactly it, Commander," Mitchell said, entering sickbay just as Burgoyne had been talking. "At least, not as it was explained to me . . ."

Sounding almost apologetic, but firm, Pheytus said, "No, that is *exactly* it." Mitchell fired him an annoyed glance, but Pheytus continued, "Yates was in Ten Forward. I walked in, endeavored to start a conversation, and Yates . . ." He cleared his throat. "Yates began laughing at me. At my name." He scowled as he looked at Yates.

"Is this true?" Burgoyne demanded of Yates.

Yates took a deep breath and let it out unsteadily. "More or less."

"In Yates's defense," Mitchell said quickly, "he was kind of drunk."

Burgoyne looked in astonishment at Mitchell. *"That's* 'in defense'? Just out of curiosity, what would you say if you were trying to prosecute him?"

"He *was* off duty, Commander. And the beverage in question had been sent to him by his family, as a gift. In fact, he offered to share it with Ensign Pheytus."

"You offered to share it with him," said Burgoyne, feeling more confused than before.

"That . . . was where the problem came from," sighed Yates. "I was . . . not drunk, but a little tipsy, and I offered him some, and then I said . . . at least I think I said . . ."

Burgoyne waited. Yates didn't continue. "I'm starting to lose patience here," Burgoyne informed him. "What did you say?"

It was Pheytus who replied. "He said, 'Oh, wait, I really shouldn't, because alcohol can damage a fetus.' And then he laughed and laughed . . . and that's when I hit him."

"So you threw the first punch," Burgoyne said.

Pheytus, normally possessing a calm demeanor bordering on the supernal, pointed with outrage at Yates. "He acted in a contemptuous fashion to my name. Do you have any idea how seriously we Bolians take our names?"

"I'm beginning to get a feeling for it," Burgoyne said drily.

"So I had no choice in the matter."

Clearly wanting to take charge of the situation, Mitchell said, "There's always a choice, Ensign."

But Pheytus said firmly, "No, sir. There isn't always. Among my people, in this instance, there was absolutely no choice at all. I did what had to be done. And with all respect, I very much doubt that Starfleet would endorse the notion of my not living up to the demands my society puts upon me."

"I'm feeling a bit put upon myself," Burgoyne muttered. S/he glanced over at Doctor Selar, who was standing there with her arms folded and clear disapproval on her face. "May I help you with something, Doctor?"

She held up an epidermal patch kit. "Not at all, Commander, at long as you do not care whether I remove their bruises or not."

Hir eyebrows knit a moment, and then Burgoyne said with an air of wry amusement, "As a matter of fact, I *do* care. Leave the bruises."

"What?"

"I said leave them," Burgoyne told her with growing certainty. "I want them to keep the bruises, so that they have to explain them over and over again. Until they're so sick of repeating it that it drives into them both just how absurd this entire situation is, and how unacceptable their behavior was."

Both Yates and Pheytus began to protest simultaneously, but Burgoyne turned hir back to them, making it clear that s/he wasn't paying attention to them. "Is there any reason they can't leave, aside from the skin contusions?"

"None. I would frankly prefer they departed," Selar remarked. "I am concerned their stupidity might turn airborne, like any other virus, and contaminate my staff."

"You heard the doctor. You're both confined to your respective quarters for the balance of your off-duty time. Pull something like this again, you're going to be off-duty far longer than you bargained for. Now get. Chief, a moment of your time," Burgoyne said to Mitchell. Mitchell tilted his bearded, bushy head in acknowledgment as Pheytus and Yates departed. Burgoyne drew hirself up, standing a good half a head over Mitchell. "Chief, this is unacceptable."

"I know, I know," Mitchell said, sounding rather miserable. "It's just . . . that name . . ."

"I'm aware that having an ensign named 'fetus' has some amusement value, but this has gone way too far," Burgoyne told him, shaking hir head as s/he spoke. "This is Starfleet, for gods' sakes. We can't have bickering over something as petty and inconsequential as a crewman's moniker, no matter how unusual and unintentionally amusing that name might be. Work with Lieutenant Beth and get a handle on this situation. If you see a similar situation developing, I want to make sure you—"

"Abort it?" Mitchell expression was one of wide-eyed innocence.

Burgoyne winced. "Very droll," s/he said. Wanting to sound as reasonable as possible, s/he tried a different tack. "Look . . . Craig . . . I don't want to make too big a production about this. I mean, hell, for the sake of peaceful coexistence, I could bring in an entirely new engineering team if I felt like it. But I don't want to do that. Do you know why?"

It was obviously an opening Mitchell couldn't resist. As deadpan as before, he said, "Because you don't want to throw the baby out with the bathwater?"

Burgoyne growled low in hir throat and was pleased to see Mitchell take two steps back at the noise. "Chief . . . if this happens again, I'm going to shoot you out a photon torpedo tube in your underwear. Leave. Now."

"Aye, sir," Mitchell said quickly, and bolted.

Burgoyne rubbed hir eyes and could practically feel

Selar's gaze drilling through hir neck. "Don't say it. Please don't say it."

"You never should have accepted the post of first officer."

"So naturally she said it. What part of 'don't' was unclear?" Burgoyne sighed.

"You were a better fit as chief engineer, Burgoyne," Selar told hir firmly. "Your organizational skills were more suited to it. Crewmen are not quite certain how to react to you in your new position of authority, and in the meantime, your engineering crew is becoming unfocused and obsessed with nonsense."

"Number one, they're neither unfocused nor obsessed," Burgoyne replied, turning to face Selar and trying to look even more annoyed than s/he felt. "Number two, crewmen are reacting just fine, and number three . . ." S/he frowned. "What was the third thing?"

"Organizational skills."

"Right. The fact is that I'm perfectly organized as first officer. The crew respects me—"

"Perhaps," Selar said neutrally. "That is open to debate. What is not open to debate is that the engineering department is the poorer without you."

S/he leaned against the edge of the bed. "It was never my goal to fashion an engineering department incapable of acting without me there every minute. If I can't appoint good people to step in and take over for me without missing a beat, then I've failed miserably in my job. And by the way, why aren't you on my side? You're the mother of my son. You're my mate."

"Is that what I am?" asked Selar. Despite the seriousness of the discussion, there seemed to be the slightest twinkle in her eye, a faint glimmer of genuine affection that she was always careful to let no one but Burgoyne see. It was the closest that Burgoyne ever got to an admission of love from her. "And where is it written that 'mates' must always be aligned on all issues?"

"I'm just saying you could be a little more supportive, Selar. That's all."

"I am supportive, Burgoyne, of that which I find supportable. There may well be no one else on this vessel as familiar with you as I am, and while I find Captain Calhoun's choice of first officer to be in keeping with his famed sense of whimsy, I simply am unconvinced that you are the best person for the job."

"Because, of course, not everyone is as fabulous as you at their job."

"This is not about me," the doctor said.

"Oh, come on, Selar," Burgoyne said scornfully, although s/he kept hir voice down so as not to attract undue and potentially annoying attention from the others in the sickbay. "Even the most unassuming of Vulcans holds up his or her race as the model for efficiency on other worlds. And you are hardly an unassuming Vulcan. Admit it: You think I can't do as good a job as first officer as you do in your position of CMO."

"It would be illogical of me to make surmises—"

"Ohhh, take a whack at illogic. Just for me. Just for laughs."

"Logic is never 'for laughs,' " she informed him. "And if you are insisting on total candor: Yes, I find it difficult to believe that you could build an operation that would be on a par with what I have here. My sickbay is efficient, tightly run . . . a model of organizational mastery. I know precisely where everything is, where it has been, and where it will go. Every single person in this sickbay knows precisely what their place is, precisely what their responsibilities are, and precisely how to carry them off to the best of their potential. And now, if you will excuse me, it is time—right down to the second—for me to begin my rounds. You see, Burgoyne? Organization is not at all difficult. One simply has to be aware of everything around one. That describes me perfectly. In the broad sense: I see everything."

She turned, started to walk away, and tripped and crashed

to the ground, going down in a tumble of arms and legs with a small boy, who let out a yowl of protest.

Immediately several med techs were heading in the direction of the mishap, but Burgoyne was already hauling the confused Selar to her feet. Still lying on the ground, looking dazed and confused, was the boy she'd tripped over. "Mook!" Burgoyne snapped out. "What are you doing here?"

"Moke," the boy said, as one of the med techs stepped in and easily righted him. "My name is Moke." His eyes were deep-set, his skin still retaining the golden brown that had been baked into him from his native sun, and his somewhat disheveled hair hung in ragged braids, which he had not had trimmed.

"Where did you come from?" Selar demanded. She shook off Burgoyne's help and picked up the medical utensils she had dropped.

"The planet Yakaba," Moke promptly replied. "My mother died, and Mac adopted me as his son after—"

"I know all that," interrupted Selar. She did not come close to losing her sanguine Vulcan exterior, but, nevertheless, her irritation with herself and him was quite evident.

"Then why did you ask?"

Selar didn't quite seem to know what to say, so Burgoyne stepped in and inquired, "Does Captain Calhoun know you're down here?"

"No."

"Then why are you down here?"

"I—" Moke glanced around nervously.

Selar, however, wasn't exactly in the mood to allow him to explain himself. "Your reasons for being here are irrelevant," she said flatly. "This is sickbay. If you are not sick, you should not be here. This is not a playground. The fact that this is not a playground should be easily discernible by the absence of climbing equipment, a merry-go-round, or a seesaw."

"What are those?"

"Ask Captain Calhoun to explain it to you. Ask him in person when you see him. Not here." She leaned down, almost bending her tall frame in half so that she could be face to face with him. "Go. Away."

Moke's lower lip quivered ever so slightly, and then he turned and bolted from sickbay. Burgoyne watched the door slide shut behind him, and then turned and looked at Selar with obvious disapproval. "You could have handled that better."

"You are correct. I could have simply picked him up and physically removed him. It would have saved me twenty-nine point three seconds of pointless discourse."

"You know something, Selar?" sighed Burgoyne. "There are times when you make it very difficult for someone to love you."

"I am aware of these times," she said with no trace of sarcasm. "They are called 'daytime' and 'nighttime.' "

" 'Physician, heal thyself.' "

"Meaning?"

"Take a guess."

"Vulcans do not guess," she told him.

Burgoyne was about to respond to that when hir combadge beeped. "Burgoyne here," s/he said.

"Need you up here, Burgy," came Calhoun's voice. "We've arrived at Thallon 21, and I need you to take the conn while Si Cwan and I go down and have a nice chat with the planet's leaders."

"On my way, Captain. Burgoyne out."

S/he started to head out when Selar said abruptly, "Burgoyne."

The Hermat turned and waited. "Yes?"

Her face softened ever so slightly as she said, "I never said you could not do a solid job as first officer. I am quite certain you will be more than adequate to the task."

"Why, thank you, Selar," Burgoyne smiled slightly, displaying hir sharp front teeth.

"Or, at the very least . . . adequate, if not more than. Yes . . . definitely adequate. Or as close to adequate as one can come."

Burgoyne sighed. "You just don't know when it's better to stop talking, do you?"

"You," Selar informed him imperiously, "do not know how fortunate you are that I truly am on your side."

Staring in amusement at Selar, Burgoyne said as s/he walked out, "I'm almost ready to argue with the captain that I should go down to the planet instead of him. My guess is, compared to you, reasoning with the Aerons is going to be a snap."

11

AERON

WHEN STUDYING FOOTAGE of old Earth history back at the
Academy, Calhoun remembered one image that had leaped
out at him from old Earth, circa the mid-twentieth century. It
had been an angry statesman, sitting at a long table, bang-
ing—of all things—his shoe on the tabletop and howling
about some outrage or another.

With that in mind, the captain was almost tempted to remove his shoe and hand it to Burkitt, because the Aeron warmaster certainly looked as if he wanted to hammer
something on the table.

"We were attacked first, not they! This was our retaliatory
strike!" shouted Burkitt. "We are not the aggressors! The
Markanians, in addition to waging a physical war, are also
waging a war of public relations! A war of perception! And
you are foolish enough to fall for it!"

Calhoun bristled slightly, but he kept his calm high and
his voice low. He reminded himself that he was standing on

the surface of a backwater planet, facing nine scowling Aerons who collectively referred to themselves as the Counselars. They were in a large room in the imperial mansion, the nine of them seated around a sizable circular table with a wide space in the middle. The edges of the table itself were decorated with all manner of emblems that meant nothing to Calhoun, nor was he in the mood at that moment to learn what they meant.

Calhoun was standing in the open area within the desk, and Si Cwan was next to him. The Counselars had made it clear that they would not convene nor speak with him at all unless he stayed in the "Place of Address," which was where he was standing at that moment. Calhoun did not particularly want to be in the Place of Address. Just then, he'd have far preferred to be in the Place of Beating the Crap out of the Counselars, had such a location actually existed. Particularly he would have liked to obliterate the one called Burkitt.

Burkitt was doing all the talking; apparently the others seemed content to nod and smile grimly before deferring to him. They might as well not have been in the room for all the contribution they were providing.

Burkitt, meantime, was displaying enough rage for a dozen warmasters. "We received a communication from the Markanians . . . they told us what happened, why our justice-seekers did not return through the Gateway . . . the Markanians were the most insufferable, smug collection of—" He became so overwrought that he had to stop speaking for a moment to compose himself. When he did talk again, it was with an overly exaggerated calm. "You have a ship, the same as this Shelby person. You tell her to keep out of our affairs!"

Si Cwan and Calhoun exchanged a glance. "You know," Calhoun said, "that is amusing on so many levels, I am not entirely sure of where to begin."

"She is your woman, yes?" Burkitt said, eyes narrowed.

Surprised, but not wishing to let on, Calhoun said carefully, "In the sense that we're married, but—"

"Then it is very simple: Control your woman!"

"Oh, good, I'm glad you said 'simple.' Here I thought it would be difficult." His attention had been splintered because he'd been trying to concentrate on all the Counselars at once. Now Calhoun decided to discard that tactic and instead focused entirely on Burkitt. His gaze bored into Burkitt's, and he was pleased to see that the warmaster looked slightly taken aback by the intensity of Calhoun's stare. It was nice to know he still possessed that intimidation factor that had always served him so well. "Let me make this quite clear to you: Captain Shelby is a Starfleet officer, with the exact same rights and privileges as I have. She is fully entitled to act in whatever manner she sees fit, and it is certainly not my place to gainsay her. Further, from what I'm understanding from Si Cwan . . ." He looked to Si Cwan, and the towering Thallonian nodded for him to continue. "From what I'm understanding," repeated Calhoun, "Captain Shelby did nothing except defend herself."

Burkitt walked back and forth. It was clear, considering how the gazes of all the Counselars were upon him but they were not endeavoring to interrupt, that he was speaking on all their behalf. "The fact that she was on the planet surface at the time our troops attacked is . . . slightly unfortunate."

Calhoun bristled. "She could have been killed. I would hardly call that 'slightly unfortunate.' "

Unbothered by the acerbic comment, Burkitt continued, "And her actions went far beyond self-defense. If she had been concerned about her own safety, she could simply have returned to her vessel via matter transport. She did not do that. Instead she chose to render unconscious all of my people!"

The truth was, Calhoun found that somewhat surprising as well. Shelby had always been the first, and loudest, to maintain the sanctity of the Prime Directive. Technically, since this was an interracial dispute, the argument could be made that she should have stayed the hell out of it. Nevertheless, not the slightest flicker of doubt passed over his face as he said firmly, "Starfleet captains have a certain amount of latitude. Obviously Captain Shelby felt that the situation warranted her taking more extreme measures to control it, rather than running away from it."

"She had no business doing it!"

"By that logic," Si Cwan spoke up, in that manner he had that sounded both disarmingly casual and yet dangerous, "Captain Calhoun has no business stepping in now, at your behest. He would be well-advised to stay out of it, too, would he not?"

"We are seeking your help in order to balance the scales."

"Two wrongs don't make a right," Calhoun replied easily. "Furthermore, before I do any balancing, provide any help, or do anything except laugh in your face and tell you that you got precisely, no more and no less, than what you deserved, I strongly suggest that you reconsider your approach to the matter."

"How dare y—!"

Calhoun's tone turned to ice. "Reconsider it. Now."

Burkitt's face darkened. "I am the Warmaster of Aeron!"

"And I am the Warlord of Xenex," shot back Calhoun, never coming close to losing his cool. "I've spent my life conducting campaigns, while you've been sitting here on Thallon 21, spoiling for a fight and accomplishing nothing otherwise. And suddenly someone has handed you a potential weapon that you know little about and care even less about, except where it will serve to gratify your dreams of war and glory. So I would respectfully suggest that *none* of you attempt to cross swords with me, verbally or physically. Instead it will be to all our advantage to be reasonable with one another, before the situation deteriorates to the point where I would have to beat you senseless."

Burkitt, rage seizing every muscle, rose from his seat,

trembling, bare inches away from Calhoun. There were calls of warning from the suddenly nervous Counselars, but he ignored them. "Defend yourself, sir," he snarled.

Calhoun's arm moved snake-fast. Burkitt never saw it coming. The fist hit him square in the temple, snapping his head around, momentarily halting the supply of blood to his brain. Burkitt still managed to stand for a moment, wavering like a great tree in the wind, and then he crashed to the floor.

There was a stunned silence in the chamber, during which Si Cwan looked quite mildly at Calhoun and said, "You're slowing down."

"Am I?"

"I actually saw the punch. Usually it's too fast for me to spot."

"Age comes to us all," Calhoun sighed. He looked down at the insensate warmaster and then said to the rest of the Counselars, "Shall we wait until he comes to and then try again?" He got a uniform nodding of heads for his answer, and smiled thinly. "Very well, then. Got anything to drink around here?"

In his private office in the Counselar's building, Burkitt lowered the cold pack that he was holding to his head. He handed it off to a rather fierce-looking officer standing next to him, who had been introduced as Commander Gragg. Burkitt looked up at Si Cwan and Calhoun, touching the side of his head gingerly. "How bad does it look?"

"Discolored," said Calhoun. "If you'd like, I could pummel the rest of your face so that it'll all match."

Gragg immediately started to take a defensive posture, interposing himself between Calhoun and Burkitt. But Burkitt laughed softly, and then winced as the laughter caused him some mild pain. "I'll pass on that, if it's all the same to you." He put the cold pack back on his face. "I am many things, Captain, but a fool is not one of them. Nor am I unwilling to admit when I've encountered someone who could best me.

You are a true warrior. I do not see how I could reasonably resent you on that basis."

"I appreciate that," replied Calhoun.

"You certainly have a direct manner about you."

Calhoun shrugged. "That's the way I am. I see a problem and I tend to try and cut through extraneous garbage in order to solve it. I certainly hope I haven't caused you to lose face."

"Lose? No. Acquire a swollen one, perhaps, but that is my doing, not yours. Nor should you be concerned about the perceptions of the Counselars. They fear me. Because you so easily dispatched me, they do not fear me less. . . ."

"They just fear me more?"

"Correct, Captain."

"Unfortunately," Si Cwan said, with a slight sideways glance at Calhoun, "discussions and negotiations are not best conducted in an atmosphere of fear. It is imperative that we convey that message to your Counselars."

"So we are going to discuss and negotiate," said Burkitt, looking somewhat cheered. "Over how you're going to help us . . . ?"

"I didn't promise that," Calhoun reminded him. He was feeling far more relaxed than before, as he usually did when he felt solidly in control of a situation. By the same token, he certainly wasn't going to make the mistake of thinking that everything was a-okay. Taking control was one thing; maintaining it required an entirely different set of skills. Fortunately enough, Calhoun was confident that he possessed both.

Burkitt took a long, unsteady breath and then let it out much the same way. "Captain . . . we simply seek parity. We seek justice. It doesn't matter how one might wish to talk one's way around this. Nor does it matter how many times you can render me unconscious with a lucky punch—"

"Lucky punch?" Calhoun sounded extremely put-off.

"The irrefutable point," he continued, "is that the Markanians started this. They launched the vicious sneak attack.

They are the ones who annihilated most of our imperial family. We are simply seeking to retrieve that which we lost."

"You cannot bring back the dead, no matter how hard you try," Si Cwan pointed out.

"No. No, attacking the Markanians will not bring back the dead, that much is true. However," he continued more forcefully, "it will help restore to life the dispirited nature of my people. Their welfare, both physical and mental, hangs in the balance."

Calhoun was glancing around Burkitt's office. There were portraits and busts of what he presumed to be famed Aeron soldiers and officers, men and women of war throughout the ages. It etched Burkitt's personality ever more clearly for Calhoun. This was someone who dreamed of greatness, and who wasn't going to let a little thing such as common sense get in the way.

Apparently Si Cwan was thinking the same thing, because he took a step forward and said, softly but firmly, "War between your people will solve nothing, Burkitt. You did not know that when we first separated the two of you. Have you not acquired that simple bit of wisdom in the intervening years?"

"If your Federation were attacked," said Burkitt, "would you simply accept the attack and not strike back?"

"We would try and respond in a way that would not make matters worse," Calhoun said. "And we would not allow ourselves to be used."

"We are not being used."

"That is not what I hear," said Si Cwan. "My understanding is that you cooperate with a being named Smyt. One who is enabling you to operate with technology you should not have, and have no right to utilize. Is that true?"

"We have as much right as the Markanians!"

"Don't you see?" asked Calhoun, working to keep his frustration well under control. "That's what this Smyt is focusing on. He is playing the two of you, one against the other."

"I do not believe that to be so," Burkitt said so carefully that it was painfully clear to Calhoun that that was exactly what Burkitt believed, except he was too proud to admit it. "Furthermore, whatever the motivation of Smyt . . . and how did you learn of him, anyway?"

"Oh, you'd be *amazed* what eight other Counselars would be willing to volunteer while they're watching their warmaster sleep off a right cross," Calhoun said blandly.

"Ah. Very well, as I was saying—whatever Smyt's motivation, it is beside the point now. We must show the Markanians that we are not to be trifled with."

"What you 'must' do," said Calhoun, "is turn Smyt, and his Gateway device, over to us."

"On what grounds?" demanded Burkitt. "His actions, and ours, are no crime against the Federation, and the Thallonian Empire is fallen."

"Yes, thank you for reminding me of that," Si Cwan said dryly.

Burkitt continued, "You do not have the authority to make demands of us, one way or the other. You came here, and we have welcomed you to our world. We have asked for your aid. Provide it or do not, that is entirely up to you. But do not act as if you can bark orders at us and we are obliged to obey, because we both know that is not the reality of the situation. Now . . . you could, of course, overpower us and try to take what you wish. Is that what you intend to do?"

For the briefest of moments, Calhoun considered saying "Yes," just to see the expression on the warmaster's face. But before he could decide whether to give in to the impulse or not, Si Cwan stepped in. "Although we may not have authority in this matter . . . the simple truth is that you do not, either."

"I disagree. I am warmaster, one of the Counselars—"

"Whose power is superceded by the imperial family," Si

Cwan reminded him. "The family may have suffered heavy losses, but one of them remains alive."

"True, but Tsana is not functional."

"We would like to see her and determine that for ourselves."

"That is unacceptable."

"Unacceptable?" It was now Calhoun who spoke up. There was something about Burkitt's attitude that was starting to sound alarm bells in his head. Up until that point he was willing to chalk it up to nationalistic pride, but now it seemed as if Burkitt was—and there was no other way to look at it—trying to cover something up. "Warmaster, if you refuse to let us see Tsana, we are going to be forced to the conclusion that you and the Counselars have, in some manner, usurped control of this world, and that you have done so over the body of a young girl. That will fall under my discretion as captain to attend to, and although the Prime Directive may have something to say about whether or not I can get officially involved, I assure you, I will personally get involved. And you will not like how I do so."

"Are you threatening me?"

"Yes. Is it working?"

"To perfection," said Burkitt, sounding surprisingly agreeable to Calhoun. "I have nothing to hide, Captain, and certainly that nothing is not worth getting into a squabble over." He turned and said to Gragg, "Commander . . . lead our esteemed guests to Tsana, if you would."

"Yes, sir," Gragg said, drawing himself up and saluting smartly.

Calhoun and Si Cwan followed Gragg outside. Calhoun tossed a glance over his shoulder at the warmaster, who was keeping a pleasant expression plastered on his face. Calhoun didn't trust it for a moment.

They went down a courtyard, across a square, and walked to a remarkable looking structure that Calhoun correctly took to be the imperial mansion. It was a gorgeous day, the sun warm and temperate, and well-groomed foliage lush. It did not remotely fit Calhoun's preconception of what a war-like planet should be like. Then again, he was guided mainly by his personal experience. He had his native Xenex in mind, a hard and not particularly charitable world. Furthermore, although the people of Aeron may have passionately desired war, it was not yet reflected in the reality of the world around them. They had been attacked, they had struck back, but it had all been quick and brutal and very contained. And, ideally, it was something that Calhoun would be able to short-circuit before it went much further.

Furthermore, he hoped that Soleta would be able to make his job a bit easier. Before he'd even come down, he'd ordered the *Excalibur* science officer to start sensor-sweeping the planet to try and pick up the energy signature of the Gateway. He wasn't sure how long-lasting it was, and whether it would be detectable if the thing wasn't on. Then again, they might have a good chance at detecting it if it went into use. Or they might not. It was so difficult to know what was what when it came to this very alien technology. For a moment he was nostalgic for his days as a Xenexian warlord. It was much simpler then. The enemy came to them, and they kept killing them until the enemy stopped coming. For all the credit he received for liberating his homeworld, it really didn't boil down to much more than that.

Once inside the imperial mansion, Calhoun immediately saw the damage that had been sustained during the raid. Blast marks, pedestals where statues had no doubt once stood. Walking past one room, his nostrils flared slightly, and he glanced in to see exactly what he thought he would: very faint blood stains on the wall. Burkitt noticed that he'd stopped walking, and drew up alongside him. "It's always difficult to get those out," he said neutrally.

Calhoun nodded, but said nothing else.

They kept walking until they got to a room outside which two guards were standing. They made eye contact with

Gragg, who nodded and gestured with his head that they should stand aside. Both of them looked with extreme suspicion at Calhoun and even more suspicion at Si Cwan. Calhoun couldn't blame them. Indeed, he approved. If you couldn't count on guards to be suspicious, what was the point of there being guards?

Calhoun had no idea what to expect when he entered the room, but what he saw made his heart lurch. A young girl, certainly no more than ten or so Earth years old. She looked like she was asleep . . . except she wasn't. Her eyes were wide open, as if she was caught on the edge of wakefulness but couldn't quite get past that point. Her arms were crisscrossed across her chest, her legs curled up and tucked under them. She was breathing shallowly.

"We inject nutrients into her," Burkitt said softly. "So she is neither dehydrating nor starving. Otherwise, though, she is unreachable."

Calhoun walked over toward her, realizing as he did that he was holding his breath, as if afraid to wake someone sleeping lightly. He crouched in front of her and snapped his fingers a few times. Nothing. Not the slightest stirring. She might just as well have been a porcelain doll. Every so often her eyes would lower in a slow blink, but that, along with the slight breathing, were the only signs of life.

"I've never seen someone in such deep shock," said Si Cwan.

"She witnessed things that no child should have to witness. She has retreated as far from them as she possibly can, short of taking her own life. For all we know, if she had the opportunity to do so, she would." Burkitt shook his head sadly. "I only wish I knew whether she is, in fact, hiding from the events that she witnessed . . . or whether her poor mind is trapped into a cycle of reexperiencing it. If it's the latter . . . well, certainly not the most vile sinner imaginable should deserve such a fate, don't you think?"

Si Cwan was standing behind him, and he said gravely, "Can we do anything, Captain?"

"You? Me? No . . . but . . ."

"But what?" asked Burkitt.

Calhoun straightened up. "I'd like Dr. Selar from my vessel to take a look at her. Come down here or, better yet, bring her up to sickbay."

"Impossible."

The flat denial came not from Burkitt, but from someone behind him who had just entered. He was tall and cadaverous and had an arrogance about him that Calhoun immediately found off-putting. "Impossible, I say."

"Yes, I heard you the first time."

"Who do you think you are?" said the newcomer, and he actually took a step toward Calhoun. For a moment, Calhoun was sorry he hadn't brought Kebron down with him. The mere presence of the massive Brikar security guard was enough to put down any thought of threats from most people. Indeed, if Shelby had still been serving as first officer, she'd have insisted on Calhoun having a security escort just as a matter of form. Calhoun's boundless confidence in his ability to defend himself was leaving him open to strangers thinking they could do whatever the hell they wanted.

All of this quickly became moot, however, when Si Cwan interposed himself between the newcomer and Calhoun. The man was clearly taken aback; Cwan was eye to eye with him, and apparently he wasn't used to someone being as tall as he. Si Cwan had moved with impressive grace and minimal effort. One minute he'd been standing nearby, the next he was blocking the man's path, and it hadn't even seemed like he'd taken a step.

The man gasped. "A Thallonian!"

"Not 'a' Thallonian. *The* Thallonian," said Cwan, allowing himself a bit of self-satisfaction. Calhoun, smiling to himself, couldn't blame him. "I am Ambassador Si Cwan, formerly of the Royal House of Thallon, currently attached to the starship *Excalibur*. That," and he inclined his head toward Mac, "is Captain Mackenzie Calhoun, thwarter of the Black Mass, nemesis of the Redeemers, he who has returned from the dead and has been worshipped by some as a messiah. And you are—?"

"Tazelok," he said, his voice uneven as he clearly tried to rally to the occasion. "Head of the Healer's Hall."

"A doctor."

"Not 'a' doctor, *the* doctor," he corrected, endeavoring to mimic Si Cwan's voice from moments before, and not doing a half-bad job. "And Tsana is my patient, under my care, and you will not remove her."

"Why, Tazelok?" asked Calhoun. "Concerned that my people will help her where yours failed? Valuing your reputation and self-esteem above her best interests?"

Tazelok bristled in such a way that Calhoun instantly knew he was exactly right in his supposition . . . not that Tazelok would remotely admit to it. "I am her healer. I was personally selected by our Hall."

"I don't care if you were personally selected by an eighty-foot flaming hand from on high," said Calhoun. "This girl's been insensate since the attack, so I'm told. Whatever you're doing for her obviously isn't helping."

"Are you a healer, sir?" he asked stiffly.

"By profession, no. It's more like a hobby."

"Well, I take my responsibilities very seriously, sir. Very seriously, as do my brethren. If you attempt to bring your medical personnel here to poke and prod this poor child, it will be nothing less than the deepest insult to our Hall. We will not stand for it."

"You won't? What will you do?" asked Calhoun, genuinely curious.

"Captain, a moment of your time, please," Burkitt interrupted softly. Calhoun stepped toward him as Si Cwan remained face-to-face with Tazelok. Lowering his voice even more, Burkitt said, "We have a delicate balance here on Aeron. There are a variety of Halls, and we of the Counselars have to respect them all and treat them with due deference. Otherwise we would be enveloped in chaos."

"Chaos?" Calhoun couldn't quite believe what he was hearing. "Burkitt, you are currently sending your people headlong toward a war. You have absolutely no concept of what 'chaos' is until you're thrust into one of those."

"Be that as it may, I am asking you to respect our political situation."

"And you think maintaining your political situation is more important than the welfare of that young girl?"

"I have to keep the big picture in mind, Captain. Certainly a man in your position can understand that philosophy."

Calhoun considered it a moment, and then slowly nodded. "Yes. Yes, I can. Very well." He headed back toward Si Cwan and said briskly, "Ambassador . . . we've done all we can here."

"Have we?" asked Si Cwan. He sounded a bit surprised.

"Yes, we have. Warmaster Burkitt . . . I will be in touch with Captain Shelby on the *Trident*. I will explain to her the nature of her . . . error . . . and request that she cease and desist involving herself in your interplanetary squabbles."

"You have no idea how much we appreciate that, Captain," Burkitt said. He looked like he was deflating slightly, so great was his relief.

"Shelby's a . . . young captain. Young captains are prone to try and bend or break the rules. Ignore procedure in favor of their own instincts. They can be very, very difficult to control. Very difficult. We at Starfleet depend upon individuals such as yourself to keep us apprised of any wrongdoings on the part of our officers, so we can take proper actions."

"I have no desire to cost her her command," Burkitt said, striking a conciliatory note. "I just want her to keep her distance."

"I'll attend to it. Tell me, Warmaster," and he rested a friendly hand on Burkitt's shoulder, "do you feel as if I've treated you as a valued customer?"

"Yes. Yes, I do," said Burkitt, pleased. He glanced at Gragg in a manner that seemed to say, *See? You simply stand firm with these people, and they'll respect you for it.*

"Well, good. That's our aim at Starfleet." He tapped the combadge, the pleasant expression still on his face. "Calhoun to *Excalibur.*"

"*Excalibur,* Burgoyne here."

"Burgoyne . . ." It was at that moment that Calhoun paused less than half a second. In that half second, something in Calhoun's demeanor—in his voice, something—obviously tipped off Burkitt, for his eyes narrowed in suspicion and he started to take a warning step toward Calhoun. And then Calhoun fired off the next words, "Emergency transport, three to beam out. Energize."

Even as he spoke, he grabbed up Tsana in his arms as if she weighed nothing. He backpedaled, cradling Tsana, Cwan leaping to his side. "*Guards!*" bellowed Burkitt even as he went for his gun.

Too slow. Calhoun lashed out with his booted foot, snagging the edge of Tsana's bed with his toe and kicking the bed directly at Tazelok. Tazelok lunged to get out of the way; unfortunately, the lunge was too powerful and Tazelok stumbled into Burkitt, both of them falling. Burkitt started to scramble to his feet, the sounds of running feet were pounding down the hallway, and everything was happening so quickly. That was when the distinctive whine of transporter beams enveloped Calhoun, Si Cwan, and the unconscious Tsana.

"*Calhoun!*" bellowed Burkitt in frustration.

"Just trying not to lose sight of the big picture!" Calhoun called back to him, and the three of them sparkled out of existence in a burst of transporter particles.

"He . . . he kidnapped her!" stammered Tazelok. And then his confusion turned to ire, and he pointed a quavering finger at Burkitt and snarled, "Do something!"

Burkitt stared at him with open incredulity for a moment. Then he faced the empty air that had been occupied by three bodies moments before and, mustering all his authority, pointed angrily at the vacant space and said, *"Come back here!"*

The air did not seem intimidated by his stridency. He looked back at Tazelok and inquired, "Any other suggestions?"

Tazelok sighed.

12

TRIDENT

M'RESS SIGHED.

Caitia was just as she remembered it. The ground thick and sandy, the air warm, the perpetual gentle breeze that tended to shift direction, but never blew with any real ferocity. And the people—everywhere, her fellow Caitians. It reminded her of the clumsiness of the vast majority of the humans, or pretty much every other species, she met. She had gotten used to it, and no longer dwelled on the fact that when humans walked, they did so with big, wide strides as if to announce to the entire cosmos, "Look at me, here I am, notice me!" This was as opposed to M'Ress and her fellow Caitians, who walked with elegant delicacy, one foot in front of the other, sliding through the world as if they were moving across glass. When Caitians walked, you never heard their footfall. If it weren't for their acute ability to scent things, and consequently know that someone was behind them, they would very likely be forever startling one another.

The buildings were low to the ground, which was sensible, since her home village was prone to the occasional earthquake. M'Ress blended in perfectly, and all her old friends were walking past her and greeting her by name. At least, they sort of looked like her old friends. They were as close to her recollections as she could make them, and for all she knew the voices weren't quite right or the looks were a bit off. But they were the best she could do.

But the scents . . . dammit, the scents were all wrong. No, not just wrong: missing. Every time someone else would approach her, and look like an old friend and greet her by name, her nostrils would flare, and the utter absence of reality as defined by her olfactory resources would bring her up short.

And then, just like that, a scent leaped out at her, so distinctive and so abrupt that it was almost like a physical thing. Startled, she looked around, knowing what she was going to see before she saw him.

"Quick reflexes," said Lieutenant Commander Gleau. The Elf had gotten startlingly close to her without alerting her to his presence. She found that just a bit disconcerting.

"What are you doing here?" she demanded, and then instantly regretted her tone. Her tail twitching, she said, "I mean, not that you shouldn't be here . . . you're directly over me in the chain of command, you can be anywhere you want, so you don't . . . I mean . . ."

"Calm down, M'Ress, good heavens," said Gleau, his gleaming eyes seeming to dance in amusement. "Don't be so jumpy." He was looking around. Passing Caitians gave him interested looks, but kept walking. "I was just trying to see how good a job we'd done. I was one of the programmers who helped put this scenario together for you, off your specs."

"You . . . you were?"

"Yes, of course," he said mildly. "I mean, you're not exactly accustomed to our holodeck technology, are you? It would have been a bit much to expect you to program something so specific and custom-made with a tech that's so new to you. And since you'd been assigned to my department, I thought this would be a way of making you feel a bit more at home."

M'Ress didn't know what to say. "That's . . . that's so sweet," she finally managed to get out. She felt a low purr in her chest and promptly stopped it; she didn't want to give the wrong impression.

He spread his arms wide, taking in the entirety of the Caitian city. "So how did I do?"

It's wrong, it's all wrong. It's like watching phantoms, ghosts of the dead walking through the land of the living. It's a cruel reminder of all that I've lost, and it saddens me more than I can find words to express.

"It's wonderful," she said. "It's like stepping back through time."

"Good," he smiled. "I'm glad."

"But . . . I shouldn't be here," she said quickly. "I should be back on scanning duty."

"M'Ress, you worked through three straight shifts," he reminded her. "We haven't yet turned up any signs of something 'non-Markanian,' as the captain put it. We can't be expected to work round the clock."

"But—"

"No 'buts,' " he said firmly, raising a scolding finger. "If you work yourself into a stupor, you could find a non-Markanian bioreading the size of a meteor and still not recognize it for what it is. Sooner or later, you run into the law of diminishing returns. You're supposed to go back on duty in . . ."

"Four hours," she said.

"Four hours. At the very least, you may want to go back to your quarters and get some bed rest."

"Would you like to join me?" blurted out M'Ress, even as, inwardly, she was horrified to hear herself say it. *Gods, what will he think of you? He's your superior officer, and you haven't worked with him all that long, and . . . gods!*

Gleau laughed softly at that, and for a moment M'Ress felt totally mortified, because not only had she just made a fool of herself, but clearly the thought of interest from her was so ludicrous that he was laughing at it. Then he said, "It's an interesting notion, but I suspect that if I joined you, we wouldn't get much rest in the bed."

She felt slightly dizzy, and there was a light buzzing in the back of her head, all of which translated into a soft laugh that actually sounded kittenish. Suddenly feeling emboldened, she said, "Well, Mr. Spock used to say that there are always possibilities. . . ."

He shook his head, looking impressed. "I keep forgetting the caliber of people you've worked with. Probably because you certainly don't show your age." He paused, and then added, "That was a little joke."

M'Ress obediently laughed.

"In any event," Gleau said, "some rest for you. Then when you go back on shift, we hit the scanners again, and this time I bet we find something."

"I bet you're right," M'Ress said, suddenly more cheered than she had been in ages. Amazing how just one person can make you feel as if you actually belonged. Then she looked around. "How do we get out of here ag—oh! Right. Uhm . . . *close program!*"

Caitia remained serenely right where it was.

Gleau chuckled even as he said, "End program." Caitia promptly blinked out.

"Thank you," she said.

He took her hand and touched her knuckles to his forehead. "It was my pleasure. And, M'Ress . . . I fully understand the adjustments you're trying to make. Would you like to know something that is antithetical to the Elf philosophy?" Without waiting for her to say "yes," he continued,

"Loneliness. Isolation. To us, it is simply wrong. There are far too many intelligent beings out there ever to excuse the feeling that one is alone. We Elves believe in crowds. The more, the better. So, as long as I am aboard this vessel, never be concerned that you are alone."

"Thank you," she said again, the words feeling so inadequate.

He smiled, turned, and walked out of the holodeck, now filled only with the typical glowing lines crisscrossing the floors, walls, and ceilings. And M'Ress couldn't help but notice at that moment that he walked like a Caitian, one foot delicately in front of the other.

This century is starting to look marginally better, she thought.

Shelby sat up in bed, bleary-eyed, as the chime buzzed insistently at her door. *I used to be able to sleep an entire night,* she thought bleakly. *Why did I want this job again?* She drew the bedclothes around her as she called out, "Yes?"

The doors hissed open and she blinked against the relative glare of the corridor. Standing framed in the doorway was Mueller, in full uniform, arms folded. "My God, Kat, don't you ever sleep?" asked Shelby.

"No," Mueller said so matter-of-factly that Shelby was hard-pressed to determine whether Mueller was kidding or not. "There's trouble down on Thallon 18."

Shelby was immediately alert. "What sort of trouble?"

"We're detecting energy bursts, flashes in the main city . . ."

"Aeron?"

"No," Mueller said. "Discharge readings are wrong. We're talking local weaponry. There's some sort of major fighting going on, and as near as we can tell, it's an internal dispute, being backed up by some heavy-duty firepower."

"Give me five minutes," said Shelby, tossing the bed-clothes off.

"As you wish. But you'll only require three," Mueller told her, and she walked away as the doors slid closed behind her.

"Insufferable know-it-all," muttered Shelby.

Three minutes later Shelby strode out onto the bridge. The night shift was still on, but Arex was working double-duty at tactical. Gleau, whose physiology allowed him to work eighteen-hour shifts (and sometimes more if he felt like it; he seemed impervious to exhaustion) was at the science station, operating the scanners and frowning. Shelby looked at him and couldn't help but think that a face that stunningly gorgeous should never have so much as the slightest crease, the mildest grimace in it, lest it mar its loveliness with unsightly lines for all times. Then she wondered why the hell her mind was going in that direction and chalked it up to being awoken early. Mueller, seated in the command chair, yielded it to Shelby as soon as the captain arrived. "Status?" she said.

"The energy discharges seem to have tapered off," Gleau informed her.

Mueller said, "We have been endeavoring to raise the Ruling Council, with no success. . . ."

Suddenly Arex said, "I'm receiving a hail from the Ruling Council of Markania."

Mueller's lips thinned slightly. "Go ahead, make a liar out of me," she murmured.

"What time is it down there?"

"Middle of the night," Arex told her.

"Hmmm," said Shelby thoughtfully, getting an uneasy feeling in the pit of her stomach. "Something tells me whatever's going on, it's a bit outside of standard business hours. All right, Lieutenant: Put them on screen."

The viewscreen wavered for a moment, and Shelby was not overly surprised when someone other than Furvus, Vinecia, or Clebe appeared on it. It was a slightly younger member of the Markanian race. He still had the "madness of leadership" in his eyes, just as he had earlier.

"Greetings, *Trident*," he said.

"Greetings, Ebozay," she replied with a distinct lack of enthusiasm. "My understanding is that this message purported to be from the Ruling Council."

"It is. The *new* Ruling Council."

"I see. And would it be too much to hope that I might speak to one or more of the representatives with whom I've already established diplomatic ties?"

She fully expected the response to be a resounding "no," but much to her surprise, Ebozay shrugged as if the request was the most natural, and easily accommodated, in the world. "Not too much at all," he said easily. He looked off to the side. "Furvus . . . the captain desires to speak with you."

The pessimist in Shelby thought that they'd wind up bringing in Furvus's corpse as some sort of twisted game, but no, there he was. He seemed unharmed, although that in and of itself didn't necessarily mean anything. "Are you all right, Furvus?" she asked.

"As well as can be expected." He actually sounded slightly amused. "We've had . . . a bit of an incident down here."

"Incident?" she echoed tonelessly.

"Ebozay and his . . . rather sizable number of followers . . . have made it clear that they are dissatisfied with our leadership. The discussion turned a bit . . . violent. But I am pleased to say that all is well at the moment."

Shelby felt the hair prickling on the back of her neck. This was so calm, so matter-of-fact, it was like speaking to an automoton. "Define 'well,' if you would."

"Well, Captain, it has always been my philosophy that one should never overstay one's welcome. And it has been made quite clear, to myself and my associates, that our presence on the Ruling Council is no longer desirable. My fellow Markanians wish to go in a different direction—"

"Straight to hell, no doubt," Mueller said very softly. Shelby ignored it, but privately agreed with the assessment.

"—and they felt that we were not the ones to guide them that way. So, after a brief consultation with my associates, we elected to step down voluntarily, rather than force a general . . . election."

"Election? Or war?" asked Shelby, with no trace of amusement.

Ebozay, who had been standing to the side of the image on the screen, drifted closer to Furvus and smiled as if he found the entire matter to be hugely entertaining. "What is an election, Captain, but a war fought with words instead of armament?"

"As I said, Captain, all is well," continued Furvus with a glance toward Ebozay that seemed a rather nervous one. "Truthfully, I prefer it. My position was becoming somewhat stressful . . . my mate was complaining that I never see her . . . you know how it is . . ."

"I have some small familiarity with that," she said quietly.

"Frankly, I can use the rest that this, uhm . . . early retirement will provide me. And really . . . it seems the only reasonable choice, Captain. Consider, if you will: I have been a staunch advocate of the ways of peace. Would I not be putting the lie to all my philosophies, my very way of life, if I were to make a precipitous decision that would lead to fighting? Well? Would I not?"

"Yes, I suppose you would," Shelby said. She knew what she had to say next, and she was determined to be as judicious as possible in saying it. "Of course, you do realize that—if you had a personal problem . . ."

But he raised a hand, stopping her before she could really

get started. "I know what you're suggesting, Captain. You are trying to tell me—in as cryptic a manner as you can—that if I am in peril of my life, you will provide me sanctuary on your vessel. That is very generous of you, but I assure you, such is not the case."

"He speaks truly, Captain," said Ebozay, and although the general air of superiority was still there, there was also an air of—annoying—sincerity. "The former Ruling Council members provide no threat to me or my peers. There was some . . . initial resistance . . . from those who were unwilling to accede to our view of things, but that spirited disagreement is now over."

" 'Spirited disagreement'?" Shelby couldn't quite believe the double-talk that she was hearing. "Is that how you characterize weapons discharge?"

"You have very skilled detection equipment," Ebozay said, unperturbed. "However, Captain, I do believe that how we choose to settle disputes internally is really none of your concern. Am I correct?" Without waiting for her to respond, he continued, "In fact . . . it's my belief, as new head of the Ruling Council of Markania, that your presence, as requested by the previous Ruling Council, is no longer required. So, you may be on your way to wherever it is you go when you're not harassing worlds that don't want you."

"I don't do well with being dismissed out of hand, Ebozay," Shelby said icily.

"Really? Then perhaps I'd best contact your Federation and tell them that you appear to be in violation of . . . what is that rule . . . ?" he inquired of Furvus.

"The Prime Directive," Furvus told him in a low voice.

"Yes, that's right, the Prime Directive. Noninterference. As long as you're in orbit around our world, Captain, it seems to me that you're on the verge of interfering. After all, you might lose your temper and do something rash, such as beam me out into space as an array of free-floating molecules. Can't have that."

As options go, it's looking better and better, she thought, but wisely restrained herself. Instead she said, "Very well, Ebozay. If you're so inclined, contact Starfleet. And they will tell you exactly what I'm going to tell you: The Gateway that you accessed poses a potential security threat not only to this sector of space, but to the Federation as a whole. And until such time as we know exactly where that Gateway is, who's in control of it, and what it's going to be used for, I have the authority to stay right here and keep looking. And furthermore, Ebozay, if you get in my way while I'm acting in that capacity, you will wind up with my bootprints in your face."

He didn't look especially intimidated. "Gateway?" he said innocently. "I've no idea what you're talking about, Captain. But please, feel free to look around as much as you wish . . . from up there. By the way . . . do you have the capacity to shift your viewer? To look at a particular area?"

"Yes," Shelby said slowly, not quite certain where the conversation was going.

"Then would you be so kind . . . as to look at the exterior of this building? We'll wait."

Shelby felt her blood grow cold. "Arex," she said, with a sick feeling that she already knew what she was going to see. "Do as he says."

The screen wavered, and the image of Ebozay was replaced by the outside of the Council building. Gleau gasped, and there was a sharp intake of breath from Mueller, and a whispered, "Oh, my God" from someone else on the bridge, although she didn't notice who. As for Shelby, she hadn't known the precise details of what she had thought she would witness, but she had certainly intuited the gist of it.

The heads of the Aerons who had been captured earlier, and spared at Shelby's behest, adorned the outside of the building. Their eyes stared sightlessly at nothing, and yet Shelby couldn't help but feel—as unreasonable as it was—that every single one of them was staring at her.

"Put me back on with Ebozay," she said, her voice carefully neutral so as not to betray the emotions within her. Moments later the screen shifted and Ebozay was smiling at her.

"Well?" he asked.

And to Ebozay's surprise—and to her own, to some degree—she laughed softly. "Did you think to shock me, Ebozay? Did you think I would cry out in horror at your ruthlessness and go running for fear of your wrath? Sorry. When you've looked down the gun barrels of as many Borg weapons as I have, the dead eyes of disembodied heads just doesn't inspire the amount of terror you'd think it would. It does tell me something, though," she continued, leaning forward in her chair, her hands resting on her knees, a hardening edge to her voice. "It tells me that you're more concerned about satisfying your own ego than leading your people wisely."

"Oh, I will lead them, Captain," he said with an air of confidence that Shelby would have loved to drive right down his throat. "I will lead them to Sinqay. I will lead them back to our promised world. But I will not bring them there so that they can live in fear of the Aeron attacking them. Sinqay will be a battleground no longer; I owe them that much. The Aeron will know, once and for all, that the Markanians are not to be trifled with. They will know that, even if we have to wipe out every single one. It has been a pleasure speaking with you, Captain." With that, the screen blinked out.

There was dead silence for a moment. And then, very coldly, Shelby said, "XO—inform Starfleet of the situation on Thallon 18. Apprise them of the change in government, and that we are continuing with our search for the Gateway we believe to be here. Once we have found the Gateway, we will proceed along the best possible course circumstances will permit."

"That being—?"

"Ideally?" There was no hint of humor in her face. "We take the Gateway and ram it up Ebozay's ass."

"I see. Would you prefer that I—"

"Edit that out, yes. But keep the image locked near and dear to your heart, XO," she said grimly. "I certainly know that I intend to."

13

MARKANIA

EBOZAY LAUGHED, his voice echoing off the walls of the now empty Council Room. He spread his arms wide, as if he could drink in the power that was now his. Power that he was going to use to benefit all his people, no matter what that foolish Starfleet captain thought.

"She doesn't understand," he said. "She doesn't—"

Then he heard a soft footfall, and he turned . . . and gaped at the newcomer. "Smyt!" he gasped.

Smyt, yellow-skinned, chinless, leggy, and curvaceous, smiled from the doorway. "Everyone has to be somewhere," she purred, her eyes sparkling with amusement.

The amusement, however, quickly faded, because Ebozay was across the room cat-quick, one hand at her throat, the other shoving her shoulder, driving her back until she slammed up against the wall with teeth-jarring impact.

"Have you lost your mi—?" she started to say.

"Traitoress!"

"Is that even a word—?"

He pulled her several inches from the wall and smashed her against it once more. *"You deceived us! Used us! You gave aid to our enemy!"*

Her air of detached amusement, which she'd managed to maintain for a brief time even as he was slamming her around, had quickly disintegrated. "What are you *talking* about?! How did—?"

"Did you think we were *stupid?* Did you think we wouldn't—?"

There was a sudden howl of energy being unleashed, a quick blast that lifted Ebozay off his feet and sent him hurtling halfway across the room. It was as if he had been yanked back by a large, invisible string attached to the back of his clothes. He hit the floor, and not gently. He was in superb condition, but even so he felt jolted and momentarily confused by the impact. But then he shook it off and staggered to his feet. Through eyes that were both bleary and yet coldly calculating, he peered angrily at Smyt, wiping away a trickle of blood from a gash his lower lip had taken upon landing. "How did you do that?" he demanded sullenly.

Her arms were folded, her hands tucked unseen into large, draping sleeves. Her billowing shirt hung loosely about her; it was voluminous enough that she might well have kept an entire armada up those sleeves, let alone some sort of handgun that could knock him around like a pebble. The copious blouse was a stark contrast to the tightness of the leggings that adorned her from the waist down. "You don't seriously think I'm going to tell you all my little secrets, are you?"

"You betrayed us . . . how could—"

Impatience flashed across her face. "Why do you keep saying that? I've betrayed no one. No one."

"The Gateway opened here, with Aerons pouring through like sewage through a tunnel."

"Now there's a pleasant image," muttered Smyt. She looked pityingly at Ebozay for a moment, then walked over to him, crouched, and took his head in her hands, one hand on either cheek. "Listen carefully: I did not aid the Aerons in any way. I did not bring the Gateway to them. Why would I do such a thing?"

"Riches."

She snorted derisively. "Riches? Is that all you think I care about?" She released him and stood, looking down at him imperiously. "Ebozay, I possess a Gateway. I can go any place I wish. I desire to be compensated for my time and trouble, yes, but if all I wanted was riches, I could rig the Gateway to put me into the heart of the greatest treasure vaults in the galaxy."

"Then why haven't you?"

"For all you know, I have," she replied easily. "All the more reason, then, to take my word that I have no financial interest in playing one side against the other." Anticipating the question he was about to ask, she said briskly, "I am interested in justice, Ebozay. I'm interested in what's right. I travel around the galaxy, meeting different races, discerning the injustices that may have been done to them, and righting them. That is what I do. That is who I am. And you, Ebozay . . . you are selling yourself short."

"In what way?" he demanded, one eyebrow cocked curiously.

"You are underestimating the passion, the fire within you when you speak of how your people were ill-used. Have you forgotten? We met . . . you were intimidated by me at first . . ."

"I was not intimidated in the least."

". . . but when you realized I intended you no harm, you spoke of the things you wanted for your people. You spoke angrily of the wrongs done to you by the Aerons. In short, Ebozay . . . you convinced me. I knew that I had found an excellent leader, a worthy cause, for the gift of the Gateway. And now . . . ," she looked stricken, "now you would accuse me of duplicity? I . . . I don't know what to say. . . ."

"Why don't you say where they got a Gateway?"

"I don't know," she said impatiently.

He had risen from the floor and was now approaching her, although far less belligerently than before. "So we're just supposed to believe it was coincidence?"

"Perhaps. I don't know."

"Smyt, I have my own followers to answer to. And they are not happy. They are also wondering, very loudly and very aggressively, whether you betrayed us. Fortunately, I was able to channel that aggression into constructive purposes . . . namely 'convincing' the Ruling Council to step aside. But if this duplication of technology is not explained in some sort of satisfactory manner, their anger could become redirected at me."

"So what you are saying," she said thoughtfully, "is that, for better or worse, our fortunes are tied together."

"That is what I'm saying, yes. The fortunate thing, at least, is that we still have our Gateway, safely hidden away and under guard. So at least my people know that you did not take it to the Aerons. That has proven the only mitigating factor to those who would believe that you have been duplicitous." He shook his head. "I do not understand how the vessel above has not detected it."

"I have it shielded . . . just as I myself am shielded against whatever life-form scans they may be using to try and detect my presence. If the Gateway is activated, they will detect that; there's no way of preventing it. The energy signature is too strong, too unique."

"But you said," and he stabbed a finger at her, "you said that the Gateway was one of a kind."

"I said the portable Gateway that I possess is one of a kind, yes. To the best of my knowledge, that remains true.

On the other hand, it is possible that the Aerons found a permanent Gateway constructed somewhere on their world. I'm not omniscient, Ebozay. I do not have a map nor record of every Gateway in existence."

"And they happened to discover this Gateway and make use of it just after we did the same thing with yours?" he said skeptically.

Leaning against the large conference table, she scratched her brow thoughtfully, almost as if his presence in the room were an afterthought. "If coincidences never occurred, Ebozay, we wouldn't have the word 'coincidence,' now, would we? Still, it does trouble me. But I have no means of investigating it at the moment; the only way I could is if I activated the Gateway, and if I did that, the starship in orbit around this world will zero in on it."

"Why should you fear the starship?"

"I don't *fear* it—neither its crew nor commander," she said dismissively. "But they can prove aggravating, and I endeavor to minimize the aggravation in my life. I shall have to think on this. However, Ebozay, if it will smooth your personal situation, summon your lieutenants, your followers . . . whomever you wish. I shall speak with them personally, explain to them how I am firmly on the side of the Markanians. How I have not, and would not, betray you. How I will not cease working on behalf of the Markanians until you have managed to eliminate the Aeron threat entirely, and the Markanians are able to return, once and for all, to their beloved Sinqay. Would that help?"

"It would."

"And you . . ." She gazed at him with a look of wicked amusement. "What could I do . . . to help you . . . ?"

She wrapped an arm around the back of his neck and brought him to her. Her lips, as always, tasted papery, and her skin was so cold it was like making love to a corpse.

But he simply reminded himself that she represented a great ally for his people, and as he pushed her back onto the table, sliding his hands down her sleeves, he mentally counted to a thousand. When he was done with that and she was still not done with him, he proceeded to compose his grocery list.

14

EXCALIBUR

"NO, CAPTAIN. Absolutely not."

There was no anger, no sense of indignation or defiance in Doctor Selar's tone as she faced a clearly annoyed Captain Mackenzie Calhoun. But Calhoun was being careful not to let that annoyance overwhelm him, or prompt him to act in a precipitous or bullying fashion. He knew that he was treading on dangerous and delicate ground, and being overly forceful wasn't going to help in the least.

They were in Selar's private office just off sickbay. Through the clear but soundproof partition, he could see her technicians going about their business. Here and there throughout sickbay were crewmen who were having the standard range of ailments treated, from a broken leg to a raging head cold (although word was down from the Starfleet general that there would be a cure for the common cold by the end of the century. Then again, they'd said that last century).

And there, lying off in a corner, monitored by instruments

but otherwise not doing anything other than breathing, was Tsana.

It was impossible to say whether she knew she'd been taken off her world. It was impossible to say anything about her, really, because she was lying in the exact same position, exact same state of mind, as when she had been on her homeworld, before Calhoun had transported her off it. Technicians were, even at that moment, taking readings off her, studying her, speaking about her in soft, understated voices (since it wouldn't do to have any negative prognosis spoken within earshot). In fact, they were doing everything except causing any sort of change in her condition.

"You realize I could order you to, Doctor," said Calhoun.

But before Selar could reply, Commander Burgoyne—standing to the captain's immediate right—said, gently but firmly, "No, Captain. You cannot."

Calhoun turned to face his first officer. "I cannot?"

"No, Captain." S/he folded hir arms in the classic stance of one who was taking up a defensive position. "Starfleet has taken pains in recent months to make that extremely clear. There were apparently one or two disputes about it on other vessels."

"You're saying that I cannot order Dr. Selar to attempt a Vulcan mind-meld."

"That is correct."

"Because it's against Starfleet regulations."

"That is also correct."

He considered the situation. "Is that the only reason?"

"No, sir," said Burgoyne politely. "I would also be obliged to tell you that you are being an insensitive cretin, and that not only would I not permit Selar to be bullied in such a manner, but anyone who did attempt it would answer to me."

"I see." Despite the gravity of the situation, Calhoun had to fight back a slight smile. "And you'd say this, even though it may be the only method that might succeed in bringing Tsana out of her coma. . . ."

"She is not in a coma, 'Dr.' Calhoun," Selar interrupted him coolly. "She is in shock. Her mind has withdrawn into itself. I am not especially familiar with this race. For all I know, that is not an unusual reaction for this species to undergo when faced with situations of great trauma."

"Not unusual?" He pointed at the insensate girl lying on the other side of the room. "That child is in pain, Doctor."

"You don't know that, Captain."

"I believe I do." He kept looking at her. When he next spoke to Selar, it was with his back still to her. "Ever watch a cat sleep, Doctor?"

Selar stared at him blankly, then glanced at Burgoyne. S/he shrugged, no help at all. "A cat," she repeated. "Small earth creature?"

He nodded. "You can tell when they're having hunting dreams. You watch their ears twitch. You watch their paws move, thrust ever so slightly as they dream about stalking some helpless prey. Well, two-legged individuals have the same sort of telltale body language sometimes, Doctor, even when they're not part of the waking world. You tell me that Tsana is not in a coma, and I'll take your word for it. But watch her carefully. She twitches every now and then—"

"Muscle spasms," Selar said.

"Possibly," he allowed. "But watch. See? See how she seems to put her hands up a bit, there . . . right there, she just did it." And indeed, just for a moment, a sudden slight convulsion of Tsana's hands occurred, palms up.

"I saw, yes. Very minor. I do not see—"

"No, you don't. But I see. She's warding something off, Doctor. She's trying to keep something away from her. Something that terrifies her."

"Captain, that is pure supposition," Selar said.

"Possibly," he admitted. "Or possibly she is in a state of

deep shock, kept where she is, blocked by something she is so afraid to deal with that her only choice is to stay deeply hidden within herself so she doesn't have to face it."

"Either way, the result remains the same."

He pivoted on his heel to face her. "Only for as long as you *allow* it to remain the same."

"Captain, I really must insist—" Burgoyne started to say.

But Selar interrupted him. "The captain is endeavoring to instill some measure of guilt within me, Commander. He will not succeed. Vulcans do not feel guilt."

"Or pity," said Calhoun.

"That is not necessarily the case," she said. "At the moment, I pity you for making these pathetic efforts, endeavoring to have me override not only my concerns for my own privacy, but also that which makes medical sense. She is a species I have not yet encountered, Captain. I said it before, but I do not think you fully comprehend it." She leaned forward, her elbows on the desk. Her face was cold and hard. "Allow me to explain it to you. If we approached a planet with the notion of going down to its surface, would you insist on a full sensor scan to ascertain—to the best of your ability—whether it was hospitable? Even survivable? Or would you simply take a shuttlecraft to the surface without any sort of prior analysis and just hope that the away team didn't die from . . . oh, I don't know, methane poisoning . . . the moment they opened the doors? Ideally—and I certainly hope this would be your answer, for if it was not, I may recommend you be relieved of command—you would endorse exploring the world before setting foot on it."

"And this is similar, is what you're saying."

"Any alien mind is *terra incognita,* as cratered and dangerous as any other. It must be carefully studied, catalogued, and understood. For all you know, Captain . . . for all any of us knows . . . I could wind up doing that girl more harm than good. There are Vulcans who are absolute masters of the mind-meld, who have honed it to such a degree, through years of training, that they could thrust themselves into any sort of mental situation and survive it. I am not one of them. I am a doctor, not a psychic. My job is to heal bodies, not reconstruct fractured minds."

"I thought your job was to help people," Calhoun told her.

Her eyes narrowed. "And I thought, Captain, that your job was to maintain amicable relations with races, not kidnap members of their ruling class. I have refrained from telling you how to do your job. Kindly extend me the same courtesy."

There was so much more Calhoun wanted to say, so many ways he felt he could approach the question in a manner that might convince her. He even opened his mouth as if he was about to reply, but then he saw the way her face was set, the inflexibility in her eyes. So he closed his mouth and instead simply said, "Very well. Do all that you can to help her." Whereupon he turned and left without another word.

"How fortunate that he told me that," she said dryly. "Had he not, I might have done less than I could to help her." She looked up at Burgoyne and said, "I appreciate your support."

"Thank you." S/he dropped into the chair opposite Selar, straddling it. "Selar . . . the mind-meld is the only way."

She moaned ever so softly. "Burgoyne . . ."

"Selar, listen to me. As you yourself pointed out, Captain Calhoun removed this girl against the will of the Aerons. She had been here for some time. There is no question in my mind that the Aerons have already contacted Starfleet. We may be hearing from them before too long. The odds are that Starfleet is going to frown on the captain's actions and order him to return Tsana to the Aerons."

"Certainly that would be the captain's concern rather than mine."

"It should be your concern, because she is your patient. If she is returned to that world, she may never recover."

"We do not know that, Burgoyne. I do not know that, nor

do you. What I *do* know is that it is my responsibility to tend to her medical needs and to do her no harm."

"No, Selar," s/he said intently. "That's your *job*. Your *responsibility* is to help that girl. You know that."

"Kindly do not tell me what I know."

"All right. I'll tell you what I know. There was nothing in Soleta's job description saying that she should help you when you were in emotional turmoil months ago, remember? But she mentally merged with you to—"

"Stop it." The tips of her ears were flushing green ever so slightly. "I do not wish to speak of that, Burgoyne. It was an intensely personal situation, and I do not feel that either it, or Soleta's involvement in it, are appropriate for discussion."

"I'm your lover, Selar, and the cocreator of our child. It doesn't get much more personal than that."

"That," she said, "shows how little you truly understand me."

"I understand you, Selar. I understand you well enough to know that when you needed help, Soleta was there for you, and when that girl needs help," and s/he pointed at Tsana, "you aren't there for her. All because you're afraid—"

"It has nothing to do with fear."

"It has everything to do with fear. The thing you hate more than anything else in this universe, Selar, is opening yourself up, even a little bit." Despite the tension in the air, s/he actually smiled slightly, revealing the edges of hir fangs. "The fact that you have done so with me, even the small amount that you have, is a source of great pride to me. You don't want to try and probe Tsana's mind because it means you'd have to let your guard down slightly, and you hate that. Hate that with a passion, which is doubly aggravating, considering you acknowledge neither hatred nor passion as part of your psychological makeup. But we're on the clock now, Selar. If Starfleet steps in, and the captain refuses to obey—which, knowing him, he might do—they could court-martial him. You won't have helped him, the ship, or Tsana. You'll only have helped yourself stay safe and sound in your cocoon of logic and imperviousness to emotion."

Her eyes narrowed. "Did you put this together? You and Calhoun?"

"What? What are you—?"

"Are you working in tandem with him?" she said. "First his approach, more strident, and then yours—"

"Selar! For the love of . . ." In utter exasperation, s/he stood and said, "Look, I'm telling you what I think. I'm sorry if you believe that I was somehow coerced into saying it. I would like to think that, in the future, I would be able to tell you what's on my mind without it being second-guessed as having some sort of sinister motivation."

"I was not saying it was 'sinister.'"

But Burgoyne wasn't listening. Instead s/he said briskly, "I'll see you this evening," and exited Selar's office and sickbay.

Once in the corridor, s/he walked about ten feet and then stopped. Calhoun was leaning against the bulkhead, arms folded, waiting with one eyebrow cocked. "Well?" he inquired.

"She figured it out," said Burgoyne. "That you and I were working together."

"*Grozit*," muttered Calhoun. "Well, we thought that might happen. . . ."

"*You* thought that might happen, Captain," Burgoyne reminded him. "You asked me to aid you in this, and I cooperated because I'm your second-in-command, and because I really do feel she should help the girl." S/he glanced around to make sure no one was coming from either direction, then lowered hir voice and continued. "But I feel as if you were trying to manipulate her through me."

"I would say 'influence.' 'Manipulate' is a harsh word. . . ."

"But wholly inaccurate, Captain?"

Calhoun looked levelly into hir eyes, and then admitted, "Not . . . wholly, I suppose."

"Captain . . ." Burgoyne paused, trying to determine the best thing to say. "I am very anxious to do whatever I can to accommodate you. I want to serve you in the capacity of second-in-command to the best of my ability. But so help me, if you ever attempt to utilize me in that fashion again—"

"Understood."

"I will resign the post."

"I said, understood, Commander," Calhoun repeated.

"With all respect, Captain, I know you say you understand . . . but that's not the same as a promise that you won't."

"No. It's not," said Calhoun. "I can't read the future, Burgoyne. I don't know what will happen in times to come, nor do I know what I will be calling upon you to do. All I can promise is that I will certainly take your sensibilities into consideration, and be aware of the consequences of anything I might request. I certainly hope that will satisfy you."

Burgoyne considered it, then sighed. "I certainly hope so, too, Captain."

It was an hour later when Selar became aware of him.

He had entered so silently that he had eluded the notice of not only the doctor, but all the technicians in sickbay. She finally noticed him though. Surprisingly, he was standing next to Tsana, looking at the insensate girl. She strode over to him, her normally deadpan face slightly pinched to display her annoyance. "Moke," she said, "we have been over this. If you are not ill, you should not be here."

The boy glanced up at her, looking chagrined, taking a step back as if he thought he could scamper back into the shadows and elude detection. Apparently realizing that was a hopeless prospect, though, he stayed where he was. He didn't apologize for his presence. He didn't say anything; just kept shifting his gaze from Selar to Tsana and back again.

A thought crossed her mind. Watching his eyes very carefully for any sign of prevarication, she said, "Did Captain Cal—did your adoptive father send you here?"

He looked puzzled. "No. Why would he do that?" And there was enough sincerity in that question, in that whole clearly befuddled attitude that she was immediately satisfied that he had come of his own initiative. She could not know for certain, of course, but every instinct told her that the child was as incapable of duplicity as she herself was. However, that still left her with an obvious question, which she promptly asked.

"Then why are you here?"

He did not answer immediately. Instead he looked at Tsana. "What's wrong with her?"

"I am not quite certain," admitted Selar, bound by Vulcan society and culture to answer truthfully in all things when it was remotely possible.

"Oh."

"Are you here because of her, Moke?"

"No."

"Then why?" Indeed, part of her wasn't the least bit interested in the "why" of it. She wanted him out and gone, and that would be that. But another part—the hated, "less logical" side—wanted its needs attended to.

"Because of you."

She stared at him. "I do not understand."

"Okay." And apparently that, in Moke's opinion, was that. The fact that she didn't understand seemed to be—as far as he was concerned—solely her problem. Instead, his attention was back on Tsana. "What's wrong with her?" he asked.

"It is very complicated, and you should not be—"

"Can you make her better?" he asked with some urgency.

Well . . . there it was. The question, stripped of all its second-guessing and rationalization. She wanted to lie to the boy. She wanted to lie to herself. But she could not. "Possibly, yes," she said.

He had been standing behind Tsana. Now he walked around the medscan table, his chin barely coming up to the edge, and his eyes were directly on level with Tsana's open but unseeing eyes. He blinked owlishly, stared into them, then looked up at Selar and said, "Then you should."

He said nothing more, just left that three-word statement hanging in the air. He left almost immediately thereafter, but Selar did not move from the bedside. She simply stood there, staring down at the immobilized child.

There was a footfall by her side, one of her associate physicians approaching, a petite, redheaded woman. "Dr. Selar . . . ? Has there been a change in the patient's condition?"

"No. No, there hasn't, Dr. Scasino." She turned to the physician. "Stay near, would you, please?"

Scasino looked at her oddly, obviously a bit confused by the tone of Selar's voice. "Yes, Doctor. Is there a prob—?"

Selar did not wait for the question to be finished. Instead, she turned to Tsana and gently placed her fingers on either side of the girl's forehead. "Our minds are merging, Tsana . . .

". . . merging . . .

". . . merging . . . do not be afraid . . . merging . . ."

She slid through easily, like a melting drop of snow dancing between the breaks in a rock face. There was no resistance, none.

All around her was darkness, a void. She tried to visualize herself, to see her self-image of her hands, feet, legs, anything, but there was nothing. By this point in the merge, there should have been enough illumination for Selar to put together a coherent version of herself. Then she quickly discerned why she was having trouble. A merge literally drew upon the abilities, the thoughts of two minds, working as one. Each mind drew strength from the other.

But in Tsana's case, there was nothing to draw from. She had withdrawn so fully, so completely, that it was like melding with a black hole. As much as Selar was putting forward, she was getting little to nothing back again.

It was a daunting moment for Selar as she weighed her options. Her natural caution told her to retreat rather than hurl herself into a situation that was increasingly fraught with danger, since she didn't know or understand the parameters of it. . . .

"Then you should." *Moke's childish, innocent comment still hung upon her. It was irritating, and she could only think that she was ascribing any sort of importance to it at all because she was looking at his quiet, troubled eyes and seeing an image of her own son as he got older.*

She pushed further in. Still there was no resistance, and she began to probe with almost reckless abandon, trying to find some aspect of the girl that was salvageable, approachable. **You're hiding,** *she called through the void.* **You're hiding . . . I can tell, Tsana. I can sense it.** *Which was not really true; she could sense nothing save the emptiness around her, but she was hoping that somehow, in some way, the probe would draw her out.*

She heard something . . . well, not heard. *Not technically. It was a sensing of something that simulated auditory stimulation in the meld. She glided toward it, a deep sea diver with an endless (or maybe not so endless) supply of oxygen, spiraling into the depths, and there was shouting, and feet running, and crying out, and sickening splats like raw meat being thrown against walls. . . .*

Existence and nonexistence lurched around her, and suddenly she was hauled in and down, like a roller coaster that had been quietly cruising along and suddenly hit a drop. She hung on, fighting the urge to scream, because such reactions were counterproductive to the success and smoothness of a mind-meld. She needed to retain her core, her essence; she needed to remain focused, damn it. There was always a danger, when merging with a strong personality, that one could virtually be consumed by it. There was a similar danger when merging with one who was so vacant that there was pure emptiness everywhere. Just like a diver, she could lose track of which way was up or down, which way presented escape, and unlike a diver, she couldn't simply release a few air bubbles and follow them to be guided to the surface. . . .

She kept hearing the sounds, the same sounds, over and over, and then she realized that it was not simply a continuation of the noises, it was a repetition. The same set of noises, repeatedly. Tsana was reliving something. She was caught in a loop, her mind shutting down, not allowing her to depart from it.

*The sounds grew louder, as if Selar were approaching a battlefield, and then she was gone, that was all, just gone, sucked down, sucked away, and she saw Tsana, and she **was** Tsana, and the terror was overwhelming, and the floor under the bed was cold, so cold, and the dust under the bed made her want to sneeze, but she knew if she did she'd be dead because they were dead, her brothers were dead, she had just seen it happen, the man had been there, the man with the big gun, and when her brothers had seen him they had almost laughed because they'd been so relieved, except he'd shot them and she heard their bodies fly backwards and pieces of them hit the wall, and pieces of them splattered to the floor in front of her, and there was blood coming down from everywhere, as if she was in a rainstorm of blood, and all she wanted to do was scream and scream and keep on screaming forever as the blood pooled around her, but she didn't dare, she couldn't make a noise, Selar couldn't make a noise, couldn't move, couldn't breathe because he would come again, the man would find them, and she wanted to* *run, and she had run, and more men were chasing her, and she couldn't take it anymore, she just couldn't, Selar couldn't, Tsana couldn't, they couldn't, she couldn't, it was safer here, safer, safer . . .*

Mackenzie Calhoun, seated in his command chair on the bridge, felt a vague sense of unease, and then promptly attributed it to the next words out of Robin Lefler's mouth.

The ops officer turned with a look of concern to her captain and said, "Sir . . . communiqué from Starfleet. It's Admiral Jellico, sir."

The bridge crew had been engaged in its normal pattern of discussion and chat as they orbited the world designated Thallon 21 and called Aeron by its residents. But upon hearing that bit of news, the crew immediately quieted.

Calhoun considered for a moment retiring to his ready room and taking the call there, but then dismissed the notion. A crew functioned based on its confidence in its captain; he did not need them thinking that he was so afraid of what Jellico might say to him, that he had to hide behind closed doors. Besides, he did not regret for a moment any of the actions he had taken. Still . . .

"Lieutenant," he said to Lefler, quite calmly, "tell Admiral Jellico I'll be right with him . . . have Ambassador Cwan come to the bridge . . . and then put him on."

"Preparing to stick your head into the lion's mouth, Captain?" inquired Burgoyne.

Calhoun smiled wryly. "And me without my whip and chair."

Tsana did not understand why part of her wanted to emerge from hiding. It was crazy, the bad man would find her, hurt her, the bad man and the other men . . . but mostly she was afraid of the one who had slain her brothers in front of her, the man whom they had been glad to see. She had ac-

tually heard their voices choke with terror, and then those sounds, those horrible sounds. Yet she felt something trying to push her out from under the bed, something telling her that it was safe, that she need not fear anything, but she knew better. Because she had thought herself safe when the man was there, and now she wasn't, and she didn't know what to do, because she wanted to be safe, but she knew she never would be if she came out, and she pushed away the little voice screaming within her, pushed it away where it wouldn't hurt her, where nothing would hurt her, where . . .

"It's time to come out."

The voice was so firm, so serene, so determined, that naturally it snared her attention. Still, she remained afraid to move, even as her inner voice urged her to trust this newcomer, but it was a trick, it could be a trick, it had to be a trick. . . .

"It isn't a trick. I am here. You are safe."

"You're . . . you're lying . . ." Her voice sounded small and terrified to herself, a pathetic and puny thing.

"Vulcans never lie."

That stopped her. She knew that it was foolish to ask, because speaking was going to give away where she was hiding, but something prompted her to ask, *"What is a Vulcan?"*

"If you wish to know, look out from under there. I know where you are. I knew the moment I entered this room. So hiding is fairly pointless, right?"

She knew this to be true, so she peered out ever so slightly, and there was the strangest woman—she thought it was a woman—she had ever seen. Ears tapered, eyebrows swept upwards, thick black hair piled on her head and some sort of an odd emblem in the hair, pinning it into place.

"Who . . . are you?" *And then, before the words were even out of her, she knew the answer.* *"Soleta."*

"Soleta," *affirmed the Vulcan.*

"How did I know that?"

"The answer would be somewhat complicated, and you

probably would not understand anyway." She extended a hand. "Come, Tsana. Come to me."

"I don't want to. The bad man will hurt me. . . ."

"No one can hurt you. You're not where you think you are. Come with me and let me show you your true whereabouts."

"Are my parents there? And my brothers and sister?" She looked at Soleta, and again, she knew before Soleta could answer. "They're dead. Aren't they?"

Lying was not a possibility. "Yes."

She was silent for a moment. Then she said, "If I come with you . . . will you help me kill the men who killed them?"

"I cannot promise that."

"Then I don't want to come. I don't want a world without them."

"You have a world without them already, Tsana," said Soleta, not unkindly. "The question is . . . do you want a world without you? I don't think your parents, or your siblings, would have desired that. They would have wanted you to live, and grow, and act on their behalf and keep their memory alive."

"How would you know what they would have wanted or not wanted? You don't know them," said the child with bubbling anger.

Soleta approached her slowly, crouched before her. It seemed as if there was light spilling out from behind her eyes. She brought her hand, almost ethereal, to the girl's forehead and touched it ever so gently, her fingers seeming to go right through.

"I know them now," she said.

And suddenly there was another Vulcan standing right next to Soleta, and she was looking slightly disconcerted. "How did . . . ?"

"Dr. Lili Scasino. She was concerned. She called me. I was concerned. I am here."

"Hmm. I must be certain to put Lili in for a pay raise."

Soleta looked back to the girl, and held out her hand once more, this time with a certainty that would not be ignored. "Tsana . . . it is time to go."

"I'm not sure . . . I'm not . . ."

"Very well. If you do not wish to come with us . . . then we will leave you, all alone. Forever. It is your choice."

There were two images on the screen, side by side: one, the Starfleet transmission, with Admiral Jellico's pinched, annoyed face on it, and the other, beamed up from the planet surface, with Burkitt looking rather smug. It was obvious to Burgoyne that Burkitt was looking forward to seeing Calhoun squirm under the white-hot glare of Starfleet's disapproval. Even more obviously, Burkitt didn't know Calhoun—or what made him squirm—in the least.

"So you're saying it's true, then," Jellico said, still sounding incredulous.

"Yes, sir," replied Calhoun. "I brought Tsana up here to the *Excalibur.* I felt that her best interests would be served—"

Jellico cut him off, both verbally and at the knees. "Captain, you don't *get* to decide what her best interests are! That was kidnapping!"

"Actually, Admiral, the kid was more unconscious than actually napping."

Burgoyne was surprised to hear a genuine chuckle from Zak Kebron standing behind him at the tactical station. The huge Brikar security chief rarely responded to anything with much more than a grunt, if that.

Jellico's face grew even more taut. "Do I appear amused by your quip, Captain?"

"No, sir, but with all respect, I don't feel I should be penalized simply because you cannot appreciate a good quip."

"Do you see, Admiral?" demanded Burkitt. "Do you see what I've had to deal with? The arrogance, the—"

"I will handle this, Warmaster Burkitt," said Jellico forcefully. "Captain Calhoun, you will return the child to the care of her people immediately."

"Her condition remains unchanged, Admiral—"

"That is not our concern."

"Dr. Selar needs time to—"

"And *that* is not our concern," Jellico continued. "Captain, unless you do as you are ordered, I will instruct your first officer to have you arrested and bound over for court-martial. I cannot make it any plainer than that."

The only sound that broke the silence on the bridge in that moment was soft, triumphant laughter from Burkitt. That was when Si Cwan said, very quietly, very dangerously, "Admiral, the child will be killed if she is returned to her homeworld."

From both Jellico and Burkitt there was a simultaneous expulsion of *"What?!"*

Si Cwan kept speaking, easily raising his voice above the infuriated and indignant shouts of the two people on the screen. "Admiral, we Thallonians know how the Aerons operate. We know their history, their character, their culture. The Markanians were foolish to attack the imperial family, because, traditionally, the imperials have kept the military in check. The abrupt termination of most of the imperial family presents an ideal opportunity for the warmaster to consolidate his power, and the continued existence of even one of the members of the family poses a threat to that consolidation. If the girl does show any sign of recovering from her shock-induced state, I predict she will die shortly thereafter. Is Starfleet in the habit of condemning children to death, Admiral?"

"Lies!" bellowed Burkitt. "Damned lies!"

"And statistics," McHenry piped up, but no one knew what he was referring to and so didn't bother to ask.

"This is all fabrication and character assassination, Admiral—!"

"Better to assassinate character than individuals, Burkitt," Si Cwan shot back.

"Admiral, the Thallonians have a long history of hostility toward us, going all the way back to Sinqay—"

"Sinqay?" said a clearly puzzled Jellico, who looked as if he was falling behind in the conversation.

"The holy world of the Aerons and the Markanians, Admiral," Si Cwan volunteered.

"No!" said Burkitt sharply. "Ours! Only ours! The world, and the Holy Site on the world . . . our claim took precedent over the Markanians, which was something the Thallonians neither understood nor cared about! And the campaign of hostility continues to this day. Admiral, I give you my word—"

"Your word?" It was now Calhoun who sounded almost derisive. "The word of someone who has hidden a Gateway . . ."

And to Calhoun's surprise, Jellico's tone mollified slightly. "Yes, Captain Calhoun does raise a valid point. Warmaster Burkitt, this technology you're wielding . . . it is extremely dangerous. More so than you can possibly believe."

"It is ours," Burkitt said sullenly.

"Might I propose . . . a compromise," Jellico suggested. "You give this portable Gateway to the *Excalibur* for safekeeping, and Captain Calhoun will return Tsana to you—"

For a moment Burgoyne thought that Calhoun would take the way out being proferred by the admiral, but s/he subsequently realized that s/he really should have known better than that. "Unacceptable, Admiral," Calhoun said immediately.

"Captain," and Jellico's tone sounded very ugly indeed, "believe it or not, I am doing you a favor here. This may get you out from under and save you from court-martial."

"I will not turn her over to the Aeron."

"That, Captain, is an option you do not have."

"No, Admiral. Returning the girl planetside is the option I do not have. Everything else is negotiable."

"This isn't," Jellico said firmly. "Commander Burgoyne . . . arrest Captain Calhoun."

Slowly Burgoyne turned, hir gaze locking with Calhoun's. Calhoun's face was inscrutable. Burgoyne would have hated to play poker with him.

"Captain Calhoun," Burgoyne said slowly.

But before s/he could get the next words out, the turbolift doors slid open. Burgoyne turned in response to the noise, and hir jaw dropped in surprise.

Science Officer Soleta and Dr. Selar had entered the bridge, which in and of itself was not all that remarkable, although they appeared rather wan and exhausted. Walking between them, however, on unsteady legs, looking drawn and a bit scared but otherwise all right, was Tsana.

"Tsana!" Burkitt blurted out, answering Jellico's question before he could even ask it. "You . . . you are recovered! This is . . . this is a great day for—!"

She took one look at him and let out a scream so shrill it made everyone on the bridge wince; Soleta and Selar clapped their hands over their ears, since their hearing was that much sharper.

And then, just like that, her cry of terror turned to one of pure, undiluted fury, and she howled, *"You killed them! You killed my brothers! They trusted you! We all trusted you! Damn you! Damn you to hell!"* and she ran toward the viewscreen. Lefler tried to stand and intercept her, but she twisted past and threw herself against the screen, uncaring of the fact that it was only Burkitt's image. *"Damn you, damn you, damn you!"* she howled repeatedly, at first clawing it with her fingers and then balling her hands into fists and slamming them repeatedly against it. Sobs were torn from her throat, all of her grief pouring from her, and it was hard to say whether she was aware of it when Dr. Selar wrapped her arms around her and gently pulled her away from the screen.

Burkitt sat there, speechless.

And with an air of supreme serenity, Captain Calhoun said to Jellico, "If it's all the same to Starfleet, Admiral . . . I don't think we'll be sending Tsana into Burkitt's tender mercies any time soon."

15

TRIDENT

M'RESS WAS READY to smash the equipment, rip it to shreds with her bare hands. She moved to do so, in fact, just out of sheer frustration, and it was only Gleau putting his hands gently upon her wrist and quelling her anger that prevented her. Yet, despite all her anger, she felt a guilty thrill of pleasure from his touch, and the fur on the back of her neck prickled.

"You mustn't let it get to you, M'Ress," Lieutenant Commander Gleau assured her. "It's . . ." He paused, frowned. "What is that . . . odd noise? It . . . seems to be emanating from around your chest cavity."

Of course M'Ress knew it immediately for what it was: his skin against hers was making her purr again, dammit. It was a reflex action, and she immediately cleared her throat loudly to try and cover it. "My apologies, sir. The Caitian . . . digestive system . . . is rather loud." She couldn't help but feel that it was an extremely weak excuse to make, but it was the only one that occurred to her.

Fortunately, Gleau made no indication that he found the excuse remotely implausible. "Amazing, the way species are so different, one from the other, isn't it?" he said, sounding for all the world as if he really thought it was a marvelous thing. "So you are hungry, is what you are saying?"

"No, sir," she assured him, deciding that this would be a good opportunity to send the conversation away from her. She rose from the scanning station in the main science lab and stalked it with obvious annoyance, her tail whipping about . . . so much so that several crewmen who were walking about, working on other projects, were constrained to give her a wide berth so they wouldn't be smacked in the face. "Sir, I'm not picking up anything. Not a damned thing. The only conclusion I can draw is that if the Gateway, or the Iconian, is down there, they've managed to find a way to shield themselves from our probes."

"Would that be possible?"

She shrugged. "Lieutenant Commander, before what happened to me happened to me, I would have been the first to tell you that a Gateway that hurls travelers into the future would have been impossible. Yet there it was, and here I am. So who am I to say what's possible and what isn't? All I know is, I'm getting nowhere, and I'm getting the sinking feeling that I'm going to continue to get nowhere."

"All right," said Gleau after a moment. "The captain is in a holoconference with Captain Calhoun, so I won't disturb her at the moment. However, if your recommendation is that we quit . . ."

"I didn't say that," M'Ress quickly informed him. "I'm going to keep looking, even though it may be utterly futile, for as long as we're in orbit around this hunk of rock. As long as there's still an opportunity."

He smiled approvingly, and it seemed to M'Ress as if his smile illuminated the entire room. "That's good to hear, M'Ress. Very good to hear." He raised his voice slightly and said, "That's exactly the sort of attitude I like to hear from my people." He rested a hand on her shoulder, squeezing it slightly, and she felt as if a little jolt of electricity had entered her and was dancing around, lighting shadows she didn't even realize were there and chasing them away. She wasn't even aware when he had left the room, because she was still embracing the warm feeling his presence had brought to her.

Her ears picked up as she heard chuckling. She glanced at her coworkers and saw what she felt were patronizing grins or pitying looks. "What is it?" she said. No one answered. Just more looks, more chuckles, and this time, more forcefully, she repeated, "What is it?"

"Nothing," one of them, a veteran and slightly grizzled officer named Chesterton said.

"There seems to be much amusement being generated at my expense for 'nothing,' " M'Ress said tightly. "Would you do me the courtesy of telling me what is going on?"

The laughter stopped, and then, more seriously, Chesterton said, "Nothing is 'going on,' Lieutenant. If something struck us as whimsical . . ."

"I will not see others provided their dose of 'whimsy' at my expense," M'Ress snapped, much more harshly than she had intended. "If you're going to enjoy your little games, do it elsewhere and with someone else."

"There are no 'games' involved here, Lieutenant," replied Chesterton, "and to be honest, I can't say I appreciate your taking out on us your feeling of frustration over your failures—"

"Failures!" She was becoming angrier by the moment. "Would you care to tell me what you're talking about?"

Matters had spiraled out of control far more quickly than anyone would have liked, and there were uncomfortable looks among the others in the department. Another technician, a woman named Brennan who had a sweet face and almost supernaturally patient disposition, said, "I don't think there's really anything to—"

"I'm getting the impression that there is," said M'Ress, her eyes glistening, unaware that her hackles were rising, "and if any of you had the slightest shred of courtesy . . ."

"All right, fine," said Chesterton, getting up from his station. "If you want to know—"

"Bill, this isn't—" Brennan started to say, placing a hand on his forearm.

But Chesterton shook it off. "I'm not speaking for everyone else here, all right, Lieutenant? Just me. But as far as I'm concerned, you're making it abundantly clear that you don't want to be here, and you don't want to be with us."

"What are you talking about?"

"Your tone of voice, your body language, everything makes it clear that you wish you were elsewhere . . . or else-*when*," he said, his voice low and gravelly. "And you constantly bring up how it was on the *Enterprise* under Kirk, as if we don't measure up somehow. Meantime, you're constantly playing catch-up, trying to remember how equipment works, and trying to cuddle up to Lieutenant Commander Gleau—"

"You're crazy!"

"No, I'm just fed up." His voice softened, but only slightly. "No one here is denying you got a raw deal, Lieutenant. Everyone understands you wish you were back in your own time. And frankly, I'd be lying if I said that any of us knows how we'd be acting, if we were in your boots . . . well . . . paws," he amended, looking at her bare feet. "But, bottom line, it's wearing pretty damned thin. There. Happy? Glad I told you what was on my mind?"

M'Ress had risen to standing as Chesterton spoke, and all she could see in her mind's eye was herself lashing out with her claws, slashing across his stomach, and taking grim pleasure in the expression on his face as his innards splashed out onto the floor. There was a satisfaction to the mental image that appealed to her primal Caitian instincts. Just as quickly as it presented itself, however, she forced it away, taking slow, steadying breaths.

And when she spoke, the voice came from so deep within her that it sounded like a barely controlled roar, with such depth and ferocity that Chesterton paled slightly and took a step back.

"I'm going on break," she said, and left before anyone could see the tears of mortification and rage that were starting to work their way down her cheeks.

Shelby had to admit that she far preferred this holoconferencing technology to simply staring at Mac's face on a flat screen. She even—although she would never have admitted it—was strongly considering assigning her science team to developing new technology so that the holo incarnations would be able to have actual physical contact. The possibilities seemed fraught with . . . well . . . possibilities.

In the holoconference room, Shelby and Mueller stood side by side, facing the images of Calhoun and Si Cwan. Si Cwan's face seemed a bit darker, ruddier than she had recalled, and she wondered if she was simply misremembering, or perhaps it was a natural aspect of Thallonian aging. "So it seems you dodged a bullet," Shelby told Calhoun.

Si Cwan looked quizzically at Calhoun, who murmured, "Bullet. Old earth projectile weapon before the development of energy-discharge weapons."

"Ah," said Si Cwan, trying to sound like he understood, and clearly not doing so. Shelby wisely chose not to try and explain further.

"And, yes, Captain, we apparently did just that, if you're referring to the situation that was developing between myself, Jellico, and Burkitt," Calhoun continued. "However, as I'm sure will not surprise you, Burkitt denied Tsana's assertions. That is going to have to be attended to."

"Do you think the girl is telling the truth?" asked Mueller.

"I think she has no reason to lie. We would have granted her asylum in any event," Calhoun said. "I think she's telling the truth, yes. The problem will be convincing the Aerons of it."

"Let me guess: They're saying that you brainwashed her somehow," said Shelby.

"Exactly. Fortunately enough, not even Jellico was stupid enough to fall for that. Starfleet is reserving action at this time . . . although Jellico did make it clear that he will step in if he feels the need. His confidence in me is truly heartwarming."

"Face facts, Captain . . . you've hardly worked overtime to worm your way into his good graces," said Mueller.

With a cocky air, Calhoun replied, "I consider that to be one of my best features."

"But this still leaves it a case of her word versus his," Shelby said. "They may do whatever they can to discredit her. Is she contending that Burkitt was responsible for the entire attack?"

"No. It's her belief—and ours—that Burkitt was simply being opportunistic. The attack by the Markanians was genuine enough," said Calhoun. "But Burkitt decided to finish what they had begun so that his path to power would be unobstructed. And he thought that the deaths of the brothers would be blamed upon the Markanians, just as the others were. Except he was unaware that Tsana was hiding under the bed. According to Dr. Selar, that was one of the main reasons the girl was in shock: seeing someone who was trusted as the murderer of her brothers."

"As if the murder itself wasn't enough," Shelby murmured. "But if this Burkitt is really responsible . . . it may just be possible that he could still escape retribution."

"If he is responsible," Si Cwan said slowly, "it means that he is carrying a certain degree of guilt within him. He can hide his actions from others . . . but he cannot hide them from himself. So what needs to be done is to have him brought to a point . . . where he can hide them no longer."

"And you know a way?" Mueller inquired, looking Si Cwan up and down thoughtfully.

"I have some resources available to me, yes," Si Cwan said. "I shall make a query or two before speaking of it at greater length, however."

Calhoun cleared his throat. "None of this, however, serves to resolve our immediate problem: the Aerons, the Markanians, and these mysterious Gateways. We've been unable to find any sign of one on Thallon 21."

"Nor we on 18," said Shelby grimly. "Science Officer Gleau informs me that scans are continuing, but he's not tremendously optimistic. The problem is, the only thing that's preventing these races from tearing into each other with the Gateways is our presence. They don't want to activate the Gateways because, once the energy signature is released, we can pinpoint them, and they obviously don't want us to do that. But we can't stay in orbit forever. The moment we're out of sensor range, they'll fire up whatever Gateways either world has and go at each other again."

"This sort of irrational, single-minded hatred is the reason my people separated them in the first place," said Si Cwan.

"And it all seems to stem from this place called Sinqay," said Calhoun, trying desperately not to let his frustration show. "Their homeworld . . ."

"Yes . . . yes, they've talked to me about it as well," Shelby said, pacing. "You have to be impressed by the hubris, that two races would consider their homeworld literally sacred."

"Not just the homeworld itself," said Cwan. "One particular area of it, which they refer to as the Holy Site. Both races have ancient writings that declare that the Holy Site is promised to them. It became the major flashpoint of their disputes."

"And what is significant about this Holy Site?" asked Mueller.

"Well, it's . . . it's holy," Cwan told them.

There were looks exchanged among the others. "That's *it?*" said Shelby.

"Yes."

"It's holy."

"Yes."

"Otherwise there's nothing there of any value?" said Shelby, obviously trying to wrap herself around the concept. "No . . . no minerals, no latinum mine, no rare artifacts . . . nothing like that?"

"Well," Si Cwan said thoughtfully, "there are temples and such, dedicated to worshipping their varied gods. But the temples have no value outside the fact that they were built to offer prayer to their gods. They fight over the temples, too."

"Because they're holy," Shelby said once more, clearly trying to make sense of it. "Other than that someone centuries ago declared this particular area to be holy, there's no intrinsic worth to it."

Calhoun replied, sounding faintly amused. "For many people, Captain Shelby . . . the holiness of a place is all the intrinsic worth it needs. You understand that, don't you?"

"No," she said flatly. "I cannot comprehend the mentality that would have millions upon millions of people fighting and dying, all because each of them believes that some sort of unseen being wants them to be in a particular spot. It makes no sense to me."

"It makes sense to them," said Cwan, "and, unfortunately for our purposes, that is all that matters at the moment. The question remains: What is to be done?"

There was silence for a moment, and then Calhoun said slowly, "If we continue to try and stop the people from fighting with each other, we are attacking only the surface aspect of the problem, rather than the cause. The cause is Sinqay. It may be that we have to address the situation on that level instead."

"Mac, are you suggesting we offer to transport both races back to their homeworld? Undo the Thallonian separation?" asked Shelby. "It's not logistically feasible. We'd have to requisition transport vessels—"

"Even if it is somehow manageable," pointed out Si Cwan, "once face-to-face, the fighting will simply start again. It would be pure folly."

"That's not what I'm suggesting," Calhoun said. "This, however, is . . ."

And he started laying it all out. . . .

Arex was heading down a corridor, having an amusing discussion with two attractive young yeomen, both of whom seemed to be hanging on his every word.

"So there we were, Captain Kirk, Mister Spock, and I, and the captain turns to me, and he says, 'Arex . . . how do you think we should handle this? So naturally, I—"

That was when M'Ress stepped from the side corridor, snagging Arex by one of his three arms and pulling him toward a turbolift. "Wha—?" he managed to stammer out.

Instead of addressing Arex, M'Ress said to the yeomen, "Excuse me . . . matter of some urgency. You understand."

She hauled him into the turbolift and, as the doors slid closed, she said, "Deck nine." The lift started to move.

"Why Deck nine?" asked the befuddled Arex.

"No reason whatsoever. It was just so I could say this: Computer, halt turbolift."

The turbolift immediately slid gracefully to a stop. Arex was now more confused than ever, staring at M'Ress as if she had grown a third eye or started howling or tossing about convulsively. "What is—?"

"How are you doing it?" she demanded.

"Doing what?"

She was so agitated that at first she couldn't even get the words out. Her tail whipped around in the lift; Arex was relieved it didn't have a barb or club at the end, or he'd have been in serious trouble.

"Fitting in!" She paced back and forth, which, considering the relatively small area of the turbolift, made Arex feel as if she were stalking him . . . except she wasn't looking at him. It was almost as if she was looking inward. "I see you. I watch you. If I didn't know better, I'd think you were born into this century. Everyone seems to accept you. You're good at your job. You make friends easily. Me, whenever I walk through this ship, I feel as if I'm having an out-of-body experience. As if I'm here, but not really here. I keep waiting to wake up and discover that it was all a dream."

"That's not going to happen, M'Ress. And going through your life like a sleepwalker isn't a particularly good way to exist."

"Do you think I'm unaware of that!"

"I don't know, M'Ress. I don't know what you're aware of or not aware of. All I know is what you're telling me." He thought a moment. "I hear they have ship's counselers these days. Perhaps you should—"

She shook her head. "What's some counseler going to tell me, Arex? This isn't a case of homesickness. This isn't depression. It's not like I just miss my family or my homeworld. *My family is dead, Arex!*" and the words burst from her, the emotions all in a torrent. "My friends are dead! My homeworld might as well be populated by strangers! What is a counseler going to tell me, eh? Get used to it? Learn to live with it? I don't need a counseler, I need a time machine. I need to go back."

"You can't."

"I have to go back."

"You can't." Arex took her firmly by the shoulders, and with his third hand held her chin firmly, forcing her to look at him. "Shiboline, you can't. There's no way—"

"There is a way," she said. "The Guardian."

"What?"

"The Guardian of Forever. I can . . ." Her thoughts were tumbling over themselves. "I can simply go back to where I left off. Or . . . or I can find myself at an earlier time and just tell myself not to volunteer to go to the planet's surface. To stay away from the Gateway. That's all."

"That's all," repeated Arex, sounding both amused and sad. "Risking the space-time continuum, and you say 'that's all' . . ."

"I'm just one Caitian!" she said urgently. "How much possible difference can one person make?"

"Captain Kirk learned the answer to that. Do you want to risk the lives, the existence of everyone here, just because you're convinced you can't make any difference to the order of the galaxy?" Arex said. "The M'Ress I knew would never do that to these people."

*"The M'Ress you knew **died** a century ago!"* she cried out. "And these people . . . they're like walking shadows to me! If they vanish, I wouldn't give it any more thought than I would a dream when it vanishes upon waking!"

She pulled away from him, throwing her arms around herself as if she was trying to protect herself . . . or perhaps hold herself together. She sank to the floor of the turbolift, despondent, and then jammed the base of her hands into her eyes to keep back the tears.

Very softly, his voice sounding uncharacteristically deep, Arex said, "You don't mean that, Shib."

She drew in a long breath and then let it out, trembling. "I don't know, Na Eth. I don't know what I mean anymore."

"Perhaps . . . perhaps you want to consider transferring off ship . . . leaving Starfleet . . ."

"You mean quit," she said.

"Leave of absence . . . just for a while. Perhaps trying to adjust to the new surroundings in a starship was a mistake.

Because all it does is remind you of what you don't have anymore."

"And go where, Na Eth?" she asked miserably. "Where would I go? What would I do?"

"I . . . don't know."

"Neither do I." She took another long, deep breath, wiping her fur dry of tears, and then said, "You still haven't told me . . . how do you do it? How do you blend in so easily?"

"Because to me, nothing's changed."

She laughed curtly. "Nothing's changed? You're not serious."

"I'm perfectly serious. Sure, technology has progressed, uniform styles have developed . . . but that's nothing new. Because the more things change, the more they stay the same."

"There's an original notion," she said dryly.

"All right, it's a cliché, but like any cliché, it's true. Because what stays the same is people, Shib. People don't change. They still laugh, love, fear, cry . . . whatever. There's a constancy to that, and I find security in it. But you . . . you can be slow to warm up to people. It's not that you distrust them automatically, but you don't trust them, either. That's okay. It's the way you are . . . the way many Caitians are."

"So . . . so what do I do?"

"There's no one thing to do." He scratched her under the chin, and she wanted to tell him to stop because it felt so good when he did that, and she didn't want to feel good just then. But instead of offering protest, she made a soft, pleasant growling noise. Arex continued, "It's not as if I can present you with an easy answer and, like a lightning flash, it solves the problem. Just give it time. And make people feel as if you're glad to see them, instead of resenting having to share a universe with them, or acting as if you're just visiting."

Arex's combadge suddenly beeped. He grinned, stopped scratching her, and pointed at the badge. "Don't you love this convenience?" he asked and—as M'Ress smiled in spite of herself—Arex tapped the badge. "Arex here."

"Hey, Arex, this is Hash up at ops. Uhm, Arex, is there any particular reason you've been sitting in a turbolift for the past ten minutes? You and . . . Lieutenant M'Ress, according to the readouts?"

"We're just talking, Lieutenant."

"And I've got no doubt about that, son. But considerin' that you're jammin' up the lift traffic patterns somethin' fierce, we all would be terribly obliged if you might get yourselves in gear."

"Will do, Lieutenant. Sorry for the delay." He looked to M'Ress expectantly.

She sighed, nodded and said, "Computer, resume." The turbolift promptly slid back into action. "Thanks for taking the time to talk to me, Arex."

"I'm always happy to make the time for someone who imprisons me in a turbolift and gives me no choice but to talk to her," he replied, and he bowed deeply.

The turbolift came to a halt, the doors slid open and Arex stepped out. "Deck five," said M'Ress, and she tossed off a half-hearted wave as the turbolift doors closed.

Arex shook his head, distressed at M'Ress's plight, started to walk away, and suddenly said, "Wait a minute . . . I don't have any reason to be on Deck nine." And with an annoyed grunt, he turned back to the turbolift so he could head somewhere useful.

16

AERON

To a CERTAIN DEGREE, it was déjà vu to Calhoun. Once again he was standing before the Counselars of Aeron. Once again he found himself in opposition to the warmaster (what a pretentious title).

This time, however, the circumstances were slightly different. Standing on either side of him were not only Si Cwan, but his sister, Kalinda, who was developing into quite an impressive beauty. Directly in front of him was Tsana. Considering everything she had been through, the girl was holding up well. Dr. Selar had overseen her being nursed fully back to health, although Selar had advised against bringing Tsana down to the planet's surface at this particular time. It had been her contention that Tsana needed more time to heal, to rest up.

Tsana, however, would not hear of it. There was certainly much of the imperious in the youngster. It was as if, having finally wakened to a world in which she was the only living member of her family, she was forcing herself to adjust to that harsh reality and deal with it as straightforwardly as possible. Part of what was keeping her going was her burning desire to seek vengeance against the man whom she believed had slain her two brothers, betraying their trust and committing treason against the imperial family and the Aerons at large.

Standing directly behind Calhoun was Zak Kebron. Calhoun found it grimly amusing that—despite the presence of two Thallonians and a young girl who was, basically, the new ruler of Aeron—the one who was getting the most looks from the Counselars was Kebron. Perhaps they were afraid that the Brikar was going to go berserk and plow through them, smashing them apart with arms the size of boulders and skin so tough that he could likely laugh off whatever weapons they tried to throw at them. He studied them with a stare as dark as an approaching thunderstorm, and they looked suitably daunted. Well . . . good. Let them be afraid. If it put them at a disadvantage, so much the better.

The only one who did not appear the least bit put off by the assemblage of opponents was Burkitt. Naturally, he would not want to show any fear; that alone might be enough to be interpreted as guilt, and Burkitt would know that he mustn't do anything that could worsen his situation.

Instead, Burkitt smiled generously, even looking concerned over Tsana's current condition. "Are you sure you would not rather sit down, Tsana?" he inquired solicitously. He turned to Commander Gragg, who was standing a few feet away, and said, "Would you mind getting the young lady a pillow to line a chair—?"

"The young lady is your new Zarn," Tsana said icily. "I prefer to stand."

Burkitt shrugged slightly. "As you wish. Captain Calhoun, I must tell you that I do very much appreciate your returning the 'new Zarn' to us—"

Calhoun was about to speak, but the girl clearly showed

no reticence in speaking her own mind. "He has not 're-turned' me, Warmaster. I will not dwell here until you have safely been brought to justice."

"You fear your own people?" He made a slight, sad cluck-ing sound with his tongue and, as laughter arose from be-hind him, said, "A true pity that you would. That certainly does not sound like the stuff that Zarns are made of."

"Your view of Zarns is of no interest to me," said Tsana. "Only your being arrested and tried for your crimes is."

"My crimes," he echoed.

"Yes, Burkitt," said Calhoun. "Your crimes. The ones that she is calling you to account for."

"The ones you told her to say," retorted Burkitt. "Or the ones you planted in her fevered imagination. This is a truly pathetic ploy, Captain, and I do not appreciate it. I will not have my reputation stained——"

"Perhaps," Si Cwan spoke up, "the only stains you care about are the stains of blood on your hands."

Burkitt rose, body trembling in righteous indignation. "How *dare* you . . . I do not have to take accusations from a deposed Thallonian and a Starfleet captain who would toy with the memories of a helpless girl!"

"Sit down," warned Calhoun.

"Or what?"

He chucked a thumb behind him. "Or I'll have Mr. Ke-bron here break you in half."

"For fun," Kebron added.

Burkitt assessed the situation a moment, and then slowly sat, never taking his gaze off Calhoun. "Is that how you get your way, Captain? Threats? Intimidation?"

"Yes. Bribery, on occasion," Calhoun said helpfully. "In this instance, I was hoping the simple truth would do the job." He turned and addressed the Counselars as if Burkitt were not in the room. "No one is endeavoring to diminish the crime that the Markanians committed against you. But enemies within can be even more destructive than enemies without. Before anything else happens, Burkitt must admit his culpability and his brutal murder of Tsana's older brothers. She witnessed it herself."

"Any testimony she might offer is tainted!" Burkitt said loudly. "It is not reliable! My fellow Counselars . . . there is not enough evidence here even to proceed to some sort of trial. Commander Gragg—"

Gragg stepped forward. "Yes, Warmaster."

"I was alone with young Tsana, was I not? I have had opportunities to eliminate her, have I not?"

"Yes, Warmaster."

"And one would think," he continued, the smug expression on his face becoming more insufferable by the minute, "that if I were concerned about being implicated in murder, I would most likely have disposed of her."

Calhoun was watching Gragg very carefully, and couldn't help but feel as if wheels were turning within the commander's head. As if things he hadn't seen before, assumptions or conclusions he hadn't dared make, were suddenly becoming clearer. However, Gragg's words didn't match up with what Calhoun believed was going through the commander's heart. "Yes, Warmaster," he said, sounding very stiff and formal. "I myself bore witness to the fact that she was helpless before you, and you were alone with her after my departure. She could not have offered testimony against you, were she dead."

"And yet . . . here she stands!" said Burkitt, as if concluding a magic trick before an appreciative audience. "Here she stands, hale and whole."

It was Kalinda's very quiet, but very firm voice that spoke up. "Tell me, Warmaster . . . how would you have known she posed a threat, since you did not know that she was hiding under the bed and saw your murderous actions?" Si Cwan nodded approvingly.

Burkitt's smile diminished ever so slightly. "I would have

desired to play it safe . . . had I anything to hide. I did not. Furthermore, if my goal was to seize power for myself, the fact that she lived would have precluded that."

"And the fact that you could not kill her without having any Markanians to blame it on would have precluded you finishing the job," Calhoun pointed out.

"I will not even dignify that accusation with a defense." His eyes hard, he said, "And I hope, Captain, that you are able to live with the consequences of your actions."

"And what would those be?" Calhoun asked mildly.

He rose once more, pointing a trembling finger at Calhoun, saying, "You are forcing a governmental crisis! Tsana is the last of the imperial family. You are tainting her, turning her to *your* priorities, causing her to lash out against her own. If this continues . . . if this divide is not resolved, and soon . . . the Counselars will have no choice but to do away with the rule of the imperial family entirely!"

"You would not dare," Tsana said. "The imperials have ruled the Aeron for centuries."

"Things change, young one . . . my apologies . . . *Zarn,*" but he said it with such sarcasm that there wasn't the slightest hint of respect in his tone. "If you have been turned against us, then your mind is addled. You are not fit to rule us. Another shall have to."

"Another being you," said Si Cwan.

He inclined his head slightly. "I would not presume to predict. That will be up to my fellow Aerons. You, Thallonian, are not one of my fellows. Instead, you represent the race that has brought us to this difficulty."

"Oh, did we?" asked Si Cwan, sounding more amused than anything else.

"Yes! Had you not taken it upon yourself to separate us from the Markanians, to deprive us of our beloved Sinqay and the Holy Site, none of this would have happened. We are the stronger race; we would have eliminated them in time. And then, as promised, the Holy Site would have been ours." There were grunts of agreement from behind him. "But we will not be deterred in our quest. We will triumph over the—"

"Oh. Right. The Holy Site," said Calhoun, almost as if being reminded of an afterthought. "I'm planning to destroy it."

There was dead silence in the Counselar chamber. Burkitt's mouth moved with no sound emerging for some moments before he finally managed to get out, *"What?"* in a hoarse whisper.

"I won't have any trouble finding it; Si Cwan can bring me right to it," and he nodded toward Si Cwan, who bowed slightly in a rather mocking manner. "I haven't quite determined how," Calhoun told them. He continued to sound very casual about it, as if discussing the best way to gut a fish after catching it. "We could just scourge the entire surface with phaser fire. It would take a while, heaven knows, but it could be done. Basically make the entire surface uninhabitable." He was pleased to see that the smug expression was now entirely gone, to be replaced by something akin to mounting panic. Not easing up, he continued, "Then again, if I wanted to go the expeditious route, I could simply plant some matter/antimatter in the planet's core, bring them together, and just blow the place up."

"But . . . but the Prime Directive—!"

"Applies only to civilized worlds. Sinqay, so far as we know, is devoid of life. I mean, all right, there may be some cuddly, fuzzy animals living there, but unfortunately for them, cuddly fuzzy animals have almost no voice in the UFP, so I doubt there'll be much protest raised. There's nothing to stop me from going around and blowing up all the uninhabited worlds I want." In point of fact, there was, but he hardly saw the need to mention that.

And that brought all of them to their feet, all the Counselars shouting at once. And loudest of all was Burkitt, bellowing, *"It is our Holy Site! Our promised world! How dare you—!"*

"How dare I?" Calhoun's voice easily carried above theirs; he was someone who'd developed the lung power to address armies while still in his teens. Shouting above nine men was no challenge at all. *"How dare I?"* he declared again. "How dare *you?* How dare you put so little value on life, that thousands upon thousands die in pointless warfare, all because you care more about a piece of territory than you do about the lives of your own people? More die, and more, and more, and it doesn't stop! It never stops!" Inwardly, Calhoun was telling himself that he should be more restrained, that he shouldn't do anything that might come across as losing control. But he was simply too angry, too fed up to tolerate any more of the tripe that he was hearing. "The bickering, the warfare, and children die, and men and women die, all because you're more concerned about words written by people long dead than you are about the rights of your people to live long and happy lives!" His voice harsh and condemning, he swept the room with his arm as he demanded, "How dare you stand there and defend your rights to be brutal to each other? You're like children! Children pointing at each other and crying, 'He hit me first! He was mean to me! He took my toy!' Well if that is how you are going to behave, Burkitt, then that is how you are going to be treated. You will be treated as if you were children. The toy you cannot agree to share with your brothers and sisters will be taken away from you, for good. Perhaps in doing that, you will finally shift your focus away from pointless bickering and instead put your energy towards such esoteric considerations as compassion, and loving your fellow man."

Burkitt looked ill, but he rallied himself as best he could. "We are not children, no matter how much you would paint us as such, nor are you our parents. This attitude of yours bespeaks monstrous arrogance. *Monstrous.* You are in no position to judge us."

"Perhaps. Perhaps not. But I am in a position to carry out my own judgment. And you, Burkitt, and all of you, will have to live with this. Unless, of course, you choose to open up peace talks with the Markanians. That is the only course you can take that will prevent me from doing as I have said I will."

Turning his attention to Tsana, Burkitt said coldly, "And do you endorse this action of your newfound allies, oh mighty *Zarn?* Even you, a child, know what the tradition of Sinqay means to us. Do you endorse this action on their part, and in so doing, close the door—now and forever—on whatever claim you may have to leading us?"

If Burkitt had been intending to intimidate Tsana, he was totally unsuccessful. "A planet whose surface wasn't walked on by my father, or his father, or his father before him, is of far less interest to me than the cancer in the soul of our people that you represent, Warmaster. I care about justice."

"And justice demands the Markanians pay for their crimes!"

"As they will. But you will pay first for yours. Even engaging in peace talks, we will still demand those responsible for the death of my family be called to account for their actions. But our own hands must be clean, Warmaster, and yours are covered with the blood of my kin. Until such time as you admit to your misdeeds, and that you Counselars," and she addressed the entirety of the room, "agree to open peace talks with the Markanians, we have nothing more to talk about."

Burkitt turned back to Calhoun. "So is this your strategy, Calhoun? Try to bring pressure to bear upon me? Hope that I will confess to a crime I did not commit, in exchange for saving our Holy Site? Well, it will not happen! I will not bow! I will not yield! Take the child and be damned!" He stabbed a finger at Calhoun. "And know this: You will be declared an enemy to all Aerons, and we have a long memory. Sooner or later, you will be made to pay for the actions and threats you have made here today."

"As will you," Kalinda said.

Apparently he had almost forgotten she was there. "I have nothing to pay for."

Kalinda approached him with slow, measured tread. It seemed as if her eyes were drilling through him. "So you say," she said.

"So I know," he retorted.

"Yes, you know. You know the truth." Her voice lowered, and in that unearthly calmness was even greater menace. "And the dead know it as well. And they are angry with you, Burkitt, most angry indeed."

"I see. And you know this . . . how?"

"Because they speak to me, Burkitt," she said, as if it was the most natural thing in the world. "They speak to me . . . and I have told them to speak to you. And they will. You have my utmost assurances on that. They will speak to you . . . and cry to you . . . and howl to you . . . until the only way to assuage your conscience is to confess your sins. Then, and only then, will they leave you in peace. But I warn you, Burkitt, do not delay overlong. Because if you do, it may reach a point where even your confession does not assuage, and they will be with you, always . . . always . . ."

"This is nonsense!" snarled Burkitt. "The lot of you, with your threats and predictions . . . and your betrayal!" That last was directed at Tsana. "Get out. All of you! This audience is over! We are done with one another."

"You may be done with us," Calhoun replied, as calm and collected as Burkitt was agitated. "However, I assure you, Burkitt . . . we are not remotely done with you." He tapped his combadge. "Calhoun to *Excalibur.* Five to beam up."

Moments later, they shimmered out of existence, to rematerialize aboard the starship. Calhoun immediately turned his full attention to Tsana, going to one knee so he could look her in the eyes. "Are you all right, Zarn?" he asked.

She looked at him with a world of pain in her eyes. "My

family is dead and my people think me a traitor. How could I possibly be all right?"

For that, Calhoun had no answer.

It was evening, and Burkitt still had not managed to calm his fury. He had a bottle of half-consumed liquor before him, and offered it to Commander Gragg, who politely declined. For what seemed the hundredth time, Burkitt muttered, "The audacity! You saw it all, Gragg. You heard! They accused me . . ."

"Not just 'they,' Warmaster. She. She did."

"A dupe. A mind-controlled dupe."

Gragg, standing stiffly, his hands behind his back, had heard Burkitt say that so many times. Perhaps it was the sheer repetition, or the lateness of the hour, or a growing unease . . . whatever the cause, Gragg opined, "She did not appear mind-controlled to me."

Through the haze of the alcohol in his brain, it took a moment or two for that observation to penetrate. Burkitt slowly turned his full attention to Gragg. "What . . . are you saying?"

"I am simply saying . . . how she appeared to me, Warmaster."

He rose unsteadily. "Are you telling me you *believe* her? That you think I would have—?"

"I do not know what to think or believe, Warmaster," Gragg said, all in a rush. "You made such a point of showing me how you were not going to harm the girl while she lay in her coma. . . ."

"Yes! What guilty man would have done such a thing, spoken so freely—?"

"On the other hand, Warmaster, it could be argued that who but a man who felt a lack of innocence would feel the need for such a display?"

His mouth twisting in fury, Burkitt snarled, "You . . . sidestepping, double-talking coward! You dance around without committing yourself! Do you trust me, or do you not? Answer!"

"These are dangerous times, Warmaster," said Gragg cautiously. "Trusting no one would seem to be the wisest course."

Each word thick, Burkitt said, "Get out. Get out of here before I kill you with my bare hands. And pray that I am sufficiently with drink that by the morning I will have forgotten this entire exchange."

Gragg bowed stiffly at the waist, turned, and exited.

Burkitt continued to drink and talk for another hour. The conversation wasn't really all that different than when Gragg had been in the room; now, though, there was no pretense that he was addressing anyone else. Finally, the drink overwhelming him, he slumped forward at his desk and fell into a deep sleep.

He remained that way for less than an hour.

And then he woke up screaming.

17

MARKANIA

SMYT HAD BEEN PLANNING to surprise Ebozay when he returned to his private quarters. She lay draped across the bed
in a fairly scandalous outfit, the type designed to make sure
that he didn't think about such things as her motivations or
where she'd come from or Gateways at all. *They are so easy
to manipulate,* she had thought with some degree of satisfaction.

But when Ebozay had entered, she had immediately been
able to tell that something was wrong . . . something was
very, very wrong, in fact. He was barely looking at her; indeed, he was looking through her. "Ebozay?" She said his
name tentatively.

He sat on the edge of the bed, but didn't appear to be registering her presence. "Ebozay," she repeated, this time more
intently. "What's happened?"

"The meeting . . ."

"Yes, yes. You had a meeting with Shelby and her people.

I know that. Why do you look so concerned? What could she possibly have said that—?"

He looked at her, haunted. "Captain Calhoun has lost his mind."

"What? Calhoun? But he's the captain of another vessel, isn't he?"

"Yes. The *Excalibur.* But . . . but he has . . ."

"But he has what?" Smyt did not always have a great deal of patience when dealing with less-than-sophisticated beings, and she was having no more patience now than usual. "Did you meet with him instead of Shelby?"

"No, we met with Shelby. But . . . she related the details of a meeting Calhoun had on Aeron . . . things he said to them . . ."

She felt relieved. "Who cares what the captain of another ship said to your enemies? It cannot possibly have any relevance to—"

"He's going to destroy Sinqay."

Smyt blinked in confusion, not quite able to grasp what he was saying. "Destroy . . . Sinqay? What are you talking about?"

"Shelby . . . Shelby said that he'd always been a bit unstable . . . but—"

"Then she's lying to you," Smyt said flatly. "Starfleet would never put an unstable individual in charge of—"

"She said he didn't start out that way," and he turned, his gaze seeking hers, searching for some commiseration in his agitated state, "but became more and more out of control since she ceased being his first officer. He now seems to feel that he can do anything. And he said he was ready to destroy Sinqay because the Aerons and we cannot share it."

"Sounds to me as if he's treating you like children."

"That appears to be his goal, yes."

"Well, you just won't tolerate it, that's all. You just won't—"

He grabbed her hand so forcefully that he might have broken it had he gripped it any tighter. *"We cannot stop him!* How can you not see that? We cannot stop this madman! The only one who possibly can is Shelby, and she is reluctant to go up against him. She says she doesn't agree with his actions, but she doesn't want to challenge his autonomy. I think she's a bit afraid of him."

"Please . . . Ebozay . . . you're hurting my hand," she said through gritted teeth.

Without even thinking about it, he released her. "How can this be happening? How can this be spiralling out of control? Shelby said . . ."

"What did she say?"

He looked at her with vast concern in his eyes. "Well . . . she said that she would be on our side, and that she would be willing to represent our interest in a peace process. That we would have to make concessions, and even give over those who killed the imperial family . . . but if we did that, she could—"

Smyt began to laugh.

Racked with tension, Ebozay saw nothing worth laughing over. "What is so funny?" he demanded.

"Don't you see?" She shook her head in obvious sorrow. "She is attempting to play the two of you against each other. You and the Aerons. She and Calhoun must be working together, conspiring. She is not the least bit afraid of him. She is painting him as some sort of a wild man, uncontrollable, to be feared by all. She figures that you and the Aerons will see Calhoun as a common foe, and will want to unite against him in fear. Then she, the moderating influence, attempts to broker a peace settlement between you and your enemies. It could not be more obvious."

"We do not know that for certain."

"Yes, we do, if you would not let yourself be intimidated—"

"I am not intimidated!" he said heatedly.

"Yes, you are." She leaned back on the bed and sighed in

a most disappointed fashion. "I thought more of you than this, Ebozay. All your talk, all your boasting. And you did perfectly well when your opponents were three tired, frightened pacifists who were willing to cede power to you rather than cause a fuss. But now you're faced with the first true challenge to your leadership—"

"This is more than a challenge. Don't you understand that?" he said urgently.

"I understand that the stink of fear is rolling off y—"

And then she let out a yelp as Ebozay's hand lashed out. He snagged the hair on the back of her head and yanked, snapping her skull back. *"This isn't about fear,"* he snarled right in her face as she gasped. "This is about Sinqay! This is about an unpredictable Starfleet officer embroiled in an incendiary situation! You may very well be right in everything you say! *But I can't afford to be wrong! Because if I am, I will go down in history as the person who lost Sinqay for all time!"*

She did not appear the least bit sympathetic to his distress. Her breath coming in short gasps, she managed to give a snicker of contempt. "So brave . . . so brave against pacifists . . . and women . . . have you forgotten what I did to you before? What I can do to you again? Release me, Ebozay . . . or you shall pay for it dearly."

With a disgusted grunt he let go of her. She turned her head this way and that, relaxing the neck muscles, and then smoothing her hair back into place. "That was very impetuous, and very foolish of you."

"Traits I can ill afford when discussing the fate of Sinqay."

"And you have no wish to go down in your history as the one who lost you your precious Sinqay."

He stared at her as if she were daft. "Of course not! Why would I possibly want to be remembered in such a way?"

"Because at least you *will* be remembered. Better to be a spectacular failure than a merely modest success."

Ebozay shook his head, obviously stunned. "That you

could believe such things . . . that you could have such little regard for—"

She took one of his hands in both of hers. "They're bluffing. I assure you."

"My comrades are not so well-assured," Ebozay said woefully. "They share my doubts. Even if you sway me to your way of thinking . . . they will not go so easily. You did not see Captain Shelby. She looked fearful, truly fearful, of what is to come. Perhaps it was great acting. Perhaps not."

"You have to decide," she told him firmly. "You have to decide whether or not you're going to let yourself be bullied in this situation . . . and then act accordingly. I cannot do that for you. All I can help you do is obtain the revenge you so greatly desire."

"What point in defeating the Aerons . . . if that which spurred our enmity all these years is gone for good?"

"You'll find another enmity," she said. "I have confidence in you."

The amusement in her eyes, the tone in her voice, was too much for him. He pushed away from her, stood, and drew himself to his full height, squaring his shoulders very proudly and a touch melodramatically.

"This," he said archly, "is obviously something you're never going to understand." With that acid comment, he pivoted and stalked out of the room.

Smyt flopped back onto the bed, draping her arm across her face. "Lords of Chaos, Lords of Light, save me from amateurs who speak a good game but have absolutely no idea what they're on about."

18

EXCALIBUR

As Dr. SELAR HEADED OVER toward the exam table where Tsana was lying, she slowed and blinked in disbelief. Standing next to Tsana, once again, was Moke. This time, of course, she was not insensate as she had been before. Indeed, the discussion they were having seemed rather animated. That, however, did not deter the Vulcan doctor from approaching them and—in her most professional mien and sternest manner—saying, "I do not recall giving you permission to come down here, Moke."

"I thought anyone could come to sickbay," he said a bit defensively.

Selar had had it. She was far too logical to do something as illogical as losing her temper, but nevertheless she pointed one arm stiffly and said, "Wait in my office for me, if you please."

She expected the boy to protest. Instead he shrugged slightly, nodded to Tsana as if wishing her a good day, and walked quietly over to Selar's office. Even from where she was standing, she could see him sit carefully on the chair. No slumping, as with other children. And he kept his hands folded neatly on his lap.

"What was he saying to you?" she asked Tsana.

"We were just talking, about families," she said. She wasn't looking Selar in the eyes. Since Selar was unaware of any Aeron custom that would have precluded a speaker making eye contact, she had to conclude that Tsana was endeavoring to conceal something.

"Families," echoed Selar, and then waited for Tsana to continue.

"He said that his mother was dead, and he never knew his father, although he has an adoptive one now. My mother's dead, too, and I knew my father, but not as well as I would have liked to."

"Few of us do," Selar said, and then felt a momentary surprise at herself that she would say such a thing. She shook it off and then asked, "Anything else?"

"Nothing much. Am I done here, Doctor?"

She glanced at the medscan one more time and then nodded curtly. "Yes, you are done here. Thank you for returning to sickbay so that I could monitor your progress. There seem to be no indications of . . . problems."

"What sort of problems?"

"Any sort of brain pattern disruptions." She hesitated and then, deciding honesty would be preferable, she said, "The . . . technique I used to bring you to wakefulness . . . and the fact that another of my kind aided me in the endeavor . . . that can be a strain on the untrained mind."

"Oh," she said, looking thoughtful.

"But there is no need for concern. You do not seem to have been done any lasting damage."

"I appreciate that." Then, to the Vulcan's surprise, not to mention her stony disapproval, Tsana reached over and threw her arms around Selar in an aggressive, almost needy hug. "Thank you," she whispered.

"You . . . are welcome," she said. "Now that is . . . quite enough." Gently she disengaged the girl. "You may return to the temporary quarters assigned you by the captain. I can assign an escort to guide you if—"

"No, I can get there. It's just down the hall." She hopped down off the examining table. "Thanks again."

"You are welcome. Again."

She watched Tsana bound out of sickbay, and then became aware that various medtechs were looking at her. They were smiling. It bothered the hell out of Selar, because she didn't want her people to think for a moment that she was endorsing unprofessional behavior or maudlin bedside manner. So she gave them a look of cold dismissal, and they all immediately found something better to do. Satisfied, Selar went to her office, where Moke was waiting for her. She walked around the desk, sat, and scrutinized him. "Your continued presence here in sickbay is simply unacceptable. If you are not ill, you cannot be here."

"You're here," he pointed out.

"I work here."

"Can I work here?"

"No. Moke . . . I do not understand this desire of yours to be in my presence."

He shrugged. "I like you."

"Why?"

"Because you're a mom. You have a son, and he's strange, and so I thought—"

"Wait, wait," and she put up a hand. "I have a son . . . and he is 'strange'?"

"Yes."

"Who has said that?"

"People."

"What people?"

"People who were talking about him." Before Selar could tell him that this was not a tremendously useful answer, he continued, "They say he grows fast, and he's not like any Vulcan they ever saw, and how difficult it must be to be a parent of a strange child like that. So I was hoping—"

"Xyon is not a 'strange child,'" Selar told him, surprised and annoyed at the vehemence of her own voice. "He is . . . he is . . ." Disliking her tone, as it seemed to border on being flustered, she reined herself in and superimposed, once more, her customary detached demeanor. "He is . . . none of your business, in point of fact. Yes. That is correct. His nature is none of your business, and you would be well-advised to remember that. And you were hoping what? What were you hoping?"

He looked down.

"Moke? What were you hoping?" The question was not asked gently.

He took a deep breath and then let it out unsteadily. "That you could be like a mom to me."

Selar's breath caught a moment, but she composed herself before allowing any of her momentary confusion to show. "What?"

He raised his gaze to look into her eyes. "Don't get me wrong, Mac is great . . . and I know that nothing can replace my mom, because she was the best, and I'd never forget her, or anything like that, but I . . . well . . . you see . . ." Then the words came out all in a rush, as if jockeying for position. "It's just that the people in the town where I lived thought I was strange, and it couldn't have been easy for my mom raising me, and she was able to handle people, and she never stopped loving me, and I know you don't know me and I don't know you, but you've got a strange kid, except he's not strange like me because I kind of blew some people away in the town, but they were bad people and deserved it because they hurt my mom, so I hurt them, and I'm not sorry about that, I don't think, and anyway she loved me even though I was all of that stuff, weird stuff, so I thought maybe you could love me a little, too, not a lot, not like she did, but just a little so I could remember what it was like and stuff . . ."

He didn't so much stop as run out of momentum, and once he had, Selar just stared at him for a time and tried to figure out what to say. "I see," was all she was able to come up with.

"It's just . . . you remind me of her . . . a little."

Selar felt as if she were running just to keep up. "Your mother had pointed ears?"

"No, but she could get all firm and stuff . . . and when she did, her voice sounded like yours. And I . . . well . . . they say that when someone's dead for a while, you forget what they sound like. Forget their voice. And I don't want to forget her voice. So . . . so that's why. Please don't be mad."

Finally something she could address. "I am . . . not mad, Moke. I am . . ." She didn't want to say 'surprised.' That would not be appropriate. Drawing herself up, she managed to say, "You have given me . . . much to contemplate. I thank you for your candor."

He frowned. "I didn't give you a 'candor.' "

"For your honesty. Candor means honesty."

"Oh. Okay. Mom said honesty was one of the most important things in the world. That if people couldn't believe what everybody was saying to everybody, how could anybody ever get along?"

"Your mother was very wise."

"I know. You are, too."

There was a long silence, and then Selar said softly, "You may leave now, Moke."

He paused, as if afraid to voice the question. "Can I come down here sometimes?"

"I will . . . discuss the matter with your . . . with Captain Calhoun."

"All right. Thanks," he said.

Selar was quiet for a long time after Moke left, her hands

steepled in front of her. When Dr. Lili Scasino stuck her head in a few minutes later, Selar had not moved. "Doctor . . ." she said cautiously.

Selar looked up at her. "My child is not 'strange.' "

Scasino blinked, then said, "Wait'll he's a teenager. And you can take that from personal experience."

Selar shook her head and said, "My pardon. My mind was . . . elsewhere. What do you need?"

"Uhm, Captain Calhoun just called down, wanted to know the results of your exam of Tsana."

"Tell him she shows no signs of—no. On second thought, I shall speak to him. There are . . . a number of things we need to discuss."

19

AERON

BECAUSE THERE WERE so many people at the Great Rally . . . a thousand or so, crushed into the courtyard outside the Counselars' Hall . . . there were naturally many different accounts of why exactly the rally went wrong, and what was the true meaning behind Burkitt's mental breakdown, and blame was ascribed to everyone and everything. Furthermore, as word of it spread, so many more people claimed to have been there to witness it firsthand that, had they been, the courtyard would have been filled twenty times over. . . .

Gragg bolted down the hall, positive from the screams he was hearing that the Markanians were once again attacking. Perhaps they had somehow discovered that they had missed one of the imperials and—falsely believing Tsana was still in the mansion—were instigating another assault. As he drew nearer, he came to the realization that the screams were coming from the quarters of the warmaster. That, of course,

236

would make perfect sense: Where else would the bastards strike but at one of the most powerful of the planet's leaders? Obviously, though, the warmaster was putting up one incredible fight, for the shrieks could only be torn from the throats of the cowardly Markanians, as they discovered their intended victim was not going down quietly.

The blood was pounding in Gragg's temples as he thought of the possibility of having another shot at the Markanian bastards. Perhaps . . . oh, gods, how wonderful would it be . . . perhaps he would be able to get his hands on the ones who had taken Jylla from him. He had been among the first to find her beautiful body splattered on the courtyard, and it had been everything he could do to suppress the howl of vengeance that sought to escape him. The sight of it haunted him still, and the joy that filled him with the thought of exorcising some of those ghosts through the blood of his enemies was almost more than he could bear.

Other troopers were converging from the opposite direction as Gragg arrived at Burkitt's quarters. The door was locked from the inside. Gragg didn't hesitate, blasting it open and charging in. He didn't just run; he leaped with a shoulder roll, making himself a moving target so that any resistance he encountered from within would have that much more trouble pinning him down.

He needn't have concerned himself. He came up, weapon extended, while the other troopers pushed in at the doorway, only to see that the room was empty save for himself and Burkitt. Burkitt was upright in his bed, eyes wide, arms flailing about as if swinging at phantoms that only he could see, and those remarkably womanish howls that Gragg had heard were being torn from none other than the throat of the warmaster.

"Get away! Get away from me!" His eyes were fixed at some point within his own mind, and he swung desperately, futilely at nothing. *"Get away, I told you! Get away! Stop looking at me like that! Stop! Stop—!"*

"Warmaster!" shouted Gragg, grabbing him by the shoulders and shaking him violently. Burkitt didn't respond at first, struggling in Gragg's grasp. Ordinarily Gragg wouldn't have stood a chance in combat with him, but Burkitt was hardly at his best as he writhed and struggled. Impatience growing, and feeling a certain degree of humiliation on the warmaster's behalf, Gragg decided that immediate action was needed. He drew back a hand and cracked it across Burkitt's face. He didn't really have to do it with much more force than was required to jolt him from his fear-filled slumber, but Gragg used a bit more strength than was needed. Consequently, he hit Burkitt so hard with his backhanded swing that he knocked the warmaster right out of his bed. Burkitt hit the floor, bedclothes tangled around him. He sat up, still thrashing, looking everywhere at once, and finally managed to focus on Gragg. His chest was heaving violently, as if the air in his lungs was threatening to explode.

"Wh—what . . . ?" he managed to stammer out. "Where are the—?"

"The what, Warmaster?" said Gragg. Part of him, the morbidly curious part, wondered whether Burkitt was about to say something incriminating.

But as if he'd read Gragg's mind—even in the throes of the dream that had so obviously terrorized him—Burkitt promptly pulled himself together. He looked around, apparently rather chagrined when he saw the puzzled guards standing in the doorway. "Nothing," he said. "It was nothing. An ill omen, that is all."

This caused a mild buzz among the troopers, for omens were serious business to the Aerons, and not to be taken lightly. Gragg has his own suspicions as to just how legitimate these "omens" were, but he was willing to take Burkitt at his word . . . at least for the moment. "What sort of ill omens, Warmaster?" he asked with great concern, and there were anxious looks from the others as well.

Burkitt studied them thoughtfully for a moment, and it was hard for Gragg to tell what precisely was going through Burkitt's mind. He might have been endeavoring to find a way to summarize what he was thinking. Or he might have been mentally scrambling to try and fabricate something. It was impossible to know for sure. Finally, though, Burkitt pulled himself up to the edge of the bed, draping the bed-clothes around him in a manner that looked vaguely imperial. "I saw the Markanians," he said grimly. "They were flooding over us, like ravenous insects. While we have been proceeding with caution because of the starship overhead . . . while we have been struggling to determine who truly guides our destiny because of the confusions and calumnies provided by the child Zarn, Tsana . . . I have foreseen the Markanians facing no such tribulations. They are directed and they are focused, and their focus is upon us. We must attack."

"Attack?" said Gragg with obvious concern. "Warmaster, to the best of our knowledge, the other starship—the *Trident*—remains in orbit around the Markanian world. If we launch an attack, there is nothing to stop them from thwarting our assault this time, just as they did the last time. Furthermore, if we utilize the Gateway, the *Excalibur* will likely be able to locate it."

"I have a plan, Gragg. That, too, has come to me." He now rose, the bedclothes still wrapped around him, and he gestured angrily to the other troopers that they should depart. They did so, and the moment the door shut behind them, Burkitt turned to face Gragg. "I know you have suspicions, Gragg. I do not blame you for this; the Starfleet men have cleverly managed to plant the seeds of doubt. And once those seeds have taken root, they are extremely difficult to pull out. But I," and he clapped him on the shoulder, "I still trust you, Gragg. I trust you to keep my plan secret until the time is right to strike."

"And . . . what would this plan be, Warmaster?" asked Gragg, intrigued in spite of himself.

Gragg laughed low in his throat. "We are not going to use the Gateway to invade the Markanians."

"We're . . . we're not?"

"No, Gragg. We are going to use it . . . to invade the *Excalibur*."

Smyt gaped at Burkitt. "You're insane," he said.

After explaining his plan to Gragg, and being rewarded with growing excitement bordering on hero worship by the young commander, Burkitt had sent Gragg to summon Smyt to him. The Iconian, however, did not look the least bit worshipful. He looked dumbfounded.

"You're insane," he said again. "You *cannot* be serious."

"Oh, I am very serious," said Burkitt. He was now fully dressed, even though the sun would not rise for some hours. He was too excited by the notion to go back to sleep anyway, pacing his quarters because standing still was simply not an option. "The plan is perfect."

"The plan is madness!"

"It is foolproof."

"And you're just the fool to prove it!"

Burkitt chuckled slightly. "A worthy jest. See? I can laugh at those, even when they are at my expense, so long as they are truly funny." His face darkened, and he added significantly, "And infrequent." He gestured, not for the first time, for Smyt to sit and make himself comfortable, but Smyt remained rigidly standing.

Nevertheless, Smyt, sensing Burkitt's mood, bit back an angry reply. Instead he shrouded himself in a cloak of calm and said, oozing patience, "With all respect, Burkitt, I don't think you've thought this through. I mean, if I am understanding you correctly, you want to use the Gateway to send your troops into the *Excalibur*."

"Yes."

"And you will take over the *Excalibur*."

"That is correct."

"Then you will transform the *Excalibur* into, essentially, a troop transport ship, sending your army through space to Markania where—if the *Trident* is still there—you will destroy her, and then rain down destruction upon the Markanians."

"You see?" said Burkitt with undeniable cheer. "You understand the plan perfectly."

But Smyt was shaking his head, remaining immobile where he was as Burkitt continued to move around the room like a bird exploring a new environment. "Burkitt . . . there are things you do not seem to understand. The *Excalibur* is a sizable vessel. There will be resistance; they have their own security forces."

"Forces that will be caught utterly off guard," Burkitt said firmly. He finally stopped his endless movement and instead pointed triumphantly to Smyt, as if the Iconian had finally grasped the brilliance of his plan. "You will send us directly to their bridge, where their key operating systems are. Then you will send us into their armory, so we can lock down their weapons. Then you—"

Smyt gestured helplessly, as if trying to explain the concept of snow to someone who had spent their life in a desert. "You are asking for pinpoint precision with the Gateway! It is not designed to function in that manner! I simply do not know if I can do what you are asking."

"I have every confidence in you, Smyt. And do you know why?"

"No," said Smyt hollowly, "why?"

"Because you value your own skin above all others. And believe me . . . your skin is riding on your ability to perform the task I am setting for you."

Slowly Smyt took a step back, as if seeing Burkitt for the first time. "I do not respond well to threats, Warmaster," he said.

Burkitt laughed as if the very notion that he had been

threatening was preposterous. "Threats? *Threats?* My dear, dear Smyt . . ." he said heartily, "that was not intended to be a threat! No, no, not at all. Not a threat, not in the least little bit."

"Well, that is certainly good to—"

The sword hanging at Burkitt's side was suddenly pulled from the scabbard. For the most part it was intended to be ceremonial, but that didn't render the blade any less sharp, and that blade was now at Smyt's throat. The Iconian gasped as the metal touched just under his chin.

"Now this . . . *this* is a threat," Burkitt informed him, as if explaining the difference between land and sea to a child. "And a very nasty one at that."

Smyt licked his lips, stalling for time as he composed himself. "I was . . . unaware of the fervency of your desires in this matter," he said carefully.

"Now you know."

"Yes, yes, I do. Tell me, Burkitt, if it wouldn't be too much trouble . . ." He cleared his throat. "Let us say, just for argument's sake, that you accomplish your goal. That you seize the *Excalibur.* How do you intend to operate her? Fly her? The functions of a starship are far beyond anything that your people have ever handled. You don't even *have* vessels capable of traversing interstellar distances. How do you propose to cover this gap between the ship's ops and your abilities . . . or lack thereof?"

"Oh, that will be simple," said Burkitt. "We will find crewmembers who will do the jobs for us."

"And if they refuse, which they most certainly will . . . ?"

"I expect them to refuse, at first. But not all creatures are made from the same resolve of character . . . not even Starfleet officers. The higher-ranking officers will not comply, to be sure. So we will execute them, one by one, until we get down to crewmen who *will* do our bidding."

"That . . . might work," Smyt allowed. As he said this,

Burkitt smiled and lowered the sword, although Smyt couldn't help but notice that he didn't sheathe it. Still proceeding with utmost care, he said, "Then again . . . you might be underestimating them. It might not work."

"In that event," Burkitt shrugged, "we have a dead crew but a functioning ship in orbit. Our scientists can pore over it to their hearts' content, and our knowledge will jump ahead by decades. It would require an adjustment in our plan, but at least we'll have a starship for our troubles. You see, Smyt . . . it is a win/win scenario, really."

Smyt obviously wanted to rub his throat where the blade had touched, but he kept his hand at his side. "Tell me this, then: If you are so anxious to capture a starship, why not use the Gateway to take the *Trident* instead? That, after all, is in orbit around the Markanian world already."

"It is a valid point, and an option I strongly considered," said Burkitt, and his face darkened, his eyes glowering with barely suppressed rage. "But Calhoun humiliated me, Smyt. He dared to strike me. He dared to remove Tsana from my care. He has shown nothing but contempt for me, and part of what brought this plan into focus for me was the cheerful mental picture of cleaving Calhoun's neck from his shoulders. He shall not be among those given the opportunity to cooperate, Smyt." His voice rumbled like an oncoming thundercloud, and was just as ominous. "His swift execution will instead serve as an example to the others of what will happen to them if they should choose not to cooperate."

"You know," Smyt said appraisingly, "I'm beginning to think that you could pull it off."

"Yes. I can."

"Very well," said Smyt. "Let me work on it . . . determine the coordinates. It will not be the easiest matter in the world, because the *Excalibur* is, after all, a moving target since it's in orbit. Then again, any planet is in orbit. It's just a matter of making the adjustments."

"Can you be ready by tomorrow afternoon?"

"I believe I can, yes. Why?"

"Because," he said with great amusement, "I am going to take matters one step further. I will organize a rally. I will inform the good captain that I am doing so in order to allow the people to make their voices heard in the matter of the Zarn and her 'allegiances.' He will come down here—"

"He won't. He'll suspect a trap."

Burkitt smiled grimly. A brief haze, a tiredness, enfolded his brain for a moment, due no doubt to his sleepless night. He shook it off as he said, "I have the measure of him, Smyt. I know his type, for I have seen it every time I've gazed at my own reflection. We are very similar, truth to tell. Oh, he will come here . . . escorted, most likely. He'll have that manmountain with him, no doubt, and between that and his ability to return to his vessel at a moment's notice, he will think himself safe enough. And Tsana . . . she will want to come. She is like her father, that one, I can see it already. There was that cold fury in her eyes that so reminded me of the late Zarn. She will want to confront me, for my lies—as she perceives them—," he added quickly, "enrage her. She will want justice. A tragic thing to see, really, in one so young. And I will—"

He turned, just in time to see the late Zarn shambling out of the shadows. His face looked longer than it usually was, for his jaw was hanging lifelessly, swaying slightly from the rocking motion of his gait. His face was covered with blood, and his eyes had crystalized so that only two shining white orbs remained in the sockets.

Burkitt let out a scream like a damned soul and lunged backward, and it was only when he hit the ground that he was jolted awake. He looked around frantically, and when his eyes came to rest on Smyt, he saw the utter confusion and open incredulity in the Iconian's face.

"What . . . just happened?" demanded Burkitt, trying and failing to pull his shattered dignity together. He was lying flat on his back, his arms and legs splayed, and he didn't have the faintest idea how it had come to pass.

"I'm . . . not quite certain. You . . . were talking, and then your head nodded slightly and you fell asleep, but before I could awaken you, you . . . started screaming. Are you . . . quite all right?" asked Smyt, tentatively.

Burkitt looked to the shadows that obscured the farther reaches of the room. Nothing seemed to be lurking thereabouts, including the angry shade of the Zarn. He cleared his throat and straightened himself up. "I am . . . perfectly fine, yes. Do not be concerned about me. Worry instead about making certain that the Gateway is functioning correctly. Because when I give you the signal during the rally . . . you will open the path to the *Excalibur,* and our mission of vengeance will proceed."

Later, after the disaster, there would be many who would claim that they weren't the least bit surprised over what had happened. That the strain was obvious, that the guilt was so clear to anyone who bothered to look. In short, no one wanted to admit to the fact that they had been totally stunned by the events in the square outside the Counselars' Hall. Everyone wanted to be the first to say that they had seen it coming.

Amazingly, of course, all those pundits and diviners who had had such foresight to see the stunning conclusion of the rally never actually spoke to anyone else beforehand about it. There had been no vocalized predictions of what would come to be referred to simply as "the Breakdown." It happened with absolutely no one predicting it. One would have thought that would put the lie to those who maintained they saw it coming. But whenever those who were not pundits would point out this lapse, those who were pundits would simply shrug and say, "It would have been impolitic/impolite/unwise to voice such hazardous sentiments in advance of the actual occurrence. These are, after all, dangerous times."

Which they always are.

"This is a trap," cautioned Zak Kebron as he, Calhoun, Tsana, Si Cwan, and Kalinda materialized on the surface of Aeron.

It was not a pleasant day for a rally. Dark clouds had rolled in, and it felt as if rain was in the offing.

Privately, Calhoun shared Kebron's sentiments, but he didn't need the massive security guard saying it out loud . . . particularly within hearing of Tsana. When Tsana heard Kebron's dour assessment of the situation, her fierce determination wavered ever so slightly. No one else noticed it save for Calhoun, and he scowled at Kebron. Before he could say anything, though, he took note of the crowd.

Somehow the word "crowd" seemed inadequate to describe it. It was a solid mass of living beings, packed in so tightly that they could barely move. Their individual words were not discernible; instead the noise they were producing was virtually a solid wall of sound. Their volume had heightened when the hum of the transporter beams had deposited the starship's away team on the front stairs of the Counselars' Hall, and when they caught sight of Tsana, a roar went up that clearly intimidated the child. She shrank against the captain's leg, and it was all Calhoun could do not to pick her up, pat her on the back, and assure her that everything was going to be fine, just fine, and he would make all these awful people simply go away. He had to remind himself that this barely contained mob scene was *her* people.

Nor was Calhoun able to get any feeling for whether they were happy to see her or not. It seemed to him there were some cheers, but there were catcalls as well, and accusatory shouts dubbing her a traitor, or worse. He protectively hauled her within the Counselars' Hall, and for no reason that Calhoun could determine, no one from the crowd attempted to follow them in. "They're well-trained," he muttered, but no one heard him.

"This is a trap," Kebron said once more, as if he was proceding on the assumption that no one had heard him the first time. Calhoun was even more inclined to believe it now than he was before. That odd inner-warning signal, that eerie prickling on the back of his neck that so often tipped him off on an unconscious level as to some degree of jeopardy, was shouting to him now. But there was no point in trying to back out of it.

"That's enough, Lieutenant," he said, straightening his uniform jacket as if it needed it. "It is Tsana's feeling that it is not appropriate for her to hide aboard the *Excalibur.* I'm not about to gainsay her on that."

"It was not 'hiding,'" Kebron retorted. "It was safekeeping."

To Calhoun's surprise, it was Tsana who responded, interrupting before Calhoun could reply. "While the voice of my people cry out for leadership—and while those who were trusted retainers stand revealed as traitors, and yet walk around with impunity—I have no business being kept safe."

"Just what every security head likes to hear: 'I have no business being kept safe.'" It was one of Kebron's longer sentences, and a sure indicator of just how strongly he felt about the matter. To some degree, Calhoun was surprised by that. It was so hard to get a read off Kebron. He seemed to be someone who enjoyed doing his job well, but his rocky exterior gave his emotions even more concealment than the average Vulcan enjoyed. Usually, Kebron simply went about his duties with quiet and occasionally deadly efficiency. The identity of whomever he was guarding never seemed particularly relevant to him, be it old classmate Soleta, for whom Kebron presumably held nothing but affection, or Si Cwan, for whom Kebron was known to harbor almost palpable hostility. Kebron always displayed about as much passion as a rock.

But for this girl, Tsana, Kebron actually seemed emotionally involved. At least that was how it sounded to Calhoun. The words he had just spoken would normally be laced, at the most, with quiet sarcasm or a put-upon air. Kebron sounded genuinely worried, though, as if he was determined to do his job, and Tsana's attitude was concerning him because he might not be able to. If it were Si Cwan or Calhoun who had been insistent, Kebron would have made efforts to the best of his ability, but ultimately would have held himself blameless beyond that.

Not for a moment did Calhoun think there was any romantic interest from Kebron for the youngster. The notion was absurd. It did, however, present hints of a few chinks in Kebron's physical and emotional armor, and Calhoun found that to be considerable food for thought.

"I have every confidence in you, Mr. Kebron, to protect those in your charge," Calhoun said, giving no hint of everything that had just been passing through his mind. Kebron simply grunted in return, which were about all that Calhoun would have expected.

There were rapidly approaching footsteps, and for just a moment Calhoun's hand drifted toward his combadge, just in case it was a troop of soldiers with potential arrest in their eyes. But his inner warning system didn't appear to indicate immediate danger from those coming toward them, and when the originators of the noise turned the corner, Calhoun could see that it was simply the Counselars. They were interestingly positioned, moving in a sort of *V* formation, with Burkitt at the leading point of the *V.*

"Captain," Burkitt said briskly, with the air of someone who wanted to get down to business.

"Warmaster," replied Calhoun. "You requested our presence, and we have come. The crowd outside, however, is not what I would have liked to see."

"The crowd comes and goes as it will," said Burkitt with a bland expression, shrugging his shoulders as if it was of little consequence.

"Really?" spoke up Si Cwan. "Here I had the impression it went as *you* willed."

Burkitt wasn't looking at Si Cwan. He was instead gazing at Tsana, and there was something approaching suspicion in his eyes. "The people of Aeron know that I wish to address them, and they know that the girl who would be Zarn also wishes to address them. Now, of course, she could likely do so from the friendly confines of your vessel. . . ."

"Yes, she could," said Calhoun.

"But how would that look?" Burkitt sounded almost sympathetic to her "plight." "The Zarn of Aeron, hiding from her own people, while making accusations against one with a long history of service who is out in plain sight, for any to judge."

Tsana spoke up. "None can judge you," she informed him tightly, "because none but I know what you have done."

"Well, then," he said, never losing his air of insufferable calm, "it will be up to you to convince them of that." He took a step toward her as if he was about to drape a friendly arm around her, but she reflexively took a step back, bumping up against Calhoun. Calhoun's face darkened when he saw Burkitt smile at that, as if the Warmaster had won some initial skirmish. "One should never retreat in the face of someone who is perceived to be an enemy," he told her in a disappointed tone. "One might be perceived as weak."

Calhoun took a quick step forward, fist cocked, and as he'd hoped, Burkitt reflexively backpedaled. Realizing what he'd done, Burkitt stopped where he was, but it was too late, and Calhoun laughed just loud enough for Tsana to hear it. Realizing what Calhoun had done, Tsana broke into a smile that was quite a contrast to the abruptly sour look on

Burkitt's face. Burkitt quickly composed himself, and gestured toward the great front steps ahead of them. "After you, 'Zarn,' " he said. "I'm sure you're most anxious to present your case to your people."

Calhoun wanted to strangle the other Counselars. They kept silent almost as a unit, watching impassively. It was impossible to get any feeling from them as to what they believed to be the truth, although the fact that they had appeared to cede all authority to speak for them over to Burkitt was certainly not a good sign.

As if he were conducting a guided tour as they walked, Burkitt said conversationally, "The elevated stairs at the front of this building actually have quite a history, Captain. I don't know whether Tsana informed you of it, but that area has traditionally been known as Oratory Point. Some of the greatest speakers in our history have traditionally come to the front steps of the Counselars' Hall and addressed our people. Tsana certainly has a grand tradition to maintain. Tell me: Do you think you'll be up to the task?"

Before Calhoun could reply, surprisingly, it was Kalinda who spoke up. She was walking next to Burkitt, with such economy of movement, drawing so little attention to herself, that even the always-attentive Calhoun hadn't noticed her. Sounding disconcertingly friendly, Kalinda said, "Oh, I'm certain that—despite whatever difficulties may present themselves—all who are involved in this situation will perform according to their best abilities." As she spoke, her hand brushed against Burkitt's bare arm. He looked momentarily startled, although not only was Calhoun unable to say what jolted him, but obviously Burkitt appeared a bit unclear about it. He seemed to have trouble focusing on what was going on, but then the moment passed and he was himself again. Kalinda smiled up at him in a most fetching fashion. If the apparent friendliness toward Burkitt troubled

Kalinda's brother, Si Cwan, the enigmatic Thallonian gave no hint of it.

They stepped out to Oratory Point, the *Excalibur* group forming a protective semicircle around Tsana. Calhoun scanned the crowd, looking for hints of someone who might be ready to indulge in violence against Tsana. It seemed a hopeless task; faces were either scowling or unreadable, and because people were packed in, their hands were down so he couldn't see what they might be holding. He glanced over at Kebron and saw that the security officer was doing the exact same thing, his face its usual unreadable stone, so Calhoun couldn't tell whether Kebron was having any more luck than he was.

He's outmaneuvered you, Calhoun, he said to himself angrily. *You've put not only yourself but Tsana into a hazardous situation, but if anything goes wrong, it's going to be your fault. You let your ego, your overconfidence, bring you to this point . . . and sure as hell, Shelby wouldn't have let you.*

He'd had a conversation with Burgoyne about it. Burgoyne had at first seemed a bit nonplussed about the prospect, and expressed extreme hesitation about it. But later, surprisingly, Burgy had turned around on the subject and actually endorsed the notion. When he asked his first officer why s/he had reversed hirself, Burgoyne had simply shrugged and said, "I would not want you to think I didn't have confidence in your decision-making ability, Captain."

Calhoun sneaked a look at Tsana, who now appeared to be growing exceptionally nervous as she faced her people. The child had inner reserves of strength, he was sure of that . . . but she was still a child. He started to wonder if perhaps, just perhaps, he had been transferring over to her his own recollections of what he was capable of accomplishing as a youth. That he had just automatically assumed the girl was as capable of persuading a crowd at her age as Calhoun had been at his. And if he had underestimated her capability, he might well have made a cataclysmic mistake.

"Doubt" was not a familiar emotion for Calhoun. He couldn't say as he liked it all that much. And he was starting to wonder if perhaps he wouldn't have been better served if Burgoyne had had just the slightest bit of distrust in Calhoun's decision-making ability after all.

Burkitt looked solicitously down at Tsana and said, "Feel free to address your people, my dear Zarn. They wait eagerly for your every word. And then . . . I shall provide them my words . . . and we shall see what happens."

Smyt was feeling distinctly uncomfortable.

Overlooking the site of the rally, safely secured in a high building with an excellent view, Smyt was surrounded by Aeron soldiers who appeared to be regarding him with a combination of fear and suspicion, the latter doubtlessly giving birth to the former. Smyt, for his part, was busy making the final calculations and adjustments to the Gateway's controls, and wasn't especially thrilled with the sensation of dozens and dozens of eyes upon him.

Foremost among the watchers was an individual named Gragg, who Smyt well remembered from his first encounter with Burkitt. Gragg moved confidently among his men, apparently able to discern with a glance who appeared nervous or uncertain or just generally cranky. He would mutter a few words in their ears, pat them on the back, and they would laugh as if everything were utterly normal.

They were standing in what Smyt could only consider an auditorium, although Burkitt had referred to it as a troop-assembling center. He had spoken with great seriousness, bordering on pomposity, and Smyt misliked everything about the present situation. But he wasn't really in a position to do anything about it.

"What do you get out of it?"

He jumped, for he had not realized that Gragg was nearby, and Gragg's voice was almost in his ear. "I?" he asked.

"There's more to you than meets the eye," Gragg said softly, so softly that none of the others seemed to hear him. "I do not pretend to know what that might be. Nor is Burkitt willing to look beyond his own ambition to question it. But I am questioning it now. Would you care to share with me your . . . particulars?"

Well . . . it began with my becoming trapped here, in this dimension . . . and there was this Giant . . . and the Giant knew things, things no one should have known, and he told me to . . .

No. No, somehow he didn't see the point in spelling all of it out. Instead he simply said, "I believe in your cause, and that is sufficient for me. Have you never believed in anything, Commander?"

Gragg gave a soft grunt. "I used to," he said. "But things change. People change, until you wonder what it was you ever believed in in the first place."

"How much longer, Commander?" one of the soldiers asked. There had to be at least a hundred of them, by Smyt's count, all of them armed and armored, all of them fingering their pulsers as if they were lovers.

Voices were floating toward them from Oratory Point, even at the height of their present location. It was Tsana, speaking in a loud, clear tone that carried hints of the breeding and privilege to which she'd been raised and accustomed. Speaking of her family, speaking of what they had meant to her personally, and to her people in general.

"She speaks well," Smyt murmured.

"She has her sister's voice," said Gragg.

There was something in the way he said it that caught Smyt's attention. His brows knit as he said, "Her sister . . . were you and she—?"

Gragg snagged Smyt's face by his nonexistent chin,

snapped it around so that he was looking him dead in the eyes, and snapped at him, "Tsana's sister and I were separated by station, birth, and destinies, and you are not to ask such questions again. Do you understand?" Smyt managed something akin to a nod, and Gragg released his face. As suddenly as Gragg's temper had flared, it subsided, and as if no time had passed between the trooper posing the question and his answering it, Gragg turned to the one who had inquired as to how much longer and said, "We will move when the Warmaster gives the order. He will do so right from there, right from Oratory Point. The moment he does, Smyt will activate the Gateway, and our invasion of the *Excalibur* will commence."

He looked over his troops. "I see doubt in your faces," he said, sounding a bit disappointed. "That is unfortunate. It should not be there. The plan will work. In their own way, the denizens of the *Excalibur* are as arrogant as the Markanians. The crew of the starship will fall, and the Markanians will fall. Never doubt that. Never."

There were approving nods from all around, and then Gragg turned back to Smyt and said in that same low voice, "And if something goes wrong with this device, never doubt that you will not live to see another sunrise."

Smyt didn't doubt it at all.

". . . nor did I ask for this," Tsana said. With every word out of her mouth, there was more confidence, more poise, as if her greatest fear had been that she would not be able to get any words out at all. "You . . . you have had your leadership snatched from you. But I have not only lost my parents . . . my brothers, my sister . . . but I've also lost my childhood. I can't—" Her voice choked a moment, and Calhoun listened for the slightest hint of interruption, of derision, but there was none. The crowd seemed spellbound by the spectacle of the young girl rallying all her strength, mustering all her defenses so that she could accomplish the simple task of speaking to her people. "I can't pretend that I'm going to be able to return to pleasant childhood diversions of playing with toys. Of seeking out small spaces to hide, giggling to myself as my siblings play the game of trying to find me. I can't pretend I'm going to carry anything but sorrow with me for the rest of my life, but there's no use complaining to you about it, or making a public display of mourning. What is . . . is. It must be lived with."

And suddenly she was pointing at Burkitt with a trembling finger. "What will not be lived with is treachery. Before we address the question of the Markanians—before we consider whether we are to go to war—we must operate with those whom we can trust. And I tell you all, now . . . that Burkitt is a poison in our body."

That was when the voices started to shout out from the crowd, and Calhoun was ready to tell Kebron to do whatever was necessary to silence them, even if it meant stepping on a few select faces. But it wasn't necessary, for Tsana seemed to reach into depths that Calhoun couldn't have guessed she had, and her voice soared above the catcalls and the open expressions of disbelief. *"I saw him!"* she cried out. "As I lay hiding under a bed, the last bits of my childhood being washed away in a wave of blood, I saw him kill my two older brothers. They smiled when they saw him, confident that they were safe in his hands, and he took that confidence and crushed it. The Markanians have never pretended to be our friends, but he, Burkitt, would be your leader. He would discredit me, he would lie to you, he would lead you down a fiery path to total destruction if it suited his purposes. You must not believe that he is anything except the greatest threat that this world has ever faced! You must join me in demanding a full hearing, a full trial, a full redemption of—"

And then Calhoun saw that, apparently, Burkitt had had enough. He stepped forward, raising his arms and calling out, "All right, my little Zarn. That is sufficient rhetoric from you for one day."

Certain sections of the crowd started calling Burkitt's name, chanting it over and over. Calhoun had no doubt that they had been planted by the Warmaster, but that wasn't going to make any difference if their sentiments spread. Crowds could turn very, very quickly. Yet again he felt a chill, and was certain it was more than just the air giving it to him.

High above, watching, Gragg turned to Smyt and said, "Ready that contraption of yours. The order will be given very soon, I think."

"I mustn't activate it too early," Smyt reminded him. "The *Excalibur* will detect its energy buildup, and I've no way of preventing that. And if they detect it, it may warn them."

Gragg nodded slowly, clearly understanding, but he said firmly, "Do what needs to be done to be prepared. We do not want anything going wrong."

Burkitt had never felt so confident. It was as if there was an energy filling him, elevating him above all those who surrounded him. For the first time, he actually felt sorry for poor, pathetic Calhoun and his entourage. They would never know what had hit them.

"We must understand," Burkitt said, knowing beyond question that the crowd's will was in his hands, "that—"

Then he stopped.

Suddenly he could feel nothing in his face, and he knew why: It was because all the blood had drained out of it.

They were coming.

Not just one. Not just two. All of them.

Despite the crush of people facing him, they were moving through with no impediment whatsoever.

Burkitt looked around desperately, tried to see reactions from the others, tried to see if they were as horrified as he.

But there was nothing, just blank, even slightly puzzled expressions as they stared at him. He knew he must have looked a sight, with his mouth moving and no words emerging, and his skin was undoubtedly reflecting the absence of blood in his face.

It was still dark and overcast, but here there were no shadows, and here there were no dreams, nothing haunting him in his sleep, no guilty concerns clouding his slumbering brain. Here it was, out in the open, and clearly they approached him with no fear, no fear . . .

What did they have to fear, really? What more could be done to them, now that they were dead?

And they were most certainly dead, there was no doubt about that. Here came the Zarn, blood covering him, and next to him his wife, the beloved Zarna, dead eyes burrowing into him like maggots feasting upon a corpse. From another direction came their sons—the eldest, who would have followed his father, and the younger lads, the ones whose lives he had taken with his own hands. The daughter, the eldest daughter, she was approaching as well, her body looking hideous and broken, reflecting the fall she had taken. But his attention was pulled back to the boys he had slain. Horrifically, they had, frozen on their faces, that same trusting look that they had displayed upon seeing him, that same momentary expression of feeling secure in his presence. There, captured for all eternity, were those looks of benign faith that he, Burkitt, had betrayed. Looks that he had thought he had been able to wash from his mind in a sea of blood, but that were clearly now going to remain seared forever into his brain.

Their skin, their clothes, were burned and bubbling from where the energy weapons had struck them, and the elder daughter was working on keeping her innards from spilling out from the rents in her body that had resulted from the impact of her striking the ground. The Zarna's mouth was moving, blood trickling from it, and here came the boys, another step closer and yet another, and still those beatific smiles framed in heads that had gaping wounds and portions of their brain exposed, pink and pulsing.

It was a trick. It had to be a trick. They looked so solid, it couldn't be that they were mere phantasms. Pointing a trembling finger, he suddenly shouted, "You see them! You see them, don't you?" He whirled on Calhoun, knowing beyond question that he had to be behind it. "You put them up to this! These are . . . these are your crewmen, in some sort of vomitous guise! Admit it!"

Calhoun gaped at him. "What the hell are you talking about?" he demanded, and Burkitt could hear the confused mutterings from the crowd.

"*Admit it!*" screeched Burkitt, and he lunged at Calhoun. He didn't get within five paces, because Kebron's arm swept wide and knocked him back. Burkitt fell and a shocked cry went up from the crowd.

Burkitt scrambled to his feet, whirled, hoping against hope that the specters would be gone, but no, they were that much closer. Their hands were outstretched, pointing at him, and there were sounds in his head now. He could hear, as clearly as if he were back there again, their agonized dying screams mingling with the screeching of blaster fire, and their voices were low and mournful and terrifying to endure. He swung at them then, lunging at the Zarn, who was closest. His hands went right through, up to the elbow, and he didn't feel flesh or organs, but instead a cold that penetrated his skin, into his bones, into his soul. With a frightened yowl, he yanked clear his arms, and he couldn't feel anything from the elbow down. He could see his arms, but it was as if they weren't there anymore, so numb were they.

Burkitt stumbled back, tripping over his own feet, and he hit the ground heavily. Another cry went up from the crowd then, and Burkitt didn't bound to his feet this time. Instead he was skittering back like a mutilated crab, his eyes wide, staring at nothing that anyone else could see. He twisted around, saw his fellow Counselars, who were gaping at him in mute shock, and he barked, *"You see them! Tell me you see them!"* Several of them at least had enough presence of mind to shake their heads, while the rest just stared.

He twisted back, and they were almost upon him, and he knew then what they meant to do. He had felt the uncanny coldness of them, knew what it had done to him just to touch them, and further knew that they were now going to return the favor. They were going to sink their own arms, or even their own forms into him. No longer were they content with haunting his outer senses. They were going to insinuate themselves right into him, invade him not only from without but also from within. The Zarna's face was closest to his, and her lips were drawn back in a hideous rictus of a smile. She opened her mouth as if to kiss him in a grotesque mockery of passion, and when she did, some sort of thick, gelatinous mass started to emerge. He saw the Zarn approaching as well, and the children, all ready to pile on, and then the smell hit him. He felt his gorge rising, his stomach twisting in protest, and that was when he began to roar, in a voice louder than any could recall in the history of Oratory Point.

"Get off me! Get off me, you dead bitch! Get off me or I'll kill you, no matter how dead you already are!"

For one moment, one moment, the ghost of the Zarna looked taken aback by his vehemence. That was all Burkitt needed. With a guttural roar of fury, he shoved and rolled, and suddenly, just like that, the Zarna was on her back, looking most surprised. He still wasn't able to touch her, and the cold of her still iced him to the soul, but the white-hot fury boiling within him gave him strength. Screaming in triumph, he shouted, *"I'll kill you like I killed your sons! Like I would have killed Tsana! You think I won't?! You think I can't?! I . . ."*

And she was gone, just like that.

Burkitt let out a howl of triumph, for the others were gone as well. He let out a demented chortle of joy and triumph. *"That for you, Zarn! That for you, Zarna! That . . . that . . ."*

Then his voice started to taper off, and slowly, very slowly, he looked around. Everyone was staring at him with various looks of surprise and incredulity. All except Calhoun, who was looking at him with a grim air of satisfaction, and Si Cwan and Kalinda, whose faces were utterly inscrutable.

Then he started to rerun through his mind the things he had just shouted, for all to hear. There was dead silence in the square.

His thoughts were scattered, like broken glass, slicing him as he tried to gather them up. Forgotten was everything that he had planned, all the grand notions and strategies. Instead he focused all his anger, all his fury on one person. Pointing a quivering finger at Calhoun, he snarled, "This . . . this was all your fault somehow . . . *you did this . . ."*

"Whatever was done here was done to yourself," Calhoun said. He appeared to be speaking very quietly, and yet his voice carried across the square.

"No! You did this! You did it—!" His face twisted in hatred, he lunged at Calhoun.

Kebron was ready for him, but Burkitt didn't get more than half a foot when the shriek of a pulser blast ripped through the air. The shot took him square in the chest, knocking him back with such force that it took him off his feet. He flailed as he went, and crashed into several of the Counselars, who found themselves to be unintentional backstops. A good half dozen of them went down in a pile, Burkitt lying atop them, his legs splayed, his arms hanging to either side. A small spiral of smoke wafted from Burkitt's chest, and his head was slumped.

The last thing he saw was Tsana, a grim smile of triumph on her face.

I hate that girl, he thought before oblivion took him.

Calhoun couldn't tell whether Burkitt was dead and, at that moment, he didn't especially care. Instead his entire focus was on the new source of attack. "Kebron, shield Tsana!" he snapped as he yanked out his phaser, pivoting and trying to see where the blast had come from.

He had no trouble doing so, because the shooter was not making the slightest attempt to hide. Across the square, on one of the upper levels of a nondescript building, he saw a trooper that he instantly recognized: Commander Gragg. He was frozen in the window, still in the aiming position. Even from this distance, Calhoun could see smoke whisping from the barrel end. Then Gragg slowly lowered the pulser, stepped back from the window, and shut it.

For a long moment, no one said anything, and finally the stunned silence was broken by Zak Kebron.

"Anything around here to eat?" he inquired.

20

EXCALIBUR

"DID YOU DO IT?"

Calhoun, having just spoken, leaned back in his chair in his ready room and fixed his level gaze upon Kalinda. She sat in the chair opposite him, her hands folded neatly in her lap. Si Cwan was just behind her, looking a bit protective, and Kebron was off to the side. Standing to the right of the desk was Burgoyne, arms folded across hir chest.

"Well? Did you, Kalinda?" demanded Calhoun again. His face was so controlled, so neutral, that it was difficult to tell whether he was upset or not, which was exactly the way he wanted it. "I'll tell you right now, the one thing I have trouble dealing with is lying. Say what you will to me, but lying is not acceptable. I won't tolerate it, and you won't get away with it in any event."

"I cannot say, Captain, that I appreciate the tone you're taking with my sister," Si Cwan said.

"How fortunate, Ambassador, that I was not requiring you

to say so." It was the kind of comment that Calhoun might have made tongue in cheek, except in this case he didn't sound remotely amused. "Kalinda . . ."

"What do you think I might have done, Captain?" asked Kalinda. She didn't seem particularly intimidated by Calhoun's mood, and he didn't know whether to be pleased by that or not. "What strange and mysterious power do you think I have?"

In a tone that seemed to say, *"We'll play it your way,"* Calhoun smiled politely and said, "All right. My understanding is that you have been known to have a certain amount of—what's the best way to put it . . . ?"

"Congress with the pulse-impaired?" she suggested.

"From what I hear, yes. At least that was the report that was given to me by my chief of security and my science officer, in viewing the interaction with alleged spirits they observed in the region known as the Quiet Place. *They* reported. To *me*." His comment could not have been more pointed. He wanted to remind her—because apparently it needed clarification—just who was running this ship.

"Now, Captain," Kalinda said silkily, "I have trouble believing that an educated, knowledgeable man such as yourself would believe in ghosts. The tortured souls of the undead, wandering about, hoping and praying that someone would come along to aid them in their quest for justice? Certainly that's the sort of thing that Xenexian older brothers use for the purpose of scaring their younger siblings at bedtime."

"Kalinda, you're talking to someone who watched a giant, flaming bird break out of the core of your homeworld as if it were an oversized egg. I think you'll find there are very few things in this galaxy that I am willing to dismiss out of hand as being impossible."

She paused, considering his words, and then said, "Wouldn't you say that guilty consciences are far more common than unhappy spirits? And being overwhelmed by one's guilt to be a much more commonplace occurrence than to be tricked into it or terrorized into it by rampant ghosts?"

"Why don't you tell me?" said Calhoun.

Then Burgoyne stepped forward, and s/he said, in a tone that didn't really seem to be a question, "Captain, permission to speak privately?"

Calhoun's gaze flickered from Burgoyne to the others, and then he said quietly, "Very well. The rest of you can go. But don't go far, if you please." There were nods of acknowledgment, and within moments Calhoun was alone with Burgoyne. He leaned back in his chair and steepled his fingers, his face a question.

"I asked her to do it, Captain," said Burgoyne.

Allowing a moment for that pronouncement to sink in, Calhoun let some time pass before he said, "What did she do . . . exactly?"

"I'm not sure . . . exactly," admitted Burgoyne. S/he moved across the room in that customarily silent manner s/he had and eased hirself into the chair that Kalinda had been seated in. "As you yourself are aware, she has certain . . . abilities. Given the situation presented us, I asked her whether there would be anything she would be able to do to, uhm . . ." S/he seemed to be searching for the best way to describe it.

Calhoun, however, didn't give hir the opportunity to do so. "I am, indeed, aware that she has certain abilities. What I was not aware of, Commander, was that you had been having private discussions with her in regards to using them."

"That is correct, yes."

"And why was I not aware of these discussions?"

"Because," said Burgoyne, as if it was the most reasonable response in the world, "I chose not to tell you."

"You chose."

"Yes, sir."

"Not to tell me."

"Yes, sir."

Calhoun's face was a mask. "You made this choice, freely and of your own will? A choice to pursue alternate options without seeing fit to keep me apprised?"

"Yes, Captain, I believe we've covered that," said Burgoyne.

Calhoun felt a cold rage beginning to burn within him. What the hell did Burgoyne think s/he was doing? Where did s/he come up with the temerity to operate in secret? The temperature in the room seemed to drop as Calhoun said, "May I ask, Commander, where you got the impression that a captain and first officer being less than candid with each other was somehow a permissible manner in which to operate?"

Burgoyne never hesitated. When Calhoun thought back on this conversation—and he would—he would remember how quickly Burgoyne responded, as if s/he'd been anticipating the question long before Calhoun posed it.

"From you, sir," s/he said.

Calhoun stared at hir. "From me?"

Burgoyne nodded. "Captain, as large as starships may be, they're still no bigger than the average small town, and everyone knows everyone else's business sooner or later. The simple fact is that I know there were any number of occasions where you developed some sort of backup plan, some sort of strategy, and you kept it to yourself. You did not tell your first officer, Commander Shelby—"

"And this is some sort of tit for tat?" Calhoun was stunned; he had thought more highly of Burgoyne than this. "I didn't tell her, so you didn't tell me . . . ?"

"You determine the command style, Captain. You determine what's acceptable behavior by your own behavior. And if I—"

Calhoun leaned forward, and he could not recall the last time he'd gone to such effort to repress pure fury. "What I choose to tell my *subordinates,* Commander, in my position as captain, is my prerogative. The chain of command goes down, not up, and you are not entitled to keep plans, strategies, or passing notions from me." He leaned back, shaking his head. "I would like to think after everything we've been through, Burgy, that at the very least I would inspire that much confidence."

"Captain," Burgoyne said with obvious sincerity, "I have never served under a commanding officer who inspired more confidence than you. But . . ."

"But what?"

"You don't inspire trust."

Calhoun wasn't entirely certain what to say in response to that. "I see," was all he could think of.

"I was just . . ." S/he hesitated, then pushed forward. "I was just trying to show you that I could be an independent thinker, like you. Operate on my own. I mean . . . here you had Commander Shelby, someone on the command track for the longest time. Someone whom you had once actually intended to marry. And yet you didn't seem to trust her enough to bring her into the loop on all your plans. So my concern was, if you didn't trust her, how much less likely are you to trust me: someone who wasn't looking for command, and whom you didn't sleep with." S/he frowned and amended, "At least to my knowledge. Although I did get fairly drunk last New Year's, and there was this one fellow who *might* have been—"

"It wasn't," Calhoun assured hir.

"Ah. So the point was, I felt it imperative to show you, early on, my ability to take charge. To take initiative. To—"

"Act like me, yes, so you've said." Calhoun sighed heavily. This meeting hadn't gone even remotely in the direction that he'd intended for it to go, and he wasn't entirely sure if that was a good thing or a bad thing. "Commander, in the future, if you have any thoughts on an issue, any strategies . . . I want to hear them. I want to hear them because I may find flaws in them you haven't considered . . . or I may decide that they're so brilliant that they could save countless lives. Most of all, I want to hear them because if I *didn't* want to hear your opinions, I never would have chosen you to be my Number One. Are we clear on that?"

"Yes, Captain."

"And I shall . . ." Calhoun smiled ruefully. "I shall endeavor to be more inspiring of trust in the future."

"Thank you, sir. I appreciate that."

"Do me a favor: Tell the others they can return to their stations."

"Yes, sir."

Burgoyne rose and started to head for the door, only to stop when Calhoun said to hir, "Oh . . . and Burgy?"

"Yes, Captain . . . ?"

"If you ever . . . and I mean *ever* . . . pull anything like this again, I will bust you down so far that they'll have to invent a new rank low enough to accommodate it. Unless, of course, you think I don't mean it. . . ."

Burgoyne quickly shook hir head. "No, Captain, I absolutely believe you."

"Because I hear tell that I don't inspire trust. . . ."

"Actually, Captain, I feel abundant trust in this room at the moment . . . far more than I could possibly have believed existed."

"Oh, good."

Burgoyne backed out of the room, keeping a wary eye on Calhoun, perhaps concerned that the captain was going to remove his sword from the wall and toss it across the room. As a consequence, Burgoyne nearly backed into Selar, who was unexpectedly standing in the doorway.

"Oh! Sorry," said Burgoyne, looking momentarily disconcerted.

Selar, naturally, gave not the slightest sign of emotion. Instead she said to Calhoun, "Captain, may I have a moment of your time, please?"

"By all means." He gestured for her to enter as Burgoyne

hurriedly exited. "Tell me, Doctor," he said when she was seated, "do I inspire trust?"

She looked at him oddly. "In whom, sir?"

"In me. Do I inspire the crew to trust me?"

"Do you desire to?"

"Doctor," he asked, "are you trying to dodge the question?"

"No, sir. I am trying to comprehend why you would ask it."

"My motives aren't really at issue," he said, hoping he sounded as reasonable as he felt. "I'm just asking your opinion. You're the ship's chief medical officer; you should have some clear understanding of the crew's mindset. Do you think that I inspire trust in them?"

"I think you inspire fear in them."

He felt a bit crestfallen at that. "And is that a good thing?"

"Of course. Trust is a byproduct of fear. They are afraid to disobey because they fear there will be consequences, and they trust you to implement them."

"Oh." He considered it a moment, and then nodded. "All right. I can live with that. Was that all you wanted to talk about?"

Selar blinked in polite confusion. "I did not wish to talk to you about that at all. You brought it up."

You're losing it, Calhoun. "So I did. What can I do for you?"

"Moke."

"What about him?"

"He desires me for a mother."

Now it was Calhoun's turn to look confused. "He does?"

"He does, yes. And considering you are his father, or at least his acting father, I felt it would be best if I brought this to your attention."

Calhoun shifted uncomfortably in his chair. "If you're suggesting we should get married for the sake of the child, Doctor, I'm afraid I'm already spoken for."

"No, Captain, that is *not—*"

Smiling, he raised a hand, silencing her. "I wasn't serious,

Selar. Don't worry, I'll talk to him. He's just trying to adjust to both the loss of his own mother *and* an entirely new environment. He's seeking familiarity, an anchor. A mother figure. And my wife is certainly not in a position to provide that. He sees that you have a child, and that suggests associations to him. . . ."

"I readily understand the personal dynamics involved, Captain. I simply felt you should be apprised."

"Thank you." Apparently that was going to be the end of the conversation, but Calhoun felt as if something more should be said. Something conversational, friendly, personal . . . anything, really. "How is your son, by the way?"

"His growth continues at an accelerated rate, and people tend to look at him oddly when I pass with him in the hallway."

Well, as far as conversational gambits went, that certainly hadn't gone the way he'd hoped. "They'll get used to him."

"Perhaps," said Selar. "My concern is whether he gets used to them. At least I need not concern myself that they will taunt him."

Ensign Pheytus strode into Craig Mitchell's office in engineering, almost marching as he did so, and when he reached the center he stood stiffly and at attention. Mitchell, who'd been studying fuel consumption reports, looked up at him in puzzlement. "You look like you're in search of a parade to lead, Ensign. Should I put in for one?" he inquired solicitously.

"They're doing it again, sir," said Pheytus.

Mitchell tossed down the padd he'd been looking over, and it clattered on the desk. *"Beth!"* he shouted.

Lieutenant Beth appeared as if by magic at the door. "Yes, sir?"

"Are we having another problem?"

"No one's been in a fight, if that's what you mean," she said, sounding defensive.

"It's nothing they're doing consciously, Lieutenant Commander," Pheytus told him. "I'm simply aware of what they're thinking."

Hearing that, Mitchell rose from his chair, leaning forward on his desk with his knuckles. "You're a telepath?" he asked in obvious surprise.

"No, not at all. But I can see it in their eyes."

Beth moaned softly, nor did Mitchell appear tremendously pleased at the assertion. "You can see it in their eyes?"

"Every time they address me by name, there is silent laughter in their eyes. I do not wish to be made sport of, Chief."

Beth took a step forward, looking both helpless and frustrated. "Yes, but you're not saying that people are making sport of you. You're just saying that you don't like what's going through their heads. You can't ask people to censor their thoughts. Maybe you're just being oversensitive. . . ."

As if Beth hadn't spoken, he said, "Chief Mitchell, the head of ecostudies is a Bolian. My name does not provoke the slightest bit of mirth from him. I've always had an interest in ecostudies, and I was hoping you could arrange a transfer to his department."

Mitchell didn't respond immediately, instead rapping his knuckles softly on the desk. "I can't say I'm ecstatic about the concept that you are only comfortable with 'your own kind,' as it were."

"That is certainly not the message I intend to convey, sir."

"It's just that I feel we all got off on the wrong foot here."

Pheytus glanced down, then up at Mitchell. "These are the only feet I have, Chief."

Wisely deciding not to pursue that line of conversation, Mitchell instead said, "Are you sure that's what you want, Ensign?"

"I truly would like to explore options in the science department, Chief . . . provided I am not ruling out a possible return to engineering."

"No, no, not at all." He let out a sigh. "If you're absolutely sure that's what you want . . ."

"It is, sir."

"Very well. I'll put through the paperwork."

"Thank you, Chief." He spun smartly on his heel, faced Lieutenant Beth, and said, "I regret I was not able to serve under you for a greater period of time, Lieutenant."

"Perhaps in the future," said Beth politely.

He nodded and strode out of Mitchell's office. The moment he was out, Beth turned to Mitchell and said, "Well, we didn't exactly cover ourselves in glory on that one, did we?"

"What's this 'we' stuff?" demanded Mitchell. "You and your people are the ones who thought an ensign named 'Fetus' was so damned amusing. I mean, here I thought my job was simply to get the best people available. Little did I suspect that I had to make certain their names didn't tickle anyone's funny bone."

"It was inevitable, sir, when you think about it . . . languages, names having unintended meanings . . ."

"Well, I certainly don't think you helped," growled Mitchell. Displaying his legendary scowl, he said, "I don't want to see a repeat of this stupidity."

"Sorry, Chief. I suppose you're right." She looked downcast. "If not for me, Ensign Fetus might not have had such an abortive career. . . ."

"Beth," and he stabbed a beefy finger at her, "if there's a repeat of this, or anything like this, the lot of you are going to wind up third-grade technicians on a garbage scow. Look into my eyes: Do you think I'm kidding?"

"No, sir."

"Good. Now get out," said Mitchell.

She got out.

Mitchell sank back into his chair, feeling frustrated and also—as inappropriate as it might have sounded—wanting some measure of revenge for the annoyance he'd been put through over something as inconsequential as a name. But first things first: He only had to arrange for the transfer of Pheytus, but he was also going to have to look through the roster of available crewmen to see who might present a decent replacement.

It took him all of five minutes to know that he'd found his man.

With a grim smile, he arranged the reassignment of Ensign Pheytus and the transfer of his replacement: Ensign Neuborne. . . .

21

TRIDENT

AREX WAS JUST HEADING into the turbolift when a familiar voice called out, "Hold the lift!" But even as he moved to halt the sliding doors, M'Ress gracefully eased herself in by dodging sideways through the closing doors. She whipped her tail out of the way just in time, and the doors slid shut with no hesitation.

"Goooood afternoon, Lieutenant," she said, her face split in a wide, toothy smile.

Arex eyed her appraisingly, craning his long, thin neck back as if making the effort to see all of her at a better angle. "Well! This is certainly a different Caitian than the one I remember from not all that long ago. The one with the glum expression practically tattooed on her face. The one who was complaining about fitting in—"

"I don't seem to recall anyone like that," said M'Ress, a manufactured expression of shock on her face. She looked around. "Why aren't we moving?"

"Even in this century, M'Ress, the turbolifts aren't psychic," Arex reminded her.

"Oh. Right." She smiled sheepishly. "Deck eleven for me . . . and you, to wherever you were going . . ."

"Deck eleven," Arex said briskly, and the lift obediently started to head off in that direction. "Back to the science department?" She nodded. "Any luck with those scans?"

To this, she shook her head. She folded her arms and tried to keep her spirits at the same high level as before, but Arex could see her ears flattening, making her disappointment all the more evident. "None, and we've had enough time to survey the world twice over. Either it's not there, or the thing has got a means of thwarting our scans. I wouldn't know which way to guess at this point."

He regarded her thoughtfully. "You don't seem especially upset by that, though. Displeased, yes, but not upset. You seem so much more relaxed. Extremely so, as a matter of . . ." Then his voice trailed off a moment as his eyes widened. His already high voice jumped an octave. "M'Ress! You've been 'busy,' haven't you." It wasn't a question.

"Busy?" she said coyly. "I've no idea what you mean, Arex."

"Of course you do. I know you too well, M'Ress. Who is he? Unless you don't want to tell me."

"No, Arex. I don't want to tell you."

"Not at all?"

"No, not at all."

"Very well," he said in that reedy voice of his. He looked resolutely forward, apparently caring not at all about anything else that M'Ress might have to say.

"Computer, stop the lift." Obediently, the turbolift glided to a halt.

Arex made a pretense of an impatient sigh. "If we keep doing this, they're going to insist we walk everywhere we want to go."

"All right . . . if you really want to know . . ."

"Keep it to yourself. I don't care."

"I had a date last night with Lieutenant Commander Gleau . . . last night . . . which continued into this morning . . . ," she said with a lazy, significant wink. "And it's amazing how one's entire view can be shifted around after one glorious night of . . . " Her voice trailed off as she saw something very odd in his expression. "What's wrong?"

"How did it happen?" he asked, very softly.

Obviously she was put off by his cautious reaction. Speaking gingerly, as if uncertain which phrase was going to upset him, she said, "Well . . . it was the end of shift . . . and I was feeling a bit frustrated . . . and he started massaging my shoulders, which felt terrific . . ." The memory alone was enough to fill her with a pleasant warmth, momentarily shunting aside whatever negative vibrations Arex might be giving off. "And I suggested we head up to Ten Forward, which I have to say is a marvelous idea, and I wish we'd had one of those in our day. If we did, my guess is that Dr. McCoy would have dismantled sickbay and just set up shop in Ten Forward instead. So we went up there, and one thing led to another and . . ." Then she stopped as the pronounced concern on Arex's face grew even more profound. "Arex—?"

"Shiboline," he said, and the use of her first name was enough to worry her if she hadn't already been. "We're talking about the same person, right? Gleau? The Elf?"

"Frankly, I prefer the term 'Selelvian' myself. It sounds less condescending, if you ask me. But yes, that's him. Why?" When he didn't answer immediately, she said more insistently, "Na Eth . . . what's going on?"

"Look . . . Shib, it's none of my business—"

She stabbed a finger at him. "No . . . no, you don't get to back up now, Na Eth. You don't get to introduce some aspect of doubt into the first thing I've felt really good about since I got to this foresaken century and then say it's none of your business. If you've got something on your mind, tell me."

"Really, I think it'd be better if—"

"Tell me."

He was obviously taken aback by the vehemence in her tone, and came to the realization that prevaricating wasn't going to help matters. "Okay, well . . . I'm not saying this is a definite concern, mind you, it could be nothing. . . ."

"Na Eth," she said warningly.

"All right, it's just that . . . well, I've been doing everything I can to bring myself current with everything that new races—new, that is, since we were on active duty—are capable of doing. It just seemed a reasonable thing to do, from a security point of view. I felt I should know the average strength, any natural weapons that—"

"Arex Na Eth," she sighed, "I know you're in love with the sound of your own voice, but do you think you could, perhaps, move this along—?"

"Yes, well . . ." He cleared his throat. "The point is, I did some investigating on Selelvians as well. Not that I was trying to be invasive of Lieutenant Commander Gleau, you understand. I just wanted to know—"

"Could you possibly take *any* longer to come to the point?" she said, making no attempt to hide her irritation.

"All right, here's the point: Have you heard of something called . . . the Knack?"

"The Knack. No. Should I?"

"I think you should, yes. Because it may make all the difference in the world. . . ."

Mueller nodded in approval upon hearing the news from Shelby. "So this Tsana is back in charge on Thallon 21, then," she said, seated in the captain's ready room, her fingers intertwined and resting on her leg. "And the Aerons are accepting of this?"

"The Aerons, according to Mac, are in something of a disarray," Shelby told her, with a certain degree of almost malicious satisfaction. "No one expected their Warmaster to come completely unglued in front of the crowd and admit to having disposed of two of the ruling family."

"May I safely assume that Calhoun had something to do with it?"

"That certainly would have been my guess," said Shelby. "Now, Mac, he swears he wasn't involved in Burkitt's breakdown at all."

"Do you believe him?"

"I'm loathe to call him a liar."

"That's not an answer."

"No, that's an answer," Shelby countered. "It's simply not a definitive answer. Considering the circumstances, however, it's about the best answer you're going to get out of me." She leaned forward, elbows on her desk. "However, this does not even remotely solve *our* problems. There is still apparently a Gateway device—either on Thallon 21 or on Thallon 18—below us, or conceivably on both. As long as these two races have the means and the desire to attack each other, the danger will persist. We've got to find that Gateway; got to convince them to turn it over to us."

"The only way to do that," said Mueller thoughtfully, "is to convince them that there's no reason to fight."

"The problem is that the Markanians are still responsible for the deaths of several of the imperial family of the Aerons. That fact is not in dispute. Hell," she noted in annoyance, "they're damned proud of it. I get the impression that if they could do it over, they'd not only do it again, but this time they'd take greater steps to make sure they got every single member of the family, thereby saving Burkitt the trouble."

"Do we know who was responsible for the raid?"

"If I had to guess," said Shelby, "I'd say it was very likely Ebozay himself. But there's no way of proving it."

"Here's the problem, the way I see it," Mueller told her, leaning back, extending her legs and crossing them at the ankles. "Let's say that Tsana determines that Ebozay was definitely the mastermind behind the raid. She demands justice . . . specifically, Ebozay's head on a platter. Will the Markanians give him up willingly?"

"Of course not."

"Of course not," agreed Mueller.

"Which means the Aerons will have to attack," said Shelby grimly. "Let's say they manage it . . . and in doing so, they achieve their goal of capturing or—better yet—killing Ebozay. But that won't put a stop to it, because the Markanians will then demand revenge in the name of the fallen Ebozay. They'll want whoever heads up the raid from the Aerons . . . or—better yet—they'll want Tsana herself. And on and on it will go . . ."

"Because that's how it's always gone. A cycle of violence among the two races, both trying to balance scales that will be forever out of balance, and neither one willing to walk away from the fight."

"Can we expect them to?" asked Shelby. "Isn't it natural to want justice for the dead?"

Mueller snorted dismissively. "The dead could not care less about justice, Captain. The only justice they care about is whatever justice they're facing in the afterlife." She paused, considered that a moment, and then said, "Captain . . . do you believe in an afterlife?"

"This is not the appropriate time to discuss it, XO."

"When might be?"

"When hell freezes over . . . a sentiment that may very well go a long way toward answering the question." Shelby rose and crossed to her window, leaning with one hand against it and watching the planet below, as if she were capable of gathering up thousands of people in her one gargantuan palm. "Do you think Tsana has the intestinal fortitude simply to walk away, rather than seek further vengeance on behalf of her family?"

"Not having met her, I haven't the faintest idea," said Mueller reasonably. "I can speculate. . . ."

"Go right ahead. It's just the two of us here."

Mueller scratched her chin thoughtfully. "If I'm recalling the files on this matter properly—and I admit, the file has been growing exponentially since we became involved—the Aerons did, in fact, capture one of the individuals responsible for the assault."

"Yes, that sounds right. They caught . . ." She turned her computer screen around, scanning the file that was already up on the screen. ". . . they caught a Markanian named Pmarr. Quite the upper-echelon individual, as near as I can tell. Probably a higher-up associate of Ebozay."

"Probably. Do you think . . ." Mueller didn't speak immediately, instead tapping out a cheery tattoo with her fingertips.

"Do I think that Ebozay would be willing to write off his associate as an acceptable loss so his world can move on?" Shelby suggested.

Mueller still didn't reply hastily. Finally, though, she nodded. "That's what it seems to be coming down to."

"It puts a good deal of pressure on both of them," said Shelby. "Tsana would have to walk away from a desire to punish as many people as possible . . . and Ebozay would have to be willing to finger Pmarr as one of the major instigators of the raid on Aeron. I don't know for certain that either of them would be willing to take that step. Unless, of course . . ."

"Unless of course . . . what?" asked Mueller.

"Unless, of course, they feel as if they're being given no choice."

"You have something in mind, Captain?"

"I believe I do," she said with a slow smile.

Very severely, Mueller asked, "Is it in violation of the Prime Directive?"

"It's borderline, at best."

"At best. And at worst?"

"It's a horrific breach."

"I see," said Mueller and, after a moment, she shrugged. "Then I just suppose we'll have to hope that Starfleet doesn't find out about it."

Only yesterday, the confines of Ten Forward had seemed so friendly, so pleasant. Now, when M'Ress entered, it appeared utterly alien to her. Every face that glanced at her in cheery recognition seemed to be mocking her, laughing at her behind expressions that appeared civil. Deep down, she knew that wasn't the case. She knew that no one was thinking contemptuously about her; if anything, they weren't thinking about her at all, but instead merely nodding to her in a reflexive greeting before going back to their conversations.

She saw him exactly where she knew she'd see him: at the far end of the room. He was seated at a table, a drink in his hand, engaging in small talk with another crewman. It was all M'Ress could do not to simply leap across the room, land with her knees planted squarely on his chest, and throttle him. Instead she restrained herself, moving sleekly across the room like a stalking panther. Such was her automatic stealth that he didn't notice her until she was almost upon him. When he looked up at her, it was with such genuine pleasure at her presence that it was all she could do not to rip his eyes out.

"Shibolene," he said. "What a pleasure to—"

"Don't call me that, Gleau," she said, both more and less sharply than she would have liked.

He blinked in polite confusion, immediately discerning that her mood was not a pleasant one, but clearly not the least bit aware as to why. "Did I say it incorrectly?"

"We need to talk."

"We *are* talking."

Her glance flickered to the crewman who was still seated,

but he had already realized that his absence would be greatly preferred. "I think," he said, rising, "that the Lieutenant would prefer to speak with you privately." He glanced at her for confirmation, and she nodded curtly. "Yes, I thought as much. We'll talk later, Gleau."

He won't be doing much talking if I rip his throat out, M'Ress thought grimly as she slid into the now-unoccupied seat. The instant the crewman was out of earshot, she said, "Did you use the Knack on me?"

He smiled, understanding flooding his face. "Ahhh . . . is that what this is about?"

"Yes, that's what this is about. The Knack . . . a Selelvian ability to 'persuade' people, to push them in certain directions that Selelvians want them to go. I want to know if one of those pushed was me, and one of those directions was your bed." It was a tremendous effort for her not to speak too quickly, to let the words bubble out of her in a torrent of rage.

Gleau, for his part, remained calm . . . even sympathetic. "It's not a secret, you know. The Knack, I mean. It used to be, but as more of us have shown up in Starfleet, we've been more forthcoming about it. Everybody knows."

"I didn't."

"You've been out of circulation for a while."

"You didn't answer the question."

His eyes narrowed. "M'Ress, I'd feel a bit more comfortable discussing this if your fangs were not so well displayed."

She realized that he was right; her upper jaw was jutting out, her extended teeth quite prominent. It must have looked somewhat threatening; it was meant to. With a visible effort, she reset her teeth so that she didn't look ready to take a bite out of him. "You still haven't answered the question."

"It's not an easy question to answer," he said, leaning back, the fingertips of either hand touching one another.

"Yes, it is."

"No, it's not," he insisted gently but firmly. "And since

this is knowledge you've only recently acquired, I'll thank you not to present yourself as an expert at it. The simple fact is that I'm not entirely certain whether I used the Knack on you or not."

"How can you *not know?*"

"Because, to a degree, it's an autonomic reflex. I found you attractive, you found me attractive. In such a circumstance, the Knack kicks in, released in a manner not unlike endorphins. But it doesn't force you to do anything against your will—"

"Stop talking about it as if it's something separate from you," she said heatedly. "It's as if you're trying to divest yourself of any responsibility for it. You're responsible, Gleau. You're responsible—"

"For what?" he replied, still the picture of calm. "M'Ress, nothing happened that you didn't want to happen. If I did use the Knack, all it did was smooth the way for something that would have occurred in time anyway."

"You don't know that!"

"I know it to a reasonable certainty. You do as well, although you're too angry to admit it. But you will eventually."

"How do you know that? Are you planning to use the Knack to make me admit it?"

He sighed. "Weren't you listening, M'Ress? I told you, even with the Knack, I couldn't make you do anything that was against your will. If there's anything you should 'admit' to, it's that you did something that you felt good about at the time, and now you feel—I don't know—guilty, perhaps. And you're trying to blame me."

"I wasn't feeling guilty at all! I still don't feel guilty!" she snapped back, and then realized her voice was louder than she would have liked, because people were starting to look in her direction. She lowered her tone and said, "What I feel is used."

"That's ridiculous."

"Don't tell me that my feelings are ridiculous."

Gleau sighed once more, as if the entire discussion had

wearied him. "M'Ress . . . I had no idea you were so provincial. . . ."

"Provincial!"

"It's understandable, I suppose, coming from another time . . ."

"I may be from another time, but it's not Earth's Victorian era, I can assure you of that," she said. She was aware her fangs were out again, and this time she did nothing to pull them in. Gleau obviously noticed them, but said nothing, as M'Ress continued. "But in any time that any female comes from, she shouldn't have to be concerned that a male is using some sort of undue, unfair influence on her."

"There was nothing undue or unfair about it!" he protested. "We both enjoyed ourselves, and we were both happy. What does it matter how that came about?"

"It matters to me. And I don't see why you can't understand that."

He sighed.

"If you sigh again," she warned him, "I'm going to leap across this table and beat you senseless."

He cocked an eyebrow. "All right . . . not a more provincial time, but certainly a more violent one, apparently."

"It's patronizing."

He appeared to gather his thoughts and then, speaking very slowly and very clearly, as if he wanted to get everything on record, he said, "I did not intend to patronize you. I did not intend to 'use' you in any way. All I intended to do . . . indeed, all I thought I *had* done . . . was make you happy. If I failed in that endeavor, I most humbly and sincerely apologize."

"I don't want your apology."

"Then what *do* you want?" He sounded exasperated.

"I . . ." She hesitated, because in truth she didn't know. "I want not to feel the way that I do. I want not to feel as if I was manipulated against my will."

"You weren't."

"You don't know that! You said so yourself. Was *that* a lie? Did you, in fact, know what you were doing? Did you use the Knack on me? Rush me along when I might not ordinarily have gone?"

He looked down and started to sigh once more, but then caught himself before the sound completely emerged from his throat. She took a grim, amused pleasure from that.

"Probably," he said. "As I said, I can't know for sure, but if I had to guess—based upon your reactions, my gut instinct—I'd say probably, yes."

She took that in, absorbing the information, trying to get a grip on the conflicting emotions within her. "I see," was all she said.

He was clearly waiting for her to speak again, but she said nothing. Finally he ventured, "M'Ress . . . believe it or not, I'm glad we had this talk."

"Oh, so am I."

"And I'm glad we were able to settle this—"

"Settle?" She rose. "Nothing is settled, Gleau. This isn't over. This is just beginning." And with her tail twitching like a barely controlled whip, M'Ress turned and walked out of Ten Forward, leaving an extremely disconcerted and worried Gleau in her wake.

22

HOLOCONFERENCE

Tsana looked around the holodeck, her eyes wide. Already she had done things more amazing than any of her people . . . more than she had ever dreamt she would accomplish in her lifetime. She had moved among the stars. All right, perhaps technically not among them, but certainly being in orbit around her world counted for something. Neither her father nor mother nor any of her siblings had ever left the surface of their world, and yet here she was. Then the thought of her family, and what had happened to them, lodged itself in her mind, and it was all she could do to push it away without tears welling in her eyes.

"Are you all right?"

Kalinda was standing next to her, looking down at her with obvious concern. Tsana managed a nod. Nevertheless Kalinda reached down, took her hand, and gave it a squeeze. Tsana wasn't entirely sure what the purpose of it was, but it made her feel better for some reason.

"Thinking about your family?" asked Kalinda.

Tsana nodded, wide-eyed, wondering if Kalinda had been able to read her mind. "How did you know?"

"Because I think my face looks kind of like that when I think about my family," she said. "If not for my brother, Si Cwan, I'm not sure what I'd do."

"I don't have a brother," Tsana said softly, "and I'm still not sure what I should do."

Kalinda squeezed her hand again. "You'll think of something," she said confidently.

Si Cwan then entered, deep in discussion with Calhoun and Burgoyne. They immediately saw Tsana there, and Burgoyne went right over to her while Cwan—more reserved—hung back. As for Calhoun, he seemed rather distant, having moved off to be by himself in a corner of the room. Tsana thought that was understandable. He was, after all, the captain, and doubtlessly had a great deal on his mind.

Burgoyne crouched so that s/he was on eye-level with her. "How are you, Zarn?" s/he asked politely.

"I am . . . well . . . although I'm not exactly used to being addressed in that manner," she admitted. "I hear 'Zarn,' and my reflex is to look over my shoulder for my father."

"I can appreciate that. I'll be honest with you, Zarn . . . throughout history, people have found themselves thrust into leadership roles."

"But I wasn't ready for it."

"No one ever really is, no matter how much they think they are. But you grow into it, by doing what you know to be right. I understand that matters have been somewhat . . . prickly . . . on your homeworld since Burkitt's death."

She nodded. "The Counselars have been somewhat in disarray. I have to say, that's helped me a great deal. They seem anxious to listen to me, even if I am only 'a child.' " She said the words with sufficient distaste, conveying volumes of annoyance in doing so.

Calhoun, seeming to stir from his introspective stance, called, "There's an old Earth saying, 'Out of the mouths of babes . . .' "

She stared at him. "Yes? What comes out of the mouths of babes?"

Calhoun blinked. "Actually, you know, I'm not sure. I've heard the saying a number of times, but no one ever seems to complete the sentence." He looked hopefully at Si Cwan and Burgoyne. Both shrugged.

"Do I look like an old Earther?" Si Cwan inquired. "I would think that the only thing that comes out of the mouths of babes is drool."

"Do I seem a drooling babe to you?" asked Tsana, sounding hurt.

Calhoun rubbed his brow in resignation. "No. You don't. Never mind. Forget I brought it up." He turned away once more, and for a moment Tsana felt guilty, as if she'd upset him somehow. Ultimately, though, she was more than happy to forget having brought it up. Then she allowed worry to flicker across her face once more. "We're going to be meeting with the enemies of Aeron. Is your large security guard going to be here? I feel safer when he's near."

"He'll be so flattered to hear that," muttered Si Cwan. He sounded a bit cranky about it, although Tsana couldn't understand why.

"Security guards aren't necessary in this circumstance, Zarn," Burgoyne assured her. "This is going to be a holoconference only. The other people will look real enough, but they're simply representations. Furthermore, this is being broadcast to key members of the various governments: to your Counselars on Aeron, and to the Ruling Council of the Markanians. If you then need to confer with them privately, you can step into the adjoining room and do so."

"You've thought of everything, Commander."

Burgoyne tilted hir head slightly in acknowledgment. "I

appreciate the vote of support, although it's hard to think of *everything*. There's always a chance that something has been overlooked. Hopefully not in this case, though."

She cast a worried glance in Calhoun's direction. "Is the captain all right?" she asked. "He seems very distracted."

"Well . . ." Burgoyne looked at Calhoun once more, apparently to make sure he wasn't listening, then lowered hir voice and said, ". . . truth be told, he's been under a great deal of pressure lately. Not only is there the usual strain of running a ship this size, but also I understand his new marriage—well . . . it hasn't been going as well as he'd hoped. There's been some . . ." S/he whispered the word, ". . . difficulties."

"Difficulties?" echoed Tsana.

Burgoyne nodded, but then cheered up. "I wouldn't worry about it if I were you, though. I doubt he'll let the strain show."

For some reason, Tsana found this less than reassuring.

Burgoyne's combadge beeped, and s/he tapped it. "Burgoyne, go ahead."

"Commander, this is Lefler," came Robin's voice. *"Trident* signals ready. We can activate the holoconference on your signal."

"Captain, we're ready," Burgoyne called over to Calhoun. Calhoun leveled his gaze at hir, and then simply nodded. "Bring 'em on-line, Lieutenant," said Burgoyne.

Tsana had told herself she would be ready for it, but when other people simply snapped into existence in the room, she was nevertheless taken aback. On the opposite side of the room were two women wearing the same types of uniforms as Calhoun and Burgoyne. One woman was dark blonde, with a scar that reminded her of Calhoun's, while the other was shorter, with lighter hair and an air of command about her. Standing in between them was a Markanian, and Tsana immediately tensed up. For just one moment, part of her wanted to flee deep into her own mind, to try and get as far away from that evil race as possible. But she knew that this

Markanian, this leader of his people, would be watching her carefully for any sign of weakness. She was, after all, "only" a child, and he would not require much in the way of excuses to feel dismissive toward her.

"Captain Calhoun," said the shorter woman quite formally.

"Captain Shelby," replied Calhoun, facing her with his hands draped behind his back. "You know Commander Burgoyne, and Ambassadors Si Cwan and Kalinda. May I present Tsana, ruling Zarn of the Aeron."

"Greetings," said Tsana carefully.

"Greetings, Zarn," Shelby said with a slight bow. "This is my first officer, Commander Mueller, and this is Ebozay, head of the Ruling Council of the Markanians."

Ebozay made no motion of greeting toward her. Instead he seemed to be devouring her with his eyes, and Tsana suddenly felt extremely relieved that they were not, in fact, anywhere near each other. At the same time, though, she was concentrating on keeping her outward appearance as inscrutable as possible. She did not want to take the least chance of giving anything away to this . . . man.

"Well," continued Shelby. "Best to get started. I wish to say, before we go any further, that I appreciate both sides agreeing to this discussion."

"There is very little in this universe that cannot be discussed," Ebozay said.

"Our thoughts exactly," said Si Cwan, stepping forward. "Specifically, what needs to be discussed at this time is a peace initiative. That is—"

Ebozay snorted disdainfully. "It is a bit late for that," he said.

"There are some on my world who would agree with you," Tsana admitted. "I have been talking with them, as well as with those who feel that the enmity has dragged on for far too long."

"And they certainly don't appreciate the sneak attack you

launched against them," Calhoun said. He indicated Tsana. "Your people slaughtered this child's entire family."

"This child's family is part of a line stretching back centuries that oversaw the intended extermination of my people," retorted Ebozay.

"Carrying anger over actions centuries back is part of what's hampered any true peace between us," Tsana said, feeling herself becoming bolder by the moment. Ebozay was looking at her no less patronizingly than her own people did. But when *he* did it, it was enough to ignite her ire and prompt her to stand up to him. Without intending to do so, he might well have been doing her a huge favor just by being arrogant. "The fact is that my family—my parents, my brothers and sister—did nothing to you. They were innocent of wrongdoing. That didn't stop your people from assassinating them."

"She talks quite well for one of only nine years," Ebozay said with a bit of a sneer.

"I'm almost ten," she informed him, and then mentally kicked herself. How juvenile that sounded.

"A thousand pardons," he said mockingly, as she'd known he would.

"I don't see the need for bickering at this point," Shelby said. "I don't see how it's going to accomplish anything."

"It'll help clear the air, Captain," Calhoun told her. "And it will let the Markanians know that the Zarn won't be condescended to because of her age."

"Make no mistake, Ebozay," Tsana said warningly. "There are those of my people who are ready and willing to carry this war to the next level. We have the will and the means to do so. Part of what is holding them back is me. I don't want the cycle of violence to continue, but that's exactly what will happen if we head down this road. And I have more than a little say in this matter, for I am the one with the greatest, most personal grievance against the Markanians— for I suffered most dearly at your hands." Ebozay was clearly about to reply, but she cut him off. "Tell me, Ebozay . . . *was* it your hands? Did you lead the raid against my family?"

"Is that truly relevant?" he said, his voice icy. "After all, whether I spearheaded the assault or not, a cessation of hostilities entails forgiveness of sins. Unless you think I'm simply going to give myself over to Aeron justice because of a guilty conscience."

"You admit it, then," Kalinda spoke up.

"I admit no such thing," Ebozay said. "I leave guilt-ridden admissions to the Aeron leaders. And how is Burkitt these days?"

"Dead," Calhoun said, moving forward as if he could actually touch Ebozay. "Would you like to join him?"

"Captain!" Shelby blurted out. "That's hardly a constructive attitude to have—"

"I don't need to be lectured by you on attitude, Captain," retorted Calhoun, "especially when the man standing next to you has more than enough for the both of us." He let out a derisive snort and said, "Look, we all know what's going on here. The Markanians started a war, and now the Aerons are looking to end it with something other than more bloodshed. And we're seeing zero cooperation from the Markanians."

"Cooperation!" snapped Ebozay. "Captain, kindly confine your comments to that which you have personal knowledge of. My ancestors attempted peace with the Aerons, and were betrayed on every occasion. Nor have they been willing to yield in the slightest when it comes to the Holy Site upon Sinqay—"

"Was anyone timing that?" Calhoun said to his officers. "I was curious to see how many seconds before he brought that up."

"Ah, yes," said Ebozay, arms folded and looking rather imperious. "I seem to recall that Captain Calhoun made some 'threatening' remarks about Sinqay. Claiming that you were going to destroy our holiest of worlds. It was a bluff, of course. . . ."

Calhoun's purple eyes went wide. "Amazing how some people will use the words 'of course' in conjunction with a statement that's so completely wrong."

"I was present when he said it, Ebozay," said Tsana. "I do not think he was bluffing."

"I don't need to resort to bluffs," Calhoun said, and he walked with slow, measured tread toward Ebozay. "Bluffs are for those who don't have the power to back up their threats. I do. And I resent the notion that you're accusing me of lying."

"Resent it all you want," said Ebozay. "But—"

"Furthermore," Calhoun interrupted, "I am frankly getting rather sick and tired of your entire race. You, with your threats and condescension and murderous attitudes."

"How dare you—"

"How dare *I?*" He stepped in close and, even though Ebozay was present only in holographic form, nevertheless the Markanian leader took a reflexive step back. "Look me in the eye, Ebozay. Look at me closely. Is this the face of someone who needs to bluff?"

Ebozay seemed to rally slightly, obviously remembering that Calhoun could not possibly hurt him, and he looked Calhoun straight in the eye. Tsana watched, spellbound, waiting to see Ebozay's reaction.

And the Markanian seemed to wilt. He took a step back, as if he saw something in Calhoun's face so terrifying that even the slightest hint of proximity was too much for him to bear. Desperately, he rallied, "You're . . . you're working with Shelby . . . I know it . . ."

"Yes, I'm working with her," Calhoun snapped at him. "We're in Starfleet together. And we're married. So naturally I have to—"

"You don't have to make it sound like it's so unpleasant a task, *Captain*," Shelby said, saying his rank with a tone that could only be described as disdain. Mueller suddenly looked worried, and she started to mutter something under her breath to Shelby, but Shelby ignored it. "We're just two people trying to do a job, and you don't have to make this difficult—"

"*Me* make it difficult?" Calhoun appeared both incredulous and contemptuous. "Excuse me, Shelby, but you're the one who's supporting these murderers. At least when you served with me, you had some shred of moral fiber. . . ."

"*All right, that's enough!*" thundered Shelby, her face purpling, veins starting to protrude on her throat. "How dare you stand there in judgment of me—!"

"That's rich! The number of times you judged everything I said, everything I did, every single action I took. And now you criticize me—!"

"Captain . . . captains . . . I don't see this as being terribly productive," Mueller ventured.

"Quiet!" both of them ordered. Mueller nodded and said nothing further.

"I'm sick of this," Calhoun told her. In contrast to Shelby's visible anger, Calhoun became quieter and quieter as a dark fury enveloped him. "I'm sick of these two races arguing. I'm sick of Markanian sneak attacks in the night. I'm sick of the endless squabbling over a piece of real estate that neither of them have even set foot on in over a century, and they couldn't stop bickering about it even when they were there. I'm sick of your sanctimony. I'm sick of—"

"Admiral Jellico," said Burgoyne abruptly.

"Oh, I am especially sick of him."

"No, I mean we're receiving a transmission from Admiral Jellico."

Calhoun moaned as Shelby rolled her eyes. "Put him on," grunted Calhoun after a moment. Meanwhile, Ebozay was making genuine eye contact with Tsana for the first time in a way that seemed something other than condescending. He seemed to be at something of a loss, the entire conference spinning out of control, and amazingly he was actually looking at "the child" to see if she was on any more solid footing than he was. She shook her head slightly, looking and feeling as helplessly befuddled as he was.

Jellico's form flared into existence in the holoconference room, looking slightly fuzzier than the others. "Calhoun!" he snapped. "Epicurus 7!"

"Epicurus 7 to you, too, Admiral," Calhoun said, his face suddenly impassive. *He looks nervous. He's hiding something,* thought Tsana with sudden unease.

"The world, Epicurus 7! You were the last Starfleet officer to have contact with it, a month ago!"

"I seem to remember that, yes, sir," said Calhoun.

"It's gone!"

"Gone," he repeated. "It was there last time I looked."

"And now it's free-floating rubble! It blew apart! As near as we can tell, some sort of detonation in the core! As if someone had introduced thermal plasma bombs to destabilize it!"

"What a pity," Calhoun said, sounding not the least bit concerned. "The leadership there was so polite, as I recall."

"And as I recall, they registered complaints about you! They said they were scared witless of you! They said you threatened them!"

"Burkitt said the same thing, and the Aerons are still here."

"But he's not!"

"Gasp. Shock of shocks."

"Calhoun! What did you do to Epicurus 7!" Jellico looked on the verge of apoplexy.

"Admiral, I think it best if we spoke on this later." Calhoun could not have sounded more calm. "I'm becoming concerned about your . . . health, and frankly, if the conversation continues in this vein, you might suffer some sort of attack. I wouldn't want that on my conscience."

*"Conscience! You don't **have** a conscience! You—!"*

Calhoun didn't wait for him to complete the sentence. Instead he made a throat-cutting gesture. Burgoyne, in response, tapped hir combadge, murmured something into it, and Jellico's transmission was abruptly terminated. There was a long moment of silence, and then Calhoun turned to the others and said, with glacial calm, "Now . . . where were we?"

"I can't believe it," Shelby told him. "I absolutely cannot believe it. You've snapped, Calhoun. You've gone totally around the bend! What you've done—"

"What I've done is what needed to be done," he said with a frighteningly disarming smile. "That's always been the difference between you and me, Shelby. I'm willing to do what needs to be done, and you're willing to complain about it."

"Complain about it!"

"You heard me!"

"If I could interject . . ." Ebozay began tentatively.

Calhoun talked right over him. "This has gone on long enough. I'm sick of being judged by Starfleet and by you, Shelby, and I'm sick of the arrogance engendered by the Markanians. I think it's about time someone taught the lot of you a lesson."

"Don't threaten me, Calhoun," Shelby warned. "I don't do well with threats."

"I don't threaten any more than I bluff," Calhoun warned her. "I just do as I promise. And here's my promise: The Aerons are going to be able to live free of fear. The Markanians will never threaten them again after I'm through with them."

"Calhoun!" Shelby was almost shouting now, waving a finger angrily. "Don't you threaten these people—"

"Again you're accusing me of threats! There's no threat here. Just a pledge. I've got a big ship and a short fuse that's burned itself out. You want a fight, Shelby?"

Tsana's knees were trembling. There was no question in her mind that what she was seeing was absolutely genuine.

Why shouldn't it be? She had seen this kind of viciousness in viewing historical tapes of Aeron/Markanian peace talks. It had sounded just like this. She tried to speak, to find something to say to shut this down, but her throat had completely closed up.

"I'm not looking for a fight, Calhoun. . . ."

"Coward!" he spat out.

"Okay, that's it!" She looked like the poster girl for apoplexy. "You want problems, Calhoun? You want someone who knows all your stunts, all your tricks, and who's not going to take any of your crap? Well, good news, Xenexian, because you've found her!"

"Oh, have I?" he said contemptuously. "Well, you're in luck as well, Shelby. Because I'm coming there! Right now! As soon as I beam the Zarn back to her homeworld, I'm heading over to Markania and I'm going to annihilate the whole damned place! You think you can stop me?"

"Oh, I'm not going to stop you—"

Both Tsana and Ebozay yelped at the same time; in her case it was almost relief, where in his, naturally, it was panic. *"What?!"* they both exclaimed.

Shelby was stalking back and forth like a matador taunting a bull. "You think you're the only one who can act like the leading psycho of Sector 221-G? That's how much you know! I'm not going to hang around here like a sitting duck, waiting for you to show up at your leisure and for the Aerons to plan whatever attacks they desire. If you show up here at Markania, it's not going to matter to me, because the moment we sever this connection, I'm setting course for Aeron."

Tsana was completely discombobulated. The one shred of consolation she was taking from this was that Ebozay looked as shell-shocked as she was.

"For Aeron? Why?"

"Mutually assured destruction, Calhoun. Sauce for the goose and all that. We get word from the Markanians that you've opened fire on them, and we wipe out the Aerons."

"Now wait a minute!" Tsana cried out.

"This is absurd!" Ebozay tried to intervene.

"You shut up!" Calhoun told him. "Why should you care? You said I was bluffing. As far as you're concerned, this is all some sort of joke or bluff. Well, you go right on believing that, Ebozay, if it brings you any comfort. That will last you pleasantly for your final hours, until your city is in flames around your ears. As for you, Shelby, we have nothing more to talk about here. I'll see you around the galaxy, my dear wife."

"And I will see you in hell, my dear husband, because if you think I'm going to back down from my threat to—"

"Wait!"

Two voices—one that of a grown man, the other that of a young girl on the cusp of puberty—raised as one. They looked at each other in confusion, for the notion of a Markanian and Aeron having a simultaneous thought about anything other than killing each other was so novel a concept that it needed to be acknowledged with a moment of silence.

"This . . . this isn't accomplishing anything!" Tsana said, and then, as if needing affirmation of her opinion, she turned to Kalinda. "Is it?"

"Not that I can see," admitted Kalinda.

And Si Cwan added, "Unfortunately, they act like this sometimes. The weapons at their disposal, the feeling of power, the lack of on-site supervision—it can get to them after a while."

"Nobody asked for your opinion, Ambassador," Calhoun said.

Si Cwan pointed a bit defensively at Tsana. *"She* did."

"She's a child."

"Maybe," said Tsana defiantly. "But this 'child' knows what needs to be done . . . maybe more than some adults do.

Ebozay," she continued, looking her rival full in the face. "We need to keep our priorities in order. Do you believe that?" When Ebozay simply nodded, she told him, "I need to hear you say it out loud . . . like you believe it."

"We need to keep our priorities in order," Ebozay said firmly. "And our priority has always been Sinqay. . . ."

"That's where our mistake has been, Ebozay, because our priority should always have been survival of both our races. We've fought out of arrogance. We've fought for a memory. We've fought out of selfishness. It's enough. Sooner or later, it has to end. I say that it ends now."

"And what of your family?" he asked stiffly.

No one spoke. It was as if they were all riveted by the moment, wondering what she would say.

"Your people died," she said, very quietly, as if she were talking to herself. "My people died. I . . . don't see anything to be accomplished by more people dying. It will not benefit those who came before me . . . and it may well poison the chances of peace for those who come after me."

"You hear that, Calhoun?" Shelby called. "The young Zarn has a better grasp of what's important than you do."

"She's never had to fight a war," retorted Calhoun, but then more softly he added, "and I hope she never does."

"If I may," Si Cwan said, "I'd like to put forward a suggestion. The greatest accomplishments that have occurred in the field of diplomacy have always come as the result of summits. I suggest a summit . . . on Sinqay itself."

Tsana fancied that she could actually hear the gasps of the Counselars on her planet miles below. The very mention of the holy world's name was enough to cause a thrill in her heart. "On Sinqay?" she said, and was surprised to find that her voice had come out in a whisper.

Even Ebozay looked taken by the notion. "To trod the holy sands . . . to stand in the same area where our greatest philosophers once stood . . ."

"It certainly sounds more productive than two starships annihilating both of you," Kalinda said.

"That was . . . not our first choice when it came to courses of action. I just wanted to make that clear," Calhoun said, sounding ever so slightly chagrined, as if he was just fully realizing everything that he'd been saying.

"I believe you, Captain," Tsana said diplomatically. "Ambassador . . . if we did do this . . . what was it?"

"Summit."

"This summit . . . what would be the goals?"

"There are some matters, young Zarn," Si Cwan told her, "that cause consternation and conflict, because the participants are emotionally too close to the situation. Time and generations have passed since any of your respective races have stood upon your homeworld. It is entirely possible that, with a possible return to Sinqay in the offing—and an awareness of the tragedy that disputes can cause—you and your counterpart here," and he gestured toward Ebozay, "would be able to come to terms on behalf of your peoples. After all, you will be looking upon Sinqay in a different light, and that alone may bring new perspective and—hopefully—an everlasting peace."

There was a silence then, and Tsana felt, rightly or wrongly, that everyone was waiting for her to say something first. After much consideration, she looked up and said, "I will speak to my Counselars, but I find the proposal . . . acceptable."

"And I will address my peers upon the Ruling Council. But I will advocate its implementation," said Ebozay.

"With one condition," Tsana said abruptly. She had spoken with more force than she'd intended, but in doing so she had captured their attention firmly, and so she didn't dwell on it. "The Gateways."

"What of them?" Ebozay was suddenly cautious.

"We have one at our disposal. You do as well." When

Ebozay started to open his mouth in protest, Tsana spoke right over him. "This is no time to play games, Ebozay. Our futures are at stake, and the only thing that can save us is complete candor. My people are still concerned about attacks from the Markanians. If I ignored those concerns, not only would I be a poor Zarn, but I doubt I'd be their leader for long."

Bristling slightly, Ebozay retorted, "It's not as if the Markanians have no reason to fear assault by the Aeron! Or have you forgotten—?"

"I've forgotten nothing," Tsana said. "But what's being proposed here is a summit that will take both worlds' leaders off their homeworlds, and also remove the protection that the two starships afford. That means both worlds could be open to attack. I only see one way around it. . . ."

"Bring the Gateway devices onto the respective ships?" said Ebozay slowly.

"You don't sound pleased about the idea."

"I'm not. It doesn't please me in the least."

"And I can understand why," Tsana said, sounding quite sympathetic. "But it has to be done. It's the only way to make sure. The Gateways have to be brought up to the respective starships. Once the captains have confirmed to each other that the Gateways are in their possession, only then can they leave orbit with a clear conscience."

"That might prove . . . difficult," Ebozay warned her.

"You think that's difficult? Try going to bed as a beloved, coddled younger sister and waking up to find the floors running with your family's blood, and having to grow up overnight because of it." There was no trace of self-pity in her voice, no childish whining. Indeed, the absence of it made her words all the more chilling, even heart-wrenching.

"Even more difficult," said Calhoun softly, sounding as if he were turning a knife, "is the threat of mutually assured destruction. Certainly mutually assured existence is preferable?"

There was a long silence then, and finally Ebozay said, "I will . . . see to it."

"As will I," Tsana assured him.

He looked suspiciously at Calhoun and Shelby. "Do you think the two captains may be trusted?"

"Oh . . . I think so," said Tsana, and the edges of her mouth twitched ever so slightly as she kept her amusement, and suspicions, buried. "I think mostly they're looking for us to survive. That would certainly look preferable to their superiors, I'd think."

"Far less paperwork," Calhoun said gravely. Shelby rolled her eyes.

"So . . . Ebozay . . . believe it or not, I look forward to meeting you in person," Tsana said.

"As I do you," he replied. "And may I say, Zarn . . . with all respect . . . that I have never, in all my life, encountered a nine-year-old of such erudition."

"Well . . . I *am* almost ten," she pointed out.

"We didn't fool her, did we?" said Calhoun.

The *Excalibur* captain was in his ready room, looking at Shelby's image on his private viewscreen. The holoconference had ended an hour earlier, and they were waiting to hear back from the respective planets' surfaces regarding the transportation of the gateways.

Shelby chuckled, low in her throat. "I don't think we did, no."

"But Ebozay bought it. . . ."

"Oh yes, absolutely. You couldn't really see over the holoconference, Mac, but I was standing there next to him, and I can tell you, he was sweating. When we started rattling our sabers, he absolutely believed that we were ready to start slicing with them."

"Yet he was the first one to claim that we were bluffing."

"He was trying to convince himself of that. Or possibly," she added as an afterthought, "someone was trying to convince him. But he himself, I'm sure, believed."

"I'm not surprised," said Calhoun. "Those who are themselves capable of the worst are usually more than willing to believe the worst of others."

"Either that or, at the very least, he was willing to believe that you'd be insane enough to take your vessel and use it to annihilate his people. I mean, we may have done a creditable acting job, but bottom line, he thought you were sufficiently nuts to commit the crime."

"The holograph of Jellico helped," Calhoun admitted. "Let's hope Jellico doesn't find out . . . although part of me almost hopes he does. Just to see his face." He laughed softly at the thought, and then looked at his wife with a measure of pride. "And you played your part perfectly, too, Eppy. I've taught you well."

"Oh, aren't we just too full of ourselves," she snorted.

"You'd never have been capable of pulling it off before you met me, Eppy," he said teasingly. "Admit it. I've been exactly the sort of bad influence you needed."

"Don't overestimate yourself or underestimate me, Mac. Although . . ."

"Although what?"

She looked at him askance. "Would you be capable of such a thing? Really. Just between us. Using the *Excalibur* to annihilate a race?"

"I would never do such a thing," he said promptly.

"You wouldn't?"

"No. Because if I did, that would be a blatantly illegal act, and I would by necessity require my crew to become accessories to it. I'd be depending upon their loyalty to allow me to commit it. I couldn't jeopardize them or their careers in that way."

"So you wouldn't do such a thing . . . out of concern for your crew." She sounded a bit taken aback.

"That's right."

"But if you could do it without concern? If the power were at your disposal and yours alone? Could you take that responsibility upon yourself?"

He didn't answer at first, but the muscles were twitching just below his jaw. "I do what needs to be done, Eppy," he said finally. "I always have, and without regret. That's never going to change. I hope such a circumstance never comes around, of course, but if it does . . ." He shrugged.

"That's it? A shrug?"

"Hypotheticals are rarely worth more than that," he told her. "People such as Ebozay will sometimes push us into situations that we would have given anything to avoid. Once there, dwelling on further ways to avoid it is pointless. We do what must be done."

Shelby looked as if she wanted to pursue his thoughts on the matter, but then elected to change directons and say, "Do you think he spearheaded the attack that took her family?"

"Yes," Calhoun said flatly. "And I wouldn't be surprised if she also thinks that he spearheaded it. But if she does, she's smart enough and farsighted enough to keep it to herself. Furthermore, she did us a favor."

"About bringing up the Gateways?"

He nodded. "The one flaw in our little plan was you or I having to bring that up. It was going to sound contrived no matter who said it, and possibly tip our hand. But because it came, unsolicited, from Tsana, it was unimpeachable. She saved us having to broach it. She's quite a young lady, that one. Knows exactly what to say, and how to be brave."

Shelby smiled a moment, and then said, " 'Out of the mouth of babes and sucklings hast thou ordained strength, because of thine enemies, that thou mightest still the enemy and the avenger.' "

He blinked in surprise. "How did you know?"

"Know what?"

"That we . . ." He waved it off. "Never mind. What's that from?"

"The Bible. It's one of the Psalms."

Her immediate knowledge of that caught his interest. He leaned forward, eyebrow raised, and asked, "You read the Bible, Eppy?"

"On occasion."

"Are you a big believer in God?"

She laughed. "Now there's a surprisingly hot topic."

"What do you mean?"

Shelby waved off the question. "Nothing. Mac, I have to go. I'm getting a hail from the bridge. I'll inform you as soon as the Gateway is aboard and we set off for Sinqay."

"As I will with you. And, Captain . . ."

"My, how formal," she said, one eyebrow raised in obvious surprise.

Calhoun let the remark pass, and with good reason: He didn't want anything to distract from the genuine concern he was feeling. "There's no way that the Gateway's keeper is going to let it out of his sight. Which means you're going to have an object of potentially huge destruction aboard your vessel. Be very careful."

"I'm taking precautions, Mac. I trust that you are as well."

"I was born cautious, Eppy."

"Oh, and, Calhoun . . . I love you."

"As well you should," he said with mock gravity. "Although I would venture to say that the Aerons and Markanians are giving us the longest odds you'll ever see against our marriage lasting out the year . . . or even the week."

"Are you kidding? They probably think we won't even

last to the honeymoon . . . whenever we might get a chance to take that," said Shelby.

"You mean a *real* honeymoon . . . one where we're not fighting for our lives."

"Yes. That would be a nice change of pace."

"I'll see what I can do," Calhoun assured her.

23

AERON/MARKANIA

SMYT WAS UTTERLY INFURIATED, stomping around the room like a petulant child. "Out of the question," said Smyt.

Smyt was utterly infuriated, stomping around the room like a petulant child. "Out of the question," said Smyt.

Tsana watched Smyt's tantrum impassively. She was far more impressed, truth to tell, with the fact that she was sitting in the grand seat of the Zarn. Even though, technically, it was *her* place now, part of her kept waiting for her father to step into the room and say, in a tone that was part amused and part cross, "And what do you think *you're* doing in *my* chair, young lady?" Her feet didn't even quite touch the ground. She made a mental note to have a footrest put in, because she could feel her feet starting to get a bit numb.

Standing directly behind Smyt was Commander Gragg. Tsana had caused quite a stir when she had not only refused to have Gragg prosecuted for his bold slaying of Burkitt, but instead had promoted him to Warmaster. Although no one endorsed Burkitt's cold-blooded murder of Tsana's brothers, there was nevertheless some noise that, in putting Gragg into Burkitt's slot, she was tacitly endorsing promotion through assassination. Tsana had waved off all such complaints, however, instead simply saying, "If you have any complaints with any of my decisions or promotions, I suggest—as custom dictates—you take them up with the Chief of Complaints. Traditionally, that job falls under the responsibilities of the Warmaster." That deftly quieted protests.

Gragg simply stood there, arms folded, so immobile that he might well have been carved from rock. Only his eyes, never wavering, tracked Smyt as he stomped back and forth.

"You cannot give me orders!" Smyt was saying. "I'm not one of your people! I'm not bound by your laws!"

"You're on our world," Tsana said. "I am ruler of this world . . . and you are invited to show courtesy."

"And you are invited to kiss my bony—"

He didn't finish the sentence, for Gragg's meaty hand lashed out and settled around his throat. Tsana's expression didn't flicker in the slightest as Smyt gagged, air cut off. "Let's start again," she said.

Ebozay watched Smyt's tantrum impassively. He was surrounded by other members of the Ruling Council, and they appeared no more impressed by Smyt's ire than he was. Naturally, Ebozay had not forgotten the powerful discharge of energy that Smyt had unleashed when threatened. But neither was he going to allow himself to be intimidated by it.

"I'm afraid it's going to have to be put back into the question," said Ebozay, the picture of calm. "The Ruling Council is in agreement on this. Matters have spun out of control, and this is our first, best hope of reining them in. And if it means bringing the Gateway up to the **Trident,** *then that's what we're going to do. And you will cooperate in this endeavor, whether you like it or not."*

"You cannot give me orders!" Smyt protested. She was fuming so fiercely that Ebozay was surprised she didn't have smoke rising from her ears. "I'm not one of your people! I'm not bound by your laws!"

Ebozay rose from his place and strode toward her. He knew beyond any question that it was vital he show her he was not the least bit intimidated by her. "Then you will be bound by ropes, chains, or whatever it requires to bind you," he informed her heatedly. "We can be most inventive when the need arises. Right now your ego and your frustrations don't concern me. What concerns me is the good of my people."

"The Gateway is mine. I simply lease it to you for a price."

"Indeed you do. And you'll be happy to know that the price has gone up."

*She looked confused, which was what Ebozay wanted. "I don't understand. You're saying that **you** are increasing **my** price? You're willing to offer more?"*

"That's right. And I think it's a price you're going to have a hard time walking away from."

Tsana leaned forward, not the slightest flicker of concern upon her face. Smyt, for his part, was having no luck at all prying loose the hand that had clamped around his throat.

"We have a situation on our hands, Smyt," said Tsana, "which means *you* have a situation on your hands. You are in a very delicate position right now. In case you haven't been keeping up with current events, your sponsor—Burkitt—turned out to be a cold-blooded murderer. Two of the people he cold-bloodedly murdered were my brothers. That crime makes not only every action of his suspect, but every ally of his suspect. And right now—in case you have not been paying attention—his major remaining ally happens to be you. So your continued health is very much at risk."

Smyt gurgled at that.

Continuing in a very sympathetic tone, Tsana said, "I

would hate to see Gragg kill you. Do you know why?" Smyt couldn't get a word, or even a sound out, so Gragg accommodatingly turned Smyt's head back and forth slightly, so that it looked as if he were shaking his head. "I'll tell you why," she said without missing a beat. "Because I've had occasion to learn that, when someone dies, all sorts of really disgusting things are released from their bodies when all the muscles relax that final time. Fluids and waste matter . . ." She shuddered. "The aroma stays with you, no matter how long ago it happened. And the mess—! Well, you can imagine. Me, I don't have to imagine. I saw it. I saw it, partly thanks to your now-dead ally. And the simple truth is that the floors are newly cleaned, and I would hate—absolutely hate—to see them get soiled with your bodily discharges. I'd prefer to avoid that, if I could. Who wouldn't? So," she continued briskly, "here's the situation the way I see it . . . and you can disagree if you wish. The situation is, we're going to bring the Gateway, and you, up to the *Excalibur*. That ship will then bring us to Sinqay, where we will meet with our opposition. We could, of course, simply ask you to bring us directly to Sinqay, but—and you'll think I'm crazy, I know—I don't trust you. I'd rather trust the man who threatened to wipe everyone out. It's crazy, I know, but . . ." She shrugged. "What can one do in the face of such difficult choices? The fortunate thing is, your choice is much simpler. Do you cooperate? Or do you die?"

Smyt actually looked rather pleased at what she was hearing . . . until the click-clack of weapons being armed and charged up sounded from all around her.

From every corner of the Council Hall, armed men were stepping out. Every single one of them had blaster rifles aimed squarely at Smyt.

"I know from firsthand experience that you have your own offensive capabilities," Ebozay said. He was leaning

back against a table, looking quite calm about the whole matter. "You should be flattered that I'm going to all this trouble out of respect for those capabilities."

"You traitorous bastard," she mutterred.

"Traitorous, my dear Smyt? To whom? To my people? What I'm doing now, I'm doing on behalf of my people . . . a people that you claimed you wanted to help. Remember? This was all about improving the lot of the Markanians. Well, I am telling you now that our lot is going to be improved by traveling to Sinqay and having this summit meeting with the Zarn. You see, Smyt, I strongly suspect that it is you who is the traitor. You brought us the miraculous Gateway . . . and then, lo and behold, the Aerons wound up with the exact same thing."

"I already told you, I had nothing to do with that," she said angrily.

"Yes, so you say. And that may be the truth. On the other hand, the truth may also be that—because of you—we stand on the brink of extinction at the hands of a couple of crazed Starfleet officers. That, I think—and I believe the Council agrees with me—may be far closer to the truth. We're going to have to do something about that, and you're going to help."

"At an increased price? You said—"

"Yes, so I did. And the increased price is, we will let you live. I frankly think that's more than generous. You will be allowed to accompany your precious Gateway device on the **Trident,** and—if you're clever, as I know you always are—you may even find a way to turn a profit from all of this. The Federation, you see, is **most** interested in the Gateway. They've made that much clear. You may actually be able to sell yours to them for far more than you could ever have made in leasing it to us. And they may be willing to pay for your services as well, in terms of learning how to operate it. Make the right decision here, Smyt, and everyone can wind up benefiting."

"And if I make the wrong decision?" She spoke with the air of someone who knew the answer before she even asked.

"Why," he said, as if stating the most obvious thing in the world, "then the only ones that benefit will be the worms that eat your body when we plant it in the sod. What can one do in the face of such difficult choices? The fortunate thing is, your choice is much simpler. Do you cooperate? Or do you die?"

"I should have offered my services to the Markanians," snarled Smyt. "They would never have treated me in such a manner."

"You may very well be right," said Tsana. "The tragedy is, you'll never know."

"I should have offered my services to the Aerons," snarled Smyt. "They would never have treated me in such a manner."

"You may very well be right," said Ebozay. "The tragedy is, you'll never know."

"So . . . you consent?"

"So . . . you consent?"

"Yes," growled Smyt, and the only shred of comfort he took from it all was that this was turning out exactly the way that the giant had said it would. Which meant that, hopefully, the final aspect of his predictions—namely, that Smyt would finally be able to get home—would come true as well.

"Yes," growled Smyt, and the only shred of comfort she took from it all was that this was turning out exactly the way that the giant had said it would. Which meant that, hopefully, the final aspect of his predictions—namely, that Smyt would finally be able to get home—would come true as well.

24

EXCALIBUR

WHEN CALHOUN ENTERED the children's recreation center, he was saddened—but not surprised—to see Moke sitting off to one side, staring out the port window at the starfield outside. Moke didn't see him at first, and was so lost in thought that he probably wouldn't have at all, had not the teacher—an avuncular fellow named Dreyfuss, a civilian married to a lieutenant in xenobiology—approached Calhoun in his typical, slightly overblown manner. "Captain, good to see you!" he boomed, which naturally caught Moke's attention. "Gracing us with a visit?"

"Something like that." He walked toward Moke, nodding in greeting at the other children, who seemed most impressed that the ship's captain was actually taking time to walk among them. "Hello, Moke. You're looking a little distracted."

"We left orbit," said Moke.

He drew over a chair and sat. The chair was several sizes too small for him, proportioned to fit the children. Calhoun endeavored to maintain his dignity while being bent in half. "Yes, we did."

"It's too bad. I liked the planet. It was pretty."

"Most planets are pretty from this high up. Although I hear tell that the planet we're going to is even prettier. Supposedly it's green, filled with all kinds of vegetation, and thousands of different sorts of animals, aaaand . . . you're not listening to any of this, are you?"

Moke looked momentarily confused. "I . . . guess not. I'm sorry, Dad. . . ."

"It's all right." He patted the boy on the knee. "It's all right," he said again. "You thinking about your mom, are you?"

The boy nodded. There were no tears in his eyes. Calhoun felt as if maybe the boy had simply cried out all the tears he could possibly have shed, perhaps for a lifetime. "Is her spirit in the stars now, Dad?"

"You could say that."

He peered out the window once more. "Which star is hers?"

Calhoun frowned, studying the vista of stars before him. Finally he said, "The brightest one. You see it?"

He was not, in fact, looking at any particular star, but Moke immediately nodded and said, "I think I see it. Is it that one, over there?" He pointed at one star, which he obviously felt fit the category of "brightest."

"That's it," Calhoun said immediately. "And the nice thing is, since it is the brightest, you can find it anywhere you go. Just always look for the brightest one, and that's her, watching over you. And she'd like you to have a happy life. You know that, don't you, Moke?"

He bobbed his head with great certainty. But then he said softly, "I miss her."

"I know. Come on," and he took Moke by the hand. "I have someone I'd like you to talk to."

Moke stared up at him, confused, but he obediently walked out at Calhoun's side. They made small talk as they headed down the corridor, but it was quite clear from Moke's face that he was most curious over where they were going and who they were going to talk to.

Arriving at a cabin, Calhoun politely rang the chime. A moment later, a female voice from within said, "Come." Calhoun and Moke entered, and Moke was most surprised to see a young girl who was—he was quite sure—not much older or taller than he. Her skin was quite pale, but her eyes were dark green, with no pupils that he could see, and in the dimness of the room they seemed to glow. Standing a few feet behind her, but providing a looming presence, was a muscled and armored man, never taking his glowering gaze off Calhoun or Moke.

Calhoun had to admire the boy's resiliency. Until very recently, Moke had spent his entire life on one world, where not only had he never seen a being from another species, but the populace had scoffed at the idea that there *was* any life beyond their sphere. Since that time, he'd become the first member of his race to leave his planet's surface, had interacted with dozens of different species . . . and taken it all in stride, as if it was the most natural thing in the world. No . . . as if he'd somehow expected it. Maybe deep down he'd always known he was meant for something greater, or at least more fantastical, than any of his world could imagine.

"Moke," he said softly, "this is the Zarn of the planet Aeron . . . their leader . . . Zarn, this is my son. . . ."

"Oh. Hi. I didn't know you were their leader," said Moke.

"And I didn't know the captain was your adoptive father," replied Tsana.

Calhoun looked in surprise from one to the other. "You two know each other?"

They nodded in synch. "This is Tsana," he said.

"And this is Moke."

"Yes, I know who the two of you are," Calhoun said, trying not to laugh. Then he asked, "Do you know this man?" When Moke shook his head, Calhoun told him, "This is

Gragg. He's a very important man on the Zarn's world. He's called a warmaster."

"Why is he here?" asked Moke.

Good question, Calhoun thought privately, but said out loud, "He's very concerned about making sure the Zarn is protected. Tsana, Warmaster . . . I thought you and Moke might get along, and now I see that apparently you were ahead of me in that regard. I've also programmed some entertainment into Holodeck 4, Moke, if you think that Tsana might be interested. It's a sailboat; don't worry, I've guaranteed that the waters won't be rough, and if you fall in, the program will make sure you float."

"I don't think I entirely understand," Tsana said, clearly uncertain.

"It's similar to the holoconference you participated in before, Tsana . . . except the place shifts. It can be very exciting."

"I'll take you," Moke volunteered. "There's no need to be afraid."

"She does not need to be," the Warmaster suddenly said. There was a firmness in his voice, and a depth of volume that made it sound as if his voice were originating from around his ankles. "I will accompany her, as is appropriate for—"

"That won't be necessary, Gragg. I'm not afraid of anything," Tsana informed him, sounding a bit imperious . . . understandable, Calhoun supposed, considering who she was.

"Really? Wow." Moke was obviously impressed. And then, with that stunning candor he always displayed, he said, "Ever since my mom died, I've been afraid of everything."

"You didn't tell me, Moke . . . how did she die?"

"Some bad people shot her."

"Oh." said Tsana, and any hint of imperiousness faded. "That's what happened to my mother . . . and my father, too. And my family."

"Aside from my mom, I never had a family. At least you had one."

"At least I did."

"Come on," he said, and he put out a hand. She hesitated for a moment, then took it firmly. "Let's go sailing."

"Zarn," Gragg said warningly.

But she turned to him dismissively and said, "Oh, hush, Gragg." And immediately he took a step back and didn't move.

"Wow!" Moke exclaimed, clearly impressed. "Mac, will I ever be able to get you to do what I want like that?"

"No," said Calhoun flatly, instinctively feeling that this was one discussion best stopped before it got started.

Cheerily, Moke said acceptingly, "Okay." Then, as if the matter were forgotten, he continued, "Oh, Mac, do you think Dr. Selar will let us bring Xyon along?"

He pictured Selar, trying her best not to look haggard, dealing with the odd and rapidly growing being she called her son.

"I wouldn't be the least bit surprised," he said.

As the youngsters went off to the holodeck, Calhoun headed up to the bridge. For a moment he considered asking Gragg if he wished to come along, but the steadfast soldier made it clear that he was going to stay on station until the young princess returned.

He had barely stepped off the turbolift onto the bridge when Soleta intercepted him. "In the ready room," he said, before she could get a word out, and he walked right past her. She pivoted on her heel and followed him in. Calhoun didn't even bother to walk around to the back of his desk. Instead he simply turned to face her, leaning lightly against the desk surface. "All right, Lieutenant," he said briskly. "Your report on the Gateway and its mysterious owner? This Mister 'Smyt,' I believe Tsana said his name is. He's down in his quarters?"

"If you consider the brig to be 'quarters,' yes, he is," said Soleta.

"The brig?" Calhoun wasn't quite sure he'd heard her properly. "Why is he in the brig?"

"Because, as per your orders, we intended to place the Gateway into a secure location here on the ship. But he refused to be separated from the device."

"On what grounds?"

"That we would endeavor to subject it to various tests without his being present."

"I see," Calhoun said, drumming his fingers thoughtfully on the table. "When, in fact, had we gotten the Gateway to ourselves, we would have—?"

"Endeavored to subject it to various tests without his being present," Soleta said.

"Whereas now we—?"

"Can't."

"I see. Of course, we could simply send Kebron down to 'convince' him to turn the Gateway over to us."

"I would not advise it, Captain," Soleta warned him. "We have no idea of the device's capabilities. For all we know, the mechanism might have self-destruct capabilities that could end up blowing apart the entire ship."

"That would be bad. If we blow up another ship in one year, Starfleet might take away some privileges, such as pudding Friday night."

"We do not have pudding Friday night, sir."

"Yes, I know. It was a joke." He paused and then added gamely, "I never said it was a *good* joke."

"Nor did I, sir, for that would be lying."

He was going to pursue it further, but wisely decided that would be pointless. Instead he asked, "Why the brig?"

"Because it's the only secure area on the ship that also has accommodations. We couldn't simply stick him in the hold. Aside from the fact that unauthorized personnel are not allowed in those sections, there are simply no amenities there that would make it feasible for anyone to reside there."

"So, the device is secure and he's secure with it. All right. This may not be so bad after all. Is he an Iconian?"

"I cannot say for an absolute certainty, Captain," she admitted. "Our information and descriptions of the Iconians are sketchy. My best guess is that he is, but that is based as much on logical extrapolations from the circumstances as it is on any concrete proof."

"All right. Make whatever observations about him you can, and forward all information to Jean-Luc Picard. As for the device itself, speak with Burgoyne to—"

"Have a sensor scan done of the interior of the brig. We already tried that, sir."

"And I take it from that faint tone of hopelessness that the endeavor produced nothing?"

"That is correct, sir."

He didn't like how this was going at all. Once again he was dealing with too many unknowns, with his ship at risk because of it. "How could that be?"

"Because," she said, folding her arms, "according to our sensors, the device isn't there."

Instantly Calhoun was alert. "Are you saying he didn't bring it with him? That it's still back on Aeron?"

But Soleta was shaking her head with firm certainty. "No, Captain. We did manage to detect certain free-floating energy signatures—a residue, if you will—that match perfectly with patterns already ascribed to the Gateway. They were undetectable while it was on the planet; the planet's own natural atmospheric radiation helped cloak it. It was like trying to find a single lit match in the middle of a bonfire. But now that it's up here on the ship, we could detect it."

"So once it was in our laps, we could find it. That's what you're telling me."

Her eyebrows puckered in that disapproving manner she had. "Sarcasm ill befits a Starfleet captain."

He let the comment pass, instead focusing on her earlier statement. "But then . . . how can you say that we can't scan it?"

"Computer," she said briskly by way of response. "View interior of brig on level five, section A1."

Immediately the screen on Calhoun's desk flared to life, and Calhoun could see the being known as an Iconian sitting there, with what appeared to be some sort of large, rectangular crate next to him. Soleta tapped it with her finger. "The device is in this large case. As far as our scanning devices are concerned, aside from the trace patterns from the leaking energy, it's simply not there. As near as we can determine," she continued, anticipating his question before he managed to get it out, "the case has some sort of built-in Reflector. Basically, it's a sort of sensor mirror. A variation on a cloaking device. A Reflector sends—"

Calhoun interrupted. "A Reflector sends any sensor sweeps back to the point of origin, so that the scanning device is essentially scanning itself and its source. So ultimately, when we employ scanners on the box next to Smyt, it informs us that—in defiance of all common sense—Smyt has a starship next to him that, in terms of size, population, etcetera, matches our own."

"That's exactly right, Captain, yes." Soleta looked a bit impressed.

"Of course it's right. The reason I know it is because Lieutenant Commander Gleau, science officer of the *Trident,* just explained it to me."

Soleta looked politely confused, and even glanced around the room as if expecting to see the Elf hiding somewhere. Calhoun noticed her bewilderment, and laughed softly. "He's not here, Lieutenant. I've been in communication with the *Trident,* monitoring her progress. Ebozay and the possessor of the Gateway on the Markanian end are now aboard the *Trident,* and they're on their way to rendezvous with us at Sinqay. And the description that you gave me of Smyt's behavior, and their experiences with what you encountered, is almost a word-for-word duplication of what transpired on

Shelby's ship." He glanced once more at the screen. Smyt hadn't budged from the almost Zen-like meditative posture he'd adopted. One would have thought him carved from marble. Watching him there simply served to annoy Calhoun, and so he said "Computer, off," and the image disappeared.

"They also have an Iconian named Smyt in charge of it?" she said skeptically.

"Actually, that's the only place where there's a slight difference."

"He's not an Iconian?"

"No, he's Iconian."

"He's not named Smyt?"

"No, the Iconian's name is Smyt."

That stopped Soleta cold. "It *is?*" Calhoun nodded. "Then . . . what is the 'slight difference'?"

"The Smyt on the *Trident* is female."

Soleta considered that piece of information. "It must be an assumed name," she said after a time. "That is the only logical explanation. An assumed name, and they are working in concert with one another. That is all that makes sense."

"That would be nice."

She looked at him, baffled. "Why would that 'be nice,' Captain?"

"Because it would be simple," he said, walking the perimeter of the desk and trailing his fingertips across it. "It's a pleasant, tidy, simple explanation. And since most of the matters I've encountered in my life are anything but pleasant, tidy, and simple, this would be a much-appreciated change of pace." He stopped his pacing and sighed. "Well, I suppose we'll find out once we arrive on Sinqay. There's no doubt in my mind, though, that whatever happens, the young Zarn is going to be up to the challenge."

"Yes, I . . . wished to speak to you about the young Zarn."

He frowned. "Is there a problem?"

"There . . . may be, yes, sir."

He waited for her to tell him what it was, but she simply stood there. Deciding prompting was obviously required, he said, "Well? Are you going to share it?"

Soleta let out an unsteady breath. "Captain, as you know, Tsana was quite . . . withdrawn . . . when she came to us. Her situation was rather dire. Dr. Selar utilized the Vulcan mind-meld, and even that was insufficient. It even prompted something of an emergency situation when the Doctor was unable to break off her meld. I, in turn, stepped in and aided in Tsana's restoration."

"All right. I'm following you so far, but I'm not exactly seeing a downside."

"The downside, Captain," she said, "is that it is not customary to perform a mind-meld with one so young. And certainly not with one who is not Vulcan. A youthful mind is a very impressionable thing. Furthermore, the mind that Dr. Selar and I found when we probed was—to all intents and purposes—shattered. The proper thing to do would have been to spend months slowly, carefully, endeavoring to reconstitute it. Instead, because of the exigency of the situation—particularly in regard to Dr. Selar's own difficulties—I was forced to . . ."

"To what?" Calhoun was starting to feel a bit apprehensive.

"To cut corners, in essence."

"Cut . . . what corners? What are you talking about specifically, Soleta?" He had never seen her looking quite as uncomfortable as she was right then.

"It . . . is difficult to describe for someone who does not possess such capabilities himself. Even Dr. Selar would not fully understand; she was unaware when it was happening. I believe she was simply relieved to be out of her predicament, and was not considering the matter too closely. The simplest way to describe it is to say that the force of my involvement, my insertion into her mind, may very well have had long-term and permanent effects on her."

Apprehension was turning into frustration. "I'm not following, Soleta," Calhoun said impatiently. "What sort of . . . ?" But then, suddenly, he understood. "Wait . . . effects such as, say, a young girl speaking with a savvy and wisdom far beyond her years?"

"Something like that, yes," admitted Soleta.

"That girl," Calhoun said, pointing toward the door as if Tsana were standing on the other side, "during the holomeeting, expressed herself with such confidence and perception that I would have sworn I was standing next to an adult. Except I wasn't. I was standing next to a miniature version of you."

"Not me precisely, Captain," she corrected, sounding a bit defensive. "I haven't taken possession of her mind or laid my own personality over hers, if that's what you're thinking."

"Right now I'm not sure what I'm thinking, Lieutenant."

"I'm saying I had a sort of . . . 'influence' over her. She has some of my maturity, perhaps some aspects of myself, mixed in with her own. It will affect her higher reasoning faculties, most likely. She's not damaged—"

"Not damaged!" He was appalled. "You're telling me that you essentially robbed her of her childhood!"

Her face hard, Soleta said, "No, sir. The Markanian raiders did that. I salvaged what was left in the best way that I was able to. I will accept responsibility for the changes I may have inadvertently made on her thought processes and personality, but I will not take the blame for the ruination of her life."

Calhoun let out a long, heavily burdened moan, rubbing the bridge of his nose as he did so. "No one is trying to blame you for the ruination of anything, Soleta. The question is, can it be fixed?"

"Fixed?"

"Fixed. Repaired. Made the way it was. Is it possible to remove whatever 'influence' you might have left upon her?"

"Possible? Yes. But it would have to be done on Vulcan,

under the care of Meld Masters. It would take time. Two, maybe three—"

"Weeks?"

"Years."

Calhoun moaned again. Suddenly he was missing Shelby more and more. Something about her presence had prompted him to be more stoic, less openly bothered by things that went horrifically wrong. Things like this.

"I . . . am sorry, Captain," Soleta said, looking down. "I have failed you."

"Nooo, you haven't failed me, Soleta," he said. He reached over to pat her shoulder, but she gave him a look that prompted him to, at the last moment, smooth down his hair instead. "You did the best you could, and you gave her some sort of life . . . more than she had before. Perhaps . . . you gave her what she needed in order to survive," he admitted. "Hopefully she'll grow into the mind that you've provided her."

"Nevertheless . . . I *am* sorry, Captain."

"But you're apologizing to me rather than her."

"Because I feel a responsibility to you as my commanding officer to tell you what I suspect happened. But if you feel I should tell her what happened, I will."

Calhoun considered it for a long moment, sensing an indefinable weight upon him. Finally he said, "No. Don't tell her."

"No?"

"For better or for worse, Soleta, she's their leader now. A leader must know his or her own mind . . . must never doubt. If we give her reason to doubt her own mind, we're doing her no favor at all. We're hampering her ability to do what needs to be done. She could end up going through her entire life never being certain of anything. What sort of life is that for her, and for her people? No," he said, suddenly feeling much older than he had minutes before, "for better or for worse, Tsana is now who she is. Fortunately, Soleta . . . you're a good person. If anyone's going to have had an influence on her, at least it's someone who's honest, and trust-worthy, and isn't wrestling with inner demons or frustra-tions."

It was all Soleta—secretly half-Vulcan, half-Romulan, the product of a brutal rape, with a deep, burning resentment against her dead Romulan father that could never be re-solved—could do to keep her face utterly neutral. "I appre-ciate the vote of confidence, Captain. I appreciate it very much. And I'm sure that Tsana would appreciate it as well."

25

TRIDENT

SMYT'S EYES NARROWED as she saw the furred being peering in through the forcefield door of the brig. She was already feeling somewhat out of sorts, being forced into a position where she felt as if she were on display. On the one hand, this was not going at all the way she had hoped. On the other hand, much of what was occurring had been exactly as the giant had described. That being the case, she was well on her way to finally getting home. She supposed that it would be ungrateful of her to resent the manner in which it was happening, but she did nevertheless.

They had no security guards on the other side of the brig, since technically she wasn't a prisoner. She could come and go as she pleased; all she had to do was use the com device they'd given her to summon a guard to shut down the forcefield and allow her to leave. Smyt suspected, though, that their intent was to deprive her of any company, make her feel lonely so that she might give in and let them take the

Gateway off her hands . . . at which point, they would do who-knew-what with it? No, no, she was going to continue to hold onto it for as long as it took.

But who, then, was this . . . female, it looked like. A female with pointed ears and soft orange fur. "Can I help you?" asked Smyt with exaggerated politeness.

The furred female seemed to be considering the casual question very carefully. Finally she said, "My name is M'Ress. I'm a scientist."

"How wonderful for you," Smyt said with only slightly exaggerated lack of interest. "My name is Smyt. I'm a hostage to science." When M'Ress tilted her head in curiosity at that, she said, "In answer to your unspoken question, yes, this is a Gateway. I'm sure you've heard all about it. . . ."

"I've gone through one."

This was more than enough to snare Smyt's full attention. She'd been sitting in a very relaxed fashion, but now she stood and approached M'Ress with open assessment. "Have you indeed?"

She nodded. "But it didn't just move me through space. It moved me through space and time."

Inwardly, Smyt felt as if her heart had just stopped. It was everything she could do to maintain her outer cool, as if what M'Ress had just told her was the most routine thing in the galaxy. "Oh, yes," she said blithely. "They'll do that."

"They will?" M'Ress took a step forward, stopping just short of the force barrier that blocked the front of the brig.

"Of course they will. Any time, any place."

"Can . . ." M'Ress's gaze flickered toward the small crate in the corner of the room. "Can . . . that one?"

"Ahhhh," said Smyt, and then she lowered her voice to nearly a whisper, implying a greater sense of confidentiality between the two. "You want to know if I can use this Gateway . . . to transport you back to where you came from."

"I didn't say that."

"You didn't have to. I'd have to be fairly stupid not to realize that's what you were wondering about."

Her eyes wide . . . quite captivating, really . . . M'Ress whispered, "Can it?"

"No."

At that, M'Ress was visibly crestfallen, as Smyt knew she would be. She paused to let the statement sink in, and then she said softly, "However . . . it's possible I can locate one that can."

M'Ress was all eagerness. There was nothing in the female, Smyt realized, that had the slightest artifice. Or if there was, she certainly wasn't displaying it now. She was nothing at the moment except a sample of living, breathing, walking need. Her tail twitching furiously, she said, "Where? How can you locate it? Can you take me to it?"

"All things are possible," Smyt said mysteriously. "If I do endeavor to help you, though . . . you have to help me."

"How?" But then, very quickly, as if she suddenly remembered something, M'Ress's expression darkened, and she said, "Whatever it is, it can't be anything that would compromise this vessel or put anyone in danger. That is simply not an option."

"Already you're setting limits."

"Better to do so now," said M'Ress, "and avoid misunderstanding, rather than keep my peace and encourage it."

"All right. Fair enough," Smyt told her approvingly. "Then let us get this much understood, to start out. We'll be approaching this beloved Sinqay quite soon. I feel as if I am surrounded by enemies, or at the very least, by people who have interests other than my own at heart. I want someone there whose interests in some way overlap with my own. That would be you. When we reach the planet, make certain that you are part of the group that goes to the surface. That way if I have need of your aid, you will be right at hand."

M'Ress nodded. "I believe that can be arranged."

"That's not going to happen, Lieutenant."

Lieutenant Commander Gleau, his polite and cheery smile never wavering, strode briskly down the hall. M'Ress, however, was the faster of the two, and she was able to keep pace with him quite effortlessly, looking as if she were gliding across the floor. "I have confidence in you, sir. You can make it happen. If there's a landing party—"

"A what? Oh . . . an away team, yes. If there's an away team, M'Ress, and a representative of the science department is required, that person will naturally be me. Hello." He smiled and nodded to a yeoman passing by. She smiled back.

It made M'Ress's skin crawl, caused her fur to stand on end. But she fought to maintain her concentration on the issue at hand.

"And what if there's a Gateway down there?"

He stopped and looked at her blankly. "What an odd question. Do you have reason to believe there might be?"

"It's . . . possible."

"Oh, I suppose it's *poss*ible, yes. And it's *poss*ible that I may open my mouth and a flock of trained pelicans will fly out. But I don't think it terribly *likely,* do you?"

"I just . . . have a hunch about it, Gleau. I'm asking you to let me pursue that hunch."

"M'Ress," said Gleau patiently, "I understand." He stopped walking and turned to face her.

"You do?"

"You're anxious to prove yourself. Anxious to thrust yourself into the midst of potential danger. But you're too new—"

"I've been speaking with Smyt," M'Ress said abruptly.

That caught Gleau's attention, and he looked at her with a new sense of urgency. "The female with the Gateway?"

"Yes."

"About what?"

"The workings of the device."

His expression dissolved into one of faint disapproval. Some part of M'Ress was utterly mortified that he was in any way upset with her. But another part reminded her that her desire to please him was very likely not her own. "And you did not share what you learned with me . . . why?"

"Because she didn't really tell me anything. But I think I established a degree of trust. My presence on the away team would be, at this point, more valuable than yours."

"Your input is duly noted, Lieutenant. I'll take that under advisement."

He started to walk away, and M'Ress said, more forcefully, "I'd take it under a bit more than that if I were you."

The Elf stiffened and he stopped, turned, and walked slowly back to M'Ress. "What, may I ask, is that supposed to mean?" His tone was as gentle and soothing as ever, but there was something else there . . . warning, perhaps? Or maybe . . . fear?

"I think you know what it means." Her every instinct was now telling her to move away from him, and she did exactly as her instincts said. She turned her back and started to head off down the hallway.

Immediately he was alongside her, giving a fairly hearty—and false-sounding—laugh. "M'Ress," he said, "are you threatening me?"

"No, Gleau, I'm walking away from you. Why, am I walking in too menacing a manner for you? How do you want me to walk? Or perhaps you can simply use the Knack and make me walk the way you wish."

"I knew it. This is about that, isn't it?"

"It's about me walking, Gleau. That's all."

"It's not." He stepped around her to face her, and now she could see it without question: He was definitely nervous.

There was sweat forming on his upper lip. It made her feel a surge of validation. "You're hinting that you're going to go to Captain Shelby and say . . . I don't know what. Twist our time together into something that it wasn't."

"Something it wasn't? Such as . . . what? Genuine?"

"You can't threaten me, M'Ress."

"I'm not threatening you, Gleau," and then she smiled, baring her fangs slightly. "But you feel threatened by me, don't you? You don't know my mind. You're uncertain of yourself around me. Well, congratulations, Lieutenant," she laughed bitterly, her cat eyes burning with quiet vengeance. "You now have the slightest inkling of what it feels like for me. And if—"

Gleau's combadge abruptly beeped. "Gleau here," he said, not making eye contact with M'Ress.

"Mueller here. Your presence is required on the bridge, Mr. Gleau."

"On my way," said Gleau. He turned and faced M'Ress once more, pointing at her and saying, "We'll discuss this in more detail later."

"Not if you're fortunate," said M'Ress. And as Gleau headed off toward the turbolift looking unmistakably shaken, M'Ress could not help but emit a soft, and rather genuine purr.

26

ABOVE SINQAY

THERE WAS A DEATHLY silence on the bridge of the *Excalibur* after Soleta made her pronouncement. All eyes were upon Calhoun, and Calhoun in turn was staring at the planet over which they were in orbit . . . the planet that had once been the home of a race so fervent in their love for the world that the members of that race had been willing to destroy each other for it.

"Are you sure?" he asked, even though he already knew the answer.

"Positive, Captain."

"Kebron, get me the *Trident* on the horn." Calhoun had no need of sensors or any other such devices to ascertain whether the other starship was in the vicinity. He could see it on the other side of the planet, orbiting in perfect synchronization with the *Excalibur.*

For once, even Kebron didn't seem inclined to be flip. Moments later, the image of the planet on the viewscreen had been replaced by the concerned face of Captain Shelby. Calhoun knew, without even asking, that she had discerned the same facts that he had. Without even bothering to ask if that was the case, he said simply, "Have you told him yet?"

She shook her head. "And you? Have you informed the Zarn?"

"No, I haven't. I don't exactly see how we can't, though."

"I tend to agree. I'll inform Ebozay of the current situa—"

"No," Calhoun said abruptly.

From the viewscreen, Shelby stared at him uncomprehendingly. Even the other members of the bridge crew seemed puzzled. " 'No'? Mac, we just agreed we have to tell them. We can't just pretend we forgot we were coming here."

"I didn't say we should, Elizabeth. But I think it would simply be best . . . if we beamed down."

"Without giving them warning . . . ?" And then she understood. "Without giving them warning," she repeated, this time with full comprehension.

"Exactly, yes."

"You realize that it could be rather . . . traumatic."

One word rolled off Mackenzie Calhoun's lips, and it was every bit as harsh as he intended it to be:

"Good."

There was a contemplative silence on the bridge of the *Trident* for a long moment after the communication ended, and then, very softly, very thoughtfully, Shelby said, "Mueller, would you be so kind as to locate Ebozay and bring him up to speed with . . . as much as we wish him to know at this point?"

"Right away, Captain," she said, rising from her chair.

"Thank you, XO." It was clear from her tone that she was not embarking on the course of action lightly, but—having concurred with Calhoun that it was the most effective way to proceed—she was now committed to doing so. "An away team consisting of myself, Lieutenant Arex, and Commander Gleau will accompany Ebozay to the surface. Oh, and inform Smyt that we will be requiring her presence as well. Her Gateway device helped precipitate all this; I want her there for what hopefully will be its conclusion."

"Captain," Gleau said slowly, looking rather thoughtful, "I think perhaps . . . you may want to assign Lieutenant M'Ress to the away team rather than myself."

Shelby looked at Gleau with mild surprise. "What an unusual thing for you to say, Lieutenant Commander. Usually the only way we'd have of keeping you off an away team is with a large, blunt instrument. Why the change?"

"No change, Captain. I'm always of the opinion that the person best-suited to a particular situation should be the one who goes. Can I help it," he said with one of his customary dazzling smiles, "if I'm the one who's usually best-suited to it?"

Takahashi smiled lopsidedly from his post at ops. "The curse of being infinitely talented."

"What can I say? It's a burden I live with," said Gleau good-naturedly. Then, more seriously, he continued, "However, in this instance, M'Ress has more experience with Gateways than I do, particularly considering her personal circumstances in terms of how she came to be here. Plus, you're bringing Arex down with you, and they have a working history together. I just think M'Ress is the better fit for this particular assignment."

"All right, Gleau," Shelby said. She still had the uneasy feeling that something wasn't being said, but Gleau's expression was relaxed and neutral, and she had no real reason to assume that anything was out of the ordinary. "Inform Lieutenant M'Ress we'll be needing her for away team duty."

"Aye, Captain."

Shelby couldn't shake the feeling that something was going on . . . that there was some sort of subtext she was missing. But she couldn't dwell on it; she simply had too many other things to worry about.

Like, for starters, whether she was doing the right thing.

She found—unlike when she was first officer, and always seemed to know for sure—that nowadays, she worried about that a lot.

Ebozay could scarcely believe it. He stood at the viewing port of Ten Forward, gazing at it in reverent shock, as if skepticism on his part would cause the planet below them to vanish like a soap bubble. "That's . . . truly Sinqay?"

"These are the spatial coordinates both you and the Zarn presented us with, from your respective histories," said Mueller, who was standing behind him, hands draped behind her back. "And Ambassador Si Cwan, over on the *Excalibur* there," and she pointed at the other starship, visible a distance away, "confirms it from Thallonian texts he still possesses. There's no mistake."

"And . . . we're going down there?" It was everything he could do not to be trembling at the mere thought.

"Yes. The captains will be in attendance, as will the Zarn and the warmaster."

His face darkened. "I'm still not pleased that the Zarn brought a companion from her homeworld, aside from the keeper of the Gateway. I was not offered the same option. All things should be equal."

"The Zarn is a nine-year-old girl," Mueller pointed out, with a slightly contemptuous smirk. "It was felt by her Counselars that, considering the circumstances, she should not be without proper escort. Or are you saying that you have to be treated with the same delicate considerations that a child requires?"

"I . . . suppose not," growled Ebozay grudgingly.

"If it pleases you to do so," Mueller said, patting him on the shoulder as if they were long lost friends, "think of it this way: It takes two Aerons to equal one Markanian."

At that, Ebozay laughed in spite of himself. "I like the way you think, Commander. Perhaps later you and I could get together."

Her voice dripping with friendship, she said, "If by 'later' you mean another life, perhaps we can. Come. It's time to put all the cards on the table."

And in the brig of the *Trident,* Smyt suddenly had an uneasy feeling . . . as if everything was coming to a head.

Gragg wanted to let out a sob of joy and amazement, but he knew he had to contain such an impulse because that would certainly not be an appropriate thing for the Warmaster of Aeron to do. To cry as a child would? Particularly when the closest child, the Zarn herself, was looking upon their ancestral home with wide-eyed wonder, but dry of face.

They were in the observation bay. The viewfloor was open, giving that always-dizzying and odd perspective that made you feel as if you were standing unsupported in the depths of space—or, in this instance, miles above the surface of the planet. Standing on either side of Tsana were Kalinda and Moke. She had become quite friendly with them of late; indeed, it had reached a point during the trip when it seemed as if the three of them had become inseparable.

"That is . . . truly Sinqay?" said Gragg in amazement.

"These are the spatial coordinates both you and the Markanians presented us with, from your respective histories," said Burgoyne, who was standing behind him, hands draped behind hir back.

"And Si Cwan and I have confirmed it, based on Thallonian texts in our possession," added Kalinda. "There's no mistake."

"And . . . we're going down there?" asked a reverent Tsana.

"Yes," affirmed Burgoyne. "The captains will be in attendance, as will the Markanian, and the individual who brought the Markanians their Gateway technology."

The comment pulled Tsana's attention away from the orb below them for a moment. "That is someone I would be most interested in meeting," she said coolly. "If not for him, after all . . . my parents would still be alive."

This was enough to set off warning bells in Burgoyone's head. "Tsana," s/he said, "I can only hope that you are not considering in any way jeopardizing—"

"Are you doubting the Zarn's word?" bristled Gragg.

"No. Merely seeking to clarify it," Burgoyne said mildly.

"It is nothing you, or your captain, need concern yourself over," said Tsana. She seemed a bit sad as she spoke, but otherwise displayed a singular lack of emotion. "What's done is done. Dwelling on it will accomplish nothing, except more of the same sort of tragedies that have plagued us for centuries. It all has to stop somewhere. I can't think of a better location than here."

"Well said, Zarn," Kalinda told her approvingly. "Commander, will we be going down there—?"

"Yeah, are we going?" piped up Moke.

Burgoyne shook hir head. "Not initially. The captain wants to limit the size of the away team."

Undeterred, Moke pointed out, "That's okay, then, 'cause I'm not very tall." Moke then looked a bit puzzled, in response to the amiable laughter from around him.

"Maybe you can go down later, Moke," Burgoyne suggested, trying to sound conciliatory. Moke didn't look especially reconciled to it, but obviously he was going to have to deal with it as best he could. Then s/he noticed a frown on Tsana's face as she studied the world below their feet. "Is there a problem, Zarn?"

"Well," she said slowly, "everything I've ever read about Sinqay makes it sound so much like a paradise. I would have expected more . . . I don't know . . . more blues and greens. It looks mostly brown from up here."

"Light filtering through the atmosphere can cause tricks," Burgoyne said immediately.

"Oh," said Tsana.

And in the brig of the *Excalibur,* Smyt suddenly had an uneasy feeling . . . as if everything was coming to a head.

27

SINQAY

THE SKY WAS AS BROWN as the land that stretched to the horizon, and a mournful howling of wind blew steadily across. It was a land of broken promises, of potential unfulfilled, of hopelessness and helplessness and nothingness. There were the remains of some buildings dotting the terrain, or perhaps they were monuments . . . it was rather hard to say. There was a spire here, a statue there, but for the most part the unceasing winds had battered them beyond their ability to stand.

The hum of the transporter had long since faded. Now they faced each other, the two groups, no longer divided by outer space or distances or represented through holographic imagery. On one side of the small circle was Calhoun, Soleta, Si Cwan, Tsana, Gragg, and Kebron, whom Calhoun had brought down—at Burgoyne's insistence—for backup. On the other side were Shelby, Arex, M'Ress, and Ebozay.

Ebozay, Tsana, and Gragg were virtual mirror images of one another in their reactions. In each case, they looked past one another and saw the bleak landscape before them. It was as if they couldn't quite believe what they were seeing, or perhaps thought—however irrational the notion might be—that only the land behind their respective centuries-old enemies was brown and lifeless. That they themselves, presumably, were standing upon ground that was fresh and green and full of promise and vigor. At that point, each of them looked down at the ground beneath their own feet, and then turned to stare behind themselves, only to find a vista as depressing as that which they had just been looking at. Then slowly, very slowly, they turned to look at one another again.

There was no greeting between the two groups, no formalities. Instead they just both looked stunned. To be specific, the Markanians and the Aerons looked stunned. The Starfleet officers simply appeared saddened.

"This . . . this cannot be right," Ebozay finally managed to say. "This cannot be Sinqay."

"It is," Calhoun assured him.

"No, it's not." There was no doubt, no question in Ebozay's voice. He was simply refusing to believe it. As he spoke, his voice began to speed up, faster and faster, as if he could somehow manage to out-talk the situation that he was finding himself presented with. "Sinqay . . . Sinqay is a paradise. A holy place. At most, you have not brought us to the Holy Site, but instead some godforsaken, forgotten patch of the world, but even that is most unlikely, for—"

Then Tsana spoke, and even though the wind was strong, her voice still carried over it. She wasn't looking at Ebozay, but instead off to the side as she said, "This is it."

"It cannot be!" Ebozay told her fiercely, clearly feeling that the child was out of her depth.

"It is. Look over there. See it?" She was speaking as if from a very great mental distance, and even though she took a few steps in the direction she was pointing, she almost seemed to come across like a sleepwalker. "That's Hinkasa's Shrine."

It was almost as if Ebozay was afraid to hear what she had just said. He simply stared at her, as if the words had not reached him. "Hinkasa's Shrine," she said more forcefully, pointing in a direction that Ebozay did not want to see. "I've seen drawings of it since I was tiny. So have you. You must have. Look at it." Still he did not look, but he was starting to tremble. *"Look at it!"* she shouted.

Ebozay forced himself to look, not wanting to appear too afraid to confront something that a nine-year-old was capable of handling. There were fallen towers, some distinctive statuary that featured a female with clasped hands, raising her eyes upward. Or, more accurately, her eye, since half her face was broken away. It was obvious that once it had been a powerful and mighty statue; now it was barely a shell of itself, not impressive to anyone unless they were the type to be impressed by broken-down rubble. Then Ebozay pointed with a trembling finger toward the horizon and said, "And . . . over there . . . it's the Wall of Supplication."

Tsana squinted to look where Ebozay was indicating, and then she nodded. The Starfleet officers simply saw a few sections of a wall that had etchings, words in an ancient lettering carved in. But most of the wall was fallen and prey to the storms that had long since pummeled it nearly to oblivion.

"How . . . is this possible?" Gragg finally managed to say.

Si Cwan stepped forward, and when he spoke it was with great sadness, even resignation. "When my ancestors removed yours from this world, remember, they were in the midst of unleashing weapons of fearful destructive power. The damage, unfortunately, was far greater than any could have anticipated."

"Far greater in what way?" said Ebozay hollowly, still staring at the fallen Wall of Supplication.

Soleta spoke up in her calm, detached manner, as if she were talking about an abstract scientific curiosity rather than a situation that was personally devastating to several of the people there. "It knocked the planet off its axis. Not much, barely measurable . . . but enough to take what had once been a paradise and change it into someplace that is not even habitable."

"Not . . . not habitable?"

Shelby shook her head. "Believe it or not, you're standing on the garden spot of this world. And even here, once night falls, the temperature drops to such freezing depths that none of your people could possibly survive."

"You knew," Gragg said with dawning realization. "You knew it was like this before you brought us down here." When Shelby nodded, he continued, "Why didn't you tell us?"

"Because they didn't want us to know until we got here," Tsana told him. She almost sounded as if she admired the cunning of the plan. "They felt it would have more impact on us if we saw it firsthand, without any warning."

"Yes," Calhoun told them.

No one said anything for a time then. The mood, the environment, was simply too oppressive. When the silence was broken, it was by Shelby, who said, "When I went to school years ago . . . there was a poem I memorized . . . by an Earthman named Shelley:

"I met a traveler from an antique land
Who said: Two vast and trunkless legs of stone
Stand in the desert . . . Near them, on the sand,
Half sunk, a shattered visage lies, whose frown,
And wrinkled lip, and sneer of cold command
Tell that its sculptor well those passions read
Which yet survive, stamped on these lifeless things,
The hand that mocked them, and the heart that fed.

"And on the pedestal these words appear:
'My name is Ozymandias, king of kings:
Look on my works, ye Mighty, and despair!'

> *Nothing beside remains. Round the decay*
> *Of that colossal wreck, boundless and bare*
> *The lone and level sands stretch far away."*

For only a moment there was silence, and then Zak Kebron rumbled, "Thank you, Captain. Cheered everyone right up."

"Kebron . . ." said Calhoun warningly, but Kebron didn't seem particularly intimidated.

Ebozay still hadn't fully managed to accept that which was being presented him. "So we're to take this as an object lesson, then," said Ebozay. "That's what you're saying. That war, that conflict, that all of the things we've dwelt on all these years . . . it is meaningless, because in the end it leads to . . . to . . ."

"To this," Tsana said. "To futility, to death and destruction . . . and to everything we were, or might be, being reduced to nothing. To less than nothing. To sand and dirt and emptiness."

"More or less," said Calhoun.

Suddenly, bristling with anger, Tsana snapped out, "I want whoever brought you your Gateway to see this. And the person who brought ours as well. I want them to see what they were driving us toward. To see what's left of the mindset that caused this, and could have caused it again on our respective home-worlds if we'd used the Gateways as they were intended."

Ebozay simply nodded his head, which was enough to show his acquiesence.

"Yes, where are our 'enablers'?" asked Si Cwan.

Clearing his throat, Ebozay said, "Ours was . . . reluctant to come down at first. She anticipated a possible trap, or inhospitable environment. . . ."

"Ours said much the same thing," said Gragg. "We felt it wiser not to press the issue at first. . . ."

"I think it's time to press it now," Tsana told him. "And while we're waiting for them to come, Ebozay, you and I can discuss . . . terms of peace. Perhaps our two races can find a way to coexist on the same world—if not this one, then on one of our own, or perhaps even another. We've been apart for too long . . . and I think we are far stronger together than apart. I just . . ."

"You just what?" Calhoun asked gently.

"I just wish . . . that this lesson could have been learned without my family losing their lives."

And once again Ebozay nodded in agreement.

On the *Excalibur,* upon receiving the call from the planet surface, Smyt took in . . . and released . . . a long, unsteady breath, even as he held his Gateway close to him and headed for the transporter.

"This is it," he muttered under his breath, unheard by the security guard escorting him. "The giant said activating the Gateway there at the right time would get me home . . . and I would know what the right time was. Let's hope this works."

On the Trident, *upon receiving the call from the planet surface, Smyt took in . . . and released . . . a long, unsteady breath, even as she held her Gateway close to her and headed for the transporter.*

"This is it," she muttered under her breath, unheard by the security guard escorting her. "The giant said activating the Gateway there at the right time would get me home . . . and I would know what the right time was. Let's hope this works."

"We're in trouble."

Calhoun had walked over to Shelby, who in turn had been watching Ebozay and Tsana taking the first, tentative steps toward reconciliation. They were speaking with one another in careful, cautious tones, which was certainly to be expected, considering the history of vituperation and anger between their two cultures. All of it seemed very positive, which was why it was all the more disturbing to Shelby when Calhoun sidled up to her and made the announcement that he did.

She looked at him in confusion. "What trouble? What do you mean?"

"I don't know," he admitted. "But I'm getting one of my feelings. You know those feelings I get?"

She did indeed. Calhoun possessed a nose for danger that bordered on the supernatural when it came to detecting problems before they occurred. Although she also had to note that, despite his knack for sensing it ahead of time, it rarely helped him actually to avoid any of the difficulties. He just always knew there was going to be some sort of problem going in.

"I know them, yes. Can you pinpoint anything, though? Do you have any solid idea as to what exactly is the threat?"

"No. But I still feel as if—"

At that moment, the air was filled with the humming of two sets of transporter beams working in perfect tandem. Moments later, the shimmering ended, and the two Iconians were staring at each other with open astonishment. They were standing about ten feet away from one another, as if facing off in an Old West duel, the containers with their respective Gateways at their sides. They were dressed identically, and even looked quite similar to one another, with only marginal differences as a consequence of their being two opposite genders.

"Son of a bitch," muttered Arex, struck by the resemblance. M'Ress fired him a look, but really his sentiment wasn't all that different from her own. She saw the female Smyt cast a quick glance toward her, but just as quickly look away, returning her attention to the other Iconian.

"Who are you?" they chorused, and then once again together, they said, "Smyt," and then again, in surprise, "What do you mean, Smyt? *I'm Smyt!* Who are you—!" And then they pointed with mutual astonishment at the Gateway containers they were both carrying. *"Where did you get that? I'm the only one who has the prototype!"*

"I hope they stop that very soon," said Kebron, with the implicit threat that if they did not, he was personally going to make sure they did.

"Most curious," said Soleta. "Captain—"

"Yes," both Calhoun and Shelby said in synch.

Kebron growled.

"I believe I'm forming a partial hypothesis."

The two Smyts did not seem the least bit interested in any speculations that Soleta had to offer. Instead, they had reflexively positioned themselves behind their devices, clearly suspicious—even afraid—of the other. In unison they said, *"Stop saying everything I say!"*

"Permission to shoot them both," said Kebron.

"Denied . . . for the moment," Calhoun told him. "Soleta—?"

Soleta was circling them, her hands behind her back, never taking her eyes from them as she posited, "I believe that one of these individuals . . . and possibly both . . . is not of this universe. I believe that they are male and female reflections of each other, from one or perhaps two parallel universes. Both of them named Smyt, both of them in possession of this 'unique' transportable Gateway prototype, and both of them here by accident, happenstance, or perhaps during passage through another Gateway."

"Could they have come here through the Gateways they each possess?" asked Calhoun.

Surprisingly, it was Ebozay who responded. "I doubt it. Because if they'd come through the Gateway created by the device, they would not have then been able to bring the device itself through. The device is the generator; it can't be pulled through itself. It's impossible."

"I believe he is correct," M'Ress spoke up. "Take it from someone who fell through a Gateway."

"All right," Calhoun said abruptly. "This has gone on long enough. Whoever the two of you are, you've done more damage than any two people should have a right to do. If Soleta's right, or if she's wrong, that doesn't matter to me as much as knowing *why* you've done all this. We're here, on this world, a symbol of the pointlessness of a war that you two helped start again. Captain Shelby and I resolved to wait until everyone was together to start asking the tough questions, but now they're going to be asked: Why? Why did you do it? Why the Aerons and the Markanians? You owe them an explanation."

"We owe no one anything!" shouted the Iconians, and suddenly they slammed their respective hands down upon the Gateway containers. The cartons literally collapsed upon themselves, revealing the rather unimpressive-looking Gateway control devices themselves.

"Back away from those!" snapped Shelby.

Arex and Kebron were already in motion, striding toward the respective Smyts with determined looks on their faces. At the exact same time, the Iconians hit control buttons on the Gateway consoles, and protective shields flared into existence around them.

Kebron, a hair too slow, slammed into the outside of the shield around the male Smyt and ground to a halt.

Arex, a hair too fast, propelled by his three legs, sailed through just as the shield activated, and slammed into the female Smyt.

The female Smyt tried to fight back against Arex, but there were simply too many arms for her to contend with. But then a grim smile played across her lips, and suddenly energy was sizzling through Arex. A scream was ripped from his mouth as his body vibrated violently under the assault, and M'Ress tried to leap to his aid, but was rebuffed by the in-place shield.

* * *

The male Smyt laughed contemptuously at Kebron, who stood outside the shield. "Try to get through all you want, you great rocky oaf!" he shouted.

Kebron didn't answer. Instead he slammed against the screen, and suddenly Smyt was no longer laughing, because the impact jolted him off his feet. The screen that was protecting him was one single, solid force unit, and when Kebron hit it with all his might, the entire thing was rocked. Again Kebron rammed it, and yet again, and Smyt kept hauling himself up only to be knocked down once more.

Seeing the disconcerted look on Smyt's face, Calhoun said, quite sanguinely, to Si Cwan, "I believe Mr. Kebron is annoyed."

"I'm glad I don't annoy him," said Si Cwan.

"You do."

"Oh. Right. Perhaps I should try not to in the future."

"A good plan."

The female Smyt's confidence was fading fast, for the device she had used with such success against Ebozay wasn't having the same impact on Arex. The energy crackling through him was hurting him, no question, but it wasn't stopping him, and suddenly Smyt was being pressed backward against the console, and Arex's agonized-but-snarling face was right in hers as he growled, *"Turn it . . . off . . . before I . . . break you . . . in half . . ."*

There was no question in her mind that he wasn't kidding, and just like that, the assault on Arex had halted. The moment it ceased, however, it was as if all his strength was departing Arex's body. He sagged against her, only his body weight immobilizing her, and suddenly he lunged with all his fast-fading might and thudded a fist against the console, right where he'd seen her push to activate the force shield.

Instantly it flared out of existence, and that was when Arex slumped to the ground.

But M'Ress had been waiting on the other side of the shield, and she had her phaser out. The moment the shield was down, she vaulted the distance and was standing in between Smyt and Arex. There was cold amusement in Smyt's eyes, as if this couldn't have worked out better for her. "This is it, M'Ress. Get him out of the way, come with me . . . and I'll find a way to get you home."

"M'Ress!" shouted Shelby, running toward them. "Immobilize her!"

M'Ress had exactly seconds to act, because in no time Shelby would be there to lend a hand. Yet even with those bare seconds, she still had enough time to shove Arex out of the way, out of the range of the shield. Then Smyt could reactivate it with M'Ress safely within its confines, do whatever she was going to do, and maybe—somehow— Smyt would be able to find a way to restore M'Ress to her proper place. It was a long shot, she knew, but at least it was a hope. Otherwise she was definitely stuck there, and was going to have to accept the fact that this world, this environment, was going to be her new home from now on.

She took all the seconds she needed to consider it . . . all those seconds and more besides, and it was something of a testament to the speed of her mind and her instincts that she came up with the same answer three times in almost as many seconds.

She extended her left hand down to help Arex to his feet, and her right hand never wavered as she kept her phaser squarely aimed at Smyt. "Back away from the console," she said. "Put your hands over your head and make no sudden moves."

For just a moment, disappointment flickered over Smyt's face, and then she sighed as she raised her hands. "A shame. I had hopes for you, M'Ress. On your head, then."

"Don't touch anything," M'Ress said firmly. Arex was

leaning against her, looking haggard. Shelby was now directly behind them.

"I don't have to," replied Smyt. "It's time. He said I'd know when it's time . . . and he was right."

The male Smyt was jolted once more, and to his utter shock he saw that the field was actually starting to lose strength. Kebron, meantime, looked none the worse for wear; indeed, the challenge he was being presented with only seemed to make him stronger. Two or three more smashes such as Smyt had just endured, and the field would crumble.

"He said I'd know when it was time . . . and he was right," muttered Smyt.

"On-line!" shouted both Smyts.
Oh, hell, they're voice-responsive, thought M'Ress, and that was the last thought to go through her mind before all hell broke loose.

Ten feet away from each other, two Gateways—identical but opposite—snapped open.

Both Smyts would have absolutely sworn that they knew, beyond question, all of the different things that the Gateways were capable of, all the permutations through which the devices could go. No matter how much they might have sworn it, however, they were wrong, because neither of them had ever experienced any circumstances remotely similar to this one.

Two stars in proximity to each other never have any planets, because of the intense gravity wells between the two of them.

Two microphones, when brought close to each other, can cause earsplitting feedback.

That was what was occurring between the two opened Gateways: a combination of intense gravity and feedback.

Immediately, power levels on both consoles spiked above

anything that either Smyt had ever seen. The Gateways hung there in the open air, energy corruscating between the two, as if they were feeding upon each other. The sound was absolutely earsplitting, with M'Ress and Soleta being the hardest hit.

The open portals started to pulsate, the power so intense that everyone had to shield their eyes. The air began to roar, a vortex building between the two of them, the air starting to twist into something that looked like a horizontal tornado.

The Smyts let out a terrified shriek that was drowned out by the power hanging in midair only a few yards away. But as they lunged for their consoles to try and shut down that which they had inadvertently unleashed, they suddenly felt themselves being hauled off their feet. They grabbed for the consoles, which seemed securely anchored and immune from the suction of the Gateway vortex. Neither of them could maintain their grip, however, as they were hauled away from the consoles. Kicking and screaming, they sailed through the air and were yanked into the swirling energy field. For a moment they were still visible in the spinning vortex, and then, like a cork being sucked into a champagne bottle instead of being popped out, they vanished.

As if it were sentient, having grown stronger now that it had "devoured" two individuals, the vortex increased in intensity. Everything was being sucked up. Dirt, debris . . .

. . . people.

On the bridge of the *Excalibur,* Mark McHenry—looking, as always, like he was asleep at his post—sat bolt upright with such force that it startled everyone else on the bridge. *"What the hell—!"* he spat out.

Before Burgoyne could ask what had so alarmed the conn officer, Lefler at ops promptly said, "Commander! Picking up some sort of massive energy readings! I've . . . I've never seen anything like it! I don't know what—!"

"It's Gateway signatures."

Robin turned in her chair, her eyes wide, to see her mother, Morgan, standing at the science station normally occupied by Soleta. *"Mother!* What are you—?"

"I told the captain I was bored; this is where he put me," snapped Morgan, studying the sensors.

"But . . . but you can't—!"

"Shut up, Robin," Burgoyne said, crossing quickly to Morgan. "Gateway signatures? Are you sure—?"

"Yes, but with an intensity far greater than anything recorded," she said grimly. "Anything that's down there is going to be pulled in. . . ."

Instantly Burgoyne called out, "Bridge to transporter room! Lock on to the away team, and anyone else in the area! Beam them up here, now!"

"Unable to comply, Commander," came the transporter officer's voice a moment later. "We can't get a lock on them . . . something is interfering with—"

"I know something is interfering with it! That's what we want to get them away from! Bridge to shuttle bay!"

"Shuttle bay."

"I want a security team scrambled and heading planetside inside of two minutes! Get landing coordinates from the transporter room! I want a visual recon of what's going on, and an airlift out of there for the captain and the others if humanly possible! If not humanly possible, do it anyway!"

"Aye, Commander!"

"Incoming call from the *Trident!*" said Lefler.

"On screen."

Instantly Kat Mueller's worried face appeared on the viewscreen. "Are you reading what's going on down there?" she said immediately, not wasting time with any niceties.

"We make it to be something from the Gateways."

"As do we."

"We can't beam them up."

"We know. I've got a—"

"Shuttlecraft prepping," Burgoyne interrupted her. "We do, too."

Despite the urgency of the situation, Mueller smiled ever so slightly. "You learned fast, Burgy."

"This isn't the kind of job that provides time for a lengthy learning curve," Burgoyne said ruefully.

Ebozay was tumbling end over end through the air, screaming as the vortex pulled him toward itself, and suddenly his out-of-control tumble was abruptly halted. He hung there in midair, twisted around, and saw that Gragg was gripping him firmly by the ankle. Gragg, in turn, had anchored himself to an upper section of Hinkasa's Shrine that was buried so deeply, not even the power of the Gateway vortex could dislodge it. Tsana was wedged into the other side of the section, safely ensconced.

"Thank you! Thank you!" screamed Ebozay.

And then he saw Tsana looking at him pitilessly, with eyes as dead as those of a shark. When she spoke, even though it was relatively softly, even though the vortex was screaming, yards away, from the wind and the power it was unleashing, nevertheless he heard every word.

"We need to keep our priorities in order," she said. "That's what I had you say before, to make sure."

"Make sure?!" He didn't understand.

She nodded. "I thought I recognized your voice . . . because I heard you say those exact words . . . at my home . . . the night you led the squad that killed my parents, my family . . . my childhood . . . my life . . . all gone, because of you. . . ."

"We . . . we have to set aside our differences—you said—!"

Tsana smiled grimly. "We've had differences for centuries. What's one more day? Gragg . . ." And she nodded just once, but the meaning was clear.

"*Noooooo!!*" howled Ebozay, but it was too late, for Gragg had released him. Ebozay tried to grab at him, but it was no good as he was yanked through the air and, an instant later, hauled into the vortex.

"*Shut it down!*" Arex was screaming in M'Ress's ear as they clutched the control console. The only reason that they hadn't been hauled away was the extra traction provided by Arex's third arm and leg.

"*I'm trying! Don't you think I'm trying!*" And she was, desperately manipulating the controls as fast as she could. Not only was it guesswork, though, but she was reasonably sure that whatever the hell was happening, it was beyond the ability of the controls to rein in.

Then the console started to tremble beneath her. It had remained miraculously impervious to the pull of the Gateway up until that point, but the vortex was continuing to increase exponentially in power. It was starting to overwhelm everything. For all she knew, it would wind up eating the entire planet. To her horror, the control console—their one anchor—began to slide toward the vortex.

"*Maybe it'll be someplace better than here!*" shouted Arex hopefully.

"*Here is actually starting to look pretty good!*" M'Ress howled back, and then she threw both arms around Arex and braced herself.

"*What the hell—!*" said McHenry for the second time in as many minutes.

Burgoyne strode forward. "Now what?" s/he demanded.

From the science station, Morgan Lefler looked up and announced, "It stopped."

"What do you mean, it stopped?"

"It. Stopped," said Morgan with a trace of impatience. "Which was unclear, the pronoun or the past tense verb?"

Burgoyne said, "Robin . . . run a check on combadges and life-form readings. See if everybody's present and accounted for."

She nodded, running a scan through the ship's op systems. The silence on the bridge waiting for her reply seemed to go on forever, and then she said, very softly, "Registering five less readings than were there before it started."

"Five," said Burgoyne hollowly. "Can you narrow it down?"

She nodded. "Missing two Iconians . . . one Markanian . . ." and after a pause, she said, ". . . and . . . two of ours."

Arex sagged against M'Ress, exhausted but laughing in his high-pitched voice. "Great going!" he managed to get out. "Great going, M'Ress . . ."

"I didn't do it," she replied.

"What—?"

"I said, I didn't do it. I wasn't touching anything when it shut down. I was too busy holding on to you."

"Well . . . well, maybe something you pushed took a while to work . . ."

"No. No, I don't think so." She had untangled herself from Arex and was studying the controls again. Then she looked across the way and saw that Soleta was looking at the other set of controls. Naturally Soleta didn't allow any emotion, such as triumph or self-satisfaction, to cross her face, so M'Ress called to her, "Did you—?"

But Soleta shook her head. "No. I was at least two minutes away from working out the basic configurations. It is a rather diabolical device when one studies it closely. Particularly if certain command sequences are—"

"Okay, fine," M'Ress cut her off, then immediately regretted sounding so brusque.

Soleta raised an eyebrow in response, but said nothing.

Instead she was focusing her attention on the console. "As near as I can determine," she said after a moment, "the shutdown came from an outside source. The power source of these devices is still undetermined, but whatever that source is, it appears to have been severed from the Gateways themselves. Captain . . ." and she turned to address Calhoun.

No response was forthcoming.

"Captain?" she said again, and then, "Si Cwan . . . Kebron . . ."

"Right here," came the voice of the Thallonian ambassador. She turned and saw that Cwan and Kebron were in the midst of extricating themselves from debris that had fallen on them.

"Are you all right?" she inquired.

"I've seen better days," admitted Si Cwan, who appeared somewhat banged up.

"Where's the captain?" Kebron asked.

"That seems to be the question of the moment," Soleta told him.

Suddenly getting a bad feeling in the pit of her stomach, M'Ress suddenly called, "Captain Shelby!"

The lack of response hung there in the stillness of Sinqay's air. Attempts to reach them via combadges produced no response. For a moment, no one said anything.

"Kebron," Soleta said slowly, "notify the *Excalibur* . . . that captains Calhoun and Shelby are missing in action."

"All right," replied Kebron, adding mordantly, "but if you think I'm going to attend *another* funeral for Captain Calhoun, you can just forget it."

28

SOMEWHERE

CALHOUN HAD NEVER, in his entire life, felt as cold as he did at that moment.

When he had first been spat out of the vortex, it had been like being hit with a thousand needles all at one time. He had almost been paralyzed right then and there, lying on the snow-covered ground, the terrifyingly cold winds hammering through him. The sky above was a pure white haze, and when flakes were propelled across his face, they scored like tiny whips. It was like being trapped inside a snow globe. He had absolutely no idea how long he lay there, but he knew that he just wanted to keep lying there, because fighting against the fury of the cold around him was simply impossible.

But when his mind wandered over that word—impossible—it was enough to motivate him to stand. It took a hideously long time for the command from his brain (*Stand up! Stand up, dammit!*) to reach the rest of his body, and he felt as if he were observing himself from a very great distance as he did so, as if he were inside and outside of himself all at the same time.

Impossible . . . unacceptable . . . impossible . . . unacceptable . . . he kept saying the two words to himself in his mind, saying them so quickly that the two words became linked. No matter how many times one part of his brain—the logic side, no doubt—kept telling him that what he was facing was impossible, just as quickly another part of him assured him that to believe something was impossible was simply unacceptable.

He staggered to his feet, only to have his boots sink into the snow. He felt no ground beneath; instead, all there was was more packed-in snow, frozen solid. He stood there for a moment, trying to breathe, but every inhalation was more stinging to his lungs. *Grozit, what the hell am I going to do? If I can't even breathe, it's impossible to—*

Impossible . . . unacceptable . . .

The events on Sinqay were still a blur to him. He was not at all sure what had happened. All he could remember was that massive energy vortex forming in the air, and then the Iconians were hauled into it, and moments later he saw Eppy being yanked through the air as well, and he'd leaped for her and . . .

. . . and . . .

His bewildered mind suddenly sorted it all out, and even though the very act of inhalation was painful to him, he nevertheless shouted, *"Eppppyyyyy!"* as loudly as he could. He had no idea which way she might possibly be, or even if she was there at all, but despite the agony in his lungs, he called her name a second time, and a third. Snow was starting to whip around him, although he couldn't tell if more was falling or if what was already on the ground was being stirred about.

Then he thought he heard his name being called in response, but he couldn't be sure. It might be the wind playing tricks on him. It might even be self-delusion, or—

"Maaaaac!"

No. No illusion, no confusion . . . it was her. At first he couldn't tell what direction her cry was coming from, but then he heard it a second time, and he saw her in the distance. She was standing at the top of a snowbank, her arms wrapped around herself. It was a ludicrous gesture, as if such a thing could conceivably give her any protection, but it was a natural thing for her to do. She looked terrible, her hair already frosted, her lips turning blue, and she was shivering. Of course, Calhoun doubted that he himself looked any better.

There was someone standing next to her. Calhoun tried to shield his eyes against the snow, and then was able to make out that it was the Markanian . . . what was his name? Ebozay, that was it. He was standing next to her, and he didn't appear to be in much better shape than she was. He was hunched over, as if the wind and cold were literally beating him down. It might have been, Calhoun realized, that the Markanians simply didn't do well with cold. On the other hand, it could also be that the material of which Starfleet uniforms were made provided somewhat better all-purpose insulation. But their uniforms were certainly not designed to tolerate this level of exposure.

Shelby was starting to shout something to him, indicating that he should come toward them. Calhoun did so, and as he did, Shelby and Ebozay started to move toward Calhoun at the same time.

And then they vanished.

Calhoun couldn't believe it. At first he thought that they had simply been some sort of illusion, a creation of his fevered imagining. Except . . . why in the world would he have been imagining Ebozay? Shelby, yes, but the Markanian? It made no sense. And as he considered that, the wind finally carried the sound of crashing toward him, like something collapsing. Instantly he realized what had happened:

Shelby and Ebozay had fallen into some sort of snow-and-ice-filled pit.

Instantly Calhoun was running as best he could. He leaped, staggering, swaying, fell flat on his face, only to stagger to his feet once more. He was breathing as shallowly as possible, so as not to create even more agony in his lungs than was already there. It felt to him that he was taking forever to get there; it had seemed a relatively short distance to cover, but that had been wishful thinking. Instead the distance seemed to grow and grow and, like Zeno's Paradox, he was starting to wonder if he was ever going to get there.

Then, before he knew it, he sensed a sudden downward angle in the ground just ahead, and he skidded to a halt. Air was rushing up at him, snow swirling about even more fiercely, and quickly he amended his original assessment. It wasn't a pit; it was some sort of ravine, crusted over with a thin layer of snow that effectively hid it and practically made it a death trap.

He peered cautiously over the edge, and let out a mournful sob. There was an outside chance he might have started to cry, but he contained himself, because, naturally, his tears would have frozen on his cheeks.

The ravine wasn't really all that deep . . . not more than seven, perhaps eight feet. If Shelby or Ebozay were standing, and Calhoun leaning over, he could actually manage to haul them up without any sort of additional implements. But they were not standing. Instead they were lying at the bottom of the ravine, both unmoving. Calhoun could see at a glance that Ebozay was dead. It was not the frost or snow or subzero arctic weather. He had simply fallen badly. He was upside down, his neck twisted in one direction, his back in another. Unless he had no bones at all, there was no possible way that he could be alive. Luckily for him, his death had likely been instantaneous. *Look at everything he missed,* Calhoun thought grimly and without amusement.

Shelby was a different story. She also appeared to be in bad shape, but she wasn't lying in such a way as to indicate that she was automatically dead. Snow, however, was falling on her face with no protest from her, and her eyelids were starting to frost closed. Calhoun wasn't even sure if she was breathing. He could climb down there after her, but he doubted he'd be able to find the strength or purchase to clamber back up. Nor was there anything remotely approaching shelter down there.

"Eppy!" he shouted down to her. *"Eppy! Eppy, come on, wake up! It's me! It's Mac!"*

Nothing.

"Eppy! Dammit, wake up! You've got to!"

Still nothing.

Desperate, his mind racing, he suddenly shouted, *"Eppy! It's the Borg! It's the Borg, Eppy! They're coming! We've got to get away!"*

From below, there was a soft moan. Through cracked and blue lips, she murmured. "B . . . B . . . Borg . . . ?"

He stifled his desire to shout out in joy, and instead called, "Yes! The Borg! And you're needed up on the bridge, Eppy! No time to be lying around! Let's go, let's go!" He was lying flat on his stomach, and he was sure he was starting to lose all feeling in his hands.

"Up on . . . bridge . . ."

"Yes, that's right!"

Slowly, incredibly, impossibly, Shelby sat up. Her eyebrows were thick with frost, her eyes barely open, and when she stood, she swayed as if she were a windsock. "Up here! Let's go!" shouted Calhoun to her, his hand extended.

"Up . . . there?" Clearly she didn't understand.

"Up here, yes. Turbolift's broken."

"Oh." Remarkably, that seemed to be enough for her, and

she extended a hand up toward him. But then the strength started to go from her legs, and she almost collapsed. Seeing that she was starting to fall again, Calhoun lunged, hanging dangerously forward over the edge of the ravine, and snagged her by the wrist. He tried to haul her up. She was a deadweight. At the angle he was lying, sapped of strength as he was, there was simply no way he was going to be able to pull her up.

"Eppy, you've got to help me here! I can't do this alone!"

"Help . . . you?" she said thickly.

"Come on, Eppy! Damn it, I'd accept this from a first officer, but you're a captain now! Now do your duty and get up here!"

She blinked, still standing on her toes, arm outstretched, and then her vision seemed to lock on to him. "M-Mac . . . ?" she managed to get out.

"Yes!"

"Mac!" At least for the moment, her mind was clear, and she realized where she was and what was happening. "Oh . . . God, it's cold—!"

"I know! Now get up here!"

She brought up her other hand and he grabbed it as well. Within moments, not only was he pulling her, but she was pushing with the toes of her boots, shoving against the frozen wall of the small ravine. They did not speak, merely grunted with the exertion, and finally she was on the snow next to him, gasping and moaning.

"Calhoun . . . I've gotta say . . . this is the crappiest honeymoon . . . ever . . ."

He actually started to laugh, until the sudden exertion caused another stabbing in his chest. He got to his knees, and then he saw just how banged up she was. There were vicious bruises and cuts on the side of her head where she'd been hurt in the fall. He wondered how long she was going to be able to keep going . . . how long either of them would be able to.

"Ebozay . . . he was with me . . . he—"

"He's still down there. He's dead," said Calhoun, seeing no reason to sugarcoat anything at this point.

She nodded grimly. "We're next," she rasped out.

That was when they heard something. It was a sound like something charging up and then discharging energy. It was coming from just over a rise that seemed to be within distance.

"Come on," said Calhoun, for really, they had nothing left to lose.

They staggered, they stumbled, they fell, and this time when Calhoun stood up, Shelby was unable to move. She was whispering, and Calhoun put an ear to her mouth. "Too . . . dizzy . . ." he heard her say. "Too . . . tired . . . just . . . rest here for a few minutes . . ." Now he saw that there was blood dried just under her hairline. She'd probably have been bleeding a lot more if the arctic wind hadn't frozen it.

"Like hell," he grunted, and he hauled her to her feet. But she couldn't stay on them, and finally Calhoun lifted her up in his arms, cradling her.

She looked at him with an expression that was nearly one of disgust. "Typical . . . soooo typical . . . always have to . . . show off . . ." Then her head slumped back. Her breathing was shallow, her pulse slowing, and Calhoun didn't even bother to call her name because if she was going to die, better that it happen peacefully while she was asleep.

He trudged forward, battling for every foot of distance, and it seemed to him as if he were making no headway at all. And then suddenly, just like that, he was at the top of the rise, and what he saw absolutely stunned him.

It was a Gateway, throbbing with power, utterly untouched by the snow and ice that covered every other square inch of the planet's surface. It was triangular in shape, and there appeared to be some sort of runic lettering upon it, but it was in a language that he had absolutely no familiarity with.

Lying directly in front of the Gateway were the two Iconians. Calhoun had been looking forward to questioning them closely about everything they knew, but as he staggered forward with the insensate Shelby in his arms, he quickly realized that he wasn't going to have that chance. The female Smyt was lying there, eyes to the white sky, unmoving, unbreathing, frozen to death. A couple of feet away was the male Smyt, and he was flat on his stomach. He was likewise dead.

Why didn't they go through this Gateway? Calhoun wondered, bewildered. Then the answer came to him: It hadn't been activated for some reason. But it was certainly functioning now, the power rolling around within. The entire thing seemed to reek of age, and technologies that were far beyond anything Calhoun could possibly have conceived of.

That was when he realized that there were words in the icy surface just in front of the male Smyt. He had managed to make just enough of an indentation in it that—for a few minutes at least, before the snow filled it in—it was legible.

GIANT LIED

Giant Lied? The phrase meant nothing to Calhoun. What giant? What had he lied about? To whom? Was that *it?* Was that the only explanation he was going to get from the Iconians and their involvement in the strife between the Markanians and the Aerons? It didn't seem right.

At that moment, though, there was no more time to ponder the cosmic rightness or wrongness of events anymore. Calhoun was crouched in front of the Gateway, Shelby in his arms, and he couldn't even tell if she was breathing. No mist was coming out of her mouth, her eyes were not fluttering behind the lids. She might already be dead, Calhoun himself was barely alive, and although a great unknown sat in front of them, he had absolutely no options in the matter. *Sometimes you just don't get to choose where you're going to wind up,* he thought grimly.

And with that final, bleak acknowledgement of an unfortunate reality, Calhoun, with Shelby in tow, stepped through the Gateway, not knowing what lay beyond.

To Be Continued In . . .
STAR TREK: WHAT LAY BEYOND

Coming in November

Look for STAR TREK fiction from Pocket Books

Star Trek®: The Original Series

Star Trek: The Next Generation®

Star Trek: Deep Space Nine®

Star Trek®: New Frontier

Star Trek®: Section 31

Rogue • Andy Mangels & Michael A. Martin
Shadow • Dean Wesley Smith & Kristine Kathryn Rusch
Cloak • S. D. Perry
Abyss • David Weddle & Jeffrey Lang

Star Trek®: Gateways

#1 • *One Small Step* • Susan Wright
#2 • *Chainmail* • Diane Carey
#3 • *Doors into Chaos* • Robert Greenberger
#4 • *Demons of Air and Darkness* • Keith R.A. DeCandido
#5 • *No Man's Land* • Christie Golden
#6 • *Cold Wars* • Peter David

Star Trek®: The Badlands

#1 • Susan Wright
#2 • Susan Wright

Star Trek®: Dark Passions

#1 • Susan Wright
#2 • Susan Wright

Star Trek® Omnibus Editions

Invasion! Omnibus • various
Day of Honor Omnibus • various
The Captain's Table Omnibus • various
Star Trek: Odyssey • William Shatner with Judith and Garfield Reeves-Stevens

Other Star Trek® Fiction

Legends of the Ferengi • Ira Steven Behr & Robert Hewitt Wolfe
Strange New Worlds, vols. I, II, III, and IV • Dean Wesley Smith, ed.
Adventures in Time and Space • Mary P. Taylor, ed.
Captain Proton: Defender of the Earth • D.W. "Prof" Smith
New Worlds, New Civilizations • Michael Jan Friedman
The Lives of Dax • Marco Palmieri, ed.
The Klingon Hamlet • Wil'yam Shex'pir
Enterprise Logs • Carol Greenburg, ed.

ANALOG

SCIENCE FICTION AND FACT

Hours of thought-provoking fiction in every issue!

Explore the frontiers of scientific research and imagination. *Analog Science Fiction and Fact* magazine delivers an intellectual blend of stimulating stories, provocative editorials, and fascinating scientific fact articles from today's top writers.

Kristine Kathryn Rusch • Jerry Oltion
Vonda N. McIntyre • Catherine Asaro • Kevin J. Anderson

CALL TOLL-FREE TO SUBSCRIBE
1-800-333-4561
Outside the USA: 303-678-8747

- -

Mail to: Analog • P.O. Box 54027 • Boulder, CO 80322-4027

☑ **YES!** Send me a free trial issue of *Analog* and bill me. If I'm not completely delighted, I'll write "Cancel" on the invoice and return it with no further obligation. Either way, the first issue is mine to keep. **(9 issues, just $19.97)**

Name _____

Address _____

City _____

State _____ ZIP _____

❏ Payment enclosed   ❏ Bill me

Send for your FREE trial issue of Analog today!

We publish a double issue in July/August, which counts as two issues towards your subscription. Please allow 6-8 weeks for delivery of first issue. For delivery outside U.S.A., pay $27.97 (U.S. funds) for 9 issues. Includes GST. Foreign orders must be prepaid or charged to VISA/MasterCard. Please include account number, card type, expiration date and signature. Billing option not available outside U.S.A.   5T91

STAR TREK
—COMMUNICATOR—

3 ISSUES FREE!

FOR A LIMITED TIME you can get 9 issues of *STAR TREK COMMUNICATOR* magazine for $19.95 – that's 3 FREE ISSUES!

STAR TREK COMMUNICATOR is your source for the inside scoop on all incarnations of *Star Trek!*

HURRY AND TAKE ADVANTAGE of this offer – simply call **1-888-303-1813** to subscribe!

Or send your name, address, phone number and payment to
STAR TREK COMMUNICATOR
P.O. Box 111000,
Aurora, CO 80042

We accept checks, money orders, Visa, Mastercard, AMEX and Discover Cards.

Please reference code **TBOOK** when ordering.

Canadian 1 year subscription $22.95, Foreign 1 year subscription $34.95, (U.S. funds only)

Offer expires 3/1/01

STCM

STAR TREK
SECTION 31

BASHIR
Never heard of it.

SLOAN
We keep a low profile....
We search out and identify
potential dangers to the
Federation.

BASHIR
And Starfleet sanctions
what you're doing?

SLOAN
We're an autonomous
department.

BASHIR
Authorized by whom?

SLOAN
Section Thirty-One was
part of the original
Starfleet Charter.

BASHIR
That was two hundred years
ago. Are you telling me
you've been on your own
ever since? Without specific
orders? Accountable to
nobody but yourselves?

SLOAN
You make it sound so
ominous.

BASHIR
Isn't it?

No law. No conscience. No stopping them.
A four book, all _Star Trek_ series beginning in June.

Excerpt adapted from *Star Trek:Deep Space Nine®*
"Inquisition" written by Bradley Thompson & David Weddle.

2161

Ever wonder what to serve at a
Klingon Day of Ascension?

Just can't remember if you bring a gift
to a *Rumarie* celebration?

You know that Damok was on the
ocean, but you can't recall just what
that means?

Have no fear! Finally you too
can come prepared to any
celebration held anywhere in
Federation space.

Laying out many of the complex and compelling rituals
of *Star Trek*'s varied cultures, this clear and handy guide
will let you walk into any celebration with assurance.
Plus: in a special section are the celebrations that have
become part of the traditions of Starfleet.

From shipboard promotion to the Klingon coming-of-age
to the joyous exchange of marriage vows, you can be a
part of it all with

STAR TREK
CelebrationS

Pocket Books
A VIACOM COMPANY

3116